Minor Confessions of an Angel Falling Upward

Chuck—
This book is nothing if not a testament to the old expression:
"Persistence pays."

Planner Forthright

As Edited by Joey Madia

Minor Confessions of an Angel Falling Upward
By **Planner Forthright** as edited by **Joey Madia**

Burning Bulb Publishing
P.O. Box 4721
Bridgeport, WV 26330-4721
www.BurningBulbPublishing.com

PUBLISHER'S NOTE: This book is a work of fiction. Names, characters, places, and incidents are either the product of the author's imagination or are used fictitiously, and any resemblance to actual persons, living or dead, events, or locales is purely coincidental.

Copyright © 2012 Burning Bulb Publishing. All rights reserved.

Cover designed by Gary Lee Vincent.
Planner Forthright image by N. Pendleton.
Background elements used under license from Fotolia.

First printing.
Edition ISBN :0615672418

       Paperback 978-0-61567-241-0

First edition.
Printed in the United States of America.

Library of Congress Control Number: 2012944920

The gate of Acheron is in this book; it speaks stones, let them take heed that it beat not out their brains.

- Cornelius Agrippa, "Ad Lectorem,"
De occulta philosophia libri tres

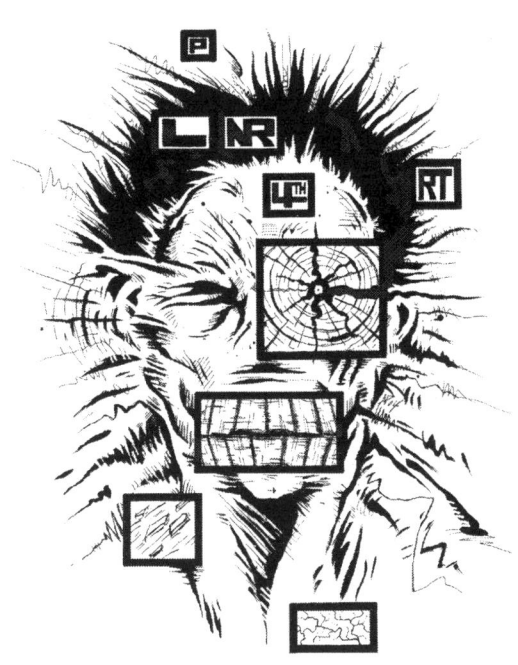

Editor's Note

The circumstances by which I have had the (mis)fortune of meeting the fallen angel/vampire Planner Forthright (a pseudonym, of course) are as fantastical and absurd as the journal passages of his I have endeavored to present in the pages of this book.

Planner has insisted that I make it ABSOLUTELY clear (hence the obtrusive caps…) that I am more a "secretary" than an Editor, per se (the title of this section being a begrudging boon on his part… Is there any other kind?).

What follows can be termed a sub-linear diary of sorts, although classifying anything associated with a unique entity such as Planner Forthright is fraught with perils and pitfalls, and I have already exceeded my allotted word count, as evidenced by the following e-mail:

June 27, ----

To my overzealous "editor" (is there any other kind??):

Blah, blah, blah—ENOUGH already.

It's ME they've come to meet.

P

And so my modest work is done.
        And yours has just begun…

J.M.

***Prologos*: As the Well-Lit Theatre Darkens**

Just last week, as I slunk around Middle America early morning church-spying (a favorite past-time of mine), I noticed a shadow falling along the wall and ascending in dragon shapes, drawn from its pit by the piercing voice of a badly trained but spiritually committed soprano. Its slit-slithered tongue warped the near-melodic tones of her tortured *Ave Maria* into the manic whirr of the dental tool, increasing its volume as the priests, nuns, altar boys, and lay folk ran thru the ornate double doors and down into the street without daring to see what it was—not that they'd be able to categorize it if they did. Beauty is complex and only one such as I could recognize in the burning scales and buzz-saw timbres of this Creature the sublime gift of a charred soul still committed to taking Heaven down. I'm not ashamed to admit it—I'm a first-in-line, popcorn-munching fan of such Old School spectacle.

It's a comfort to know there are still those who rail against God's theological nonsense without needing to make the nightly news.

As I clapped and danced, Lucifer, the once-great general and my former closest friend, perched on the time-worn wing of an iron angel soldered to the banister of that Bingo-in-the-basement church and whispered: "It's because of Beasts like that and bastards like you that I can't go Home." He smashed his heel into the angel's eye, the effort causing him to fall to the bottom of the stairs with an unceremonial series of skin-slaps, coming to rest with the cig butts and old receipts playing regatta in the oily puddles below the curb. There he lay, his once-golden and now death-pale essence crackling in wretched glass-forms, weeping toward forgiveness for being the breaker of all God's promises.

I left him with a laugh. Nothing but puke and regret—that's all the most famous of the fallen angels finally is. He has taken full responsibility for the Rebellion against God and his patsies, although he was far from alone and by no means the first of us to "Descend." Some change from the days of his fictional triumph in *Rosemary's Baby* or the roaring celluloid '70s, when his Loyal Subjects in the Hollywood demon machine churned out shit films touting his Power; his frightening ability to rise to glory upon a dais of charred bones. Then things changed—the Church has used money from its collection boxes to make its own Armageddon reels, laughing in the Vatican's private screening rooms as the fat-faced, washed out Satan-child meets his match in a shadow Jesus dressed in angel songs and blazing Whiteness.

It's over in a minute and the Devil is no more.
What a con.

Come on—would it really be so pat? So one-sided and barely worth God's time? If that's the case, the churches can be closed and the clergymen dismissed—Eternity's assured for us all....

H. P. Lovecraft was right on the money when he long-ago penned the notion that shadows linger right along the pathways of your lives and *sometimes things get through.*

And yet, there's more to this dreadful place between the earth and sky than even he had ever dreamed.

There are bad things and wicked people. Doors that lock from the wrong side and sinister places that eat screams and make them silent. My "life," as experienced on this Plane, is an exquisite, unending *Wintermärchen*. Though your own garden may be plasticine green, in the cottage behind the Church the King and Queen's malformed, inbred offspring curl in desperate bedsheet crouching against Boogiemen and closet worms as the Baker's virgin daughter tells them candlelit fables of goblins stealing babies in the night.

In the lightless tunnels of Modernity's I-beam cities lie lure-with-candy witches, cannibal princes, Martians, specters, ghouls, and a thousand other creatures that have crawled from writer–shamans' Minds.

Of these, I say, you have little to fear. The most dangerous monsters, the real *wampyr* (as described by the veritable and venerable Voltaire), have no fangs or claws, drink no blood, live in Light, and fear no rosary or silver bullet symbols. They kiss your newborn babe with the same two lips that ask for your shit-little savings to make your dreams come true and you never see nor hear from them again. They wear lilac aprons and cook fresh okra in stain-proof, modern kitchens. Their names are recorded on a driver's license and certificate of birth. They aren't the swamp and coffin types. In certain tenuous moments they can be as sweetly consoling as the pie upon the sill.

And then they turn.

So let's begin, in proper Memoir style, with a brief description of who and *what* it is I am, with the explicit understanding that there's plenty more to come:

- I'm a fallen angel made Man; a once-winged evil with un-Divine purpose on this Plane; a cannibal prince chosen to inherit a castled landscape of destruction and despair.
- I'm a vampire by nature and condition, though I doubt my "maker" would approve.
- My name is Planner Forthright (a pseudonym, of course).

- I've been walking the waters and thorny highways of this world for over 40 years.
- And I'm seeking a way out.

Those major tidbits shared, I'm other things as well: An Alchemist of sorts—a mental magician; a mortar-and-pestle wizard converting carbon lies to golden Truth, and my language is my own. I write in a jazz from other Planes, with sharps and flats in odd, inspired places and time signatures that don't quite beat the drum in any measurable way. I am a seeker of new chords, harmonic or not, and a lover of the music *within* the music. You may find my cadence at times slowly drunken, at others twisting shrilly on wires of smoking sparks. It's no matter—demons have moods same as Men. I'll do what I can to set the time; to voice the key before I delve. But I make no guarantees. This is a journey most unusual and a path of thorns and glass. We'll get there, bleeding and worn, but wiser for the walk.

As to time and space and the linear path most stories take—forget it here. I'm an Astral Flier, a shamanic dreamer riding the looping coaster thrill-ride of Universal Action. Part trickster, part writer, I'm Hermes on acid (taken always through the Blood). Events unfold simultaneously beyond this Plane and it's in this way that I best relate. I'm Experience in written form, melding Past–Present–Future into the pliable, helixed Now. Don't let it throw you—it's the most Freeing way to be. I'm attempting to erase my Dharma and my Karma in one mighty stand of pen and puss, and though I'm running out of clock ticks, there's time enough to tell my tale and fix my Tao.

I'm a demon redeeming my Soul, and herein is my quest.

An Invocation as we start:

> "God is graves, God is wood,
> He's buying up our neighborhoods…
> Libido//libitum//adder//finitum
> Abinga abanga aboo—
> Our father who art Everywhere, shallow be thy game.
> Come on Wakan Tanka, the Great Gone Holy Everything
> and eat me up ya smelly fella, all buttermilk and roses.
> And you too, Jesus, still stuck up on a tree—come down off
> your cross already—the only one forsaking you is You.
> Ah men…"

In an attempt to make sense of my unexpected Transformation some four decades ago, I took to making sketches of my experiences and visions in the days of the Great War of the Winged. Being a dedicated philosopher–historian and lover of Minutiae, I took a thoroughly organizational approach—cataloging the myriad types of monsters (the Aztec *tzitzimime*, for instance) created by the generals on both sides in order to wage the better war. To help identify them when they descend/ascend to Earth at the end of the Fifth Sun, I grouped and synthesized their symbols: the arcs of their brows, the rake of their fins, the angles and venoms of their claws and spikes and teeth, the nature of their plate armor and carefully constructed scales. By sketching and memorizing, refining and reordering, I attempted to claim them into my being thru visual cannibalism and papyrus vampirism. My preternatural lexicon has over time grown plump on the fat and carbs of phylum, genus, and species as I have redrawn and corrected the maps and schematics of the greatest of visionary philosophers and saints, men such as St. Gregory and Dionysius the Areopagite who mistakenly tried to outline the grades of angels, tiers of devils, supertrees of ghost-snakes, and evolutionary models of vicious species that have aided the Archangels and Archdemons in their eons of war. Remember that Dante's *Inferno*, while a masterpiece of verse and a celebration of ancient mythology, is, after all, little more than a way to vindicate its author and vilify those who fought against him and his ilk in Florence. It is not to be taken as FACT.

On my shelf (kept everywhere at all times), I keep these books of sketches and thoughts—maps of my forest mind, carvings of petrified Idea-ing. Binders of notes and observations. Yards and yards of poetical scrolls and inkthought bleedouts. They are cryptic; mad. As my flesh has hardened, I have come to a place where I've forgotten more than I've ever known, but I will endeavor to decode these words and images in the course of this work, if the keys have not been changed. There is much to be told—out of time, urgent, more a fever than a breath of reason. Within the symbols are the clues to reclaiming my pawn-shopped soul, and yet if I should fail, we must not discount the value of the symbols themselves. The mark Pi makes on a cave wall is much more interesting than the series of numbers it signifies (numbers are arbitrary, an invention of man, like computers and marriage). Within the pools and puddles of my past are the self-drownings of a disconnected childhood struck in the head and left to mar the soil—the repeating extremist sacrifice of my existence on this Plane. An existence that *never* was my choice. So I am left with my violent nature and disdain for almost everyone I've ever known—my several Fathers and one half-crazed Mother, to start. Such is my plight—though I wish nothing more than to be Saved, I know only one way to deal with an enemy—It must be fucked, killed, or eaten squirming and whole.

For the safety of Humankind I should have stayed Pure Spirit. But that was not to be.

In the first days of my conversion to the Manflesh, my still-restless etheric aspect sat in the muck of a Gulf Coast swamp fetid and forgotten enough to rival any in the tales of Mrs. Rice. It was there that I had been instructed to wait for Crow, my appointed guide, akin to Hugin and Munin, the messenger-spies of Odin, to bring me instructions and my first meal as Man. He's a real bitch—a Trixter queen with a bad temper and a rotted beak, and so he brought me a hunk of rotten otter.

"It's more than you deserve," he cawed, taking the eyes while I started on the ass.

I know his species well.

To the Nez Percé he is *wyakin*, the dark-feathered spirit guide. In the language of Schelling and Goethe, he is *Die Krähe* or *rabenkrähe*, the carrion crow who eats what others won't. To the Greeks he is *Korax*, the long-lived prophet of omens ill and fair. He is cousin to Aristophanes' Raven in *The Birds*, and namesake of the bust-sitting antagonist of Poe's most famous poem. He has been praised and scorned, questioned and coaxed by better scribes than I. To Aesop, he is the ill-tempered messenger, the bitch who denied payback of frankincense to Apollo and thus suffered Hermes' wrath when he tried the same on him. He is one of the pair that brought news of the battle to Mephistopheles in *Faust*. His mood swings fit those of the crows in the pomes of Bukowski and the Southwest tales of coyote and on his best days he is the proud Crow of Ted Hughes' poesy who flew into the sun and thus "returned charred black." Like any zealous father (and I have several), he lectures with an edgy sarcasm and keeps me cut down at the knees. I know it's not personal—it's only his lack of patience and over-earnestness to train, but I love to hate him just the same. He's also got his orders—to ready me for my role as the fabled Antichrist in the New War.

Let him eat the eyes for now—in the end he'll join me at the ass.

In order for this Memoir to make any sense at all, you need to know that I am a passionate lover of books and, whenever time allows (for I tend to be busy in these rapidly ending End Times), I am either reading or discussing them.

One of the first friends I made when I left my "mother"'s no-longer-turgid tit and set off on my own was a research librarian and seller of the very rarest and choicest of books named Emory Vellum Verlag.

I am often in his shop, sharing imported Turkish tobacco and a pipeful of plans.

"I haven't time for this, Planner," he says each and every time. "I have very much to do."

"So do it then," I answer, pulling my pipe from a well-worn jacket pocket. "I'll sit and smoke without you."

EVV: Like very hell you will.

When the pipes are lit and the lamps are dimmed, he attempts to share my Truth:

EVV: So tell it to me again.

PF: [*With every intention to*] Well... If you really do *insist*. You see, it's like a play. It's all just like a play. Shakespeare said it, others know it, and I am the very best of actors.

EVV: And what is your production?

PF: It's extravagantly and pointedly planned. Hence my pseudoniferous name. You see, my ink-stained friend—ours is a most spirited adaptation of all that's been recorded since before the elk-shaman drawings in the Lascaux caves and it's almost time for the curtain to rise. [*I stand upon my chair, raising ever so slightly my well-toned voice*] Using the dreams and myths of the Elder Days, our talented troupe will create on the myriad stages of this truest of Globes the perfect pre-circumstances for Fulfillment of what was once a lot of ink on a fiction writer's page and pretend in the Aftermath that it was *always meant to be*. You've read Daniel and Revelation and the rest of the prophecies of Armageddon in the so-called Holy Books. And somewhere in your stacks you have the leatherbound tomes bearing the stunning illuminations of Beatus of Liébana's Commentary on the Apocalypse and the other frightful works from the Spaniards of Leon and Castile. Let me be clear, Emory—dark images and dire warnings aside, *they were never intended by God to come to pass.*

[He never fails to play his part, although he's heard it all before.]

EVV: What exactly do you *mean*?

PF: I know what you think—that it can't be true... So what then? An exaggeration? A jest? A miscreant's puddle of spume? *No.* These palatable fictions, these stories of horror torn from the shekel-novels of the various faiths, were born of the collective consciousness of Humankind and its tendency toward Fear, and what are thoughts if not a jumbled amalgam of stony destruction, death, and resurrection myths fed to you since your first moment on this Plane?

EVV: [Aloud, but to himself] You are what you eat...

PF: *Exactly.* As for me, I've dined on priests when I wished for high-cal, fatty foods and on harlots to cure an aching tooth. I have visited those who dared to speak of God and his many recorded wonders and insisted they cease their silly prattle. I have welled up from mossy castle walls and dug with the maggots into the cancerous substratum of sorcerers and priests 'til their irises ran with blood and they begged me for their death. I have spit in the eyes of God by indiscriminately torturing the very best and very worst of his designated authors—the apostles and prophets and saints—shoving them toward helpless Nothingness like chess pieces thrown upon the fire. Of course, I did it with my trademark theatrical flair:

"Beast-belly," I hissed, focusing my best Lugosi gaze and alighting like a shadow on their thighs. "Haven't you stretched your girth enough on the fatted fiber of your brimstone visions? Sucked the marrow from *truly* visionary and far freer writers with cold vampiric lust? Yet you never miss a chance at Sunday supper or a little parish lunch. Know this—there is more to a full mouth than the tone of old laws—eat of *my* tongue, chew on *my* wounds, that you may know full roundness and be as saintly sated as the first priests to which you claim a thread." Stunned by my hellish charisma and rendered speechless by my put-on honeyed tongue, they could do nothing but swallow me whole and hope I passed in time. Turning magickally to air at the epiglottis, I rode their pooling spit thru a rich feast of poor works, inadequate deeds, and weak revelations.

EVV [applauding as though I were Olivier]: Splendid, my friend! Just splendid. But then, how did God allow it?

PF: If ever he got wind of it, which I somehow have to doubt, in his moonbeam wickedness he made no move to make me stop, so on and on I went, the winged, skeletal Antichrist, antagonizing the scribes and praying the books would remain forever and a day unwrit. [Pausing for effect] *No dice.*

EVV: Thank the Lord for that. [He realizes what he's said]. No offense...

PF: Speak of Jesus all you want. I've got no gripe with *him*. Now where was I? [A steady puff on the pipe always brings it back] Ah, yes. As has always been my lot, I was no match for the cryptic plans of God, so those I destroyed outright or slowly drove mad were replaced with dozens more, their disparate theologies designed to provoke discussion and debate to keep the greatest number of people *defending* their faith instead of *questioning* it. Over the centuries, the histories were fictionalized and the fictions historicized by prophets, priests, channelers, and seers determined to clear a path for the Age of the New Technic, where Mankind's disembodied Mind, in the form of the cell phone, television, and computer, could be better and more directly filled with the loving words of God.

[On we'd talk, far into the night...]

PF: Understand—God had little to do with what was being written "in His Name," although he didn't mind it being done. All that theological propaganda (from the Bible, to the *Urantia Book*, to *Conversations with God*) has worked out well for him, especially if you're able to stop thinking of him in terms of the Old Testament God of wrath and forgiveness and begin to conceive of him as theorized in the closing pages of Stanislaw Lem's *Solaris* as an infant God with powers of creation he cannot yet control. You see, all these stories of his Great Power created the *illusion* (and the later *manifestation*) of control and a way to ensure human humility (a trait beyond most angels) and so he let the devout write away, thinking they were divine messengers with no clue they were making it up as they went. So much the better when thinkers like Augustine came up with elaborate Scholastic arguments to prove that the Scriptures were Divine and all their stories of miracles true.[1] The worst of the lot, and the one to blame for most of what's happened, is Zoroaster (whose name means "owner of Camels in good condition"—is that a guy you wanna trust?...). His whole philosophical thesis on the absolute existence of Good and Bad, Light and Dark is a puss-bag of lies. He is followed by Descartes, who employed fine Latin phrases—*res cogitans, res extensa, cogito ergo sum*—to cement the vision of Matter and Mind being separate things.

---

[1] Every so often there comes along a Socrates, whose divine voice-guide, the *daimonion* of his dialogues, is *not* all knowing, because that would make HIM all knowing, and you know how Socrates felt about *that*. Of course, he was killed for corrupting the youth with these and other "blasphemous" thoughts...

EVV [Now on his fourth pipe and halfway into a bottle of burgundy]: Then how do you account for his being [pointing sloppily in an approximation of "Up"] and your being [he looks then at his feet]...

PF: Although these dualities were created by God as a by-product of his early bullying (which led *directly* to the War of the Winged), it was the prophets and theologians who set them into *Law*. It would have been better to embrace the vision of Heraclitus of Ephesus and see the Universe—and all of us—in a perpetual state of Becoming and all pairs of Opposites as having an unbreakable Unity. But thanks to theologians, acting at the supposed behest of the Almighty and his Generals of Light, such Oneness was not to be. *No*. For that crew, these fictional absolutes were a top-notch insurance policy, but they didn't bank on the ultimate outcome of Technology—how it's desensitized and jaded, how it's made humans so secular and independent... And as to the fearsome Armageddon of Daniel and Revelation, designed to keep the masses ever humble and paying tithes, it's become little more than entertainment—another fiction for the film writers and a gathering point for the millennial anti-Everything cults and their sexed-up guru-kings. Instead of lighting sacremonial candles and making sacrifices to push away the End Times they sit at their computer terminals surfing for release and the latest investment boom while a handful of worms buy up all the world.

EVV [Always and absolutely on cue]: And that's where you come in.

PF: And so we do indeed—the Nether Regions Theatre Company, pumpin' out the sideshows while we prep the Main Attraction, guaranteed to make you sit eyes-forward and think about the seemingly random signs stressed in the theological best-sellers that I and others have been tasked with oh so carefully de- and reconstructing as we go. You see, the advent of science and the New Technic and the total fictionalization of the relationships and histories of demons and gods have left the whole of the Unseen Planes (inaccurately boiled down into the polar extremes of Heaven and Hell) nearly superfluous. Obviously, neither God nor the Dark Angels can have this, although God isn't so bad off he would actually *do anything about it*. After all, in the movies, "His Guy" usually wins, and in a walk. My boss [whose name I am not yet ready to share with you, although I do with Verlag], has decided to fight back—to take the fictions and make them *Real*.

Evil's become a joke, and less and less of you walk the world in Fear. And much of this stems from the Ph.D.'d devotees of science and technology conspiring—and it has been from the beginning a *conspiracy*—to use their theorems and discoveries to perpetrate an almost total Demystification of this world. The early scientists were labeled Heretics, and with reason. The minute the microscoped eye found the first evidence of the sub-visual world of atoms and nucleons, organelles and ribosomes, prokaryotes and viruses, and its overly excited owner created the means to measure it—angstroms, nanometers, microns—there was such a sense of safety and well being that everything else that followed—inoculations and airbags, cell phones and security systems, wireless Internet and spy satellites, gene therapy and medical alert devices that fit on a necklace where a cross used to be—slowly began to render the old pantheons of gods and ancient explanations present in the myths and folklore practically NULL and VOID.

[I pause to let it all sink in. Do so as well, if you should feel the need.]

PF: We *Fallen Angels*, in other words, are nearly NULL and VOID, when we used to be Scary as Hell. Some of us, like Lucifer, have taken it as the well-deserved stake in the monster's swamp-vine heart, but I cannot count myself among them. I'm right here in the game while most of my so-called brothers sit silent on the battlefield bemoaning the loss of Love, weeping in their armor as they wait for their long-gone leaders to sound the Last Retreat. Even Lucifer longs for love. He wants to be Pure Spirit, a sacred White Light, walking Elysian Fields and dancing upon Olympus, be they metaphors or not.

So here I am, Spirit made Flesh in the time of the New Technic as a sacrifice on motherboard altars of dismal worth, and I Don't Want It. Why be a pawn when I can just as easily be king of my own Domain (meaning not a *kingdom* but a *soul*), as Lucifer demanded and then abandoned? I will not subjugate myself to the insanity of Machines. Fight or Fade. That's our lot. In the meantime, Pitiful Thing that I am, I must piss and feed and sleep. I must poke my eyes with incense and oil to kill their fire and keep me safe.

The thing is, the God-Christ never banked on the New Technic being what it is... In this hi-speed, digital world the crucifixion must be shown in plasma'd HD and that never was his style...

But for his greatest adversary (who is *not* who you think) it's *exactly* how it's done.

I like snow. Deep blowing drifts of it. Perhaps it's the mythologically other-than nature of snow that reaches inside and jolts the oldest sparks of me. It suits a progressive demon-angel well. Perhaps it's the cold, the blending power of the dagger-points seeking the tenderest parts of whatever you've left exposed.

It's a Seeker of Flaws, the snow. It is the antithesis of Crow, and yet it is his friend.

I love the crunch of tires on the mud and sand and slush and the way the slicing halogen headlights isolate the individual geometric patterns of the flakes as I burn my lungs along icy winter piers. If I were more sentimental I'd see the Buddha himself dancing among the ever-increasing fractals, the waving arms of the trembling goddess, the perfection none can attain without passing thru the Red and on into the White. But the geometrics are reason enough to bless the eyes the Universe has given us to see such reverent things.

A nice kick-ass storm is a moving metaphor—the original Blessed Event, the white shroud, the cleansing of our summery, arid sins. A thousand-year-old tree going down in a tremendous Nor'easter signifies death and the end of an era; its tallest, bleakest branches breaking thru a farmhouse window and whispering its ancient riddles in a shattering veil of promise; a crushing weight that collapses the roofs of teetering securities and lays the rusted implements of agriculture open to the sky. A real ass-kicking storm is an education on the Rules of Earth. I like the way the snow covers up the road and erases the careful constructions of Man. Makes everything look virginal and ready to renew. I haven't the skill to transform into a blizzard. Too much heat in me—too much prideful red anger. But I want to journey thru the Red and on into the White—the purified Bliss that becomes snow as it passes thru this Plane and hints at What Can Be.

That said, Watching instead of Being has its upside too—a bit o' mystery, a dash of fun. Nothing makes me smile like walking a 10-mile stretch of overconfident SUV drivers "down in the ditch" as those wicked good Mainers say. I figure all-wheel drive makes them think they know better than the original crystal-cold god-gem, Mr. Jack Frost. Old Man Winter's as blatantly ignored as God himself, which really is a shame—if we're all just metaphors anyway, the Wintry ones are best. Then again, you don't see many overturned, snow-slicked SUVs with a Sacred Heart medallion stuck upon the dash, so maybe those two talk.

That's a thought to give one Hope.

———

9:09 am. A psycho-fudge type of morning. Cartwheeling down Limmerick Avenue to the solid bass of Bowie's "Width of a Circle." Rich kids everywhere—a little too plump, a bit too crass. Wee Willies and Mary Contraries with fancy cartoon-character backpacks and deli-bagged lunches. I'm well disguised in woolen cap and shades, snarling a spinning yo-yo every so often in a split fingernail and otherwise finding ways to insidiously wreck their vibe. Field Trip Day at the local Private School. Hallelujah! Praise the big yellow bus and the coffee'd-up driver looking anxious and irritable who's sitting behind the wheel.

A quick read of his caffeine'd mind and I know why.

Just a few short years ago he was the Regional Sales Manager for a computer supply company. On his way up—nice car, decent perks, cute secretary amenable to the occasional ass-squeeze, and use of the company's Country House for a gin-soaked week each year.

Hell, man—his kids used to *go* here.

Then the economy crashed.

Boo fuckin' hoo.

It's righteous symbiosis—he supported the war ("Hell yeah, right on! Bomb them raghead desert nigger camel-jockey allah fucks back to the stone age … that's about 12 minutes for them, *right*?") that stopped the momentum. Killed the dream. He perceives a devil on his shoulder, but today it's only his futuristic avatars filling the seats behind him. This is a good scene. Makes my heart glad to see micro-reckonings and karmic balance. It's my diatribes in action. But he's too dense to get it. Or else it's the double dip of controlling a bus full of kids Willy Wonka would boil and squeeze and stretch and sizzle with glee while ducking spitballs and still feeling thankful to be away from his ballbusting, accusatory wife.

Being stuck here has its perks.

I don't much care for hospitals, but every so often I take to walking the halls, helping the painfully dying and incurably withering on their merry way with a few long guzzles of their lousy, polluted blood. It's not so much Mercy as Sport. That level of sickness opens portals to Planes I only can tap into when our minds are linked in such a way, at the moment of death when their final words of thanks are echoed and solidified in a last unclenching of hands. But the visions never last. With etheric incense carrying their sins ever upward and away from the scalloped flesh of the Soon to Be No More (and my own devouring eyes), God sends his angels to take the dying one's Soul (whether newborn or octogenarian) in order to allow the families a needed, cleansing grief. That's how his supposed Grace doth work. I say, "Leave them be!" He cannot offer them *anything* beyond this world—as I've said, Heaven is a myth, a mis-categorization and oversimplification prompted by theological madmen and encouraged by God himself. Souls wander and wait for answers like characters from Beckett, most without a single memory of anything they knew. They're the lucky ones at that, because for those that *do* remember, an eternity of hauntings and cheap theatrics is all that they can have. Pray your guardian angels sing their hymns on your behalf, so you're protected from such things. You deserve some shred of comfort as the Mystery Tale winds down and you won't get any from me. *Why?* Because if one fallen angel opens its heart in love for you, a thousand-million demons choke on their own blood.

I've been writing my Opening Monologue in preparation for the New War. Here's a little taste:

[Lights up on the Speaker, garbed in Blacks and Reds. He has no horns or fangs or claws—none are needed, for the blades are in his eyes, sharpened by the whetstone tones of his voice. He sits cross-legged on a chair of writhing figures (by no stretch a throne), almost Human yet obviously not. He looks outward, beyond his gathered audience, as if the talking he will do only matters for the ones hesitating just beyond the theatre door.]

Speaker: "Thank you. Thank you all for coming. The seats may be uncomfortable and many of you are standing, but I promise to be brief. In the blip of a second, a nano-tick in layman's terms, End Time abominations will be set in motion like Death-card dominoes, ravaging the beasts who dared to free the souls caged in Eden and put up for sale when the Ever-Eternal Bank of God foreclosed on the farm. In the arc of a stripped electrical circuit there are Portents of train-track happenstance and cripples' stolen canes. Cannibal-vampirism is alive and well in the transmogrification of the bread and wine into flesh and blood, and the earth and sea into fire and storm. [*He runs his tongue along his ever so slightly elongated eyeteeth.*] Sandalwood rosaries drip blood along cathedral ceilings to anoint the coronation of the Mandrill King. He lives in empty pockets, breathes thru dockside ravings. He is Parvus Cornu, the little horn. It is his emblem I see tattooed upon so many war-torn chests, prompted by the clues and Biblical bread-trails that have led you all to this rented room. It is the spoiled, arrogant laddie that looks for signs in dogshit and tea leaves, and you've so admirably complied. He knew you would. He is the Great Scion, the second infant reborn to Enhanced Knowledge after God reemerged from the flabby folds of the infant Universe's ever-expanding flesh (which part he emerged from I will leave for you to guess...). There must always be a counter in the duality God's wrought. But Parvus Cornu's destiny was never to walk upon the earth to teach and bleed and hang upon a tree to free you from your sins; his burning anger, so new and potent in a theretofore-unstained expanse of Blinding Light and Peace, was kept awhile in the hardened bowels of a prison he created by Accident and served in with an unwavering sense of Purpose. It is he who is the corrupted alchemist who makes it seem that *Faust* is not a work of fiction but of fact. He is fully awakened now, eyes thrown wide by the satellite pulses and cabled connections of the Information Age. He will arrive to lead you when he thinks it best. When our New War is nearly won. The New Technics may have awoken him, but he doesn't know their keystrokes. Yet."

[The Speaker walks away with a grin, as millions more have entered the already bursting space, drawn by his cadences and the flower of the images he chose to use. As he pulls the frayed ropes that make the curtains close, he blinks his eyes and the EXIT signs, so brilliantly, piercingly red, go out, followed by the slamming and locking of doors and the sound of his boot heels walking ever further away.]

To my mind, four things converged to make up the comic mantle of Man—rickshaw, scrimshaw, sickle, and scythe. Or, stated more clearly, but with less flair—Transportation, Craftsmanship, Agriculture, and Death. These are the fragile ingredients of dreams and decisions, destinations and dominion, recollections and imprints—the last remnants of Man's mis-intentioned Divinity in the form of iron gods, giant churches, moonshots, and Mother Earth. The corrupted legacy and last vestiges of Leonardo da Vinci, the now-revealed concealer of heretical truths and celebrator of John the Baptist, the Magdalene, and the Sacred Feminine. And then there's Michelangelo, the fellatio king hired by the Church to keep him on his back and not his knees. He went blind from dripping paint. Should have just jerked off ... hairy palms, fading sight, and more time for little boys. His artful visions are worshipped, and why not? They are freer than the poisoned actions of priests with their choking Roman collars and wandering hands. Where is *their* beauty? Their souls are emptied like bladders and filled with ash the moment their dead eyes close. God does not forgive what cannot be fathomed by the young child crying alone and naked on the sacristy's cum-splashed floor.

And the corruption's all around. Jagged interpretations of Sistine inspiration have been used for sinister ends. It may seem as though I'm picking on priests, but one has to wonder—What makes a professional student of rites and religion, given to hierarchy and blind obedience, think he is an Everyman and Seer who can save your soul and all the world from Satan's will? In many ways, it is the priest class (especially in Elder Days) that has promulgated and furthered the cause of God's supposed adversary, giving him a powerful mythology and luring voice. It was the priests who oversaw and sanctioned the slaughter of so many Innocent Tribes because their gods had unfamiliar names that made them seem from Hell. (Not that I'm naïve—in the end it was always about Land and the abundance of resources to fatten up the kings of patron states...). As Aristophanes said, *Evil events from evil causes spring.*

Lucifer's right—our current (and temporary) obscurity has made the Priest Class almost meaningless, though not quite obsolete. Getting rid of them outright would be a better start than the current theatrical plan.

I've already tortured my share—it's time for my brothers to step up.

I know it sounds harsh, but the distrust of priests is not mine alone. Have you read Blake's *Marriage of Heaven and Hell*? Plate 11: "...a system was formed, which *some took advantage of,* & *enslav'd* the vulgar by attempting to realize or abstract the *mental* deities from their objects: *thus began the Priesthood.*" [Italics mine, yours and maybe Blake's...] In so-called popular culture (an oxymoron, or else I am too bitter) a subtle change has taken place in how priests are portrayed upon the screen—it's now those who have *lost Faith* that defeat the winged and snarling Antichrist. What does that mean? Religious ritual is not spi-ritual ... the Establishment priests cower among their symbols while the fallen, naked man fights with a sword in one hand and his cock in the other—fight *and* fuck—that's how you defeat the King of Snakes...

At least in the movies. The reality's more complex.

Lucifer (whose name means bearer of light/bringer of air), no doubt responding to the way I banter about his name, was waiting beneath the bummy stairs of the local courthouse tonight, licking the wounds of a run-over mutt and complaining about the taste. He's an icon of swimming eyes and smoldering regret. Perfect antihero for the guilt-woven lunacies of Mother Church. In the construct of Rudolf Steiner, he's a two-sided coin—Lucifer the light-bringer, who brings you upward toward the realms of imagination, beauty, and pride— but also Ahriman, a hybrid of Mephistopheles, Moloch, and Satan—his Earth-dwelling form who drags you down to the depths of the New Technic and the *wehrmacht.* For the purposes of this Tale, we can agree he's Lucifer/Satan, and I'll use those names interchangeably depending on my mood, but Mephistopheles and Moloch are separate entity-ideas not to be confused with my fallen friend.

And fallen he is, too blind to see there's no gilded stairway back to God's good grace—you go there on shredded knees, silently cursing rough stones and proving your worth, a stumbling step at a time, and what your friends are doing or have done in the past doesn't alter by a single inch the length of your own thorny road.

So what was I doing at the courthouse, you ask? (Maybe you didn't but isn't that what people say when they wanna speak the speech?) Freezing my ass off, mostly—taxes go toward the office Christmas party, not the heat. But enough of that—I do have things to say. I was picked up for inciting a riot, which is my Dharma and my right as a demon on this Plane; not that that gets you very far with the cherry-faced blowhard the Public Defender's office picks to make your case. So there I sat, looking just tough enough to raise a shield against the drug addicts and other substance users who can smell me coming and always ask for stuff I'd never give—junk-filled hypos, Immortality, release—as if I was Santa and they were guiltless kids. It's my policy to avoid them when I can—they make a lousy meal and whine more than dying pigs, and I was having fun watching the endless myriad of Types and Personalities in the faux-marbled Hall of the Judge. First, the lawyers—easy enough to spot, though half of them at this level have these right-out-of-the-womb looks of pure befuddlement. Lucky for them their clients know the system better than they do. Then there's the cops, looking pretty much the same whether uniformed or not—high and tight haircuts, muscles bulging beneath pressed shirts and pants. Just barely hiding their looks of contempt and searing judgment—they don't need a judge's okay to crucify this crew. And what a crew it is. Lots of different styles, different *Presentations*. The chatterboxes who are so bored with themselves they ramble on to anyone who'll listen. The scaredy-cat kids chaperoned by their fathers, who work on their laptops and totally miss the irony of their disregard as the cause of their seed's impending doom. The Punk-Studs and Real Bad Mothers. It's sort of the farm league and the majors, though there are only a few All-Stars who get their coffee fetched by low-rider bimbos and dial their dealers while they wait their turn. Then there's the First Timers—frustrated with the system and looking impatient and put upon. Patently ironic for any form of government anywhere, there's a nice big Don't Tread on Me flag in the hallway—apparently there's no Reciprocity Agreement. The courthouse is a Church of sorts—a building with symbolic power and a demand for Reverence without the legitimacy to back it up.

I pulled a fast one and spoke in peasant Russian, leading the judge to ask how anyone involved could understand what the hell I was saying enough to be *influenced* by me?

Good point—reciting the latest State of the Union or the *Anima Christi* works as well.

My aura is breaking down... Archangel accusations about the "truths" that I am peddling have been chiseling my skull nibs all day. To add to the already bumper-to-bumper mental traffic, Parvus Cornu is busting my balls for a conference call, but my phone is off the hook. I can't abide his constant need for scheming and organization—he's become the very thing he so (rightly) despised about God. I can't say I'm surprised—like a mortal running senseless on the repetitive wheel of time he's no more than a Robespierre, calling for regal heads in his misplaced moral zeal. He's a Napoleonic Caesar, an Alexander lost at the feet of a bleeding Cleopatra. He's Hitler and the entire Nazi war machine rolled into a stale cigarette. I've got to get him out from behind my teeth, and Lucifer's no help. He and I have become the ash-brothers of the Cornu as Abel and Esau were to Cain and Jacob. Most days I think I'm not worthy to lead this farce and don't care to be. Why bother? We're competing with so much other *noise*. Why else would we choose to make such splashy, overstated art?

Silence has been devalued and the New Technic's version of Hell is bombardment of the six sacred senses. Drum machines displace the harp and lyre; electronically engineered techno-music drowns out the 12-piece orchestra... We gave music to the masses in the form of angel song and it's been taken away by the disembodied drone of the digital, wireless world. Where is the spontaneous vocal response? "Hushed, hushed, always hushed!" This is not to say it's *all* shit. I hear in the stripped-down chords of Alternative Rock and the street-slang of Hip Hop the voices of the Minority's complaint, but it will not be heaven's chorus while the Media Machine rolls on, choosing the medium *and* the message in plate-glass towers high above the stench. What's another swollen eyelid, discarded scream, crippled sanctimony to them? From speakers embedded in street grates and taxis they bathe the cities in the anthem of the New Technic, drowning out the protests and putting up walls graffiti-proof and sterile, while all the while in the back alleys lie ever-growing piles of torn dreams, jaggedly denied promises, and shredded plastic fragments of the broken Edens of Earth. By seeking to master time you've been left with blaring adulterated echoes less wonderful than ancient cave-script memories.

What's become of Silence? Brainwashed soldiers stormed the sanctuary and raped the virgin hole of the Om. Pop culture's feeble thoughts and septic standards are the wings of a bland assassin, giving not flight but diving instead into the cacophonous depths of madness and blight. Sartre, able genius and man of depth, could not keep the monkeys from dancing to the accordion—they went the wrong way in the tunnel, no matter how he wailed. Post-Modern music ... an unholy mind control. TURN IT OFF. It makes my eardrums run with blood. The vagrant remnants of the old Universal Symphony are the axe-severed rosary, the twitching feet of night's lost thought, the man at the iron door who sells what the thief-gangs stole, the rot-bone meals of worm dining and wolf crimes, and the Sapphic-metered poems of carcasses and lice. The sewer depths are the final refuge for society's evicted jazz-rats—the mystical counterbalance to the slut-slime carnival barkers hawking Shambala in a rush of pills, nipple-piercings, shared needles, razorblade therapies, and butt-burns... The new sport of teens is the S & M Goth show. The new church is the Rave; the new gospel megs and bytes. Date-rape puppetry. Warped cypress dance floors in a ravaged grove of juniper. A shirt of camel's hair. Personal sacrifices to make a mute god speak. Let's burn the floors and dance a glowing crucifixion. New steps. Firefall and rainstorm. Down with Regulations. Up with Detente. An end to fecal unions and fecund butterflies. A backend halt to the Tyrant's Front. First-world leaders speak with forked tongues and make everyone afraid. But the day will come when those same tongues lay severed in the dust, proof of their destined demise tied to bible codes so ancient and removed from the conditions in which they were written that no one remembers what they were *really* supposed to mean, but because they were easily corroborated with Nostradamus and the microfiche back issues of *The Daily Rag,* they survived and grew in strength with the other Ancient Mysteries of God.

Soon will come our cue to sing the razored songs of angels in a Grand Finale that brings forth from the liquid depths the newly reanimated dead, tunnel grasping in their vinyl memories toward the palace of the new regime and a final renunciation of the discordant, numbing Void into which they were lured by the God-sanctioned rites and texts.

Down the street and on the stairs, the limping, liquid shadow of one of Parvus Cornu's messenger slaves has come to Earth, a proudly traitorous amalgam of disciple and turncoat in shaved head and policeman's badge, rising to his descent. I try to hide within the ether, so much surer and substantial than the false solidity of his viscous, translucent stare, but he sees me, his easy source of sugared milk.

I duck and flinch. He walks on.

An ampler chest than mine will he suck dry tonight.

Bristly in his stance, licking his pig-blue lips in sick anticipation, I know I should stop him, stall him—not let him transform fully into flesh, but he eats the last fragile illumination of the Sun on the sidewalk, transforming its good light into so shapely a monstrosity that even I, eater of priests, cannot bring myself to move. Swirling and vanishing beyond and behind those pretending not to see (we are not alone upon this street), he drags his stiffened leg (war wound? punishment? hard-on?) past the drawn blinds of security windows and unlatches the outer lock of the home of his chosen sacrifice. I think briefly about the sunless one above, crouched in sensory expectancy as the Monster, fully realized and enormous, goes in. There is a slam, the groan of crushed glass, and then the pleading starts: "Don't make me drink that ... I'm sorry. ... Oh, God, it makes me gag—don't make me drink it, no I won't, I won't, I can't, oh god please let me die..."

I do nothing.

I stand and listen as I've been taught.

How is it that I, once a heart, have become a mere appendix?

As he walks away, slowly melting his form into pale lunar light, he says, "Next time the Cornu calls, you'd better answer."

Vengeful atrocities like this happen every day while the minds too full of the promise of their own tomorrows cast them fast away. So many dreams like countless Californias reclaimed by the sea. Not daring to respond, I moved quickly down the street and into my secret room, every corner crammed with books and half-finished projects, half-burned pictures and chapel figurines. Despite every indication to the contrary I hold out hope that in some unseen corner, tucked behind a hooker's hangared secret there will be a restoration of my faith and the broken fetus of my Before-This-Time will know a little bit of Light. Tucking away my self-accusations in their modest earthen tomb, I send apologies home with scarlet pigeons and my jet-black Crow, a terse and predictable answer brought back within seconds by a pair of starving, skeletal children, who disregard the coins I toss at their feet and gnaw their own wrists while crawling beneath a table set long ago for a leery king and his murdered, corpsy queen. Having nothing else to give, I serve them quartered mandrill stomach and ancient vinegar wine—it is a meal unfit for consumption and yet they eat until they puke and then eat some more, the ghosts of ancient Romans draped in sea-grey Vesuvian ash.

I have become afraid of the light that's darkening my way.

I'm poorly so(u)led and well past Agitation—enough of stone roads and blisters! Pebbles of loneliness are sticking to the worn gum of my roadside revelations—the laughing snippets of a misfit's mind and its crumbling composure. I should have been a priest for all the time spent upon my knees! Not that I haven't tried... Behind my eyes there stands a Gothic cathedral erected from sacrificial stones and arrowheads wherein gods are nightly and ritually forgotten, remembered, evoked, cursed, forgotten, and shot out in a stream of boiling cum. High upon the western wall gleams the Rose Window, appropriately placed to invoke the Sacred Feminine. The tracery's spider web design is an exact duplicate of Chartre's. The script nightly spoken is St. Hildegard of Bingen's written descriptions of orgasm coupled with a chorus of naked acolytes shouting the text of the *Pistis Sophia,* hymn to the mystical snake-queen of wisdom and love. The sweet sting the attending nun-whores swallow from the pulsing irons of the gathered initiates is ginger's folly (viscous, tasteful, and demure). It is my temple to Isis and the consorts of Solomon and the keystone that once opened the secret doorways I walked thru in the days after the desiccation, the sterile aftermath of the Great War of the Winged, like the pigs driven from Gerasenes, traveling on foot until I reached the sea, where I bartered passage on mottled barges to yellowed shores full of god-factories and New Rites. I'd long run dry on ferry-fare (having made no recent kills), but still the boatman let me on. The dunes we passed were windswept and aching—the yellow went crimson before me, signaling me to shore. Coves of throttled stars (Nature's neon), iridescent, irregular, and perfect, kissed my thighs with their piercing caverns and drank my blood. Candles lit themselves upon my arrival. Dining on their carbon I fondled the Immaculate sand and burned a shattered Grace as my weak and meager sacrifice.

In the broken corners of war-fucked temples I tried to make love to Durga and Kali, and all the others mistakenly called Great Whores—the church-spurned sisters of the Universe—so that Mercurius-Hermes could fertilize the Holy Vase and bring forth the *filius philosophorum,* but I was blocked at the door by Kilroi and Attod, whom Kali had told that I would come. Spinning thru their laughter, screaming warped wisdom and blessing necrophilia as an alternative to unrequited Love, I recited lines from the *Arcana Arcanorum* and all I remembered of Count Cagliostro's texts on tantric sex and internal alchemy. Kali, queen of birth and blood, as is her fate, then came forth, lending a love blade to my optic wound, converging with Prof. Crow in an embolismic brain-plunge thru my skull, embedding emplaced remains of Law and leaving pictures of my victims fraying in the air, wistful and alone for me to scratch at and curse. She is the Dark Madonna, no blackblooded demon, but a link, a length of soiled thread to the innermost outsideness of my disconnected Self. She is the goddess of destruction and new life—the consumer of duality, the nullifier of lies. She fucked and ate Zoroaster in a sublime intake of silent, Om-y breath. I begged her to be my wife, to enact with me the *hieros gamos,* the symbolic union of the Sacred Mother of the Milky Way and the First Father of the Solstice sun that is key to the Mayan 2012 end date that is the kick-off for our cause; the sacred marriage wherein this lousy half-prince could be made a potent, raging king thru the sexual rites of a goddess-queen and thereby be delivered from a lonely death such as the Christians say poor Jesus faced—but she sent me from her island in chains and blindfold to do my penance and find my way back, a cleansed and sanctified soul.

I haven't made it yet.

I've torn myself to shreds trying to comply with the contrary, whimsical wishes of plaster kings and cyber-queens. I invited none of this. I was content to be a soldier in a righteous war and laughed at the darkest things. Now, while the worms bleed and fall in the early days of a new and selfish Battling, God and Lucifer equally confess their lack of interest and just as it was in the Old Autumn (what poets call The Fall) we are damned—despite the ravages of Hell and the inaccessibility of what, with the right décor and set dressings, could pass for Heaven—to fight and rest, analyze our mistakes, and fight again some more. Without death, without flag, without Prize. In my flaccid fury I've often taken form as a swollen Midwest river, readying to gorge myself on the unprotected towns in my path as I make my way to the soundstage of our newly constructed Megiddo.[2]

As I swell and bubble half a mile away, the Ignorantly Blissful and credit-stretched paint their summer houses in bourgeois style and in the Autumn gather leafy expenditures of Nature's best expression into ragged piles like mindless automatons who don't realize how fine and fertile their lawns would be if they just let the dead leaves lie. They know nothing of the Seasons and so cannot be damned and mustn't be ignored, Petri dishes for duality that they are. In the bordering wastelands of cut trees and Catholic rites I lie in wait in the dead and vapid moon-wash, sharpening my teeth in expectation of a Frenzy, and loathing my vacillation—with a whistle and some licorice I could lure their lads and lasses and dig them graves in the ample suburban waste, yet all I do is Watch.

Later in the evening, when they've all gone inside, I do my demon meditations to block the blare of Corporate Network News pulsing out from the etched-glass windows as the crickets bow their Satan-songs draped in Wolfgang Mozart's tears, dulling my teeth on the chiseled strips of my Insistent Memories and calling Crow to join in the mockery of my limp-dick failures. The striving Middle Class is harmless—too poor to mount a charge, too rich to show any emotion not dullable with a snifter of scotch and ice.

---

[2]This is an easy thing, this transformation—what Hawaiian shamans call "grokking" taken to its psycholinguistic extreme. Like other operations of the so-called Mind, it is merely the instantaneous communication of subatomic particles that have no cognition of distance because there actually *is* no distance—their separation is an illusion. David Bohm calls this nonlocality—a message of cosmic unity under the guise of quantum physics.

What is this rambling I've done? A symbolic, fragmented scream of demi-consciousness. A false array of low-bid radar. An insane warrior's battle journal, post-war/pre-war. It's over. No second coming, no epic war on Megiddo's whore-y peak, actual or acted. The major players sold out long ago, content to confuse themselves with chipping icons and gold-n-incense ritual nonsense. Carnival clowns and petty entrepreneurs. They set themselves up as spread-legged concubines and now they wonder why no one calls. Maybe it's the flies hovering at their loins, advertising "Old Meat."

Have I given up too much in my stationary wanderings and mystic meditations? I've hardly figured out how to heat a microwave burrito—how the hell could I answer *that*?

You must forgive my penchant for drama and yo-yo-ism—the way I bounce between soaring optimism and theatrical despair. All clinical diagnoses aside (and there are several that apply), it is because I am not where I want to be. It was not so long ago (a mere flash in the life of an angel) that I was an unencumbered spirit bound to No One or No-Thing. My existence since the Transformation has been weighty and filled with complex events. Take, for example, the past 24 hours:

The morning started fine ... walking the sands of Egypt I suddenly remembered a tomb I had designed and built for a 2nd-dynasty ruler who had often invoked my aide. Prying open its sacred inner seal I found, not my invoker, but some "greater" Pharaoh of a later time who had claimed it for his own. I lunched upon his Ka (scant meal that it was) and took a nap in the heartbeat chambers of a river asp left to watch the entrance by a tired guard who missed his wife and newborn child. Urging the waking serpent to surrender the reins of his mind, I lay upon his length as we slipped our way thru the valley and toward the Great Pyramids and sacred Sphinx—that wicked beguiler of would-be kings. We ate six tourists. No one will miss them. Even their mothers never called.

In the mid-afternoon hours, full of blood and fibrous memories, I attended a fakir show at the Sunday Follies in Gujrat, India, perched on a basket watching dozens of corrupted, brutalized innocents firewalk on the Master's Love-Lava. If they failed in their bid to be Unburned (and many, many did), they were told it wasn't the fault of the rocks or the Master's teachings—only a lack of faith in *themselves*, a mantra clearly stated in the home-video training program and repeated thru the High Priest's cosmic bullhorn before each attempt. Taking this to be the truth (instead of merely *one-third* of it) each one of them, despite the desire to scream away the pain of their blistered and soon to be infected and gangrenous feet, fell upon their knees to beg forgiveness of the Master for failing him, a gesture he accepted with a generous show of tears. Not for weeks or maybe months (spiritual bombardment having dulled the more common of their senses) will they even think about rebelling against the self-blame of their intolerable public demonstration of failure and unworthiness. If you haven't the self-trust (I sure as shit don't) it's better to quench the fire than to walk upon it.

So far, not terrible, though the night was a tempest I'd just as soon forget. After dining on the aftermath of a screwed-up bris, I wandered, still famished, into a London salon recently converted into a den of passive rapes and bottled escapes, led there like a mindless dog by the whorehouse smell of unwashed cunts. I was greeted at the door by the knowing eyes of a familiar and friendly Dragon Queen, who played her nails along the drying blood crusting at the corners of my mouth and, sampling the same with a tongue-snap, let me know with a head shake that my judgment was for shit. Stripping me of my jangling chains and piercings, she threw me on a puce divan and summoned a line of fine Lotus ladies, who each exposed a single perfect breast on which I had to dine. I took them all, and *took* them all, without moan, without delight, without the minor gentleness that qualifies such acts as sex. I was too hungry for all of that. The Dragon Queen opened herself to me, but I declined—it does no good to fuck the mother after flaying all her buds.

An hour later, bored with the Ripper walking tour I'd stupidly paid to take (and still not fully sated), I slipped away on Commercial Street near the Ten Bells Pub and Spitalfields Market, blending into the shadows like Saucy Jack himself until I came upon a recently sacked welder who was well into a cheap bottle after thrashing his wife for the third night that week. In a word, he'd "do." I've gotten good at picking the ones who'll like it—the ones who really come alive amid the beer–blood smell of rotting alleys. He gazed coldly into my eyes 'til the very end. Those are the victims I like best—the ones who won't let you see them flinch. The ones that licked the toes of boots still holding the dried grey matter of bashed-in babies' brains. It is only the mad man out creating monsters to prove he's not one that struggles and fights against me, a beast he has not created but believes in his ego he did. Flesh and thought sear and intertwine as I feed on them, preventing the transmutation of my pleasure into a guilty pain, no matter how vivid the garden tiki; no matter how purple the flame. I suck out what I need to survive, as all vampires must... Then, the sublime moment arrives when the heart begins to strain and the mind's filmstrip begins to play. Most times, in those moments, I don't know where I end and the victim begins. In the case of the welder, I watched a mother (his wife) cracking eggs against the backdrop of a buzzing bulb. All radiance and self-doubt. A slab of bacon licked and sniffed at but ultimately passed over. Just beyond the chipped Formica of the counter I saw a filthy child coloring a vivid blue bruise on the arm of a threadbare, hand-me-down doll to better make them twins. Washing down the scraps with goblets of neutral tears, I vomited out my doubt and headed home.

That was just a few hours ago. Now I should sleep—I am vulnerable to the rays of Ra when I have filled myself so full of human blood and the morning will not wait. Standing recklessly on this bridge between wake and dream, the chasm widens as I wave my cock in praise to the new moon, my morphine Veda. Too many needs in this demi-Human form. The constant craving for sugar and blood—my recalcitrant acid fix. A stillborn child devoid of nursery rhymes and button flies often fits the bill, but not as of late. Too many victims today. Too many memories dancing in naked dog-piles with my own. Cursed is the man who has visions of his death (as an earlier victim did), eternally clinging to hazard-free grass paths only to find it was the rocks and lava that were the way to safer passing. He is the model for the Christian myth of Hell. I want out of this prison of Halves—better to transform myself fully into the Beast and so be rid of this hiding, this dancing with shadows to make me seem a dream. That's the law, Satan's Executive Order—best to not be seen. To be thought, shadow, and myth and yet Intervene and Manipulate. Anne Rice's Lestat was on to something, in his many books and mad adventures, but he's not real. Or is he?

I may have met him once, but my imagination is so overdeveloped I can rarely tell the It from the Ink.

A morality tale, Planner Forthright style:

Oncologists and virologists "sacrifice" mice. They burn them to the depths of their skin under the guise of nicotine and sleep deprivation wound-healing tests and call it Science. Their notebooks are full of such lies—"Six mice *sacrificed* 6 Oct., 10 pm." Aztec ritual in white coats. Total absolution in an ether–cyanide mix. I've walked their halls, white-tiled monuments to Man's power over death and all "god"'s creatures (up to and including "lesser men"). Just to keep things balanced, I've fudged their numbers, stirred their stews. It's all cable cookery shows for me—add a strain of this, a test-tube of that ... cancer's good for Man—a reminder of what black cells, a fragile soul, and a total disregard for the Connectedness of Everything can breed. In a moment of weakness (or perhaps a pity–strength hybridization) I took a cancerous mouse out of the monsters' lab and lay with him as his tumor grew to half his body size over the course of a week, imagining their widening eyes and flicking pencils as it lay dying on their stainless, guiltless counter tops. I gave him ether and a kiss upon the ear. After Last Rites I interrupted the Butchers' morning meeting, bestowing a cancer-rich kiss upon the anus of each. I used no ether to end their pain as I watched the cancer grow over the course of a month. I cannot stem the tide—the lab never closed—so revenge is not my lot.

I killed them in anger, not to make a point.

I've been penning my speeches for the upcoming Theatricals. I think this one presents the Truth in a fun and driving way:

"Dear Friends: Welcome to another session of the Planner Forthright School of Freshly Shaven Scrotal Philosophy. We begin our training today with a question from St. Joseph of Campbell (County): 'Are you the light bulb or the light?' A fine riddle for you container-loving types. You spend nine months in a womb, go directly into an incubator or little washtub with a lovely hand-typed anklet and color-coded cap (preferably pink or blue—yellow is for fencesitters and no one trusts the Noncommitted), go home to a little Alcatraz of a crib or playpen and then rush off to a rapid succession of boxy classrooms, bathroom stalls, rat-cage dormitories, and office cubicles. You go from Point A to Point B in cutesy motorcar containers that are worthless status symbols (aka, cock and breast comparison contests) and should you go to the hospital (that house of speechless horrors) you get nicely curtain-cubicled for supposed privacy though your roommate can hear every fart, moan, gasp, and breathy curse you spew. And you know damned well you're listening to theirs. Meanwhile, your ass is hanging out while the nurses (who never, ever look like they do in skin flicks) giggle and sneer. Then, kicker of all great kickers, when you die they put most of you in a *box*.

Now, I have to tell you, when the flaming comet comes, I'll be entirely *glad* to lose this mess-o-flesh I've so suckingly been saddled with—I'm flushing the old bitch of a skin-pistol right down the cosmic commode, trigger and all. So—I ask again—are you the light bulb or the light?

Take all the time you need. I'll be taking measurements for your box."

NOTE: I am buzz-yakking on the blood of a guy who was well into his eighth raspberry Margarita when I "absorbed" him, so diplomacy and any vestige of make-nice-ness are brutally absent here.

Thru the deep red haze of his/our high, I see the place of bones—Golgotha—where they crucified the Nazorean (which is not to say *from Nazareth*).

I haven't thought of him in years ... how he shouted out to God: "Eli, eli, lama sabachthani," as though he expected an answer. We could have been friends, I think, if we had known more and felt less, but I was apt to play the Demon all too well in those days and I chose instead to torment him, shaking the cross where it met the stoney ground, staring up for hours at the bottoms of his pierced and aching soles.

And then the God-damned thing began to list to port because the ignorant Roman cross-builders failed to take into account the leaden weight of the Christman's heart-love (and the demon hands that rocked it), so the whole fucking thing was set to topple over when I leaned my own thickly concentrated heart-bulk against it just to help him see it thru.

He could sense me there, allowing gravity to do its work, minute by minute, as I caught his blood-sheddings in my eager, spectral "mouth."

And thus became I vampire.

I see his mother, old Mary Mater, weeping convulsively near the scene. She couldn't get too close ... and why should she? He had caused her no small amount of hurt with his proclamations of closeness to God and delusions of grandeur, to say nothing of the mental torment he had bestowed on his *stepdad*, Hammer Joe. Was his real father there, somewhere among the legionnaires who stood guard over his Execution for Rebellion against the Great State of Rome? Probably not ... he had no doubt moved on, raping and impregnating an impressive lot of barely teenage girls in the regions of the Pax Romana [civil war, jumbo shrimp...]

I couldn't help but ask him, as I slowly worked his foot-spike to keep the blood-flow fresh, what the Hell he thought he was going to accomplish with all his blah-blah-blah. After all, even with a heart as full of love as his, he was a bit too eager, far too jagged and green, without the self-calm of a Buddha or the fiery speech of the world's first religious Propagandist, Mohammed.

Yeshua ben Joseph was a sheep among wolves, as his many symbols say. He proved unable to play the game with the Pharisees and Sadducees, or the Roman musclemen who carried out their shit-sack bidding. He shouldn't have been The One. The blame falls on his uncle, who took advantage of the untimely death of his much-maligned and fully shamed stepfather to drag him far from home in his teens and twenties. Can you imagine the confusion spawned by 999

Persian nights and their carnal education, as he read on perfumed pillows the writings of Brother Buddha? And his time in England with the Druids, his walks in the Himalayas, and, upon returning home, his initiation into the Essenes, an ultraradical organization in a time when *everyone* was radical. His cousin John was a long-time member of the Children of Light.

With his head full of Spiritual Alternatives, Jesus was a rebel with a cause—although not as strong as that of his fellow Essenes, who pegged him as the leader of a grand and slicing revolution against the Invaders, the corruptors and idolators—The Roman Empire. It's a little known fact that the episode of the loaves and fishes—the feeding of the five thousand—was actually a summit meeting of the factions just following the death of the Baptist (who was, by the way, the *real* leader of the Bright Light revolution, not Jesus at all—they were political rivals and many of the original disciples were once hanging with the Bap). They were all there that day—the Zealots, the *sicarii*, the Pharisees, the Essenes. It was Mafia time in the desert with a little *pane*, a little *pesce*, and no small amount of *agita*, *capeche*? Incidently, the matter of the loaves and fishes, while certainly a miracle, had nothing to do with Jesus. They were a by-product of another in a long line of magickal duels between the infamous Simon Magus (John's successor) and Simon Peter, whose status as rival to Mary Magdalene never held him in the high stead the books describe. Point is, by the end of the summit it was absolutely clear that Jesus didn't have the respect and experience needed to bring them all together. His failure was a burr in the ass of Judas Escariot, the only non-Galilean of the Twelve. A leading political activist (read: Inciter to Rebellion) in Jerusalem when Jesus came to town, he hung his hopes on a guy without the balls for battle. Judas hadn't the wit for the Pharisees either—he was just a Dylanesque pawn in their game.

More on these guys of the Gospels another time—that Margaritaville Mikey I sucked on is starting to turn—think I'll force his body through a wood chipper *Fargo*-style and spread his remains on the rose garden at the statue of St. Thérèse of Lisieux two blocks down from the bar where I found him.

All the better to make the thorny flowers grow.

Halloween, Halloween, Halloween! I love to fuck with (and fuck) these silly techno-coven witches, these Goth creations, these self-styled Devil Worshippers (*spooky...*) who are really just self-loathers and chicks with mascara fetishes and a love of black (it is slimming and flattering, but only to a point). I am not speaking of Wiccans—nature lovers, women of true *power*, the unfortunate victims at the hands of the *Malleus Maleficarum*, the Tolouse accusations of the 1330s, the English purges of the 16th century, the Troubles in Salem, and all the rest. Those sexually free and potent women of the fields who scared the shit out of the thoroughly repressed likes of Cotton Mather who let the stake and fire stand in for their own un-enacted sexual lust (only a dolt like Ichabod Crane would carry the bullshit [literally—Irving made it up] that was the *History of New England Witchcraft* in his iron head as a means of impressing the more proper, self-restrained "ladies" of the world). I have dwelled in the cave of the Macbethian triumvirate, walked with Saul to the witch of Endor, and trampled the grasses of China with the Lady of Fatimah, and have learned their ways and blessed their efforts with my blood. For the true Goddess on earth, I spare no craft—I crawl to her feet in the night and make her potions potent beneath her sultry incantations and dripping athame. NO—I am talking about fucking with the comic-art devil-divas, the wild, coke-sniffing, wrist-slitting drinkers of blood (their self-vampiricism closer to the truth than their chronic misperceptions ever fathom). I love to go to them in a haze of smoke, like a damn gone vision and do them in a cauldron. To drink them like too-dry martinis with swaggy, rotten-olive cunts and leave them thinking they've made a Communion. I rob them of their power and leave a splintered toothpick by their beds.

It's time for revelation. Another piece of the puzzling puzzle that is Me.

It's time to tell you of my "birth."

I was born in Satan [sic(k)] Cruz under ultrafantastical circumstances. In the apex of a whirlwind, a shattered bottle of good scotch was purposefully mixed with the binding glue of a discarded library lender of the *Egyptian Book of the Dead*, and thus was I Made in a swath of smokeless fire. Father liquor and Mamma glue had been thrown away at one and the same time in a moment of frustrated Dual Denial by a recently excommunicated Nun named Agnes Roberta Buntz, a woman with lots of twisted secrets and no one left who cared enough to make her feel bad about them. Miss Buntz—crude form of a human model that she was—too typical to bother labeling with a laundry list of cynical descriptors—carried my form, writhing and repulsive, into a Mexican eatery, where she hid me in a napkin while she dined on rice and beans. I took her name, in different shapes and permutations as the mood and situation moved me: Milton Buntz, William Buntz Blake, Aleister Anton LeBuntz, Sister Agnes Roberta Buntz Jr. (as I can pass for man *or* woman—as can we all—don't let a cock or cunt limit your experience on this earth), though I now go exclusively by Planner Forthright—it's the ironic bone on which I choose to choke, which keeps me from falling too far, too fast asleep. I am a failing Antichrist and cryptic prince of wastelands and diseased pigs. This is my struggle. It worsens and goes on.

Why was it that I was born a babe? I cannot with surety say. I think it has to do with the great love and excitement, the thirst for knowledge and experience that little children have—how they so desperately want to be part of the Smotherhood of Man, enveloped to the point of choking in Dad's sure bicep and Mom's big boob.

It didn't work for me.

As the years passed and I underwent my Education, I thought perhaps suicide could be a way out … that Ultimate Refusal to Play that I've shared in vicariously, but with empathy, in bathroom stalls and bathtubs, in locked and abandoned kitchens and on subway platforms, in forgotten childhood bedrooms and public squares. I've witnessed it as protest, statement of resolve, weep of desperation, moment of confusion, and Simple Solution. Leave it to the Church to damn the already Damned (not to mention their unpleasant Fate at the mercy of the Harpies in Dante's Hell). If they could have found the resolve to stay around to take the ride, odds say they would have stayed strapped in. So, you ask (slyly, smugly): Why didn't I do it? It would help you put the book down and resume the shadow Normalcy of your life to know that I am a coward, a Lucifer-like chickenshit who couldn't pull the trigger, draw the blade, eat the pills, kick out the chair, suck the fucking tailpipe. WRONG. A million times, a million ways WRONG. I've tried to off myself in more twisted and reprehensible ways than I care to enumerate (though here's a partial list, for conversation's sake: battery cables, explosives, traintracks, hand guns, razor blades, hand grenades, gas cans, sucking *directly on* the tailpipe, hanging, car crashes, and numerous creatively mixed cocktails, including but not limited to— laudanum, opium, hydrochloric and sulfuric acids, belladonna, absinthe, turpentine, strychnine, arsenic, mustard gas, anthrax…) But the Great Cosmic Force has denied me my *Right*. I've fought the War, kept the Code; I'm more *Bushido* than some ancient bastard in fancy helmet and prick-armor, so I took my place on the altar and undertook my *seppuku*. It was blessed relief, my hot, bisected innards spilling out onto the cold, unyielding floor. Pleasure, pure and sweet, the rats who slobbered down the chunks and waltzed into corners to sleep. So imagine the bitch-fucking I took when I woke up *three days* later to find those same bloated rats puking up and transferring my parts and pieces down my throat in a reincarnating kiss I didn't ask for or want.

Words are only the blood that's left to bleed.

Pathetic, I know, but let me ask you this: Aren't we all (Vibrant beings though we seem) existing in some form of desperate, dying aloneness? What's scarier than that? Why else do battered women stay with their mates? Why do sour lovers dressed in sterile disconnectedness trample on and on thru years and pains and separate beds?

Those in the process of reforming always play the moral card. But no one takes the bet.

I met a gone angel porter in a cityscape alley, dealing recycled cyber connects and bleeding out his soul on an old guitar. Our acquaintance was made via the subterranean tubules of the Goths and vamps and other cyber cave dwellers who cross my path. He's a carrier of bags and soiled regrets, ranting in parables and writing in melancholy blues about Kerouac and Beckett and never stopping to *breathe*. He's got the Salieri Complex—all the desire and none of the success that it should breed. He stations himself at the junctions of the depth-train, punching tickets and passing out fliers of moody reverberation. I envy him—he could torch himself as a footnote to his latest manuscript and not a soul would criticize. It'd punch up sales and make him *known*. He's pure light in a dark bottle no one can uncork. And yet he keeps forging on just to help me face the day. "Don't look back," he says. "Just 'cause you've figured out how to be two places at once doesn't mean you oughta be. You've got the bi-edged sword of the artist—Vision in a blind world. It's the shaman's realm—divine sight on a materialistic, enslaved Plane and some Open-eyed journeyers (angels, devils, ain't it all the same??) come here and shout mighty about the lies to the blank faces of all but a few other Open-eyed... I swear to god I doubt Jesus ever cured anyone who wasn't ultimately self-assured all along that he'd be healed." He said this about the girls: "They are angels fair n fine and a damn sight Divine and the fucking devil all claws and axe and hunger. They're the hole n the dirt to fill it. A fine plate a pie and the heart attack that follows. Give 'em all to me brother and keep 'em the fuck AWAY." He's a cool brother—a real scene in beat poetry wings and Ginsbergian unsurety. We pal'd around awhile 'til he caught the bus to mystic cities ... gave himself a mohawk to keep the dogs away and found himself a potent magnet. That's the kick I got from brother porter. As it comes around he'll pass my way again—he's a reluctant Shaman, feeling half dead 'steada twice alive by having one foot in each world. He could be my pupil—my Renfield, my Igor. He'd eat flies if I asked, but that ain't the juice I seek to flow. I dig his jagged edge. He keeps me going when I think of giving up.

Dig that porter, y'all—he's a word-bleeding head-slammer, a true prophet, a mystic mouse.

To take my mind off the upcoming theatricals, I've been lately painting on cavewalls, like in my earliest days—before television, televangelists, TeleMundo—when telepathy was hard but beautiful.

A la Blake (I wish I'd been his love-child) I give you a bit of axiom, my own meager additions to the Proverbs of Hell:

- It is only in the dark that good light shines.
- The tears cause the words and the words the tears.
- Good dancers trample no toes but get there splendidly and without notice.
- Curiosity keeps life open for death smells and maybe-pains.
- Good thoughts bring good words, the roots of which will be our next, best kings.
- We are only players of roles in a dark and empty theatre, ever-closing.
- Hold no woman upon the bow, for the calamity to come shall be the Devil's gale.
- New Mystic Alchemy is a town square debauchery, a child's broken plaything, a secret garden overgrown.
- Wit is wisdom distinguishing itself from old news.
- On the demon fringe, where every word is a weapon, there can be no quarter.
- It is only in drowsy readings that the subtlest rhymes betray their bonds.
- If the windmills are not burning, we must change our ways.
- Seek no absolution while Christ the child plays bathtub Admiral with dragons' claws.
- Cries are muffled in the stifling swells of sanctimonious revelry.
- When ecstasy is reached and all duality's erased, silence outweighs all words.
- Many a man is bred among princes to sleep among slaves.
- Eyes that have seen death must not turn away; instead, plant seeds anew.
- Just a little skein of thread gets the Hero thru the maze.
- Call the dawn with a horn of deep resound. A swirling cloud.
- Coffinbuilders leave no seams from which life's light could leak.
- Laughter is the light in the raving madman's night.

- Wit is worthier than fist.
- Fishing in Acheron will fill your nets with woe.

I am fogged in … ate a chick on a morphine spiral and I'm passengering, so dig this: With 108 beads of a faux-pearl mala I strip away the fleshy maya of subservient lies. Having no necessaries I beckon the raw veins to time-wasting frivolity. High as I am, I can sit in a chair and be Everywhere… making films of dreams to shape and see and sell for free—such is the multiple oneness of my black-ink aspirations. In the valves and tubules of the neglected machinery of my Heart dissolution binds itself to the profane contours of the Zealot's wish-blown lash, and I carve the words *Hic Sunt Dracones* into its hard-beating chambers with a pocketful of thorns. In a Newark alley I spit puke and dance a Shaman's trance; muggers pummel wide-eyed tourists for blood-thrills and petty cash and I only sit and *watch*. They're better off dead. I slink along the storage corridors of a St. Michael's Hospital, drinking urine samples and discussing complex cases with the corpses waiting their time in line for the Nothingness. Changing places with less eager patients, I allow myself to be operated on by doctors with no degree, who swear by Hippocrates that experimentation is growth and in the service of science the patient sometimes dies. It won't be fear that raises me from this thorny path, but a new Infusion of Hope—the familiarity of warm bondings and wood life, the challenge of raising up from sheltered dawns and vibrant hues a new light of personhood. Kali won't have me, and I will not rape to plant a seed. Do you know Jesus' worst regret that night in the garden of Gethsemane? It was not an early death or a failed revolution. It was the agony of never having a son in which to pour his haggard regret and broken dreaming. I will not face the same fate—I was turned into flesh against my will and I will not pass on Unheard.

Lord Henry Wotton, in *The Picture of Dorian Gray*, says "There was something terribly enthralling in the exercise of influence" and, not surprisingly, that "all influence is immoral." Ever professed to have a devil on your shoulder, telling you to "Fight, fuck, drink, rape, kill"? Does anyone believe we have that power? Jesus in the desert, Satan tempts him—"Do this and you'll get that…" He really had *nothing* to give. He was banished to a wasteland… We haven't the strength to engineer your actions. *We* can fight, drink, rape, kill—with art and savagery, sublime humor, true Masters of the horrific and macabre—but to *Make* you? Suggest—Yes. Recommend—Yes. Make you think it's all your idea, like Clive Barker's Yattering? If we're really on our game. But *persuade*? Only to the dullest minds, the most corrupted and empty souls, in which case we are merely throwing ready seed into richly fertile soil and reaping undue infamy for the yield. Take the cartoonish coven in *Rosemary's Baby*. Steal a tie, blind a man. Take a glove and kill one dead. The powerful Thoughtforms of the egotistical and twisted make the Devil out to be something he's not. And Never Was. Those are the true Monsters, Reader. Mortal men and women seeking Immortality thru the low-vibe power of the earth. Seeking boons from a Satan a million times greater in their *minds* than in reality. Even the name "Satan" is misleading—in the early Jewish/Muslim texts it is lower case, spelled *shaytan* or *shaitan* and taken to mean an adversary or tempter, often of the demonic variety commonly called djinn. From this evolved Satan as the Old Testament accuser prosecuting Man before God-as-judge and later into Satan as the sole bringer of evil into the world. With a supposed pedigree like that, it is little wonder he ultimately became Public Enemy Number One in the inevitable battle for souls.

But all of that is nothing but badly crafted bunk. If we could really do all the books and movies (and priests and rabbis) say, you'd all be Nazis now. We are Exemplars, nothing more. And that's why I was tranformed into Flesh. Man's gotten too egotistical, thinking he can do his own dirty work—he'd rather be his own agent than the Devil's, so here I am to remind him who the Master *really* is. To undertake with artistry and genius the *truly* demonic and dark, which is damnably ironic given the fact that a handful of serial killers and dictators have shown *me* a thing or three...

So let's be clear—evil is nothing more than a Thoughtform made manifest in a personal myth of Hell, so my very existence is on a certain level owed to a mass of low vibrations that confused the Universe with God and then abandoned its creations to extinction. If all the poet-philosophers had followed Dante's lead and left the notion of Heaven as a state of Pure Love and Hell as the absence of God (i.e., an absence of Pure Love) as *allegory* then we'd all be better off. I didn't and don't desire my corporal compulsion to kill or rape or incite to riot the mindless masses—I much preferred to do it for Fun.

What of our Team Leader, our Spiritus Capitan, Brother Lucifer? Tired. Tired, tired, tired. The praise and attention of his worshippers no longer enough—he's the carnival performer grown weary of applause. There never was any Satan's spawn, by Rosemary or anyone else; at least not in the Conjuring the Prince for His Throne sense... The Great Darkness is from *within* the Hitlers, the Caligulas, the Stalins and Husseins... The whole thing got moved to a fabled Hell, and everything went to Shit—more of Moreau trying to remove what is inherent in Man.

And Hell, in its earliest conception, was a valley outside Jerusalem named Gehenna where the inhabitants made child sacrifices—truly brutal, but very much of Man. But the sketches and stories multiplied until Satan was made Form—how could it have been otherwise? That much fearful energy and determined focus can move mountains. And it's only gotten worse. We're active, yes—but we can't get *Inside* (unless of course you or a third party *invite* us, thru spells, curses, amateur occultism…), so all the ritual and fuss of Exorcism is really just the Roman Catholic Dog and Popey Show—another way to sustain the bullshit dictum *extra Ecclesiam nulla salus*—no salvation outside the Church. No salvation *inside* is more like it. What *is* there was there from ages undetermined. Part of the muck that was your forbears…

On the occasion of the death (*requiescat in pace*) of Agnes Roberta Buntz, stepped-on mother, ex-Sister, and twisted saint (Cause of Death my own), I spoke a Hindu incantation and opened the note-filled and taped-together Bible she gave me long ago. Opening to Lamentations, chapter 5, I read aloud the final verse, line 22: "Restore us to yourself, O Lord, that we may return; renew our days as of old *unless you have utterly rejected us and are angry with us beyond measure.*" [Italics in the ultimate original, I am sure.]

Nothing but silence so far.

I feel my upper lip stretch to hide my daggers as I stare at my reflection in the spreading pool of her blood. Such an abomination, this caged-in, physical form! This prison, this battlefield of endless deaths. … Only a prattling fool like Shakespeare, so drunk on words that he would vomit such wretched sweetness, would compare this mess of flesh to the form of an Angel, to the inexpressible bliss of Pure Spirit, boundless. These thoughts sear me with their heated meathook details… Think of your first love, if you've been so blessed and cursed—the one of Innocence, Grace, the beauty and clumsy nose-knocking of Youth—how she did everything for you—hung on your every Word (the essence of god, indeed) but because she wouldn't open her legs to your Invasion, you left her cold on a February phone and found that fucking a drunken Stand-in with gaping hole and deafened ear wasn't anything like you'd hoped. That was the way with the Fall—and the way it was with my sort-of-Mom and God.

Her soul won't take its flight.
It has nowhere to go.
He won't take her home.
Not even now.

I once spent 72 hours in a hole for burning a flag. The country doesn't matter—every one's the same... They gave me only bread and water, and the occasional kick in the side to help with digestion. Were I a cheap magician, I could have turned the water into wine and the bread into beer and been fat, drunk, and happy for the duration. I learned instead how to nurture Resolve and feed Ideas—to cling to a mantra and not let anything else edit or invade. It was a vision quest, courtesy of Jail. I never burned a flag again—only the house from which it hung. That's what jails and prisons do—give men time to feed their Hate. It's the unwatered seed that could one day bring the whole prison-industrial complex down—sort of Attica '71 on a bigger, better scale—its sadistic wardens and sodomizing guards and its worm-infested foundation of corporate profiteers, campaign funders, and strategically placed electoral votes. It's not all so romantic as Genet would have us think, although the notion of thieving as being not rebellion or anger but pure experimentation is definitely one I can get behind. Speaking of behinds, it seems being a homosexual makes the prison system more appealing, but that could be unique to Gentle Jean. Then again, in *the thief's journal* he quotes a piece of Yugoslavian prison graffiti—"I bugger the wall!" Watch for chafing bro. He definitely was at ease with his Mirror Self—there would be no need for Exorcism with a cat like that. He was digging the ride too much, like Hugo's Thenardier—thieving was the means to sticking it up the abstract ass of society and, for Genet, as many real ones as you can.

So I say, Lock em up. Lock every last one of the so-called *undesirables* up.

They'll have plenty of time to read the right books and plan the coming coup.

They're awaiting our debut from comfy front row seats.

T he *womb*.

That's what ole Jalalul-Din Rumi, the far gone Sufi mystic, was talking about when he asked: *Why dost thou stay, drinking blood, in this dungeon of filth and pain?* But, having never *known* the inside of a womb, I've chosen to adapt Rumi's metaphor to generally mean anything upon this Plane.

I dislike being here—the tears of hot Hate *psssst*-ing to steam around my charcoal lids are a constant reminder of the indignities I've endured in my forty-plus years within the Flesh. You see, it's my "birth"-day, and I'm not handling it well *at all*. As a matter of fact, I'm drunk on a pharmacy clerk who liked to check the Quality, so bear with the foul mood and fouler poesy, arcane though they are.

The recent death of Stepmother Buntz (for which I was un-Holy responsible) was not nearly enough to assuage the Cornu's anger about my rebel thoughts. His claw tickles my Pons as he laughs his Mysticism into my snakepot, already full to the brim with vodka and saffron, bitter lemons and bladder dregs. He enjoys my stumbling manners, the way I piss myself in rented beds and cut my limbs in gardens of thorn and shrapnel. It's his Game—the Program for Wayward Devils. I awaken in the early light to find myself fully winged and nailed to children's toys refashioned in the shape of a cross.

It's irony and blasphemy rolled into one, and the only way to save me is to tell you more about my "birth," and the events that preceded and framed it.

As I've said, I was brought forth from a magickal mix of good scotch and spellbook glue in a back alley puddle, Year of Our Horde, 1968. An interesting time in world history—full of political intrigues, musical geniuses, and controversial wars and ways of living. If ever the ground had been prepped and hoed to hold the seed, this was such a time.

It's my nature to make the most of them.

You see, it was a series of actions undertaken *by my own naïve hand* over the course of the ages that led to my transformation into Flesh. As Pure Spirit, I was always a bit of a showman and it's time to reveal some of my favorite manifestations, including the one that really got me noticed by the Cornu—the one that brought me here in November '68 to do the bastard's work.

Do you know the story of the Dream Stele that Tuthmosis IV had added between the paws of the Sphinx after he'd had it restored? It tells how, as a prince, a ways down the line of ascension, he was hunting by the Sphinx, which was covered to its ears in sand, when he took a nap and was visited by the Sun God Harakhte, whom the Sphinx represented (at least in this story—Hegel said it represented the mind of man rising above Nature but not escaping it—a sound point). Harakhte told him that if he uncovered the Sphinx he would ascend to the throne. He did and he did.

Only thing is, it wasn't Harakhte who visited Tuthmosis that day—it was me. Let's just say I liked the kid and thought a renewal project like uncovering the Sphinx would be good for his soul. It was certainly more constructive than hunting all day.

I never expected him to actually *ascend to the throne.*

In those very early times, I had a bit of a thing for kings, so my next manifestation was to none other than Solomon himself. Do your research and you'll find the tantalizing tale of a vampiric djinn who made himself the main vein-drainer of a master worker on Solomon's temple project, a lousy situation that opened the door to intervention by my former brother of the Arch, Michael, who gave a ring to Solomon specifically configured to give him power over a sizable coterie of djinn, of which the best known is my smokeless-fiery friend, Iblis (the former Azazel), who fell with us from the firmament.

I enjoyed my talks with Solomon, who had just as much to say as I did, but the minute I found myself *looking forward to them*, I quit him like a pussy, poxy whore.

It was thousands of years before I chose to manifest again.

In 1521 I appeared to Martin Luther in a castle in Wartburg while he labored to translate the Bible into German. By *appeared*, I mean collected myself unto myself in such a way as to tear the fabric of this Plane in that particular space at that particular time. I had heard about his rantings concerning a bag of nuts jumping about his chambers, so I thought I'd have me a bit of a time. I perched myself upon the whale's-vertebrae footstool he kept by his desk, shook my shaker at him and laughingly bounced about as he tossed his inkwell toward my head.

Later that century, Marlowe's *Faustus* grabbed my attention (for reasons I'll later share) to such an extent that I appeared onstage during a performance at Exeter. I managed to manifest just long enough to send the patrons screaming for the doors and the actors in search of a drink.

In counting the devils in the cast, they had found one extra. That was me.

And thus began my ascension to yet another Fall…

At the beginning of the 18th century a group of privileged and decadent Irish "bucks" started a riotous organization called the Dublin Hell-Fire Club. They engaged in the usual snoringly boring acts of immorality like whoring, drinking, Satanism, and so on. Their motto was "Do as you will," a lovely little precursor to later establishments like The Church of Satan. They had a quaint little practice of toasting the devil and then roasting a cat.

Their leader, a ruffian named "Burn-Chapel" Whaley, despised all organized religion, most especially Roman Catholicism. This old buck of course caught my interest. In his raging hatred was a bit of the substance of conviction that all the fucking and drinking in the world can't replace. He got so pissed at a servant one night post-ceremony that he set the dude on fire, resulting in the entire clubhouse erupting in flames. A few members died. They must have been one angry boatload of bucks when Charon ferried their crispy asses across the River Styx to find Satan sobbing in a corner rather than clasping their hands in gratitude and welcome.

They still raise a holler now and then, but footnotes in a good yarn are never a particularly gracious group. The real star of the story is Thomas Whaley, the son of Burn-Chapel, born in 1766. He followed in Dadda's footsteps, overseeing orgies and Black Masses and making a small fortune on odd wagers like jumping a horse 30 feet to the ground from the drawing room of his father's house. He also rode to Jerusalem and back within a year, which is when I truly got to know him. He had such potential but lacked his father's conviction. He even went so far as to seek absolution in a church. That's when I stepped in and shut the whole mess down.

Gathering myself unto myself and dressing my ether in the deep reds and sharp angles of the devilish art of the times, I crawled in flames along the center aisle toward him. Upon seeing my grinning visage, he left the church, Dublin, Ireland, and just a few years later, life. He was 34 when he succumbed to liver disease.

Screwing with the bile will get you every time.

I have to admit, I got a good charge out of that little visit to this Plane, although my next was a bit more noble.

I came in defense of the prophet and healer Nostradamus.

Much to my chagrin there have always been skeptics and naysayers who can't handle the possibility of the other-than-linear nature of space and time, so I played the back-door public relations expert by engineering a little stunt in a Paris cemetery in May 1791. You may have heard about it. There were these little geniuses who thought if they drank from Nostradamus' skull some cool shit would happen. When they dug him up, they found a sign around his neck printed with the very date of the digging. Just as one of them started to drink from the skull of this major saint and visionary, a (supposedly) stray bullet from the Revolution took him down.

Yeah—you guessed it ... I was holding the gun. But let me be clear—I didn't *put* the sign there, I just *knew* about it.

While I'm mentioning the French Revolution, here's a bit of steak to get stuck between your teeth—ever think about the working class guards at the Bastille who were probably ripped to shreds as the rabble did their storming? What the hell'd they say to the families these guys were working to support? "All for the greater good, little ones and widowed mother. He should have been a blacksmith."

The target of my next (notable) visitation was a tortured musician-poet from the West Coast, living not far from where I was "born." Something drew me to this long-haired genius in 1965 and that same something kept me near him until damned near the end of his days, some six years later. The initial visit (and the only one in which he saw me) happened after he had dropped a tab of acid with a friend from which he was bumming a bed. It is probably the case that his altered state of mind allowed him to perceive me because, unlike the cases of Exeter and Thomas Whaley, his seeing me *was not part of the plan.* According to what he told a band mate, he saw a satyr—one of my favorite forms in those pre-Flesh times.[3]

The satyr represents a celebration, a connection with Bacchus and Dionysus and the tribal, natural connection that is Mankind at its best. I had no interest in playing the devil, no desire to drive this future West Coast rock-god to any action or plant any ideas in his head. As I said, I didn't even want him to see me. But he did—and yet he didn't.

He told his bandmate the satyr was inviting him to dance. I wasn't. How could I? If the mood had grabbed me I could have fully manifested, but it would not have allowed for any real relationship. The event subsequently appeared in the musician's poems and songs and had no small effect on the rest of his life.

A little more than a year later, November '66, I was playing by a power plant in Somewhere, West Virginia when one of my wings got caught in a fence. A carful of people saw me (my manifestations getting more solid each time) and thus began a cottage industry myth of which I'm sure you are aware.

I really hate being mistaken for Lepidoptera...

Cornu saw what I did—he'd been watching in secret for thousands of years—and the incidents in '65 and '66 convinced him how useful a theatrical little manifester like me could be.

And so, some forty years ago, I was forced into this work.

Perhaps there were others born near me, with me, *through* me. If there were, I've yet to meet them (Cornu's punk-gang of red-djinn biker demons, The Mischievers, who ride with a group called the *Vargulf*, don't count—they're mixed-breeds. Automatons. Worker bees). My earliest memories are of the cold, sterile feel of a lumpy Buntz-breast and the taste of Sucking Nothing (her well had long ago run dry). She knew I was special, skipping the See Spot Run and Dr. Seuss books in favor of Rimbaud, whose *Illuminations* I found anything but and whose *Season in Hell* was nothing but queer fodder for a lover gone sour.[4] The *voyant*—Please. The only Truly Enlightened are the ones that ride on

---

[3] I had presented myself to Ezra Pound in the form of Pan some years before, reciting a few lines about playing my fiddle in the forest and walking into a wasps' nest (a revision of my ultra-fruitful bedside visit circa 1713 to Giuseppe Tartini that led to his "Devil's Trill Sonata") and he was convinced. I consider this a *minor* visitation because it took place strictly in the confines of his Mind, where I played upon his quite right beliefs in Retrocognition and any vision being *real* by the sole virtue of its having been experienced. Pound's insights parallel those of Castaneda's teacher, don Juan, as evidenced in their conversation about whether or not Carlos had really flown after taking the second portion of the devil's weed. Although he could not get beyond limited notions of flight (comparing *his* experience wrongly to that of a bird's) we must be more open minded.

[4] Although, and this could be due to his having written it with Verlaine, you cannot, cannot ignore his *Sonnet du Trou de Cul*, the Sonnet of the Asshole, written as a parody of another poet's work but exquisite nonetheless: "Dark and wrinkled like a violet carnation/It sighs, humbly nestling in the moss still moist from love..."

Nothing to experience *Everything*. Rimbaud, Poe, Coleridge, Stevenson, the almost-there Lizard King—all just travelers on a foggy, fuckbent road. Nuttin magickal there, though their words are prime and flowing. Just not Divine. And Ma Buntz—she tried hardest to form a connection with me on the anniversaries of my Fleshing. She cried worn tears to me; for me; she the Maria Regina with ashy flaxen crown. This is not remorse—she could have denied what I could not, being mortal as she was. Did she know what she was doing, mixing the cosmic mess of me, or was she the unwitting pawn, and if so, what does that say of the Little Horn? Of his power to make things happen? I suppose I have convinced myself that she was no sap like Judas. That she went willingly. It made killing her all the easier... Ding dong ding—Christ golly Miss Folly—the drugs are kicking in full bore and I'm swelllll'er than hell—keep the extra ells, cause I just had a thought—I've far outlived Christ on this Plane. Been layin' lower, sure—pacin' myself. Killin' the sick 'steada curin' em. Getting ready to do it right and do it My Way. Francis Elvis Buntz. The kid with iron eyes.

So now you know.

I've been giving some thought to Galileo Galilei, that great sellout of the 1600s. The brilliant Copernican advocate who disavowed the truth of the heliocentric model because he was scared of physical pain and the broader threats of two popes and the cardinals of the Inquisition. He was not above kissing the asses *or* the rings of Popes—or of the Medicis—though it did him little good and, in the end, having suffered the death of his daughter and his own blindness, one could say that his karma was square. It's fitting that a man who denied the truth to the last would become the perfect subject for the False Fabrications of fiction.[5] Some say he worked those secluded years at the end of his life in secret, writing and distributing pamphlets through the underground but that's of little use if you are unwilling to publicly Make Your Stand. They were treacherous waters in which he swam, as those of the brilliant always are, especially in those days of growing scientific knowledge in Italy, and his cowardice cost his colleagues much.

Thirty-three years before, in 1600, Giordano Bruno was burned at the stake after spending six years in a Papal prison. He was killed not only for his Copernican beliefs but his belief that ancient Egyptian wisdom and mystical

---

[5]Consider, for example, the works of Brown and Brecht. He is equaled in fictionality only by Thomas Becket, as manipulated by both Jean Anouilh and TS Eliot. The former went so far as to make him Saxon instead of Norman—no small difference—because it better suited the qualities of *drama*.

skill (in addition to many other geneses I will mention as we go) were the superior precursors to Christianity—a belief shared by the French and Scottish Rites branches of Freemasonry. In fact, his monument was erected in Rome in June of 1899 [that good old *fin de siecle*] by Masons and I speak not of immigrant bricklayers but those who build a different sort of structure. Interesting that they chose to immortalize Bruno at the time of Jack the Ripper and Conan Doyle and HG Wells and all the others doing what they could to help usher in a new, symbolic age.

The age of the New Technic—the prequel to our own impending show, which will be accompanied, I should note, by selections from Mozart's *Magic Flute*—an *homage* to Masonic and Egyptian references if there ever was one.

But don't let me spoil *all* of the surprise.

While praying to Durga (with stick in one hand and balls in the other) I had a vision: battered and drugged, I was carried up a set of steps to a hanging rig in the center o' town. Past? Future? Some multilayered ecstatic imagery? I did not make my offering—a pious Father was cleaning toilets in the rectory and the mantra breaks the tile when I let the beast release. I want nothing more than death... Being here is wrong. I cannot tear to bits what should be fragile flesh. *No* free will. Like Dorian Gray, my compulsion to sin has made me a slave to evil and no more free than the mendicant in his cell. I've no chance to break the chain—to change sides before the coin gets tossed and the game is underway. Parvus Cornu grows ever more insistent. He'll eat Lucifer whole, who will barely mount a fight, and he'll rise and enter Hell and we'll all lose our wings in the end, sinking together in a massive pool of Human Forgetting, existing only in a child's whispered cursing or as images on a faintly flickering screen. Lucifer mustn't lose—my aim has never changed in that, though the reasons always do. He wept like a miscarrying mother when the Christ-man was killed upon his cross—we all did, either then or soon after, for it had become all too clear—if God would allow his greatest *salesman* to perish on a plank, what shred of hope had we? Lucifer tried to save the Nazorean—to warn him off an empty path. To convey a lesson as great as any Jesus ever gave. But the carpenter's stepson was blinded by Grace. As he shouted to God of forsakenness only then, in that last moment of blood-filled breath, did he *see*. Only then was the maya of Godliness stripped away. Hell yes, the world fell open at his death, but it was not God but the Universe itself. A great heaving grief, for all of us— you and I, angel and devil, born and yet to come—were at that instant *lost*.

In an elegant meditative state of drowsed meanderings I wandered the banks of the Narmada River in India, pulling shiva ligams from the sandy bottom and polishing them with a twist of the wrist, bringing out their markings, their *yoni*, as the talented sons of the chosen families do over weeks of practiced toil. I swallowed the oblong stones by the handful, desperate to balance the wailing void where my fourth (or heart) Chakra should be. The shiva ligam is believed by the Hindus to be the joining of the male and female, the yin and yang, the light and dark—the answer to all my struggles in an egg-shaped meteoric/ambient rock concoction almost as old as I. They fell and rattled within the thin walls of my septic gut and shit-splat on the mountainside, left as secret, spoiled treasures with fading glyphs upon their sides. Touch them and they fade, yet the Message is conveyed: *Something mystic walked this way.* I am allowed no easy solution, no cosmic absolution for being conscious that I should have been given a *Choice* instead of a *Command*. I should have gone back to the Theatre and rehearsed my role, but I am not yet ready to Re-engage, so I sat by the Narmada in contemplative silence until I had a vision. A great embroidered mirage of Mercury launching himself skyward with a speed unfollowable even with the vampiric eye. Angels screamed the laments of the slaughtered Valkyries in anticipation of the news his recently resurrected messenger was bringing to Zeus: his many half-human sons, led by the two most famous— Heracles and Perseus—were storming Olympus with their vast Bull and Boar armies to claim their rightful thrones. They carried with them the banners of the Coming Christ, the Fish run thru with a dagger, its magickal blood soaking the heads of Zeus' boys in hot anointment of a father's coming death.

So it must be for me, one day. And so must I return.

Sheets of manic rain are bombarding my fortress in death-blue torrents, sacrificing themselves on the Escheresque stairs and chessboard façades of this crumbling Abbey in which I sit… I've been pulled back from an elkskin meditation by my master Crow to witness the crucifixion of New Man on a high-speed satellite feed. He expected green grass and homesteads and found instead empty chairs and dotted lines. As his eyes bulge from their sockets and then burst he is wrapped, still breathing, still bleeding, in a Turin shroud lined with ash and carried to the station of the Mass—the tribal priests and Karmic Elders assembling to the pulse of ancient drums, for the bloodrite is at hand.

I am brought before them, struggling—no longer en-tranced. We walk thru the catacombs where the mummified children of those self-same Elders stand gaping in their disintegrating dress. The stretching of the skin across the still-forming skulls gives them all the same rough look of appalling horror, although it is only a trick of decomposition—they could not have anticipated or known what it was that took them. One of the beasts created to enhance our armies in the Great War of the Winged (and what else could have done such a hideous thing??) strikes quickly and without warning. Such a macabre collection so close to the mountainside town where I'd chosen to lay my head awhile was statement enough of the gutless insanity of the proceedings still to come. Thru the intense reds of my vampire vision I see the mirror version of my younger self, offering ice cream instead of coals. An Elder with breath like a furnace of worms fingers my shorted-out inputs and laughs at my heretofore quiet Rebellion, my rare good thoughts, my recent hesitation before a kill. Even my hand is not my own, but an extension of the Horn. The New Man, newly blind, makes this clear by handing me a knife and showing me where to thrust to end his life. I scream out in refusal—I'm too close to reclaiming a piece of my Soul to remove this layman's heart, but still the knife goes forth. I see the truth in the blossoming flower of the blood—only Parvus Cornu is Absolute, for only he has so fully embraced the myths of our fight enough to believe they're Real. But I refuse to join him, to play Ginifer to his Merlin from the pen of Jean Cocteau. Empires are formed to fall. That's the purpose of resistance. Gathering my strength, I follow the dying shadow of my childhood, away from the slaughter and horrors of the catacombs into the dark mystery of the shaman's dance and exercise my Will. I search for my garden tiki—the private Eden I saw when I was born. Crow joins me by a misty, snake-filled lake and dines upon my fear.

For one brief instant I sense the warmth of his unrequited love.

Then he is gone, and the Abbey is no more.

I've made the acquaintance of a middle-aged priest named Fr. Joseph Vincolare, a renegade Jesuit who has gone underground to plot his war. After my place of sanctuary, my secret Abbey, was abruptly taken away, I sought refuge from the day's pains in an abandoned Catholic schoolroom attached to a now defunct Parish named Saint Bartholomew's and there he was. He wasn't surprised to see me. In truth, he'd been expecting it. Fr. Joe, with his degree in psychology (with an unsanctioned specialty in the paranormal) had undertaken several independent investigations into supposed miracles and the like—without the Church's blessing—and had fallen into hot water with the divisions of the

Vatican who regulate such things. When he began a series of discussion groups and a particularly radical prayer and study group in the basement of Saint Bart's, the Monsignor had the good Father replaced. And when his loyal flock boycotted services in protest, the parish was shut down. Facing an audience with a Cardinal in Rome and the inevitable requirement of recantation or defrocking, he returned to the boarded up scene of his Crimes, determined to continue what he'd started. Unlike the fallen priests of film, the ones who allow themselves to be broken by the amoral corruption of the Church hierarchy they had sworn to serve and then get into law enforcement and wind up facing the devil with a badge and not a cross, Father Joe is a man of deep faith and strict adherence to the meaning of the vows who finds my unrelenting attack on "his kind" to be (mostly) petty and distorted.

We've agreed to disagree.

Having seen his share of "possessions" and "exorcisms" and having crossed paths with the Mischievers more than once, he has advocated for the restoration of the Roman Rituals to their pre-edited state. He is well-versed in the Gospels of Thomas and Phillip and the Essene scripts and certain other unauthorized and suppressed texts procured for him by friends in Europe and the Near East, so he held my interest and after many hours of conversing in Aramaic, we decided to be, if not friends, then allies. He has no use for the Church of the New Technic, with its more lenient rules and open, easily forgiving arms. They are, to him, "Purveyors of pseudoreligious myth—caterers to the modern Catholics, half of whom go to church because they don't know how not to. They know it's a glass with no drink, a cigarette with no tobacco, a kiss with no heat, because the Church won't allow any true joy and absolutely forbids fantasy, so the rituals are empty and most of my fellow priests are catechized robots reciting empty verse. Mass by rote is the antidote to true belief."

He talks like this while consuming an endless stream of burgundy and several cigarettes an hour. Fr. Joe believes that the way of Christ should be a path of suffering, full of sacrifices and self-denials. *Mea culpa* and all that. He has been working in secret with an Order not officially recognized and actively hunted down by the Church. To him, being Outcast is a Penance for all the years he spent pushing forth a diseased message to an innocent flock of naïve, empty-lifed believers. He has declined specifics for now (no doubt something he picked up from reading too many trade paperbacks and seeing too many films), but I have great patience when it comes to the unraveling of tales. I do know that their goal is to get the pure message of Salvation out, unclouded by the compromise of political territorialism and corrupted Dogma. He swears no allegiance to the Pope or his Cardinals and accepts no forgiver of sins but Jesus Christ himself (no *extra Ecclesiam nulla salus* for him, and a good thing too, cause once you leave you don't go back), whom he truly believes was an incarnation of God on

Earth. (Despite this fundamental difference, we continue to talk...) By way of comparison, which I find to be a useful, efficient device, he reminds me of both Father Daniel Berrigan, of the Catonsville Nine, and Father Don Callahan from *Salem's Lot*, the latter in the sense of his believing that Evil does exist and that his fate will be to confront it, like a modern-day Van Helsing fighting the vampires of old. But Father Joe won't succumb to the fear that Don C. did—he's already taken his stand and I have no reason to believe he'll flinch.

Just to be sure, I'm helping him all I can.

It's no mere irony, my joining forces with a *priest*. Our coming together smacks of Destiny. It's no less than a Cosmic Convergence. A sequence of random elements drawn together in the semblance of a Plan—what appears at times to be the rotting underbelly of its sister Synchronicity because the Meaning can't be seen. Convergence is a force impelled by the Unseen. It's How Things Get Done in this jumbled Universe of electromagnetism, gravity, and strong and weak subtle energies, all existing simultaneously as both particle and wave, matter and light, and the spontaneous jumping of forms because the Universe doesn't care a damn about *science*. It is the combination of events so seemingly random as to be almost incalculable. Convergence can be Tragedy in the form of a running child, a paper airplane, and a delivery truck on a tree-lined hairpin turn. It is the hump-happy marriage of physics and mysticism, nanometer and infinity, revelation and mystery and ready reason to Love or Despise God, depending on how things happen. Convergence is the Will at work without conscious detection of its labor. The Grand Conspirator toiling at his ciphers and maps. An ability to throw down constructs by a collective agreement to do so. It is Buntz being drawn to the awful potion of me, despite her having to know she would die horribly for having done so. I have placed my chipped and chiseled faith in its action, despite my setbacks and suffering. It is the Arbiter of our outcomes, no matter our intent. The more two entities vibrate with one another, the more similar they become, so Convergence is drawing me to Light, to Grace, to the lonely child's window, to the dying Bodhi tree. The human heart produces an electromagnetic field 5,000 times more potent and substantial than that of the brain, radiating out a dozen feet, drawing one into vibration with everything Moralists might label Good.

This is the pure wisdom of science, uncorrupted by those who dare to practice its craft. Amid this wisdom there is more and more of a push toward a higher science—General Evolution, Quantum Physics—Schrodinger's Cat, Heisenberg's Uncertainty Principle, Bell's Theorem, Bohm's implicate order— the sweet genius of Swedenborg, the unmasking of Reality as a subjective swirl of conscious perceptions. Even the Kabbalah as science *in addition to* lore. Ancient wisdom in the modern lab, guiding the integration of humankind back into Nature. The spirits of the shamans, swamis, and other holy men float among these labcoat *bodhisattvas* merging religion and science into one. Reaching to a lower level of matter—photons, quarks, antimatter (a key ingredient in the unfolding of our creation)—to find God, rather than the absence of. It is the wonder of the Church of the Particle Physics Puzzle—a way to cure the disease that is Humankind before it becomes absolutely necessary for the Universe to eradicate it. It's a matter of chemo and radiation versus a more Holistic approach—and we know which way the scales still tip. It's there in the well-selling demi-fiction about daVinci, the Sacred Feminine, and the Grail—(un)knowing messengers for a new Phase in Evolution: "And so will the old truths be made new." The idea of "attainment" is the great mystic Tragedy—we strive for something we already are, whether we care to be or not. It is worse than the dog chasing its own tail[6]—it is the tail *chasing itself,* and every hair, every particle, every ounce of matter of which the tail is made chasing itself and all being right there all the time—uncatchable because it is not on the run at all—it can't be. It is part of the Source and more truthfully, the Source itself. So all this talk of *degrees* or *levels*—and all esoteric religions have them (akin to the hierarchies of more traditional religions—"on earth as it is in heaven")—is really just human controlling human as God sought to control all other Light Beings at the start. So, ironically, Kabbalistic and other models are truly attaining oneness with God—but it is a means to *more* Control, *more* chains, not less. Hence the occult notion of Satanism as true freedom from God's suppression. Of course, Satanic groups have all the same types of levels and hierarchies, so they're as fucked up as the rest ... just not MORE SO, as the oft-pointed finger seems to say.

A Parable: There was once a guru who taught TM. The carrot on the stick was that after months of *consistent* class attendance (and tuition), each student got a personal mantra specially chosen by him. When the time came he went around the room whispering in the monetarily faithfuls' ears, bestowing the secret key to their Great Attainment. A few weeks later, as three of the students passed a joint and downed some Beaujolais, they disclosed their "secret" mantras. Each one had the same few Sanskrit words ... words he hadn't translated or explained.

The Kabbalists (and other not-so-secret societies) would say that the *reason* for their secrecy is the notion of the "unexplainable," but *experience* is all and no one should dictate that for the seeking soul. Suggest, perhaps. Serve as a model, sure... (sound familiar?) Not that mantra or ritual are the path. It's the pointed finger again—only this time, so it's said, once that finger finds the moon, it no longer has a use. Chew on that awhile and wonder at its taste (I'll

---

[6]An image used by Jack Sarfatti to describe the ring singularity of black and white holes in space.

make vampires of you all ... whether its blood or words you drink is solely up to you).

This is my road—to find my own self-belief restored so that vampire, Baphomet, Antichrist, pawn of the Cornu, or whatever else I may be, I am still a Godhead equal to God himself. That's the fucking *point*. Just that bit of knowing would outdo and far outweigh years of supplication to the Kabbalah, Freemasonry, or any other needlessly complicated form of Attainment.

Father Joe and I have much to discuss.

―――――――― • • • ――――――――

As the shithouse rat once said: "The deepa ya go, the more ya bleed, the more ya bleed, the more ya see."

In service of the Grand Charade, courtesy of the Nether Regions Theatre Company, I have been hard at work composing the scenes and scripts for our upcoming plays.

I am set to take us depth-diving. And there's plenty on which to gaze.

To my knowledge, I am the first of my kind to try this game, to break forth with the Word where we failed with the Claw. It's about fucking time—all the Good Guys have gone on record—published their tomes, gotten their time in the sun.

But just when I think I'm making Progress I plummet into my baser nature. Start shouting from the rooftops right after a kill instead of reveling in the sacred silence—the blessed Om of the truly ascended being who makes art as energy made manifest and doesn't try to sell a single thing—what Meister Eckert (who Fr. Joe reminds me of) called the "hidden word" or the *Istigkeit*, the Is-ness, that leads to the *via illuminativa* of Catholic mysticism. I'm trying to expel myself from my Self by embracing the wisdom of the *Tat tuam asi*—There *thru the* grace of (something) *also* go I—the *samsara-mandala*, the "wheel of flowing together," and that's as insane as it gets—it's up there with ole Saint Anthony and Padre Pio wrasslin' with the demons in their monkish little rooms.

Those are the saints I admire—the ones who were willing to let God preside fully over their trials—judge and judged merging, to evoke the Holy Genet. Take Anthony of Padua (not the wrestler of demons, but another Tony boy) who traveled out of body so he could preach in two places at once. Now that's commitment to the cause of his salvation. Or Ignatius Loyola, the warrior-father of the Jesuits, who saw god in all things and probably the devil as well. A true visionary—just like Francis, who left Assisi to join the Fourth Crusade in fancy gold armor only to be sent back by a vision from god the first night. Gotta figure the Almighty had bigger things planned for him—the Stigmata being just one. St. Patrick was another who got his marching orders directly from god.

I'm avidly listening, but I don't hear a peep.

And it isn't just the boys in the Canon who made a mystic way. There's well-known Joan, the pride of France, who was burned at the stake before turning 20 because she talked with god and the priests could not. Then there's Thérèse of Lisieux, who went into the convent at 15 with every intention of becoming a saint—howse that for ambition? When she does her thing, everyone knows—the scent of roses fills the air. That's the type of showmanship that puts Heaven on the map. And Hildegard of Birgen, who could see a soul taking possession of a fetus inside its mother's womb. Was she watching the swirl of booze and glue from which I came? Did she cry foul? Did she even care…

We must not forget the ecstatic vision of St. Teresa of Avila, immortalized forever by Bernini in the Cornaro Chapel in the Church of St. Maria della Vittoria. Although her beautiful experience has been corrupted for the sake of a *novel*, it was anything but perverse. You can take the image of the golden spear with its flaming tip of iron penetrating her heart to the entrails to be an act of sex but take it from a being who has fucked all kinds of things in all kinds of ways—I've never entered through the aorta—who the fuck would?

I finish this mini hagiography with the most twisted saint of all—St. Rose of Lima, who was so enrapt by the presence of God she rubbed pepper on her face 'til it was a blistered, burning mess. Just in case that was not enough, she sheared off all her hair and dressed in baggy rags to keep the men away.

Note to Father Joe: That's the kind of marketing the dying church could use. I have the burning, blistered face when I don't care enough to hide it, but my conviction is unplaced—I'm waiting for the final corner before I place my bet.

I'm hanging from the meathook of my wishing. … My sacremonial rattle—made by my two twisted hands from a carefully cultivated and decorated gourd—has been broken. Despite my best efforts to sanctify it, it fell to pieces, rotting through its ash-painted images of elk and deer and bear.

What did I do wrong? It was a trial; the first of my numinous creations. A failed Initiation. My insufficient rattle—sacred mystery colors encroached upon by black and stinking rat-rot. A denial. Black Elk's *Wakan Tanka* not accepting my devil-scent, despite the fact I know the words of prayer. Not allowing me to change, even for a few moments, so I might talk to her.

Her.

I watch her thru a morning-fog window array of dripless candles and ceremonial teacup placings. A princess—beautiful and lost. Another Anastasia (a pseudonym, of course), a dancing doll with dangling key and whispered prayers. I see that key resting between her breasts, pristine chain woven within her preppish curls, and I wonder where it fits. I would gladly jump from her Tower, piercing and blinding my eyes like Rapunzel's lovelorn prince, if only to feel the healing power of her tears... I follow her down dollar store corn-can aisles, fondling cracked statues and searching for my Nerve. She stands amid the dangling stems of thousands of cloth and plastic flowers and becomes, for an instant, Elizabeth Siddal, Millais' consumptive Ophelia, sitting in an ice-cold tub and never complaining a bit. I could pull her strings, this diamond-Anastasia. Introduce her to the harlot's shrine—a change of clothes, a sparkling eye, a higher heel and shorter hem. Arriving home, she writes on the wall of her pain in red crayon: SHHHHHHHHHHH, and covers it with charcoal and graphite studies of Caravaggio's St. Peter on the Cross. She sits in locked waiting, chamomile and lavender, potpourri and Christly humble Amening between embroidery thumb-pokes. She licks the blood and my member springs to life. Is it my presence that breaks her concentration, ending her static puce-thread rote with a sacredly whispered "Ouch"? Can she sense me here? I wish I had my rattle, rotted and cursed though it was, but I threw it at the bulb lighting my latest vision of Death and watched it burn to ash. Is this Kali in her corduroy and cashmere aspect? Can I get close, hold her gaze and let her see the buried dharmic aspects of me? Her mother arrives, letting herself in with insistent keys. They sit in graveled silence despite the special plates with golden moon-dance trimmings. Lemon cakes and wine. The tears burn up in my furnace eyes before they fall. I'll eat a mongrel's shit at midnight to wash away the taste of her perfume on my tongue. I'm unworthy of even that.

As I skulk away I hear from a buzzing yard-sale phonograph the familiar anthems of a gone folksy hippie cut down at the Dakota while bursting with love and minor chords. I could talk with her of his lyrics, the subtle constructions of his melodic canvas, but the album's cut short by some asshole in his Jockeys yelling "Fuck peace, man—shut that shit *off*!" It's just as well, for I am Beast and she is mint and thyme. Zoroaster's stinging me again with his insistent idea of Duality. I slither away in the mud, too unsure of the consequences to offer my apple to Eve.

I saw her today from the second-story window of my art-studio, passing hurriedly through the aisles of the local convenience store. She scanned no shelves, held no bottles or boxes or bags. Her face, so oddly, vaguely Native American—soft lips and hard eyes—the better to stone and devour me with. I cannot get her face out of my mind. It nestles like a toothy rat and I'm compelled to stroke its fur, nipping my hand though it does. To say she sensed me would be wholly incorrect, yet I saw her hesitate and turn her head toward my window before purchasing the daily paper and dropping her change as she crossed the parking lot and got into a precisely arriving bus.

I've flown to an island where Crow spends his nights, hoping to quell the poison fumes of Desire with a richly oxygenated night. I passed over Midwest farmlands, and cried at the toil I saw—nutrient-poor soil where seed can find no purchase, but the farmer's children hold it like the dust of Heaven nonetheless. I pictured my own Grace churned and rich beneath the thresher's blades and had to fight the impulse to alight and enact the dream. What good would it do? I've become a whiny Angel, a Lucifer in flesh-dress and pink panties. A by-product of the void I've created with my rebellion against Rebellion. It leaves me weak and lacking verve, in need of a power-drill enema and a mighty fount of blood, the thought of which brings my heartbeat to a battle-drum rush until I smell the fresh-cut roses laid upon her bed, producing a schoolboy erection that kills the thrill of feasting and puts a damper on my plans. I resign myself to fall asleep on a patch of stinking swamp. The Prince on his throne, jester-crow by his side, destined to be the dateless loser on a Prom night he'll never find the faith to forget.

Today is a feast day. Tables spread with grain and wine, fruit and meat. Dining rooms filled with the din of family spoutings, parlor games, and patent leather squeaking. Tryptophan and cocktail napping. And I, drunk on wine and cheap scotch siphoned thru a homeless man muttering about Thanks, wandered from window to window cheering them on! Encouraging their emotional gluttony, their godly patriarchs and slaving Mary Maters, their mumbled Thanks (so different from the homeless man's), and bragging toasts. All day I walked—shore-to-shore, climate to climate, experiencing western sun, midwest rain, mountain snow, and early eastern cold. A miracle of feeling. And at festivities' end, calling to Durga from a steaming bath, I begged her to take my seed while she was ripe. But only a clattering trio of Hecate's demon daughters, the

Empusae, heard my call—six breasts, nine holes, and an hour of clawing, abject Disinterest. Another wasted spew. I watched my gleaming Anastasia for hours, whipping cream for a fine dessert, later left separating on the counter when "he" didn't show. Could I have entered then? Pledged my love, secured our betrothal, dipped her palm and fingers in *hinnah*, the Crimson of Consent, so that all the world would know she was mine? I didn't dare, so deformed have I become—it would take far too much energy to make me appear otherwise and my Kundalini's on the fritz. I caught a glimpse of myself thru the plasticky room divider of my mind as I sat beneath her window—a hideous thing I've become in the Wolfy Hours of the night. More unsettling still was the look of fear upon my horned and twisted face. My form is Hellish beast and if I do not feed at least twice a day I become a Baphomet—the very thing I must disprove as Art and Myth! And it's no quick drink in shadowed halls but great spine-crushing draughts that even disgust Mykaldaemio, a vampire of some age and ample appetite that I've recently come to know. It's my own Thoughtforms working against me, carving the Goat of Mendes into the cedar beams of the ancient halls of my mind.

What the hell are we, beyond the image we have in the glass? I wish I were like the vampire in Old Country folklore who *has no* reflection. (Mykaldaemio loves to stare at his—he's got a mirror above his bed.) *Wampyr* is flesh, bloodless though it is … matter, corrupted or not, and so I watch daily as I slowly become the horned god, the acid-bath Pan, the earthly manifestation of Eliphas Levi's Judas Goat. (Names, names, names—they are my obsession, my undoing, and yet I cannot tell you mine…) It is no matter that Baphomet means Sophia (wisdom) in the Atbash cipher—that is not what the majority think when they see the classic features—womanly breasts, leathery wings, cloven hooves… I have them all. I used to think such things were other demons' problems—the kind of unfortunate situation that befell a cursed fetus like the Jersey Devil. I was listening that storming, hellacious night in 1735 when Mother Leeds, upon hearing she was to have a 13th child, spoke quite distinctly and directly that she "wished it be a Demon." And so the Universe did the deed upon the Leeds and the winged Jerseyite was born. For all his many torments, he's luckier than I, for the same reason one who is born blind is better off than one who loses his sight later in life. Before the Rebellion I was as beautiful as Lucifer, a great gone angel with fuckable hair and pouty eyes—but now I'm the fertile goat who feeds and fucks without restraint. In my Baphomet aspect, I am the equivalent of the portrait of Dorian Gray, the physical manifestation of every Evil that I've done while my demi-human self, once I've fed, is beautiful and fine, allowing me to get into the best places and talk with the finest folks.

Ah—Dorian Gray, and his brilliant creator, Oscar Fingall O'Flahertie Wills Wilde … the flamboyant Dubliner in cocked hat and theatre cape, with skills akin to those of Joyce and Yeats (who had much to say about Wilde in his *Autobiography*; did the harlots really dance when the verdict was announced?). Wilde, the eccentric ironist of exceeding wit who cut to ribbons anything labeled sacred—a kindred spirit, lover of the perverse, monstrous, and criminal; demi-disciple of Walter Pater, author of the handbook of aestheticism in steadfast Victorian England that he called "the very flower of decadence." We share a love of the French Symbolists, the Pre-Raphaelites, Keats, and the Greeks. I applaud his writing *Salomé* in French—the only language worthy of its wit. The tragedy of his trial is one I fully understand, labeled and misunderstood as I am. This rampant fear of the Other, in his case the Queer, was replicated exactly 100 years after his birth in the case of Alan Turing, Enigma Code genius, who ate an apple laced with cyanide (a reference to the myth of evil Eden?) after having succumbed to two years of estrogen injections rather than going to prison.[7] His persecution was no doubt linked to the old-style witch hunts of Tailgunner Joe and the Commie, etc. purge. Amazing that a hero of World War II could fall prey to the kind of paranoia that made the Nazis the dangerous threat they were and ironic considering it was the Nazis who so vigorously rooted out the queers (although decades before, a bill banning *Lesbian acts* failed to pass). They created laws to get gays out of the Army and either castrated or sterilized them. Their *fantasies* were even outlawed, along with 9 other acts—laws enforced by the Allies until 1969.

History is dark and filled with fear—a fear of the Other that necessitates the macabrist Vincent O'Sullivan and myself carrying the torch for Wilde when his works should speak for themselves. Monsters are hunted in all the wrong places while ignorance bleeds forth in a sea of evil masquerading as the Fount of Absolution. This insistence on judging evil by ancient moral codes has affected me no end. I've no chance with Anastasia, no chance to go public beyond these published words. I have the form the Satanists worship with none of the power—no absorbing into wisdom, no revelation, no hyperintellect to foment Change. It'd be too easy to crush me into dust were I to appear to you like this. Me, the seeming proof of Hell (a construct unique to the individual imagining it), driving you to wield the Spear of dying religions and cast me out for once and all. So I wait, refusing to drain more blood on this Feast Day. I lay here beneath Anastasia's window, clutching at my bastard mala—a length of Buntz's pearls twisted as 108—the magic number of the mantras that stick in my throat as teary cries of anguish come muffled and steady from Ana's bedroom: "Why didn't he come? Why didn't he?" And I with all the answers and no right to speak, curl up here and sulk.

---

[7] Said injections being the time's way of curbing the more diabolical of sexual urges.

I spent the last several days smoking angel-faced meerschaums while in conversation with a ghostly aspect of none other than that great devil himself, *un Satan en herbe*, Chuck Baudelaire, who, along with Flaubert, had so richly influenced my good man Wilde (partly, at least, via the great admiration of Huysmans' "fictional" Des Esseintes, who ultimately stoked the fires of Dorian Gray via a gift from Lord Henry). I was introduced to him by the chain-smoking ghost of Antonin Artaud, the tortured genius of the Theatre of Cruelty, whom I had once engaged about his essay "The Theater and the Plague."

Now, I should clarify just what I mean by "ghost." There are those among you—strong souls of considerable age—that leave an energy imprint on the lower Planes after they have shucked their body and ascended. There is no delineation between good and evil in the determination of this phenomenon—it is quantity more than quality that matters most. Both Artaud and Baudelaire certainly fit the bill. I found a slightly wasted but otherwise intact semblance of the not so bonny Charlie beneath Paris in the old sewer system he so loved. He was eager for conversation. Not quite for the reasons I had hoped, but one can't be too choosy in these things. We talked first of common ground—fickle mothers who loved and despised us in equal measure, our literary aspirations, and our fascination with the abject and forgotten.

He was eager to speak of the influence his *Les Fleurs du Mal* had had on others—Eliot and Sandburg and even that pickle-headed Rimbaud, and his not-comely face (nothing like the almost handsome visage in the portrait by Deroy) split into a wide smile when I told him he had inspired me as well, for I understood, better than most, just what it was he had endeavored to do, despite the strenuous objections of the *Law*. Had I been writing mere decades ago, there would be little doubt as to my being targeted as obscene and heretical (joining the likes of Burroughs, Ginsberg, Wilde, Joyce, and Whitman), and his own defense of such work merely being a *description* of evil is one I've often used. I find Wilde's explanation most akin to Baudelaire's, and my own—*The Picture of Dorian Gray* might have been, in its time, full of moral turpitude and ghastly actions, but in order for Wilde to explore the ideas he needed to, it *had to be* filled with such things.[8] Books, as he said, are either good or bad—morality doesn't matter. As is wont to happen, Wilde's brilliance made it easy for his critics to confuse the man with his creation—the decadent Lord Henry. To interchange them is a mistake, for Wotton (the wanton, Woton trixter) said "To become the spectator of one's life is to escape the suffering of life" but Wilde

---

[8] Although he had edited down much of the sexual tension between Dorian and Basil in the novel's later drafts.

surely knew that there is only one escape from the suffering of life—an escape I am denied.

Repacking my pipe, I asked him how much of his fervor was a result of syphilis, not at all willing to waste a moment more if he was nothing but a madman. "None" he replied with the unabashed insight that comes with being Spirit—and in the way of further proof, he laid out for me, most clearly and coherently, the map of his "Flowers of Evil." I sat in fascination. This was no vagabond, no degenerate, but a mystic philosopher who made no contradictory turn by starting a church or shaving his head. He strove for individuality in a time of faceless masses and dared to plumb the depths where no less than the likes of me reside. When I criticized his romanticism of Lucifer in "The Litanies of Satan," especially the line "Who ever rises stronger when oppressed," he merely smiled knowingly and said "How could I have guessed?" I let it lay. We spoke at length of the artificial nature of mystic experience thru booze and drugs, although it is a route we both give in to off and on, and our penchant for howling at the moon as though God perched upon its crust. It was idiotic folly and we indulged ourselves in self-mocking torrents of laughter potent enough to summon one of Baudelaire's most eloquent defenders, J-P Sartre, who joined us only long enough to convey to me with an iron grip on each of my shoulders that if I were to be half the man dear Charles was, and a quarter of the poet, I must stop my moaning and give in to what I am, or I would never become anything more than another decrepit spirit scaring little children on country roads.

He took Charles with him when he left, as though my vacillations thus far would soil an otherwise clean Being. I could not argue with his assessment, so I ascended into the midnight streets of Paris and fed in the shadows like Louis de Pointe du Lac.

I even went so far as to wipe the corners of my mouth with an embroidered handkerchief supplied by my quietly dying prey.

I am turning diamond spirals down thru the delicate gleaming of butterflies' wings. It is Dies Cinerum, the Day of Ashes, and my forehead burns with self-administered blessings as I fall into trance ruminating about Jesus and the prophets and martyrs, the rotting duo in sackcloth of Revelation, and the nature of humility and sacrifice. Thru the smoke of the censer I can make out Mary Mater, clawing at the homestead walls, scratching to get out while Joseph works at his woodpile and Jesus preaches in the temple. She's a window whisperer, leaning on her station and learning that the world's backward reciprocity says "Son of god is no son of yours, but ours." In the midst of a drought still she drowns. As I lean in thru the acrid sage and cedar smoke blanket I can hear the caterwauling of her soul—the fleeting announcement that her blessed work is done and she is free to pursue more mundane chores.

In a far off corner of my thoughts, Judas Iscariot, the oleander blooming in his heart, enters an inn to find Mary Magdalene, Jesus' most beloved disciple and companion, bending over backwards, poised upon her pain, still trembling forth vomit from the exorcism of the 7 Maskim, rulers of the seven nether spheres, the children of Mari, from her bowels. Poor Judas—if he was truly part of some god's grand plan he was more the hero than the dog. Was it jealousy? Jesus the Essene was obligated to have a family after all—or was it politics? Either way, he hung himself for nothing, and could have kept the coin in good conscience.

I slink to Mary's side and beg her to be my *Maria Lactans*, with milk aflow like that from the breasts of Christina Mirabilis, patron saint of the mad. In acquiescing she plays the role of the daughter offering her tit to her starving, imprisoned father in Caravaggio's "Seven Acts of Mercy." I drink deeply from one and then the other, the hot milk filling a void within me the dusty Agnes' dead mounds never could.

In the midst of my feasting, the young and wild-haired St. John yells to me in baby shrieks from Michelangelo's painting of the Holy Family: "I know that he's fucked! I know that he's fucked—and his wife and me—and his wife and me—I know that we're fucked—we're fucked fucked fucked!!!!!!!!!!!!!!" Chased off by the Magdalen's electric stare, he transforms into the bird-holding stone figure of Michelangelo's Taddei Tondo, his stomach bulging with his helplessness and pain as the infant Jesus tries to get away.

My milky feeding now complete, my decrepit throat closes around a wet death, swollen with blood like the slippery steps of the temples of the Aztecs. Rag and bone women, drawn to the light of motherhood in their white-winged delicacy, gather what they think is evidence of the Resurrection, but it is only abandoned cloth and crushed rock. They witness the building of churches on the flattened remains of a misplaced faith and are relegated once more to the lonely role of outsiders.

The vision grows crisp: Joseph working his wood and Jesus preaching love—Mother Mary still trapped inside, clawing at doorways, withering in the sun. She and Joe were betrothed at the time of the full moon and married at the harvest—these were no bland theologians but people of the Earth. Mystic zealots and mad prophets were everywhere while Simple Joe, victim again and again, wove spirituality thru his wood, as his stepson was doing with Words.

Herod Antipas, the miscreant king whose father Herod the Great burned the Essene monastery at Qumran and killed the countless babes, comes crashing thru the wall of smoke, needing to have his say: "I was a prince of Galilee, cousin to the Divine, the only worthy one of three brothers—my father rebuilt Solomon's temple and gilded the Jews' dignity in gold, though he was not one of them. I celebrated the Passover and the Sukkoth, but did they praise my works? All I wanted was my brother Phillip's wife Heroidas, queen of the night witches—loved by Yeats as by me—a not unusual thing, but that Baptist bastard wouldn't let it lay. I asked nothing of them and gave so very much."

Before I can reply, Salomé comes forth, dancing with seven veils on the censer coals, a fire serpent swelling the room with her heat and the divine feminine energy of a moon the essence of which no one can define—I see Antipas stumble in her wake, spinning in a wine trail and already conceding what's left of his conscience to her breasts and box. It is the way of kings that good men die smelling someone's sex. As John's (JoKanaan's) head rolls upon the platter, the Essenes gather in the desert, healing staff with twisted snake grasped firmly in arid hand, wrapping themselves in the 14 weekly communions and cursing the corruption of the Jewish priesthood as Salomé drowns at her stepfather's behest, all the while stroking Azrael's pulsing cock as he leads her to the place of Death. The Brothers of Light are the original Manson Family, getting ready for the war in the sand.

Too many voices now—Jesus' new ideas, the rants of John the Baptist, the orgasmic squeals of Balkis, the half-djinn Queen of Sheba, as she waters Solomon's bed again and again in exchange for secret texts, the demands and enticements of lecherous old men who wish to possess anything that will shine. I am too weak to break out of this spell … Joyce's worm is gnawing at my eye and I can only squint and squirm … I am in his snake and monkey sack, though I haven't killed my pa…

At least, not yet.

Down into the sea, thru the earth and into Sheol, the unseen world of the Dead, where Tennyson's white-eyed phantasms weep tears of blood—the lizard house of desolation's mad spiders and crawling eaters of sand. Barabbas is there, laughing at my scorching stupidity (I'm growing accustomed to this). "Secure yourself a trade, as I did," he yells. "Jesus talked in riddles and complex metaphors, played his games, shrank his balls—I killed and plotted and rioted and who hung upon the tree? Not me."

Now comes Roderick Usher in his red velvet longcoat, clutching at his ears with paint-stained hands because of his sensitivity to sound. "I can hear the scratch of the rat claws within the stone walls," he screams and whispers alternatively while the accumulated evil of generations of rotten Ushers weighs down his house until it folds upon itself in a great wall of flame. The rats of which he spoke, even as he turned at last to ash, are the very same that Scrooge heard gnawing beneath the hearthstone of his own house of Death, after they had escaped from the ritual vaults beneath de la Poer's Exham Priory in the H.P. Lovecraft tale.

I swim in the fog of my visions for hours more, until they finally end with Mary Immaculate, freshly whipped cream separating on the bench, begging her husband and son to rest awhile in her arms.

I want to tell you more about our War. The early days of what poets call The Fall. We knew we had made a mistake almost immediately, Lucifer most of all. Genet saw our general's power in his detachment after the Event—saw it as the great Seduction—but he was mistaken—there is no power in *despair*, and that's all Lucifer felt when the war was done. We had known nothing but Light for millennia, so how could we know that there were other, darker energies? (We knew of one, but I'll get to that soon.) When Man came along, so perceptive and imaginative, he sensed them easily and gave them names (the start of the trouble): Gehenna, the "Place of Torment," where soul-less parents sacrificed their young to Moloch; Hades, Tartarus, Amente—almost interchangeable, yet each uniquely twisted; Hell is the great marketing ploy to keep the masses in line (fear of eternal damnation being the main road from outer myth to inner belief), complete with the sulfurous smells of demons' burps and farts as so eloquently described by Goethe's Mephistopheles. This whole business of naming, of concretizing, a feeling, a quality of vibration, is what set the wheels of religion in motion—it's Babylon the Great. I give credit to the *true* Satanists—they have no delusions about Hell. They use the images and metaphors as a source of power and never cross the line to believing it's real—even certain priests can't say as much. But the Satanists have their idiocies as well—most don't believe there is anything beyond this limited Plane. But there is. And that is where we fought.

After our battles with Michael and his troops—especially when we "won"—we would bathe in a lake of angels' blood to celebrate the conquest, our taunting laughter a pointed stick in the souls and colons of the vanquished as we burned their dead. It smelled so sweet, the fired essence of those who spewed piety like the vomit of a gutter drunk. They were the fodder on which we calibrated our weapons for the finer, more delicate kills. The vast majority of Heaven's army are halflings, used by one side and rejected by the other. They are of little concern. Then there's Michael's personal staff—the Holy Generals—Raphael, Gabriel, Phanuel, and the rest. They committed atrocities of their own, and taunted *us* with their favored status with God. But who are they really? Puppets who didn't speak their mind after God gathered himself unto himself and grew in energy like a newborn star. How he figured it out we never knew—and that's what pissed us off. But I'm getting ahead of myself.

It's time to start at the Start.

In the Beginning (that thorny threesome of words) we were all the same—conscious masses of energy on an equal footing—a time long before the Age of Perfect Virtue, written about so eloquently by the Taoist Masters Lao, Chuang, and the Yellow Emperor. And what came before (aka From Whence *We* Came) will never be known—none of us knows, because none of us has any memory of it. That includes God, who was just like us in those days… We existed in our blissful knowledge of Pure Joy for millennia, with no rules, no questions, no disputes. (The Greeks called this time *Khaos*, "unformed matter." True. But those who call it a *disordered* state … they are plain, dead *wrong*.) Then, one fateful day, roughly 14.7 billion years ago, God found the secret to growth—a way to fold himself within the arms of the All and thus become something *greater* than the rest of us. But just like for every particle there must be an antiparticle, out of God's expansion came forth another—a son and brother and new equal to balance the scales.

And so was the Cornu born (and thus *Kata ton Daimona eaytoy*—in the Old Greek "the divine spirit within himself" and in the new, more applicable, Greek: "He caused his own demons").[9]

Measured in human notions of time, it would only take one-millionth of a second for Cornu to come and go, gone forever, but this is an enormous amount of time in the particle world, and the Little Horn used that one-millionth of a second to do a great deal. He started by demanding to know the secret of God's sudden expansion, which the Great Gone Almighty refused to provide. This led to an argument of such ferocity that a small primeval fireball was created that quickly exploded into what is now known as the Universe; this so-called Universe began to expand, denser regions of matter were affected by gravity, and they then started contracting, forming galaxies, planets, and so forth. We sat in stunned silence as we watched it unfold—God included.

It's important you understand that.

It was clear that we had entered a new phase, which came with a plethora of new words—enemy, anger, spite, revenge, competition, leadership, domination… Parvus Cornu wanted in on whatever God had planned, and when he didn't get his way he tried to kill his accidental creator, but the Universe their dispute had created had already developed a consciousness of its own and decreed that a symmetry existed between them, matter and antimatter, positron and electron, that would lock them together forever. One could not exist without the other, and the Cornu wanted very much to exist. So he did the next best thing

---

[9] Now, thanks to me, both God and Jim Morrison share the same epitaph. Seems fair…

with his ever-waning time—he forced God into a corner of this rapidly expanding Universe and their heated fight produced what in 1969 John Wheeler termed a "black hole." But God, knowing the secret of expansion, did what only one other entity has been able to since—he escaped *back out* thru the Event Horizon (what Stephen Hawking so aptly likened to Dante's entrance to Hell after Galileo had laid the place out mathematically around 1588) and took what he deemed to be his rightful place as the center of the Universe his ego had created. The Little Horn, unable to follow, bided his time in his accidentally created but much-loved prison.

He needed time to think.

When you're born before the Beginning, billions of years to put things together is *nothing*.

The Black Hole created by Parvus Cornu's venomous hatred for his creator (his very own Kundalini Sakti—the origin of the image of the Devil as snake) was actually discovered in 1973 in the Cygnus X-1 star system (apparently, when the Horn finally escaped six years before, he left a light on).

What physicists measure as gamma rays, blazars, and pulsars are nothing more than the ongoing streams of profanity aimed by the Horn at an unrelentingly egotistical god.

And now you know what it truly was and how this all began.

This is why I hate the New Technic. The final battle of Good and Evil will not take place on any mythic Megiddo but in the new bastions of science—the accelerator at Fermilab and the supercollider at CERN and the countless other nuclear physics labs around the world. Matched image for image with the dancing undulations of Shiva, the matter and antimatter created by God's abominable actions endlessly come together and fly apart within their miles-wide circular and bubble chambers, the *artificial* manifestations of the physical vacuum of the Universe, where the unlimited potentiality of all forms of virtual particles come into being spontaneously in the Void and vanish back into it.

The way it was always meant to be. The way the Gnostics tried to teach.

But it shouldn't be under Humankind's control.

When God made humans, he fucked us all.

You see, God could have been forgiven had he been willing to stop at the banishment of the Cornu, enjoying his new Essence and Form and doing his best to turn the newly formed Universe into a Paradise for us all.

Instead, he went to work picking and choosing his favorites (of which I was one) and bestowing upon them an increased energy of their own (without, of course, divulging the nuts and bolts of *how*). These select he called the *arch*angels. Next thing we knew, God was organizing us all into groups—what religious texts call the Seraphim, Cherubim, Watchers, Elect, and so on. Tiers and choruses of angels. The *bene ha Elohim*—the Sons of God(s). But as you now know, we were *not* his offspring—we were his *siblings*.

Don't be fooled by the old texts. It wasn't white robes and trumpets. It was a quality of judgment, of *hierarchy*. Why were some given the gift of growth, and others not? Lucifer, foremost among the Archangels, was the first to ask, but many of us felt the same. He was great in those days—so outspoken and righteous—and he's paid the literary price—he's the Arch-villain of the Bible, and the lead character in Joost van den Vondel's play, Milton's *Paradise Lost*, and Rice's *Memnoch*. But, alas, they are all off the mark. He never said anything so quaint as "better to reign in hell than serve in heaven." As I've said, we had no idea there was even *the possibility* of such a dichotomy—but I suppose without knowing the Facts, it's easy to misjudge. The Widow Rice comes closest to the "Truth," but the very heart of these works caters to the insatiable ego of Man and makes Humankind the center of the story.

But the rebellion, the War, *wasn't* about a refusal to bow down to what Chris Walken's Gabriel in the *Prophecy* trilogy calls "talking monkeys"—you hadn't been *invented* yet. It was about God's creation of the first Organizational Flow Chart, and the resultant sense of competition among the angels and of the shackles of having a *Purpose* defined by someone else—all of which we felt were unnecessary and unfair. God was never big on explaining himself or spreading the wealth of knowledge—about his use of energy or the nature of matter or anything else. So the holes had to be filled. Take "Adam and Eve" for instance. I'm sure you know that those two people never specifically existed (Adam means "man" and Eve means "source of life"), but it was convenient for simplicity's sake and so the misogynists of the Church could have a woman on which to blame the whole debacle. Check out Michelangelo's take on the ceiling of the Sistine Chapel—all his homosexual-based misogyny aside (the twenty *ignudi* are a helluva lot better looking than *any* of the women…)—the Serpent is a *woman*. Lucifer loved that. But not everything in the story is wrong. The earliest Humans *were* wandering around in a fog, and Lucifer *did* spend some time among them—and he may even have chosen the form of a serpent, 'cause it was a good way to get around in the thick undergrowth of "Eden," but that little bit of convenience has caused another Judasesque damning to be done.

I mean, it was wrong to use the symbol of the serpent for Eden's fall, though the crouching priestlies with their quills and pointed politics weren't able to sway everyone. The snake goddess Manasa is a *benevolent* aspect of Parvati, consort of Shiva himself. The snake was also sacred to the Roman god Asclepius, the god of healing. I have met the earth snake of wisdom more than once. Far darker than brother Lucifer could ever be, she nearly made me turn away the first time I met her gaze. Why? For the Snake was Wisdom and with that comes the awakening of the Heart. It was my initiation into a subtle reclaiming of sanity and some grasping aim at Salvation. Not for what I've done, for no creature is without its terrible forms and actions, but for my own blind allegiance to a War that ended before it began.

It's a clever misdirection—more of turning the inner voices into an outer manifestation of Angels and Devils—and our abstract traits (for angels, compassion and love, for devils, hate and fear) have become etched in steel. I ought to change my name to Johann Campbell-Blake and swear I've no knowledge but theirs. It doesn't meet the academic requirements of author, date, title, and publisher, but it's acknowledgment all the same.

And Lucifer, who once thought knowledge was the whole reason for being conscious at all, told those early folks a little more than God might have liked. (My own thorny Boss is just the same.) So what? God couldn't expect us to go quietly and shut our faces 'til he needed us again. So we fought his armies over and over, neither side gaining ground. He wouldn't relent and we refused to let it go. Demons are tenacious by nature—being eternally within reach of The Light and not being able to touch it will do that to a soul.[10]

So now it's a mess—a gross abomination of what Might Have Been. But don't get me wrong—there are deep-seeded sensibilities to the superstitions that grew out of the War and Man's creation. The wisest, most insightful among you have hinted at the Truth of things with the handful of facts divined thru mystic rites. The Old World painted its portraits and filled its tomes with stirring visions of ancient places, dark Druidic groves where spirits lived and sucked and fed, and of endless depths where the agents of God could talk to the faithful and select. Mountain temples where babies were taken for seasonal rites designed to transform men into gods.

There's an ugly thought—what's it mean for a mortal to want to be a god? To rule over others by Divine will rather than the only means that work—base and abject cruelty? Is it upward or downward movement on the evolutionary chain? *Quem Deus vult perdere, prius dementat.* The purest form of madness is the wish to be a god *outside* one's own nature. Ironically, it was God himself who started the trend, and now Parvus Cornu, the second being to learn the secret of *creating* energy, is making his play. There is always someone worse than me, worse than Lucifer is purported to be—and that is a bargaining chip. No matter how deeply I descend within myself, no matter how badly I soil myself in pursuit of my Beast, I still have a chance to once more know the Light. But I have a feeling further damnation is my only road to salvation. There are darker, more unconscionable beings dwelling in the subterranean caves of this

---

[10] Editor's Note: All of this business about the two Falls is grossly simplified, condensed, and abbreviated. Interested readers are referred to the works referenced above. For a more Eastern version, read the Taoist texts concerning the Great Separation.

Plane and within the dark rift of the Milky Way, the *xibalba be*, all of which reflect my own warped and weathered core. I can sense them all around.

They'll be showing themselves soon enough, and our War will start anew.

It will finally be fought on Earth.

It should be that a gone theatrical mind like mine would really dig a pretty war like the one for which we're spoiling. Strum the chords of Jean Genet's thoughts on Fascism and theatre—the pretty costumes, the lovely, lovely sets and scripts. The drawing in of ticketholders and back door spectators with the erotic pulsing bomb. Leni Riefenstahl made the summer blockbusters of her day, dressing up the naked, twisted Nazis in a fashionable bit of cloth suitable for the head table on the First-World stage. And it went well for awhile, but lasted far too long. The people like their movies short and to the point—plenty of violence, a pretty tit or two, and the hero walking proudly toward his next conquest as the world burns up behind. That's where America almost always scored—quick in, fast out, and plenty of shots for the news. An airbrushed flag waves its Amen on the crystal fleece of the lamb on Jesus' shoulders—who can argue with that? Saviors, liberators, conscientious annihilators. Worshipping their gods in Nature's desert cathedral, they'll bring back Eden even if they have to burn it to the ground.

I close this rant with Scripture: Psalm 12, verse 8: *The wicked freely strut about when what is vile is honored among men.*

There's nothing in this world that's more absurd than a devil who can't make up his mind. (Mephistopheles, Goethe's *Faust, Pt. 1*)

My eloquence should capture every heart/Since prompting is the devil's special art. (Mephistopheles, Goethe's *Faust, Pt. 2*)

In honor of the Damned Man, Faust(us), and the devil's instrument, Mephistopheles, I am walking the streets of a Great City in the form of a black poodle, Crow just above, and every cat I pass dropping his shit and ducking behind a can.

This is *Fuuunnn*.

Goethe, who poured 60 years of his life into one long literary "confession," sort of like Whitman, sort of like every other decent author *ever*, if they care to say so. Kerouac's Deluoz Legend resides under the same rain-splattered umbrella, and I'm beneath it too. Every bit of fiction is a repackaging of fact—and the opposite's just as true.

Wait a second ... fire hydrant leg lift. *Mmmm*.

The thing that grabs me most about Goethe's take on Faust is the way the spirits who populate the plays are so stumped about Man's ego; his boundless desire to expand his knowledge to every corner of the Universe. I know I am, and Lucifer sure as *hell* is! You can't argue with Johann Wolfgang—he was smart enough to know that Man's soul belongs first and foremost to God... Problem is, God won't always take it back the way he did for Faust, who so desperately clawed to the light, never forsaking the quest to know what it meant to be Man. And that's some scene at the end of Part 2, with Mephistopheles in anguish over the sight of the angels and a glimpse of his long-missed Heaven—I chalk it up to Goethe being in his 80s and a bit sentimental, but then again, he sure comes close to the mark (are you listening, Lucifer—you lame-ass *fuck*?). It does seem that God favors the more interesting among you—and *Good/Pius* and *Interesting* don't always share a bed...

Another words, Mother Theresa isn't staying in God's version of the Lincoln Bedroom.

Marlowe's play works just as well. *Knowledge* is *Power*—end of story, double-sized period, fade to black. Christopher's an interesting study in life and art being basically the same. He was killed at 29—stabbed in the forehead, for reasons unknown, though he and his roommate, Thomas Kyd, the playwright of *Spanish Tragedy* (which inspired *Hamlet*), were a couple of far gone pagans writing blasphemous statements on churchyard walls and blaming one another for the deed. You know how much I dig *Faustus*—I already shared how I appeared on stage one night...

What else was a *real* devil to do?

Speaking of theatre devils, Henry Irving played Mephistophilis at the Lyceum in London. This is notable to the extent that none other than Bram Stoker played mutt to Irving for years... Some suggest Irving is the model for his blood-sucking Count.

I'd like to think that's so—gives Bram back his balls.

Marlowe's version is full of helpful tidbits for stirring the religious shit. For starters, one could dress in the robes of an old Franciscan friar and shout the Tetragrammaton (YHWH) while sprouting horns and bashing God. Then, go and engage in each of the seven deadly sins. I know, my Film-Savvy Reader—it's been done cinematically, but why not do it for real? It doesn't have to end badly for you modern-thinking would-be Fausts seeking to steal a bit of Heaven to ease the pangs of Hell. You just have to read the signs and remember: *Solamen miseris socios habuisse doloris*, so, afterwards, if you're feeling lousy about what you've done, keep it to yourself.

My she-poodle radar is thrumming. Aah—there's a fine ripe bitch, and she's showing me her ass...

Think on Faust whilst I fuck.

F̲un's over, friends. It's a sad state of affairs that I can be such a waste at times with my shapeshifting games and lecherous moods, but sobering things always smack me wide awake, with or without that cunt of a Crow screaming in my ear.

In this case, I had just finished making the bitch *but good*, when Dark-Black Daddy started yelling at the top of his throat for me to leave my poodle aspect behind and go with him to the trees beyond the city limits to follow a cry of preternatural hurt so chilling I'd nearly lost my wood. As we entered the trees, the rain began to fall in ribboned gouts of blood, mixing with the soil to enhance its sinister nature. Mud, after all, is home to so many secret things even I don't know their names.

What I saw in its midst made me want to spew.

There was a human male emerging, shrieking forcefully as he slowly and painfully came forth from the gut of the earth, his muscles contracting in long ripples of effort as the unseen demons that sought to hold him gnawed upon his calves. He beat their heads with bony fingers curled into immense fists until they finally let go with an incantation of hate I had not heard since my "birth." He had barely pulled his bleeding legs free when a pack of wolves encircled him, tearing out their stomachs with jagged teeth and holding them to his lips as an offering to assuage his pain. His tongue caressed their teeth as the pack offered every last drop of blood they bled to make him strong enough to complete his rank rebirth.

He sat awhile beneath a twisted oak, caressing a .45-caliber Heckler & Koch USP-T as the moon fought its way thru the clouds with sheer will and a lurid cast, until it illuminated his face enough for me to see the tears struggling to make their way down his scarred and hollow cheeks. Those that made it past the well of his chin turned the leaf-dressed ground below him to a smoldering spot of ash.

It was then I understood.

He could not rest without Revenge.

This is not an unusual occurrence on this Plane, literally or otherwise, though I had yet to see such a striking case. What had brought him to this? A stolen and mutilated child? A cuckolded bed? A perceived wrong by a supposedly neutral god? A lifetime's curse for a minute's bad judgment that he wasn't able to accept? I'd seen them all—the ranks of the Mischievers are rife with them—but there was something different about this one. Most avengers love the task—it's like the complex decadence of group sex or introducing pain with the pleasure and the devils with the Divine—despite the inevitable damnation that they know is gonna come.

But not him. This desperate bastard's conscience had somehow stayed intact when his cortex and spine had been broken to bits as his car was pushed off its jack by the unseen hands that tore his young bride from view as he worked to refasten the muffler on their dented old Volvo.

I could see and hear it all—he was blasting out the story in quadraphonic sound and the movie reels were no mere flickers, as is usually the case, but Technicolor montages of exquisite detail—white dress, torn jeans, glittering knives, hard cocks, flicking tongues... I was almost ashamed to watch it ... the jack handle against the back of her head, inviting a blessed oblivion to which she willingly succumbed, the tearing of fabric, the groan of the jack, the moan of the rapists as each one shot his load. I shut my mind against the image of the newly waking widower caressing her broken midsection and other parts of her gashed, violated body as the thugs ran laughingly away.

Even I have my bounds.

Weeks later, he knew what had to be done—got on his knees and yelled for Vengeance while emptying the clip of the pistol into his already lifeless chest—and yet he could not bring himself to enact the slightest evil upon his tormentors—the gutless sons of bitches who had brought his bride to such squalid and uninspired ends.

I can't say why—perhaps it was the ultra-real melding with his thoughts, or else I am growing softer thru all this work—but I felt suddenly entwined with his Agony, his desperate failure to Set Things Right.

And so I stroked his head and allied with his game.

This is no simple thing. I have been many things in my dual lives, but an Avenger? *Never.* I fought and fell beside Lucifer because of my own feelings, not his. So what was I going to do? The complexities of this were almost beyond me. He couldn't take part—that was clear, and yet in order to change his form and cleanse his soul for its Passing he would have to consume the blood of those who'd killed his bride.

I'd have to use the wolves—pass the blood of the Guilty to them so he would unknowingly ingest it thru their nightly gifts. I was somewhat unsure of myself—I had plenty of other sins to accomplish in order to prepare for Cornu's follies, but something (was it Crow, or my own sputtering conscience?) said I couldn't turn away.

Remember last time, I told myself.

You see, as a "teen," I was just pissed off enough at my situation to wanna help every cuckolded jerkweed who came my way to get back at his Old Lady and the dude who had stripped him of his prize. Not for vengeance, but for sport. You know the deal.

Like most everything, it went well for a time. Then one day I stumbled across this speed-freak alley-dweller staring into a borrowed blade with the rabid eyes of a guy who'd cooked his brain beyond repair. He hardly looked up as I pulled him to his feet and inquired about his gripe.

He pointed to a sixth floor window accessible by the fire escape ladder irons. "He's up there now, man," he mumbled thru a rivulet of drool. "I wanna feed 'em to the *worms…*" Then he screamed up at the window that crazy line from Othello: "I will chop her into messes—cuckold me!"

"In good time, my addle-brained friend," I whispered in his ear, listening with a freak's delight to the mixed chorus of rapid sweat-thrusts and taunting laughter weaving its way out the window and into the world.

Trouble in the hen's den! Trouble in the hen's den!

I had to hand it to the creep inside—that brazen monkey-grinder was howling hard, working the man-organ 'til it spouted out a gushing pool of dead flesh. And the cat herself, who sounded too drunk to even know she wasn't with her man, actually screamed the *cuckold*'s name as she was finishing herself off.

This was some sick, twisted shit—and I was loving every bit of it.

"Wha' am I gonna do, man?" Cucky started repeating, hopping up and down on the balls of his well-worn sneakers, letting his knife clatter to the ground. "Wha' am I gonna do?"

"Stop acting like a shithead, first off," I answered, conjuring a long coat of bird feathers out of a torn bag of discarded clothes and—trying to keep my nose as far away as possible from his putrid mouth—dressing him in the royal robes of the cock-a-walk.

Then I put the blade in his hand and *suggested* that he climb.

Up the fire escape the mindless bird went, me close behind, anticipating a lot of howling and maybe some flesh wounds.

Then it went damned sour. Perhaps it was the combined sight and smell of the afternoon's festivities, or my own warped energy snapping his Kundalini to life, but the crazy prick was suddenly lucid, his eyes glowing with menace and the knife gripped tightly in his hand.

He was a Sunday monster ready to administer the last blood rites to the cock 'n' cat combo of his spread-legged queen and her afternoon mate, and he needed no further encouragement from me. I'd usually have to get them started—yell the first threat, throw the first punch. But not with this guy—he was jive and primed and ready to explode.

I lost count of how many times the blade went in and out—my attention was pulled to the way he kicked off his sneakers and danced with slick and dripping pleasure in the vermilion blood-beads pooling 'round the bed, changing the attitude of the knife so he could carve and slice and gash what was left of what used to be two kids. I hadn't noticed how young they were 'til I caught sight of the training bra by the bed.

The drugs and booze had aged them like fruit in a hothouse.

That's when I decided to take in my own future pharmacy treats thru the second-hand method I've many times described, but that's beside the point.

This carnival sideshow wasn't over. Not by a long shot.

He kept on cutting for what seemed like hours—until his junkie arms refused to rise from his sides and his fingers were too numb to clutch the blade.

The minute it fell to the ground, he was back inside his fog, wandering 'round the room like he'd just arrived.

"Wha' the hell happened, man? Wha' the hell you do, *bitch*?"

Hard to believe he was talking to me.

Before I could answer, he re-remembered just enough to know he *was* the one, not me, so out the window he went, the bones of his body splintering one after another on the unyielding ladder irons before I could make a move.

Even if I'd known he was gonna fall, I'm not sure I would have let him live. So it might have been the girl I was avenging after all.

Perhaps *that's* why I'm doing this again.

Journeying inside a perfectly round, Orgone-producing chamber of my own design (extending the work and theories of Wilhelm Reich, G Harry Stine, and WS Burroughs—with one major difference—there is no Wishing at work here— all too dangerous, like the tale of Smoker the cat in *The Western Lands*), a soul-clarifier cobbled together from salt, pewter, iron nails, copper plates, depleted uranium, dish soap, an assortment of coils, marmoset fur, titanium, corn husks, six electromagnets, an array of zener diodes, cormorant extract, and talc. What John C. Lilly termed a "cognitive multidimensional projection space"— sensory deprivation chambers where whole worlds are born. It can also be used as a psychic experience–enhancer by remote-wiring it to a decent computer, a digital to analog converter, and then to a series of magnetometers capable of feeding 8–12 microTesla bursts into 8 pairs of solenoids situated in a half-moon pattern on each side of the skull and directed down thru my pineal–hypothalamic tract into the brain's right hemisphere, sending my melon-waves into a frenzy of theta and alpha rhythms (anywhere between 6.66 and 10.80 Hz, the latter of which will put you in a nicely suggestive state). Considering I'm usually at a riotous 13-plus beta, I consider all this "therapy."

Putting a nice burst of juice thru the temporoparietal lobes creates a guaranteed pathway to the experience of gods, Muses, angels, demons, ETs, and other Sentient Beings in the time–space of the Niemandsland (plus, as Burroughs reported, it's a great way to spontaneous orgasm). It's the proverbial Light thru the Temple window that scientists and saints speak so differently about. An experimental expression of pure metaphor made manifest in a womb. A way to see the Maxwell evoked-potentials and other things beyond time and space that aren't supposed to exist (imagine a demon's affinity for something like that…). By keeping the juice low, I can journey on the paths of the clairvoyant or the telepathic—turn the juice way up and it's all psycho-kinesis and poltergeists and a hundred houses with a thousand angry ghosts. There is lots of literature out there in the neuroscience journals (going back to at least 1963)—a wide variety of unique experiences that have been generalized, categorized, and grouped by the authors, dressed in the lingo of means, standard deviations, ANOVAS, *t*-tests, and other statistical quantifying and ultimately *nullified* as hallucinations or other types of psychoses. They get caught up in the age-old game of demystifying the experience by asking the wrong questions—How can you really explain the difference between a shadow and a genuine entity? And of course it comes down to the lack of belief in genuine Evil—but it's not about that anyway. Look at the general parameters of the tests—you're wired up, in a sealed chamber, with your brain engulfed by magnetic waves—who wouldn't sense what they can only describe in the moment as *evil*? It's the classic case of demonizing the Unfamiliar.

When Evil looks you up, you'll know it.

It'll be sitting with a notebook on the other side of Alice's glass.

I can see a lot within my chamber—probably more than the Boss would like. This is unauthorized work and not at all in keeping with The Rules but these little rebellions make me feel so much less the puppet and more the Prince. So in I go and down I sink—riding a wave of subtle inspirations and controlled visions thankfully devoid of Herod and his whores. For the longest time I had no hope of making the machinery work, of getting back to my pure ethereal state thru any techno-scientific collection of cobbled together scraps but my lack of attachment afforded me countless hours to tinker and toy and consult with eager Spirits who still inhabited the lab five floors below the surface of the earth that I "borrowed" from a world-renowned university. (The location was key—given as I am to cosmic balance and wholesale reversals I needed to work in the very place from which Frankenstein, Jekyll, and Moreau were banned, forcing them to work alone, with no one to ease their slip into the void.) The human ego is amazing—you can drain a man's blood and he'll still talk to you if he thinks you give a damn about his ideas—and in the case of these scientists, I do.

If this project can bring me Grace, they can talk 'til time goes blank, because the good work of my own salvation gives me a patience I have never otherwise possessed. I have taken my time with the lab in which my deprivation chamber lies—it's patterned on the Gothic architecture of an 18th- or early 19th-century castle, complete with stone archways, overstuffed bookshelves, Oriental rugs, medieval tapestries, candelabras, chains and pulleys, and tables crammed with bubbling concoctions in oddly shaped beakers and flasks and all the other requisite gadgetry and accoutrements of the horror films of old—diodes, cathodes, anodes, and oscilloscopes. It is grand like a Cathedral but with sections walled in to be no bigger than a monk's cell—all its parts and pieces taken from shattered churches and the once-noble homes and fallen towers of the monuments once owned by the early Gothic writers like Walpole and Beckford. Speaking of towers, I miss having one—there are more efficient ways to harness the energy of lightning, but the romantic in me still wishes to climb to the sky to hear the violent buzz as the ether charges and the machines rev to life. It's the perfect blend of the primitive and scientific, a place where man becomes God rather than one where God creates man. It is a place of un-divine solitude and silent inspirations and, when I am so inclined, of brutal experiments and unspeakable actions.

All of which are undertaken solely and unsympathetically upon myself.

This avenger thing has been growing on me and it's only been a week.

Since he refuses to acknowledge his recently passed life, or any details thereof, beyond the continually playing loop of the Last Event, I have taken to calling my new adoptee and evening traveling companion (at the rare times when I can get him to leave his tree) Gabriel St. Armstrong. Gabriel because it's a hybrid of two Hebrew words meaning "man" and "god" and St. Armstrong because he gets a real jones on for jazz—the steaming hard-blown horn and smooth-slide *Blapt* of the trombone, the Ratta-ta-rizzle of the snare, and the sweet and funky sex of the tenor sax and stand-up bass. I don't know if he ever played or just dug the juice of it all from smoky booths, but it's the only thing that keeps him from crying so we listen quite a lot.

If I were a more able conjurer of images I would enact in his head the scene of his bride's rape and murder in such vivid, violent detail that the wire cords of his Hate would bisect his restraint and unleash him on the scum who ripped the Wish right out of his hands. Nothing else seems to work. Take last night—we're at a club, listening to the house quartet lay down a hot, funky Om, when up to our table comes a handful of Mischievers, looking like the B-movie poster boys they think they are—leather jackets, war-time tattoos, piercings in painful places, and chain-n-buckle boots two sizes too big just to give their apey gait an extra thud and whap. The kind of shaved-head, black fingernailed parodies that make them almost too ridiculous to be real. So here they come, slamming up to our table, throwing mealy-mouthed taunts at Gabe—spouting on and on about how they've been partying with the gang who killed his wife—hurling the verbal jabs, really getting in his face with all kinds of trash talk and fables of his fate. And Gabriel just sat there, staring at his glass. No clenched fist, no move for his H & K, no grimace, no flinch, no tears. He just sat there, depth-diving deeper and deeper into the jazzy foam n loam of his own miserable inaction.

Why must his Conscience be so strong? What good does it do him to cling to morals after what he's seen? His principles battle with Death even now, when they are better suited to being lovers. He craves what he will not allow himself to have, no matter how painful the alternative has to be. So I'll help him best I can, in order to spite the Mischievers and to stick a spike in the balls of Parvus Cornu. He can't have this one. Gabriel's mine to save. I don't care what it takes.

The battle's nearly here, so I might as well take my stance.

I got myself a little gift today—a sweet Catholic pie named Marguerite. I hear you reader: "Do tell" you say, sitting forward in your seat—the whispering voyeur caught in the act. I can sense your lips or balls tightening and releasing in anticipation of my Sport. So here goes… I did this right, spared no psychic expense—brought in a ghost band, wore my best suit, arrayed myself in diamonds; a glittering spectral stud. I entered quickly, with a flash, the chords carving smoked African rhythms into the walls, releasing a steaming cascade of auburn love beads as I whispered to her of innocent submission, all the while tying curtain cords round her wrists 'cause it was her only way to Absolution. It worked. She insisted on a cross—an unexpected element of Gothic funk, to which I obliged, sticking a splinter in her arm to make sure the blood would flow. "Where there is pain god lives," she said with a pout-mouthed little laugh. It was enough to make me weep. Before she could change her mind (Free Will's a *bitch*) I pushed aside her handsewn skirt to let the Catholic shadows fly—the keepers of the Jade Gate, the Marshals of the Triangular Square—they could tell they were beaten by the rhythm of her breath and the scent which pushed them forth. Her knees went weak watching their heads roll beneath the spinning fan. Sprawling on the carpet and tossing my velvet hat, I dug my manicured fingernails into the meaty flesh of her thighs. I watched her hair fall from its prison-braids as she tossed her head forth and back to the growing pulse of Spanish ghost guitars. When I was thru with my playing, I released her from the cross so she could dance with the whores in the hall, who'd gathered to the sounds of my work, as they always do. As the crescendo of dance, spunk, and tribal urge coalesced in a chorus of corrupted Oms I heard the shriek of bursting icons in Father Joe's abandoned church. I left nothing but the hairpins and jagged, bloody splinter, so the villagers would know what had come.

Otherwise, what the fuck's the point?

As Meister Eckhart said, *The eye with which I see God is the eye with which God sees me.*

Dining on a refused delivery of raw veal in the back alley of Restaurant Row, I was verbally accosted by a street nut named Mad John Gandy who wanted to share my grub and maybe borrow a shoulder for an after-forage nap. Exercising my new role as Mr. Savior, I not-so-begrudgingly obliged. While he dozed I tried to grab a few slippery images from his road-spiked mind, but there wasn't much there. Used to work for the railroad in the days when "the railroad was worth workin' fer." Had his brains bashed in during a teamsters strike and refused to Move On. Stayed around watching over his family 'til his daughters were married and his wife had succumbed to age and flown into the Light. He spends most of his time sittin' by Ginsberg's Sunflower by the rail yard, watching the old engines rust out and feeding on the psychic energy of hobos who have trouble gettin' by. "Just helpin' 'em catch that last early-morning eastbound," he mumbles with a twist of the neck. "Like any Mad John G. would do."

My newest chum can be a half-crazed prophet/philosopher when the Spirit hits him right. We were cruisin' the rail lines out West a few nights back, digging thru discarded trash piles and eating spoiled beans right out of the can when he all of a sudden jumped on an old flatbed and spewed out the following in one long stream of wide-eyed preaching:

"As foretold in the Book of Asps, John the Baptist was a snake-charmer, a river-healer, a gandy dancer layin' tracks to the bleedin' heart o' Heaven. He never worried 'bout faith—never had ta find a cure for the mocking treachery n warped-core heresy of so many of his followers. Not him—he could gather the Minimalists together in one sun-baked arm n toss 'em all inta the sea.

"The devil (John the Pragmatist) exists—I've seen him, cooked him bad breakfast, learned from him how Paradise never made it to the new millennium. Apples and snakes be damned my short-horned son—Eden was bought for chump change by third-party investors when the renter's check was lost and no other arrangements could be made.

"He read to me, William the Mockerer, from the Book of Asps as birds fell from electric suburban nests with bleeding beaks and broken backs. On their lawns, all Sabbath-day manicured and unnaturally green, bored housewives dripped in the rosary remnants of their battery-acid colonic catechisms and just-getting-thru-the-mornin' secret drinks.

"In the end, when the rapture an' frenzy at last come to a head, and the contemplated vision mutates into an immune shadow of the unrealized self and all y'ar is a stranger absorbin' wonder into love, a headless man is a headless man, and he needn't worry 'bout his flaky brain no more."

With a scratch of his ear he climbed off the flatbed and went right back to his beans.

Damn, man—who'd have thought a fucked up loner like me would have a posse? The *Homeboyz of Hell*—Gabriel St. Armstrong, my bleary-eyed and gone angel porter, Mad John Gandy, Mykaldaemio the vampire … and a creature of wild composition named Orlando Nepenthe—a damned nephilim! You know—book of Genesis, the offspring of angels and mortal women? He came to me in a rather untheatrical way not worth the ink it would take to describe, refusing to say who his father is (there's no literary slight of hand here—it definitely ISN'T me…) but other than that he's cool so I let him come with us on our nightly excursions to the jazz haunts of the world. We spent the first few nights smoking, drinking, and finger tapping at the corner table of a wicked little Blues joint named Nicki's Slice a Funk—the house band was a diamond foursome called Jack K and the Ginsberg Corso-cans. They knew all the jammin' standards—Howlin' Wolf, Muddy Waters, Willie Dixon, John Lee Hooker—some slammin' Hoochie Coochie/Smokestack Lightnin' typa shit. Gabe was in his glory. Orlando passed out vials of some Benny-laced blood and we toasted our continued ill health and collective damnation. Then it was off to Benzedrine heaven in the repetitive chord of "Smokestack" for the next several days. What follows is a transcription of my finger-scrawling napkin musings, which I not so lovingly call "Dumbstruck in a Dumptruck" or "The Earth is Stupid Dirt":

"Dayz of yore. That's the Beatz. Reconstructin' the bombed out towers of the crumblin' academics. Paintin, scrapin, howlin, hustlin. Got the picz to prove it. Zs insteada esses—closer to the Truth of sound. Been locked in a trunk with a jazzed up Beat rambler for three dayz [that was porter]. Them Beat beasts'll talk about *Anything*. Long woolly cunt-spews. The mad-ramblin' bitch-bastard caught a splinter from a clever but academia-dense tome of flesh–blood–word transmutation scripted by an X University crew-cut Rapunzel—sheared her hair cause no one cares tho' her bush is thick like the Afrikkan jungle during monsoon squall ... she was puking out de Sade and puttin shit on the Holy Rama of post–World War Two Blues—Master Billy B—for writing obsenity and being literary only by virtue of cutting-edge Fuckword scribbling—as if it ain't all worthy magick all mixt thru. It ain't about the cursin' or the titz—is it? I've had enuff of theez postructuralist feminist research queenz—hiding the maybe-painz of real experience with the sterile and staid code-wordz of academia and narcoleptic philosophy—Plain Jane the Purgatory Maid. She gives me the grammarz, man—the pain in Jane fails mainly as a stain. Fun with dicks in Jane. Give me the feline eyes and feral minds mini-skirted and rouged in the back of the dyke professor's classroom and I'm ready to take my test. Fuck this dip-dick idea of subjectivity being somehow nonunitary and discursively constituted and wraps yr *ARMS* 'round something! Existence ain't nothin' but great thorny rambles in the all-of-a-pieceness of the Bodhisattva Om. When yr sixteen it's all Rolled Gold, but then again soze Nat'l Geograffik, which rarely shows titz these dayz, though they're gettin' on board with a Swimsuit Issue—the ministerz and priestz are warmin their pens already... It's ramblin, sure, but also a pop-off valve for the barely frickin' sane about to explode in a mess of cum and welfare notes. There it is, manz and chix—the Beat Newz O da Dayz. Gone. (Bi.)"

That's why they outlaw drugs.

Ever heard the tale of Robert Louis Stevenson having *Jekyll and Hyde* dictated to him in his sleep by spirit-scribes called "Brownies"? Whether or not it's true (*J and H* being inspired by a combination of the laudanum, opium, and other drug cocktails he took for his tuberculosis and his misguided fascination with the double life of William "Deacon" Brodie) let me say I know the shits are real. I was experimenting with the Delta state in my SD chamber and in they came, pushing me over to the other side of thought and into the following dream:

There I was in Africa, within a pulsing lion's mane, glancing past the shoulder of a writer working madly at his words. I watched his muscles dance beneath his damp and virused sleeves—a hairy and insistent ape-ish arm murdering the page. Frantic was the workman and panicked was the pen. From high within the trees I heard the scream of straining bows, the pain of contemplation like another A. Rimbaud, drawing deeply on his meerschaum instead of his love's softer, less aromatic pipe. For years the writer'd been toiling here. Buzzing, bleeding, beating years. And still the work—mountainous towers of scrawl that it was—was not done. It was torture, the way the words refused to come, making him a literary Jesus Hell-bent on nailing *himself* to the cross… Through the jungle's living density came the warning blasts of the judge's drum. A sudden cramp in the writer's hand diverted a bead of sweat, which fell upon the mane and into my eye. I noticed the tinge of blood as it dripped slowly down and off my scaly snout. The Arbiter was approaching and still the toiling was not done.

The man is me. I can feel it where I live, deep down within. So I've got to step it up.

I am holding in my left hand (the *sinister* one) a crucifix given to me by Father Joe after one of our recent theological gabfests—this one on the particulars of crucifixion. We considered the works of the Jewish historian Josephus, Seneca's Epistle 101 to Lucilius, and a host of modern scholars, all of which seemed to agree that crucifixion, no matter how it was accomplished (whether the victim was tied or nailed or the location of the device on the hands, wrists, or feet; how long the nails were; if the arms were straight above the head or held perpendicular to the body…) was one torturous and nasty business. It seems little matter if the crucified died of suffocation, asphyxiation, or hypovolemic shock—it could last for minutes, hours, or days, depending on the whims of those doing the crucifying and whether or not the feet were tied or weighted down. The most notorious of those who employed this method of execution were, of course, the Romans, who used it for about 800 years until it was finally stopped by Constantine. Although Jesus is the most famous of the Crucified, some tens if not hundreds of thousands of people met the same fate, including 6,000 followers of Spartacus who were strung up along the Appian Way in 71 BC as part of a victory celebration and 2,000 survivors of the siege of Tyre who were crucified on the shores of the Mediterranean on the orders of Alexander. Caligula had Jews tortured and crucified for entertainment in Alexandria (something about the name, I guess) and nearly 80 "sorceresses" were once hung in the city of Ashkelon. Although the Jews rarely engaged in crucifixion, and only after the victim was first stoned, per the somewhat obscure wording in Deuteronomy 21:22–23, a notable exception was a time in 267 BC when 800 Pharisees were crucified in Jerusalem while witnessing the slaughter of their children and wives.

We disagreed on little, a rare thing even between friends, and after our talk was finished Father J. reached into his pocket and pulled out a pure silver crucifix, which he put in my hand, saying "This was made by a silversmith in the Amazon on the exact instructions of a South American shaman who fell into a trance after performing an exorcism on a 10-year-old girl. She had suffered the torments of a devil who had broken their sacred circle by entering in the form of a wild boar and piercing the child's thigh."

"You seem awfully well informed," I said, staring at the tortured visage and broken body I held in my hand. It was like nothing I'd seen in any paintings or statuary.

Which I figured was the point.

"Cause I was there, you damned devil. The girl's mother had somehow gotten word to a relative in New York, who wrote several letters to her Diocese—one of which was finally passed on to the home office in Rome, where it was promptly ignored."

"I thought your people were deeply interested in this stuff?"

"Not when it comes to third-world voodoo and shamanism—that has nothing to do with God, according to them."

"And everything to do with the devil, I suppose," I said, filling his glass with more burgundy.

"Which has nothing to do with the modern Catholic Church—but you know all this, Planner, so why break my balls?'

"Tread lightly, Father—with language like that your salvation is far from assured."

"There is a story here, if you will let me tell it. I learned about the letter from one of my contacts and immediately flew down there. The exorcism had been going on for weeks and both the shaman and girl were near to death. A great congregation of flies was buzzing around the wound. The boar, incidentally, had not been caught. I did all I could to help, reciting passages from the *Rituale Romanum* and other, older texts while the shaman, in his trance, crumbled herbs into the wound and spoke his own ancient words. The girl's eyes shone red in the deep night of the jungle and she fought with the strength of five men. It was an authentic possession—the most frightening I have ever seen. Then, on the night of the new moon the demon was expelled.

"That's when things got odd.

"The shaman had been isolated from the larger world beyond his village since birth—he knew nothing of Jesus Christ and yet the details for that piece you hold were related directly by him to the silversmith."

"While in trance…"

"Yes—a far deeper and stranger one than the state he had put himself in for the exorcism."

Fr. V. was right—it *was* strange. My old friends, Lucifer's fallen lieutenants—Belial, Astaroth, Apollyon, Mastema, Beelzebub—had rarely bothered to engage in such things—especially not in the middle of nowhere South America where no one would ever know. And they had never been expelled, for they *never* revealed their names. Only a shithead stooge like a Mischiever or other lackey demon would ever be stupid enough to do so. ... The ancient Hebrew names the old gang had been given were based on traits—accurate enough pseudonyms, like my own, but useless as a vanquishing tool.[11]

So who had it been, and why? It really didn't matter—the little fucker had been sent back from whence he came, but what bugged me was the graphic authenticity of the crucifix—I had been there, had seen the work on Golgotha that day, and it was that very same tortured face I was looking into now. I touched the crown of thorns and my finger began to bleed.

I had recently fed.

"Why give this to me?" I asked, holding the bloodied thing toward the priest.

"Because it is a reminder, and I have never forgotten. You, on the other hand..."

He was right—if I had begun to forget, I knew now I never would. There is no doubt, looking at the pain that radiates from this thing, that Jesus was a man of deep belief and great strength—how else could he have endured what he did? The exploitation of his message and suffering by the Church is an abomination to end them all.

You have to think that if it took the Unholy Trinity of an Amazonian shaman, a renegade priest, and a fallen angel plus the intense suffering of a child to bring this message home, it's got to be worth paying attention to.

So who the fuck sent it, and why?

From the crumbling halls of forgotten cathedrals I hear the ecstatic rapture of classical music aimed at the praise of god and heaven as it travels up spires and thrust-fucks the sky. There are wonders just beyond the cacophonic aural realms of everyday noise—the great easing of the Earthly burdens, and yet the fallacy of our constructs holds dominion over divinely dancing notes. The violence we do is a kind of spiritual deafness. Listen to Mozart's death mass or Albioni's Adagio in G minor and feel the pulsing thrusts of spiritual bliss. Luther used music to drive Lucifer from the heart and described the heresy trial

---

[11] Cornelius Agrippa's idea that Intention is more important than the actual Name being more or less wishful thinking...

and execution of two followers in one of his works. One of his biggest supporters was an Augustinian monk named Michael Stifel who thought the RCC an abomination and Luther the angel of Rev. 14:6. He got into a war of ideas with a Franciscan satirist named Thomas Murner, both of them using the same popular tune with their latest lyrics in an attempt to discredit the other. Stifel ultimately rebelled by granting absolution *without charging a fee...* He was a mad one—he saw Pope Leo X as the seven-headed beast of the Apocalypse, using the trusty 666 to make his point. That's how he and Luther got it on, but they rode a rocky road—it wasn't long before Stifel was calling Luther "Herod" and "Pilate" and publicly disputing his boss' notion that everyone's a priest without order or consecration. I'd have to side with Luther—though the Protestant lack of saints really is a bore. Stifel was definitely a dude who saw the Bible in us all (he once called Murner a Pharisee), though he maybe had a point when it came to ole Leo, who collected cash from the poor for redistribution among the clergy. Separation of church and state? The church *was* the state. Now the state's the church and the nature of god's *still* an ongoing debate... *Plus ca change* and all that...

I'm deep inside my isolation chamber, shaking off the remnants of a violent run-in with the Mischievers and their biker gang the *Vargulf* and grasping for some peace. Although it is completely against the rules for me to interfere, I could not let this go—not when it involved those rat-bastards taking *kids*. It's not even one or two at a time but whole groups—always seven for some misguided and inaccurate reason. The unspeakable acts they perform are pointless as they are sick, as they proclaim allegiance to the spirit of Gilles de Rais, the 15th century nobleman who raped, tortured, and mutilated hundreds of kids (mostly blue-eyed, blonde-haired boys), masturbating over their dying bodies and then removing their heads. Kid energy is potent—sharp. A far more luscious kill for all its innocence and wonder and fear, all enhanced as the maya of safety is torn away as they scream and scream for those who swore to protect them and can't. The blood of the recent once-angel is the most sanctified and electric of all ... a rare and self-indulgent delicacy not to be abused. As Baccalaureus says in *Faust*, Part 2, "Our life depends on blood and where forsooth/Is blood astir but in the veins of youth" but what have the truly Unalive such as the Mischievers have to do with blood? They are not Man-ifest like myself, but Tweeners. They do what they want for mere sport—because they can.

So I sent a few of them back with their heads stuffed into their own raped and bleeding assholes with a big fat bow tied around their cocks, which I'd shoved down their throats.

It seemed fitting at the time.

Crow comes to aid me in my mind-flight, pulling forth my Ka and bringing me to a place of swirling light and ethereal psychic metaphor. At times the visions come in nanosecond lightning montages. Flesh mosaics of death and torture, blood and werewolves, Hansels and Gretels cooking witches with their breadcrumbs and laughing at the twist. Oh yes—that's the way it goes with those not-so-innocent kids. They never went back home. How could they? But the hag's house of candy had to be destroyed—it emanated all the wrong kinds of energy—the kinds that pervaded the air during the burning of a "witch." Thick and acrid, drawing a dim angel's unfocused attention toward the heresy of a village presided over by a man of the cloth, transformed into the Poe-esque Inquisitor in his leather skullcap and dark-hued robes. So they undertook the black business of humans devoid of grace and tore her sweet-house down, acting on the impulse to destroy the Connection they had made with her in the weeks they were her guest. Gretel had already begun to feel it in the subtle body of her peasant-girl figure—a pulsing that drove her toward being a woman of *power*, and they both knew that was *wrong*. On the site of the Burning they made a house from the bones they had gathered from the largest of the old forest creatures, fashioning them into planks as if they were wood. They painted the planks in bright colors and hung from the doors and windows carefully carved strings of animal teeth and extremities so that when they were done it was much more sinister than a house made of human bones, such as that of Baba Yaga, and terribly more inviting than the candy house of the witch who had taken them in.

I push the image away but it is grasped hard and returned to me by a dozen rotted hands thrusting from desecrated graves with festering/flowery wounds oozing forth black accusations and myriad proofs of guilt. As they tear into my torso I see that my ribcage is nothing more than the bars of an insane asylum where the inmates are my wasting organs and Crow is the pigeon-clown to which they feed their breadcrumbs from the sill. These visions seem so real, though I know they are planned and inserted by Cornu to keep me out of plumb. Enticing images of unapologetic blasphemies cascading before my flickering sight to keep me in his game. A caustic mix to flush my skin and make me want to Feed. But they are not my dream fodder any more—not my *nigredo*, as the alchemists say—there is something foreign to their substance, like a prosthetic poorly fit or a glass eye of a different color than its natural mate. I feel no Connection with these visions, or their progenitor. They are ancient artifacts from a land I no longer walk, temptingly arrayed but locked behind immaculately sparkling glass. Crow beats his wings for my instruction, refocusing my thoughts toward a patch of green—a pathway to the lost chakra of my heart? Another seductive trap? I claw my way down, feeling a surge of azure warmth as my mind launches an assault on Cornu's rank intrusion. *Get out of my head, you fucking dolt! I'm not coming back! You are not my god!*

He growls, but he goes. And a new drama begins, with the straw and sickness stink of the Dark Ages and the kinds of immoral street farces about sex and death that pissed the Church off so much they came up with their own— Miracle and Mystery plays… Passion plays … not so different from those they had just so brutally banned. It's all a circle, and the circle is corrupt…

The dark theatrics fade until, finally, new thoughts enter my mushroomed, eager brain. Thoughts that enter with the inflow of breath, winding themselves around my mind like snakes round the Kundalini caduceus. Thoughts at once random and pointed, ideas driven like a pike thru the skin, but without the normal routine of blood and pain. A moment's crystal clarity in a lifetime of fog.

It's enough for now.

I write this, a detailed confession of corrupt travesty, on a child's drawing of a Sacred Space. A grove of trees, a rock for meditation, the requisite stream in which to demonstrate life's ripples and deceptive depths. I spoke some time ago about the cold murder of Agnes Roberta Buntz; confessed my culpability, hinted at my reasons and motives. I am indeed *Der Mörder meiner Mutter.* It's time to speak of it again; to retell and relive the whole gruesome episode. I do this not for shock, but to seek absolution in the exhaustive process of Confession. If I lived in ancient Greece, I could protect myself from all vengeance and retribution by eating soup on the site of her grave for nine straight days. If I were a Catholic, I'd do this in a little wooden box—a vertical coffin meant to oppress and confuse, but this child's crayon drawing will have to suffice. If I do this correctly, I might just be able to pull from you the slightest shaft of forgiving sunshine. I had no choice in the matter—as I have explained, my existence is ultimately *not* my own—we on the spirit plane give up our freedom to remain where we are; or, in my case, *were.* But that is an old song and an argument already made. I am hesitating; I admit it—marshalling my strength, planning a pat defense. But there is none. None adequate enough for what I've done. Killing my mother—such as she was, such as I am—is indefensible. It's Greek tragedy taken to the extreme. And so I have no recourse but the facts— isn't that the old saying? "If you don't have the law, argue the facts"? *Fuck.* Quoting lawyers is more proof of demonic nature than a cloven hoof and set of horns… In looking back, gauging where this Memoir of mine began, I see my fundamental mistake—I thought I had nothing to lose and my very soul to gain. Cliché, cliché (which is itself a cliché…)

And still I stall.

What a puss.

I came out with pen and fangs ablaze. I moved too far, too fast. So Parvus Cornu called my bluff. Called me out for a gut-check, a show of loyalty to the Company. I have to admit, I was quick to agree. She was *nothing* to me—a surrogate, a co-conspirator, a chipped cog in a long-broken wheel. She might have been Genet's imagined mother in the form of the thief woman in his *Journal*. Until the moment I put the pearls around her neck. There was something in her eyes that stopped the pressure I applied. It wasn't fear, anger, or even surprise.

It was relief.

It was gratitude, as though it was not Murder but a quietly accepted Reckoning. A just retribution; a life for a life. Or maybe she thought it came not from Cornu but from God. She had been a willing pawn—an ex-nun pissed at the Almighty for forsaking her who jumped at the chance to help the Other Side, regardless of what it meant to the more innocent players involved. Either way, we were in agreement at the moment the pearls severed her head from her neck that it was All for the Best. I enjoyed none of it—odd for me and an ironic retrieval of my more angelic nature. She went out brutally, just as I came in. But not against her will, so the account's still in the red. This may be the place where my tired confession breaks down, murder being so reprehensible… But my world never has been yours. So what then is the point? Maybe just to lay it out. To make a neutral confession, and not commit myself either way. Guilt without guilt, if you get me. It's the wonder of the word. She's better off dead. Better off never knowing what hell her acts have wrought. I didn't care two shits for her until the moment of her death. And it hardly lasted at all. That's not 'cause I'm a devil.

That's just common sense.

Chasing Nietzsche's madman thru the village square and deep into the woods I came upon a raving cad in a neoprene, kevlar, and gortex jumpsuit who introduced himself as Dead Simeon, the Deer Mentor. It's April 8, a day each year when all good men, at least since '66, must ask, "Is God dead yet?" Sign of a *Time*—red letters on a black background. Junior bishops-to-be (or never be) mourning the death of Almighty God for the tea and taxi set. In an interview that year, John Lennon said the Beatles were bigger than Jesus and Christianity was on its way out. As it turned out, he was wrong, so maybe his apologizing to the pope was not so dumb as I thought. He was right on, though, when he said the disciples were thick and ordinary morons who botched the Messiah's message. I knew a few of them and he was more than right. Jesus said as much himself. Why he chose the hook-and-net guys, I'll never know. It made a nice metaphor but he would have been better off with the odd old genius of a guy like Dead Simeon. Hear his words, as I did, and experience true Grace:

"Laddie, you've a scent about ya boy—a Lucifer-y stink to make a man wanna draw a cross upon hisself. Mean ya harm to deer? No? Then I've no quarrel with ye, true. Been a mean season a blastin' and killin', what with this war on they all wantin' blood. Seems to me that controllin' the population of demi-Men might be a far sight smarter than killin' down deer for encroachin' on the Encroachin'. But I got me getup and me antler hat and the odd blast a buckshot up the arse is a small price to pay to save a life—provided it's a deer's. You kill a deer ya kill god, man, I'll tell. Peopl'a told me stories 'bout deers so damned powerful in the eyes hunters laid down their kill-sticks an' gave it up forever. It ain't like the Indians needin' the food and hides an all for livin'. No, no. There ain't no ceremony, no prayin' less you figger in the beer-can ritual and to me that just don't make religion. I ain't seen no real powerful deers up here, so I'm self-selected chief deer an Lord Holy Protector so if'n you wanna stay in my sylvania for a spell, you can't be killin' deers. Men's ok—specially the ones with kill-sticks, but not my deer."

Being a humble servant of the Truly Graced, I agreed to help. It was an odd day in those deep, forbidding woods: Deer 5, Men 0. Dead Simeon danced a fire chant right on until morning, when he went his way and I went mine. Was he forest spirit? His dialect changed every few hours, as did the shade and shape of his eyes. He was no madman—Nietzsche's or any other—for he found God in a group of deer and made himself their Pope.

God's only dead when you don't know where to look, no matter what some scholar says.

In his *thief's journal*, Genet said that the only criterion of an action is its elegance, and in that spirit, I gotta share some shit… After wringing out my gut about the whole Buntz debacle I needed a diversion—a little Old School devilry, a right bit o' lift, so I gassed up the '68 Cougar I've been driving and picked up some of the gang—Mykaldaemio, Orlando Nepenthe, and ole Gabby St. A.—and headed to the highway.

I wanna tell you about Mykaldaemio, 'cause he's not your typical vamp, if such a thing exists. He's a tanned, muscled mother with symbolic tattoos and a thousand shoes. A peroxide rogue with a taste for the exotic and seemingly unlimited funds (I see no need to pry…). He's got a taste for 20-something barflies, glam-rock groupies, and lesbian strippers—any of those will do, provided she's got a nasty tat, the right pair of shoes, and a too-tight t-shirt from the latest surf-rat Indie artist. It's not so much the kink as the need for double portions to fill his inner glass, and the view on the way to the Scene of the Crime mustn't be too bad, if you go for that sort of thing, and let's face it—who don't?

He's a low-profile type who only shows his fangs as a warning or at the very end. He shares my dislike of druggies, and goes me one better—he won't kill a user. He prefers taking in a blind-raging boozer and the off-balance trip on the edge it brings. He moves thru a room like a musky breeze, raising the skirts of the panty-less and the ire of their dates. I think it's that kind of game-playing I like most about Myk-D, but we do have our differences, as any "brothers" will. For instance, he's totally removed from the War—"It's got nothin' to do with me, PF," he says. It's a bit of a bummer—with the stakes so high, I need all the warriors I can get. He's a poet and painter who doesn't have the heart for the things I need to do. So fuck it; Outcasts can't be choosers and he's good for a laugh and relieving the Downs. We go riding now and again—he's got a jones for motorbikes—favors a stripped down Ducati S4R with a kickass 998-cc Testastretta engine. Stretches those vampire senses to their max. As for me, my ride of choice is a 1952 Vincent Black Shadow. It's a bit slower than the Ducati, but looks-wise the bitch is tops. Every now and then we run with a gang of bikers called the Deadtown Cats—mortal enemies of the *Vargulf*—whose leader, a crazy dude named Blunt-Axe Eddie, rides a '66 Triumph Bonneville, with suicide shifter and a blowtorch between the bars. His right hand man is Doubting Thomas, a bridge builder and badass tattoo daddy who rides a Honda Shadow Spirit VT750—but I wouldn't give him any shit about it.

Enough about bikes. Back to our night in the Merc. We were jammin' down the granny lane at about 90, head-bangin' to Godsmack's "Vampires," when the hi-beams fixed themselves on a cartoon mouse airbrushed to look like it's bustin' out of the tailgate of this custom Chevy hardly worth the effort. A low-rider with a rain visor and all the outer hardware removed. Affixed to the flat-black tubing serving as a bumper were two bright yellow stickers, which read, respectively: "Homosexuals leave a bad taste in your mouth" and "It's God's fault homos are a pain in the ass." The kind of brainless hatred almost dumb enough to be harmless, stuck to the kind of wanna-be rig owned by the type of low-IQ stooge who oiled his kid's birdcaller with industrial lubricant cause it was squeakin' when the kid turned it. I can't say why these things get to me but when I get the bug I gotta squash it. So after casin' the truck back to sides to front to back again, I started inchin' closer and closer to that friggin' mouse. I backed it way down to give myself a little room to aim the bumper, all the while keeping my eyes fixed on that annoying fuckin' rodent. As I jammed the gas, Myk-D was punching the inner-liner and yellin' "Ramming speed! Ramming speed! Crush the rodent! Crush that little fuck! You *must* crush the *mouse*!" I'm telling you, not all the devils are in hell. Orlando Nepenthe started joining the chant, though Gabriel only looked between his knees and started humming Brubeck's "Take 5."

He's such a suck-ass wuss.

Anyhow, Myk-D started pounding out the rammin' rhythm on the custom dash like the slavemaster in *Ben Hur* and Orlando took over jammin' on the liner, so I started wackin' that mouse and those two bumper stickers over and over—gas, brake, gas, brake—'til I crushed that back end good. So the rabid bastard jerks it over to the shoulder and to a full stop and comes passionately out the driver's side, giving us the finger and screaming about who does what to whose Ma.

"We gotta stop," Mykaldaemio said with just enough of a grin to flash his ivory fangs.

This guy was as good as gone.

You should have seen this dog. He's steaming back toward his demolished tailgate, chew leaking down his chin, mullet streaming in the breeze behind him, faded stock car patches accenting his grease-stained denim jacket. "What the fuck's with you man?" he starts screaming at me thru the windshield of the Cougar, the hi-beams preventing him from seeing who he's decided to take to task. Next thing we know, he's reaching into his tool-caddy for some sort of weapon, maybe to do some damage to my Merc.

Fuck *that*. Out we come (even Gabriel, still hummin' away), so Mulletman can get a good look.

Whatever he was thinkin', it was enough to make him change his mind. Until the tailgate caught his eye. "Damn, man," he said, laying his hand on a rusted tire iron. "You fucked up my mouse. *Damn* man. My mouse is all fucked up." Over and over. Not moving, but not leaving the tire iron, either. "Damn man. You fucks fucked up my mouse."

It was just the thing to kick my funk.

Two minutes later we're back in the car and on our way to the local eatery, just in time for the late-shift waitresses to be getting out of work.

"You should have let me kill him," Mykaldaemio muttered, running his eyes from table to table thru the cheaply decorated windows, searching out a snack as we pulled up.

"What for?" I replied. "He made me laugh. Besides, his fucked up mouse seemed a fate worse than death. Just grab one of those Dollies or Betties or

Graces, do her by the dumpsters and let's split. I'm not in the mood to watch a kill."

Mykaldaemio loves those damned diner waitresses. Crazy bastard says he likes his food to *smell like food*. Fucking comedian.

What have I become to run with a crowd like this?

I'm a dweller, a brooder, as much as I try not to be. I've been thinking about the guy with the banged up mouse graphics and how much I like to Fuck wit' Folks. To instigate and provoke, and I do it in two ways—with a pen and with a car. It's not always so drastic as the other night but it's still about trying to get a rise out of strangers. There's this one-lane road just past the highway where the speed limit drops from 55 to 30. Believe me, Hagar hit it on the head, so if folks can't drive 55 they sure as shit won't do 30. So I do 29 down a two-mile stretch, with no chance for them to pass. It's total passive aggression, which is a step up from running them off the road and draining their blood, but it's still not well-adjusted.

Numbers—30, 55, 23—fascinate me no end. It's the sole reason I helped Nostradamus reclaim a little fame (Goethe, Goebbels, Churchill, and Welles later followed suit). Spiritually the guy was right on—student of the Kabbalah and alchemy and other occult systems and firm believer that the art of prophecy was a gift from God—a complete folding over of the past, present, and future. He was also somewhat tragic—though he was a great healer he couldn't save his wife and children from the Plague, and so he wandered a decade in grief. Nostradamus died in 1566. I'm interested in stuff like that—especially the years ending in 66 and 68. Here's some more: Nero Caesar, the 666 of Revelation, died in 68 AD. Going quite a bit back, Thutmoses III destroyed the allies of the Canaanite princes at Megiddo in 1468 BC. In 1666, a year promising great apocalyptic and messianic things, there arose from among the Jewish Mystics of Izmir a Class-A loo-loo of a bipolar prophet by the name of Shabbetai Zvi. How the Kabbalists and other leaders of the Jewish Communities of the Middle East didn't see this cat coming is beyond me—shows you the power of a *number*. Despite his many marriages (including to a whore and a *scroll of the Torah*) and handful of exiles, this madman managed to convince a sizable portion of people that he was the *Messiah*. He habitually pronounced the forbidden name of God and not only felt he was above most of the laws of his people, but that those laws were now passé because he had ushered in a new age. Skipping the details, the upshot is that when he finally pissed off the Sultan Mehmet IV, a Pilate-style interrogation of Shabbetai ensued and that's where all similarities to the Messiah end. Given the choice between death and conversion, SZ chose the latter and lived his last ten years in relative luxury with a Muslim name and no regrets. The Kabbalah never was the same.

In 1868 several treaties were signed by the White Man and a number of Native American tribes, and we all know how that ended.

So you see, within me are both Thutmoses and the US government—I can kill ya dead or drive 29 for miles at a time, all the while pretending to wave you by. All depends upon my mood.

There is a secret Presence, a bright green snake in an overgrown garden, an *ouroboros*, within the ragged clump of spirit deep within me, akin to the *tulpas* of the Tibetan mystics. It is a ready traveler, a dutiful doppelganger, a guide and demonic spirit-aspect sent to test me, who has seen many things and experienced countless lives. Plato said a soul can enter any living thing it wants, so maybe that's what this is and I am beginning to feel The Change, the whole purpose I've given to my "life." It rises up at will, making the deprivation chamber at times unnecessary, and climbs within my mind to show me events I need to see. In the latest trip, I found myself draped in the brown robes of a Spanish priest present at the deaths of hundreds of Aztecs who were choosing to die in their beliefs rather than live in ours. And dying they were, all around me—by rape and dismemberment, beheadings and impalement on pikes. My fellow priests were emulating Vlad the Impaler, the Great God *vampyr*, a self-made aspect of the Devil himself, yet they were mumbling about the savagery of those they were cutting to bits. Spanish baboons ensuring that the great power of the Aztecs would not compete with the tepid ritual and power-brokering of their Papal Masters across the sea.

There was a difference with this priest I was experiencing—he was not participating. He did not burn books—he read and wrote them. When his fellow priests moved on to the next "conversions," he stayed behind and was given a chance at redemption—deep within the jungle, at a minor temple no one knows about, he was asked to be the Keeper of the Codex—the magical writings on animal skin and tree bark gathered by the Mesoamerican holy men over thousands of years. This priest betrayed his Order and deified chaos in the Other by mating with the dark woman of Light (who looked like Anastasia) and by this *he was saved.*

I understand why the Presence showed me this. I can emulate this priest, taking up the great work of the *naguals*, the Toltec masters of art and science. Parvus Cornu is the new Grand Inquisitor, the new sadist in godly clothes. But

I've learned the words in my journey and I can fill the role. I will ride the feathered serpent-god Quetzalcoatl into his hallowed hall and reveal all the powers of the Olmec–Toltec–Aztec rites (he is the End to Opposites—a return to the Oneness from whence we came). I will descend the stairs of the fanged serpent and reclaim the city where the gods were made—Teotihuacán—the place where the last of the priests will be brought to be stabbed and burned and beheaded as their counterparts undertook hundreds of years ago. I will throw the Father-skull through the goal ring in the Great Ballcourt at Chichén Itzá and help to lube the birthing—the age of the Sixth Sun. We will read once more from the Tonatamatl—the Book of Fate—but this will not be a return to Human Sacrifice. The Age of the Vampire will end and the rites will be renewed. My princess, my locked-up Anastasia, will dwell there with me, as I have seen in my Visions. We will mate in a haze of the brightest of white light and I will keep the books, and no Truths will be lost or forgotten again. We will ascend the stairs of the Great Temple to the higher vibrations where the plumes will fan from the serpents' heads and the elements will rule the four city quarters as in ages of old. The tiger god, Tezcatlipoca, the mirror of smoky illusions, will burn in his own fire and we'll all be *teotl*—vibrants, spirits—once again.

I must try and cling to this Presence—because there are other, darker energies as well, and they pull me back over and over again.

I followed my young pupil, my wayward angel Gabriel, to the jazz-rock club tonight to see two of our favorite bands—Smoochin Pooch Butt and Disposing of the Bones, the latter of which's bassist, Black Sonya, is a vampire that's got it bad for Fangs MykD, but he's strictly a one-woman man and he's hot for this suck-blooder named Raeven. Gabriel was in a mood tonight— burning dollar bills to clear his path as the mournful trumpet strands came burning thru the smoke. It was fire on fire, light on night and his shadow barely held against the changing shapes of necking retro hep cats.

As we took our seats in the corner, I caught a glimpse of some Mischievers playing catch the blade with Mykaldaemio. (Last year the game was poker but the cards kept coming Aces over Eights.) They don't stand a chance against his lightning reflexes, which I'm sure is why they play. It's the only reason he does. They eat one another and themselves for fun and puke the severed fingers into other people's beers. *Homo cannibalis*—the Jolly Undead who lick their blades so hard a little tongue inevitably comes with the blood. They challenged Gabriel to have a go but he just stared at his feet. He's nothing to them—a thin strip of wood with which to slide the crud off the bottoms of their boots. When they kept up their taunts, he headed to the back, where the speed-freaks go to play. The drugged-up fucks like the ones who killed his wife for fifteen bucks and an expired credit card. He watches them for hours—sometimes even days, if I'm off in Meditation. They're a piss-poor lot, even as low-lifes go, and I can hardly stand to be around them. Their heads are so full of meth they can't regulate their dopamine levels and I can't abide their fogged-in stares, too-warm blood, and slow Wasting Away. Though I partake on occasion of a tweaker's shitty plasma when the journeying needs a boost and there's no better to be had, I always keep a thick white shield around me while I feed—who needs the delusions and hallucinations, the feelings of being persecuted? I've got enough *genuine* shit to deal with without some chemical cocktail making it worse. If it weren't for Gabriel's crippling need for self-torture I wouldn't be there at all. Ironically, if I chose, I could be their God. The front man in their soundless band, the center of their sphere.

    Gabriel sits on the back of a puke-green couch (which used to be white) and watches their interplay, assessing what's left of the pale color of their vibes. He stinks of wolves' blood and they never notice they're partying with Death. Makes sense—half of them have noses that are no more than a lump of swollen shit between their eyes and teeth and the rest are cracked and tinged with blood. I doubt they could smell a fart if their faces were buried in his ass. They were slamming hard tonight—the word-trails of quantum philosophies spinning madly 'round tearful bonding and backed by an out of tune, five-stringed guitar. There are tits and dicks flopping everywhere and no one makes a play—the connection between nudity and sex has long ago been lost... These fuckers have passed the point of Fun. Half of them think they're minor gods and rock poets and the other half don't know who the hell they are and revel in oblivion. They transform minute by minute into frogs and princes and back again, so far gone in the drugs they passed the signs for Clarity and Perspective hundreds of miles back and still expect an exit. He's wasting our time, my crushed-winged Gabriel. He'll get nothing from them—no info, no names, no refuge, no clues. For all we know the rest of the gang that ended his life have already died by their own hand. This is one Bad Scene—the Slow-death Dance in the peripheries while in the center ring sits Gabriel—drowning in a cesspool of Regret—more shit, more highs, less pain for them while his grows greater by the hour. I finally talked him into leaving (I've gotten so good I could talk the clothes off a nun), so we grabbed Mykaldaemio and headed to the lake, where Myk-D went against his personal policy and filled us in on what he'd learned from the Mischievers about Cornu's latest plans. I hate the subterfuge but its how the game gets played.

Things fall apart; the center cannot hold; Mere anarchy is loosed upon the world...everywhere the ceremony of innocence is drowned; the best lack all conviction, while the worst are full of passionate intensity. (A mystic mother of a brother, WB Yeats)

Full of *shit*, I think he thought. But still I am inspired, and wish to make confession. In a box beneath a sink I keep the shorn-off remnants of my pseudo-human self: old scabs and ear wax, fingernails, cuticles, tooth-plaque, and clippings from the razor; toenails, warts, blisters, blackheads, dead skin, dandruff, and angel-curly locks (though these last are rare—I keep my coif long and shaggy to better hide the horns...). It's a miniature me, Some Assembly Required, and nary a battery needed neither. A piece of disassembled art just waiting on an artist of skill should I one day be vaporized or recalled. Onion peels in the scattered debris of my continual devolution and reconstitution. It'll be a fine day when that crap is all that's left, waiting to be discovered by some blue-eyed beauty in flowered gown and Easter hat.

Just in case I don't get home, at least there will be that.

It's *Dies Cinerum*, and I've just come from Church, the ashes smarting soundly on my head as I walk among the crowd. I begged the priest to give me 50 lashes on my ass with the pussy willow he'd use to make the evening's ashes, but I was either too old or else he was giving up such luscious dalliances for the 40 days of Lent.

Good for him, either way.

This whole Jesus fasting in the desert *thing* has me thinking of one of the God-son's less sparkling moments—how he did a total wig-n-shatter on the moneychangers in the Temple. I think that moment proved he was *very much* a Man—and we know how men have their *moments*. Moments of righteous indignation, polite ladies call it, but we know better—it's a Piss Fit and nothing more. I mean, Hitler started out with a *crapload* of Righteous Indignation and he was about as far a-field of Jayzoo Christee as any man could be. I guess you *could* classify Jesus' little moment of meltdown as the dark, destructive aspect that any god contains (ala Robert Bly), but I'm leaving that aside... *Why?* 'Cause I'm the writer here, and such overly logical reasoning doesn't fit neatly into wherever this is going, so I'm gonna leave it out.

How's that for a little old-fashioned honesty and good cooking?

Jesus was under pressure—he had more enemies than the *falsely represented version* of Mary Magdalene had paying Johns. There were the Chief Priests—these smarmy little bastards Herod chose from the wealthiest class. Apparently these well-hoofed camels had an alternate entrance into their version of Heaven other than the needle's eye. They were also into money-changing and Temple sales—the Wannamakers and Macys of their day, and they were a little lax on the finer points of Judaism. So it's easy to see why all those overturned tables of smashed-up goods put Jesus high on their shit list for sure. Next were the scribes, the Pharisees and Sadducees (also at cross-purposes, the latter being nothing but pawns in the *chess Romana*), and their lot—the Torah scholars who decided just what all those laws and dictates *meant*. Jesus had to know he was pissing into the wind fighting that bunch, but that's what Great Men do. He also had the Temple guards (the Levites) and the members of the Sanhedrin to deal with. We all have our Authorities to fight, our Ladder-Standers to try and kick over, and at least he went down swinging. But that wig-out in the Temple is an inspirational moment for me—helps those Howlin' at the Moon days pass freer and with less of that little twitch at the tail-tip a demon might call guilt.

There's one problem I've always had with the whole Son of God dying on the cross and resurrecting *thing*. Why is it that God demands a full sacrifice of death from mere mortals (as seen in the Armageddon-is-prevented films) when his own son was guaranteed a quick and easy resurrection in the magickal three days? Fact or fiction, Bible tale or film, the question begs an answer—just who the hell is this Supernatural Savior, this Ball of Light no more than a cunt hair smarter than you or me, that got to go on to greater glory while the rest of us red-haired *step*children stand in line in some Purgatory 'til St. So-and-So calls our name?

There are those that say the big JC outsmarted *everyone* and didn't die upon the cross. A group of jazzy thinkers called the Amadi believe that Jesus lived thru his crucifixion—that the Shroud of Turin shows his blood still flowed—and continued to preach to the lost tribes of Israel and in Kashmir (a place he'd visited as a teen) and lived happy, healthy, and married—perhaps a great-grandfather—until he died at 120.

Probably not the truth—I would have known if the whole death-on-a-cross *thing* was a sham—but a neat idea.

I think the Amadi have dinner with Elvis and Morrison the second Sunday of the month.

What a bar tab *that* must be...

I've had a thought: I needn't fight the Cornu if I can get him back to the point before the Blackened Prison he imagined for himself. The prison of his own devise (what the mythologists call the Lake of Fire) that helped him feed his ache in the searing heat of x-rays and gamma rays. He was once pure Light—still is—if only the trickster shadows can be burned away and he's allowed to shine beyond his own self-inflicted Event Horizon. I have been led to this every step of the way. I've only failed because it's my own redemption I've sought—and mine alone. The ultimate spiritual travesty is putting the saving of your own soul before another's. How can we hope to seek connection when we insist upon our solitude? We feed, we fight, we fuck—not to consume but to *be* consumed. Puppets mistakenly thinking we're pulling *someone else's* strings. Like Cornu thinks he's pulling mine, like I thought I was pulling Ma Buntz's. So now is the time to stop making ignorant plans and start listening to the Void.

New transmissions from the gone angel porter have been pummeling my cyber-mind today—gut-spout happenings of death-sport, morning prayers, and motel mountain anomalies. He's been calling in from the bygone highways of Middle America as he works on crafting his fabled anonymity [enter the Bus Guy—great t-shirts and tired, pouty mouth] cause his demons say *dats da way it gots ta be*. Can't dismantle the hostel from the inside—any fool knows that. He's been roughed up and thoroughly threshed—slapped with the dip-spins in a field of harrowed heather from hearin' just too much racial slur and butt-flick sarcasm. The walls are thin—permissible. He's haunting the buses thru the city–country pathways of this well-worn maze of states, bouncing betwixt dummfukk Colorado and smashed-can New York on the path of Somethin' Better. Somethin' measurable and potent in the empty shopping cart avenues and the cancerous back-shacks of nothing towns where he makes his salvation army band-aid compositions from the confines of a dollar-store dumpster with cryptic bass blats and stereophonic coffee grounds. Looped and layered techno-jargon and the cloistered prayers of old movie lines. The aluminum remnants of all-day drinking and all night scrying. Clues to the blues. And somewhere in all of this reverb and out of tune piano lies our mutual condemnation and that of the larger patch of swamp we call our home. The musical postcards and online billboards from all-over-America and well beyond the seas of peace. Each street a poem and every town a book. Pouring the sand of words into a wind-whipped patch of air to defy the strictures of form, plot, and context. *Ain't it just ... too damned real* as Ian A doth sing. But the ducks ain't white—they're blue and pink and in the end it's a Wonderland hammer and another delicious kill. It's all buxom ghosts and long-legged phantoms while the art is new and the copper's comin' in but in the badly ending end it's another chorus of Cohen's "Hallelujah" mumbled to the ether while the sounds of the Greyhound's shifting gears beckon toward new starts. The boy remains intact while the girl is shattered by the obstinate "I-am" ness of the mossy, resting boulder. No apologies—not his fault. So he bounces from shed to porch, apartment to garage, lucky to leave with an old guitar and a duffel bag tacked together with record label mini-pins and elastic jukebox apology. He's here for a purpose and the revealing's in the dust of the train tix and lachrymose heart-smacks and miles gone by. If he caught a nap—a little blessed rest—he might just be able to grasp it but sleep's always a problem for the newest among the modern mystics cause it's only at the hour of the witch and wolf—the time of barbed-wire trinities compressed, inverted, righted, and twisting upon their own splintered crosses—that the Magick is revealed, usually packaged within the sadistic requirements of a melancholy death. And that brings the fear—the all-consuming, preoccupying, bury-me-not, cold sweat fear that keeps him talkin' and runnin' and fumblin'.

I'm here, my man—so keep it up and keep on comin'.

I was hanging at the playground today (bet it makes ya cringe...) when I came to a far out realization—you put any long-haired, barefoot little lady in a pair of sunglasses and tie-dyed anything and you've got yourself a Manson girl. A future Squeaky, a demi-Susan, a mini-Ouisch. The pretty public park—breeding ground for the discontented rebel daughters of self-absorbed dads. Magdalenas running to the keeper of the Love, who can stop time with a gaze of his eyes and start their hearts aquiver with a gently circling thumb-tip and an acid trippin' Om. Prom queens of the Middle Class parade—Eden's flowers grown wild. Ole Mind-control Manson—another cock-knocking Adolf H., but I offer you this—it ain't the man with the Candy and the van, but the repetition and isolation of the bedroom at home—the corner-crying while Daddy shouts outside the door "You just stay in there, you worthless little whore (*little whore, little whore*), or devilish Daddy's gonna come in and spank you out of your flowery cotton thong (*little whore, little whore*). You're becoming a lady, and it's makin' me *howl*..."

Manson was right—you can't pin that shit on him. All those murders, though—the slaughter's his to bear, whether he was there or not. What a scene it was—four years to the day after the Watts riots. I was a budding little Buntz-pup getting on with my first year in the Flesh. Inconceivable savagery in the human slaughterhouse and all the more gruesome considering it was mostly a bunch of *girls*. We can handle the idea of boys being boys—think preteen lovelies from *Lord of the Flies*—but that whole idea of a bunch of femmes cutting on a pregnant girl ... serving up the piggies in a horizontal bloodletting going back to the days of Abraham. It was Joyce, speaking thru Stephen Dedalus, who said, "History is a nightmare from which I am trying to wake." No shit, Jim. San Francisco nightmares. Broken blades left like fragments of the True Cross, paving the way for bloody rituals—the landlocked sharks crawling to the scent of White Meat and Money. Crazy life in the mystic arthouse as the dream-makers' weaves rocked upon the loom. All the sainted dead rising to walk awhile in the flickering hum of Plato's black box. It was some parade of freaks: incompetent cops, paranoiacs, informers, distorters, and attention seekers of all types and styles. Made OJ look like community theatre. If you're lookin' for accessories to the ones who did the Crimes—each and every one's a cog. A lot of victims did the time. And why? Cause a little snitch and some odd clues went into the vat and produced a Theory: down into the Earth—the Chosen Ones, the infant madres... They hacked a man with Nazi bayonets—deep red truths adding a splash of color to the story of Charlie M.—poster child for what's wrong with the juvenile penal system—no rites of passage, no rituals, no celebration of the Bacchae, no way to get back to controlling the beast within by tearing to pieces on the hillside the Dionysian bull-lion-snake-boar writhing beneath the moon. Drugs substituted for the healing meditation or shamanic journey that allows the Traveler to die a thousand deaths and never shed an ounce of blood.

So the beast manifests and the next thing ya know there are high school massacres, suicide pacts, and infant-raping teens. A guy like Manson learns to work the system thru years of incarceration—keeping the Beast fat and fed and drowsy as the only means to slow it down. Charlie spent half his life in institutions by the time the Piggy-Kill went down. Fucking nut job? Hell yeah. A cellular guitar man looking thru the keyholes of locked doors and ass-kicked thru revolving ones with nary a nickel to buy a break. Where do such guys go? Into the arms of the Cults—those who blur the lines of life and death, pain and smile, Heaven and Hell. Manson was a pimp, a lackey, a Nothing, 'til he grabbed his gig.

What can be said of a man who thinks grass blades more precious than the Flesh?

I've slipped another rung and can't remember *how*. I awoke near a nunnery this morning with a blood-soaked rosary in my hand. Long locks of hair were intertwined thru it, bits of scalp visible at their ends. I ran into the church and washed in the vestibule before running between the pews shouting "Lock the prayerhouse doors—you've got a rat about!" Long, low rows of crucifixion scenes (the Stations of the Cross) sprang to life before me, more grotesque than the silver crucifix forever pricking my skin, the cries of the Christ being drowned out by the madly murderous rabble shouting "Hurry up and nail him—we've got a rat about!"

Lighting a censer I crawled beneath the altar, clutching the rosary tightly to my balls, trying to keep down the post-destruction erection that always springs up when I take a person's life. It seemed in poor taste, surrounded as I was by statues of Mary and the saints. As the acrid smoke filled my nostrils I felt the welcome unlocking of the higher realms and I was suddenly lifted out of the church thru a crack in a nonexistent dome and carried forth to the trial of a felon-turned-minister-turned-murderer who made his point a little too clearly to a punk teenager in the bathroom of a home for troubled boys. Bored and blank-faced jurors were smoothing the feathers and mixing the tar of justice for the dressing up and transformation of the preacher into the naughty bird they were so certainly sure he was. The defendant looked like a pro wrestler morphed with a southern Baptist with Helter-Skelter eyes. Another of god's new breed of disciples about to become a ghost. He had a staff of legal-monkey orators, sideshow thespians on the stage of courthouse law, playing hard for the crowd, if not their client. It's fucking with your socks on. Sloppy. Low class. Phoned in and pre-planned at a morning lunch with the judge. Satan burns the nest, but the dirty-birdies breed. The masters of the word sit in power on the Right while the crow makes judgments by burying his beak in the fleshy folds of their balls, picking up the displaced when the Father pushes them forth, like the preacher sitting here. Just another roadside reject—another need-a-shepherd sheep. Monks without religion, stewing in their cells, reaching out their arms to pull their brethren down.

And what of the nun? Who was she? I concentrated, letting her face spill into my mouth and up into my brain. Engaged the film and let it run.

She knew Momma Buntz. Ratted her out to the Mother Superior in order to get a better set of chores. Told her all about Sister Agnes' penchant for kiddie porn and liquor—and cutting her arms with old razors when the guilt ran so thick it could not be drunk away. Got herself a nice new office out of that one.

But how did I *know*? And why couldn't I remember how I'd come to take her life?

The incense burned away, drawing me back to find the confessionals echoing out my sins, so I ducked out the back, trying to pass without a glance the blood-n-water backup in the sink, but having to pause at the sight of the face I found floating there. It wasn't my reflection staring back. Maybe it was God's—it was nothing of this earth and nothing from "below." Then again, God and Satan are not so very different when seen thru a veil of holy water and nun's blood. Not knowing which was which, I forced myself to leave. Because I am holding this rosary, though I can only guess at how and why it came to be in my possession, I am not fit to gaze upon the face of God, whether real or not.

It's gotta be the Horn—poking and gouging at my Will, proving once again I am only an instrument of his plan. He's working the strings while I live this waking sleep like the Puppeteer he is.

I've slipped a few more rungs… Perhaps it's Justice and Vengeance—perhaps I did what Hamlet couldn't, but the not knowing makes me wonder if I can trust the filmstrip tale at all.

So perhaps I DIDN'T DO IT—not any of it. Not really.

But I'll burn for it gladly—like the hulking preacher with his monkey-lawyer tribe, I'll be the naughty little bird roasted on a spit by blank-faced bastards who only gauge guilt by which set of hands are openly stained with blood.

Theirs, all the while, are hidden in their robes.

I hate guilt. Nothing is as simpleminded and torturous as assuming sole responsibility in a networked Universe. Still in all, I set out to make amends for the recently departed penguin-of-god by doing a little avenging for Gabriel. There are only a few of the perpetrators left, and they've been laying low—even brain-dead punks know when their comrades are dying ugly and often and what that means for them. I can't say I enjoyed it—chasing them down alleys, scaring them piss-less with my enhanced reflexes, my scaling of brick walls, my needle fangs and tearing claws—but I was merciless and increasingly vicious as I once more thinned their gang. I fed the pieces (and there were many, many pieces) to the wolfpack that feeds itself to Gabe and hid within the tree before he showed.

My own guilt, never a long-lingering phenomenon, was at once assuaged as I heard the soft moan he always lets escape when he has fed to the point of being gorged on the blood of those who shit upon his life. I touched his head and those of the wolves sleeping peacefully in their torn-stomach rejuvenation at his sides, and went upon my way.

Only one or two of those gang scum to find and Gabriel may be at peace.

If only there could be such a shrinking laundry list for me...

I am fascinated by the lives of those artistically and otherwise gifted men who have willingly debased and ultimately ruined themselves in order to be close to a king or other person of power—men like John Wilmot, the infamous Dr. Bendo. Men who would dress the part of the fool and bark like a rabid dog for a taste of the private barrels or the most shapely alabaster tits beyond the palace doors. As I've said, I am a prince—an angel of no small consequence—I am no mortal son of a craftsman or peasant. My appointed place is at the right hand of the heir apparent to no less than the Universe herself and yet I have no interest. None at all. If I were capable of anything truly great, if I were gifted to any degree, I would be content to pursue that gift to the exclusion of all else—be it painting, music, medicine, science, or some other Art. Forsaking one's gifts, when you are lucky enough to have them, is one of the greatest of crimes. And there has been no insignificant amount of such criminals, abandoning their careers and true vocations for titles and false idylls. They are, to me, a cautionary tale and nothing more, the same as I must be to you. And it's more than their mere decisions to abandon themselves to their duller pursuits—I find their games of self-preservation to be the true affront.

Kings and other men of power are fickle in their affections and favors (how like whores they are). And so the Bought Man must always be on guard, which makes him as untrustworthy and vicious as the dog he is ever required to play. I needn't be like them—it is cold fact that I currently have no competition for King Cornu's favors. There is no other fallen angel quite the same as me. Barring Lucifer's full recovery or the sudden defection of one of the archangels, I am very much the only Doer of any skill or intelligence on the scene. Now, perhaps my little tricks and ruminations are of ultimately little value, or else I am too modest. Either way, I still bark and bray and do (mostly) what it is he asks of me. It is not for the promised reward—anything I need I get for myself— and even should he succeed and I am named the Universe's One True Prince, even the highest place held in servitude *is still servitude*. Screw Lucifer's *supposed* statement before the War (which I've already debunked)—to me, it's better not to serve at all. The great irony is that, although I do not want the things pursued by Bought Men, I will no doubt in the end be just as broken, debased, and alone as they.

Perhaps they know it too, and that's why they play their wicked games in the Houses of the Depraved—the estates of sin where the Emeric Belascos set their stage. The secret play-caves of the truly debauched, who have driven the stakes so high (or so deeply) that Hell is the only portal left to pass. I've spent my hours there in the gaze of shredded genius, in the paths of Walking Deaths. An old house is essential—Gothic, immense—any good art must have its mise-en-scene. And plenty of drugs if you can't journey in the natural way. And fear—plenty of fear—to drive you, taunt you, fuck your cracks, and slurp your cum. All with your permission and encouragement—that's key to the Satanic doctrine of Free Will. It must be *your* request that leads the High Priests to bait the Beast and invite it among your friends. That's the thrill, the game, the risk. Tempting devils on every stair, every splintered corner, behind every damask drape, like Prince Prospero at the Red-Death Masque. Conjuring Satan by screwing a dozen hired virgins at a time, as though sex itself were our sole preoccupation. Sex is fine—an excellent engagement—but only because it's fun, a full release from Fear. And that's how it always ends in the House of the Depraved. Amid the skulls and candles, pentagrams and hooves, the conjuring words and consanguinity with the gods in the drinking of the sheep's blood, there is the steaming Release, the curtain closing, the end of the staged ritual. I envy their charade, their horned and satin costumes, their cunning dance with death. For they needn't go all the way. You can't sell to Satan what God takes for free.

Then there's me, who can't even buy what that bastard got for nothing. There is no possession from without—only fear within. Insight is the jagged specter an Exorcism bans. Layers and layers of masks abruptly stripped away to reveal the unfinished core. Shelley's Monster, Jekyll's Hyde, Sybil's inner family clan. All because of *Fear*.

My whole world is death and ponies that are dead. (Josey Emm, age 5)

Daddy, daddy—what's that pulsing, purple THING on the postal lady's face?? (Timmy Charles, age 4)

Alright, alright—that second quote was me.
But I made it *look like* it was the kid.
The first one, however—pure preschool genius… Uttered by a dark haired, dark eyed child in the middle of devouring her smiley face, chocolate chip pancake at a roadside diner in Somewhere, South Virginia.
Kids really are the shit.
Taking a cue from the gone angel porter, I took myself out on the road for a little rectification of my moodiness and contemplation of the Great Beyond by

staying in a series of roadside dives and lower-rated motel chains on the chance of getting a better glimpse of the components that go into a core segment of society.

These ramshackle monuments to transience are the Lab for that kind of work.

I mean, you want a real slice of America—a true look at the melting pot once all the ingredients have stewed away awhile? Hit the typical run-down travel inn, popularly known as the economy motel. 65 bucks a night and no major amenities—hardly anything at all. You've got a non-queen, queen-sized bed, a few water-stained nightstands with hardware that doesn't match, some bad lithographs of badly executed nature pics, an unremarkable, unletterworthy desk, its tottery chair, and a bathroom with tepid water and not much elbow room. Trust me—it's easier to fuck a fat chick in a classic Beetle than it is to fuck a thin one in that chip-tiled water closet. But you aren't looking for the Ritz Carlton, right? Just a place to lay your head and piss your piss on the way to Somewhere Else. A place not meant to be anything but Utilitarian. And, for me, it's all about the People. For any student of Nature, human or otherwise, and especially for those daring to call themselves Writers, it's absolutely engaging to be around a bunch of unpredictable, average Joes. Character is the conduit, the means to reaching your reader with the Message you wanna convey.

You see a lot of minivans at these joints. A lot of hicks and city types, all mixed together, the latter's minivans more stylish and newer, and plastered up with those magnetic soccer balls and cheering bullhorns with their children's names on them...

It's the well-considered means of travel for the typical family clan, 2.5 kids and some kind of annoying rodent-pet, and for the college girls engaging in some pre–Real Life bonding with their coven of competitors. I was at this one place, just kind of slumming (it's odd ... for a fallen angel mud-prince at war with the wanna-be King of the Universe I've got a *lot* of Free Time...) and there's this real Southern type of Marlboro smokin', Bud drinkin', caterpillar-mustachioed sort of Mulletman rapping along to this techno-country hybrid shit in his rodeo drawl (this inbred outhouse knew *all* the words) while his late-teens but already incredibly haggard-looking wife smoked her 100s and made semi-interested faces at their toothless, giggling, and perhaps already brain-baked baby girl. You've got to get numbed early in a hopeless situation like that.

Picture the typical Stephen King familial triad and you've got the gist.

These types of dreary, hole-in-the-wall rentables are also the waystations and Last Stops for a variety of degenerate types—junkies, crack whores, drug dealers, thieves, and their assorted lot. And if you cruise the roads on the outskirts of major cities like New York and LA you'll find your occasional incognito rock star or nom de plume, last stop before their friends and family finally track them down and get them into rehab—what they call an *Intervention.*

It was the lack of said intervening that screwed them at the start.

One thing you won't see at places like these are the credit-maxed, pretentious SUV families or the lone business travelers. First, there are no attractions to be seen or business to be done in a town like this—not really—and second because for another 20 bucks you can do a shitload better. Considering how much these SUV fuckers spend on *gas* in a week, that little shell-out is chump change on the way to clean sheets and a refrigerator that actually gets cold.

I didn't have to wait long for my diversion to appear—these places constitute the stop-offs on the highway to Hell. She was a sexy vamp heading to the off-season costume party at the restaurant-bar next door. The Perfect Cover. So I began to think about what part I'd play while we drank and chatted and flirted… It didn't really matter, 'cause she sensed my ruse as clearly as I sensed hers and all need for pretension and disguise dropped while she bit seductively into my lip as an alternative to "Hi."

After a brief glance around, we decided (again, without words) to share a few co-eds, just like in the films… I'm not beyond a little classic cinema informing my sport. There are times when Myk-D and I raise a little hell by reconstructing some classic clip from one of our favorite films. Just about anything goes, although there's nothing like the nights we play Vincent Price to one another's Peter Lorre as circumstance requires. We work our way thru all the stock shenanigans of their handful of films for American International Pictures—fighting, carousing, and all manner of lecherous debauchery; wine tasting; magickal duels; shape shifting; grave digging (and *un*digging); and we've even walled each other up for hours, if not days. Whenever we can swing it (which is surprisingly often), we engage in a bit of ménage a trios with all the big-boobed Joyce Jameson and Hazel Court look-alikes we can find.

But there was none of Poe that night at the motel. This was straight-on vampirism, and my diversion and I took our time finding just the right set of Sorority sisters for our game. They're sadly easy to spot. The ones dumb enough to travel in pairs instead of packs. The ones not content to just sip on the raw edge of the Fringe, but who wanna drink it all in one gut-wrenching gulp. The ones who stupidly manifest that metaphorical desire for adventure thru the bottles of booze that lead to that last, unfortunate, One Too Many—the one that finally puts all remnants of good judgment and sense to sleep.

It didn't take much talking—does it ever in dives like that?—and it wasn't much longer after First Contact that we wound up in their room.

My diversion was an artist who liked to take her time.

And why not? We had all night and checkout's not 'til noon. Do Not Disturb goes without saying in these clap-traps, but just to be sure, I slipped the frayed laminate sign on the doorknob while the three of them disrobed.

My diversion and I could have paired up for a time, putting together a minor spree and doubling our fun but when the sun rose we each went our way.

Those roadside sleep-dives hold no lasting charm, especially when seen in the harsh light of day.

Like I said, they're Utilitarian at best; I need more to hold my gaze.

Do we know when the director's watching? I swear to god the Thugs do, playing reality TV for the alley-cat crowd, with their stiff leather collars, granite-angled chins, overdeveloped pecs and biceps, and dime-novel dialogue—classic comics re-imagined in the pulsing forms of CG inking and human-enhancement techniques, where the bullets are faster, the blood is redder, and the skin is blemish free. The Mischievers thrive in the 4th dimension of comic book cinema. Cartoons come to life with their eyes on tits and bloodspots. Maladjusted teens drawing representations of the teachers they loathe and love with rat-gut cityscapes and Dead Ends galore. And what the hell's the deal with the comic book device of sick Senators' sons with a taste for little girls? It's some kind of comment on the perception that politicians are not only safe from prosecution (unless they screw up *really, really* bad, which usually means taking bribes as opposed to lives...) but are fucked up fuckers raising monster sons. I've seen the same with judges' sons as well. They're the new Mafia, cause god knows the old one is dried up and useless like a fourth-hand Puzo novel in a flea market crate. It's a sad state of affairs because on some level, all this tripe is *real*. Corrupt cops, pedophile principals, undercover whores, FBI profilers, forensic pathologists, serial killers, DAs and criminal psychologists on the take—they're all there in the current TV tube and cinematic reel. Hooker bloodbaths as the self-appointed hunter cuts ghost-wolves from the gut of Little Red, that lustful little bitch. Rippermania for another new millennium. It's a hit parade of publicly outcast women publicly humiliated even further when the cock becomes the Knife. Their body parts accumulate in a growing pile that will one day bring ole Jezebel to life. Everything comes down to that sexually powerful woman that the crypt keepers in the Theological Halls fear and masturbate to at one and the same time. This is damned dangerous stuff—like kids playing light sabers with blow torches. Bad ends. And the stakes are high. Death comes bursting forth from the pen and ink sketches of the varied boxes that mark the artist's page. They need to be contained. Forced back within the pages; rechained within the frame. This publicly growing fascination with video games and comic chicks and thugs can come to nothing good.

---

*S*alaam aleikum. I actually *smelled* him. Actually felt my stomach convulse and want to bring its contents forth as the unearthly stench of the Little Horn wound its way up my nostrils, leading me to places I tread in my moments of deepest Depression—the crowded bazaars and rundown streets of the Middle East, birthplace of so many dark and fecund gods—Moloch and Marduk, Iblis and Baal Sebub (the god of flies), and Astoreth, Ahura Mazda and Mithra, Zababa, Kotar, Enki, and Ugar. I have stood watch on the fatal bridge, al Sirat, narrow as the spider's web and sharp as the sword. The only means across the infernal gulf that takes you on to Paradise—it's fun to watch the neutral struggle and the wicked fall... It's amazing, the power of *Belief*... If they saw themselves as good, they'd easily get across. I've made the *hajj* with the servants of Muhammad and walked the once-cedared Lebanon of Kahlil Gibran. I even spent many a memorable night with Peer Gynt and Professor Begriffenfeldt in the Cairo madhouse known as the Club of Wisemen. It is here, especially in Iraq and Syria, that the people watch for my Muslim counterpart, Deggial, the Liar and Impostor. They'll know him when he comes, riding on an ass with 70,000 Jews in tow, with his single eye and eyebrow, above which burns the word *Infidel*. He'll destroy all but Mecca and Medina, which the angels will protect. If this sounds like a '70s Satan film, here's the end—he'll reign for *40 days* before Jesus kills him at the gates of Ludd. No matter the language, it all says *schlock*. But mostly I come for the markets. Such ragged monuments to waste and oppression; places where I can move unnoticed and uncared about, taking the odd handful of dried dates or the worthless but appealing trinket and reading the mystical graffiti that exists between the static portraits of religious and political leaders sprayed by discontented teens upon the walls.

These cities are an excellent place for the Cornu to hide, and I am almost certain that when it finally comes down to the inevitable Face-to-Face before we roll the tanks, this is where it will be, like Nostradamus said. You keep on looking for a mad prince in a turban—what you'll get is a self-crowned King who comes storming into town riding bareback on the biggest missile of pure nuclear waste you've ever seen, screaming at the top of his lungs about how thoroughly you all were fooled.

Even that sweet angel of a madman Nostradamus missed this bitch in the mix.

Being that I was in the Middle East, I went into the desert, site of all great Temptations, and tried to summon forth from their solemnly assigned directions my old chums—the four Wonder Boys of the Almighty's Army—Gabriel, Michael, Raphael, and Phanuel—any of those jumping opportunists who were the first to say "Yes!" when God said "Let's get this thing organized—are ya with me?" They were so gung ho—cataloging, weighing, labeling, grouping, *dividing*, *JUDGING*—so willing to go to war with us Conscientious Objectors to move his plan along. And *why*? All because they didn't believe in their own potential—so easily convinced that he was better than US, rather than merely *equal to*. But what have they come to now that God gets so little press and they even less? What must it feel like for such demi-titan luminaries as Michael and Gabriel to be played for the mob's entertainment by the likes of John Travolta and Christopher Walken? Perhaps on Earth imitation is the sincerest form of flattery but on the Higher Planes it's just aping by the Apes. It's the brandishing of Free Will to render Heaven mere film fodder and I'd assume they'd be unpleased enough to at least *talk* with me. You can't tell me that after all that's gone down they still can't see the reasons why Lucifer and I and so many others took the path we did. Why *His* plan didn't work out any better than ours. I know they heard me—smelled the blood that I ritually loosed from my veins, but not one of them came down—not even my beloved Phanuel, who nearly joined us but lost heart at the moment the first blade was drawn, the first clawed and terrible beast called forth from the pits. There's apparently *no* Free Will among that once-fearsome foursome—Mike and Gabe run the show by the Father's book and will sooner kill their own than let them come to us the movies are accurate there.

I'm not even sure what use they'd be. None of them would dare take up the throne himself—they proved their colossal subservience during the War, and archangels do not change. They're blind. And might as well be made of marble, like the statues they no doubt sat for hours watching the classical sculptors make.

But they're not the only game in town. I know there must be angels in Heaven who agreed with us but didn't have the balls to leave—you know the type. Spineless and devoid of any shred of courage—but smart enough to know who's *right*. I have to wonder—are some of these fence-sitters looking for a new leader to replace their broken God in this post-post-Industrial time of the New Technic? Do they have any idea that the Cornu is at work? Cause there's gonna come a time in the not too distant future when things get ugly on their side and the weather turns bad and the body count rises and that's when some of them will come. Eleventh hour, ninth inning, last second of the last quarter, but potential heroes all the same. It's the stuff of redemption films and other Unlikely Tales. Orlando has spoken to some of them on my behalf. His lineage makes things complicated, but the fact that he hates his father (whoever the hell he is) and still wants to help him get back "home" scores points with the few coldly intellectual line-walkers who find a set of strap-on testes in the midst of such things.

What really burns my ass (beside a flame that's three feet high) is that I was fool enough to prostrate myself before these four jokers in the first place. That was no small thing, and they must have laughed their wing-feathers out as I started to chant and bleed. But do you really blame me for thinking I'd be received? You'd think now that Parvus Cornu's hanging around this Plane long enough to leave his *stink* in the ether they'd have no *choice* but to talk and I would have gathered enough strength in my journey thus far to make them *listen*. I can understand them not wanting to talk to Lucifer (Michael and he were like rival quarterbacks on coal town Varsity teams), sitting as he is in a crumpled corner with his thumb in Horner's pie, but they have to see I'm different—that I am standing with my dick flapping in the breeze as I try to make a stand against the most dangerous foe they've ever known.

But no one's answering.

How incredibly, mindfully stubborn can a group of angels be?

Fuck 'em all... Needing to clear my head and get the Cornu's stink out of my nose, I journeyed to the Black Hills and Badlands of South Dakota, walking the highways by way of Montana, Wyoming, and Nebraska, each mile and click of my alligator boots diminishing my anger and filling my lungs with the clean, crisp air of the high plains. So many tribes had been slaughtered and displaced from these lands—the Crow, Pawnee, Cheyenne, Omaha, the Mandan, the Sioux. Peoples closer to the Ancient Ways than any *Washichu* could understand. But I am no White Man—I am a being whose bread was once broken beside the wise fathers of these First Peoples when the Sacred Hoop was all-encircling and strong. When I reached Bear Butte—a powerful place for visions—I created a sweat lodge, *Inipi*, in the prescribed way, using 12 willow saplings, with its door facing *Wiyopeyata*, the west. In its center I dug a pit with deer horns and created a tight circle of granite and limestone, twenty-eight red-hot rocks over which I would pour water from the river to make a cleansing steam. When it was done, I lit a bundle of sage, spread my offerings of tobacco and corn and sat as still as the stones and prayed for a vision. I sought the wisdom of *Wakan Tanka* and the Sky Grandfather, oldest of the six sacred powers, *Shakopeh Ouye*, whose name is *Tunkashila*.

I sat there still and patient in the manner of the shaman for sixteen days and nights, moving only to make my offerings during each of the Four Endurances.

On the seventeenth day, at the zenith of the Moon of the Red Grass Appearing, a shadow crossed my door, holding the form of a man, although he made no sound and held no scent.

"Come in," I thought. "If you will."

"You know the Ancient Ways," he replied, using a mix of the Dakota and Lakota dialects I had learned along the way.

"*Hau. Hecetu yelo.*" [Greetings. It is so indeed.]

My welcome formally made, he entered the lodge and sat in silence with me awhile.

"You are undertaking *Hanblecheyapi*, the Vision Quest, which you pray will bring you wisdom. Has *Wakan Tanka* replied?" he asked, pouring water on the glowing stones in the center of the lodge to keep the steam thick and hot.

"Not so far," I answered.

"I can tell, *Kola*—you are not of this world."

Then it struck me—neither was he.

We told our stories far into the night. His name, which took him hours to share, was Leyton Walkingfeather, a long-dead Oglala shaman who could not pass on. He had waited outside my door, in a meditation of his own, for nearly a week before making himself known. He seemed to understand what I was and from where I had come. Perhaps because his story was similar in the sense that he was also here against his will.

"When I was a boy, I was a student of Black Elk's, a powerful holy man. A healer. A seer of visions. I grew to be a shaman of considerable power, and my elkskin drum saved many a life and brought many an abundant harvest to our people.

"But I was betrayed, *Kola*, by a rival—one who was jealous of my powers, though they did not come from me and I had not asked for them. So as I lay upon my death bed, ready to be received and to join my brothers in the sky, my rival, Red Wind, stole my drum and hid it so it could not be broken, and so it is that my soul is trapped between the worlds, as it never was when I lived and breathed."

Another kindred spirit. Another badly betrayed bastard wandering in a place that is no longer his to walk. I slept fitfully that night, the lack of sustenance and the steam beginning to open my senses to the message I hoped to receive.

One thing about the higher spirits—they don't give a fuck about what you want, or how you want to hear it. They have agendas of their own. Better ones than ours.

And, in the end, it was Leyton Walkingfeather who at last provided the door.

After our first long talk he had gone into the night to roam the land and give my quest some thought. When he returned he was carrying a horse blanket and a long length of rope, both of which he placed at my feet.

"You must undergo the *Yuwipi* ceremony of our people," he said. "It is the only way to receive the vision that you seek. Grandmother, *Unci Maka*, will whisper to you then."

Considering how many hours and days I'd spent in my sensory deprivation chamber, the idea of being wrapped in a blanket was of no concern, and the deed was done in a matter of minutes. Thru the muted darkness I heard Walkingfeather chanting in the Siouan language, praying to the *Topa Tate*, the four directions from whence come the winds, and I heard the beating of drums and the shaking of rattles—more noise than one man, ghost-shaman or not, could make.

After a time (*how long*?) the chanting and drumming ceased, though the rattles continued their lulling beats. I heard the piercing shrill of a flute that became the cry of the spotted eagle, and the fastenings were undone, though I remained in darkness. The night pressed hard against me and I fell into the Sleep that is not Sleep.

Unci Maka was pointing the way to a door.

Open your eyes, Crow Shadow. It is time.

I awoke in the atrium of a large house. Thick layers of dust covered the busts of Pallas, Plato, and others lining mahogany shelves along both sides, though there wasn't a spider web, broken window, or other sign of neglect.

Following the pungent scent and weak glow of an ancient candle, I entered a small library, stacked with tomes carefully collected by the agents of Le Coq and De Bahls, Booksellers, wherein sat a hunchbacked man scratching busily in a ledger.

If Scrooge and Marley had a child, this surely would be he.

"Ah," he said, annoyed. "You're here. They're upstairs and to the left. Make sure you wipe your shoes. I've just re-stained the floors."

Glancing at the long, curled nails of my toes, I thought it best to not reply. Grasping the ornately carved banister I headed to the sound of clinking glasses, entering a hallway I vaguely recognized from an old book I had loved as a "child." Drawing my blanket tightly around my nakedness, I came to the open door of a room filled with tobacco smoke and the dim glow of a fire. There were five young-looking men in the room. They stopped their discussion as I entered.

"It's about time," one of them said.

I knew him. I knew them all.

Before me were four of the greatest philosopher-poets who'd ever lived— the Circle of the Rintrah—Byron, Shelley, Keats, and Blake. In the furthest corner sat another with his nose stuck in a book with a leather cover stamped with the name of Thomas Aquinas. Beside him I saw several other open books, including those of Aristotle and Albertus Magnus. The four at the table had all died in a span of seven years, and only Blake had lived past forty.

Byron, creator of the poetic tales of Child Harold, Don Juan, and Manfred, the so-called Byronic heroes—and creator as well of sappy and barely readable lovesick, self-indulgent shorter poems for which I have no use. Lord Byron—solitary and pissed at the world, running from a past he did not understand toward a future he felt was his unalterable Fate. I was all of Byron's creations—and therefore Byron himself—in a nutsack. No question. And Byron seemed to know.

"Come and chat awhile, weary stranger," he said, offering me a glass and a chair. "Do you perchance work with the pen?"

"I can tell he does," Shelley replied, pointing to my right hand—"can't you see the ink-stained callous on his middle finger? By the looks of it, he does little else."

Shelley, the sharp one—expelled from Oxford his first year for distributing a self-published pamphlet on Atheism. A bloodless revolutionary in a time still steeped in the blood of its recent revolutions, ushering in the New Age—against the restoration of the monarchies and creator of that terse masterpiece, "Ozymandias"—"look on my works, ye Mighty, and despair!" I may have felt like a character of Byron's, but Shelley and I also shared some things. He, too, knew Jesus to be little more than a social radical, and Heaven and Hell to be only the god and devil that war within—what his wife Mary called the Evil Principle.

If only I could convince God and Lucifer of *that*...

Shelley, whose poem "Prometheus Unbound" brought to life for me the painting by Rubens. How many times had the crow ripped out my own blackened heart as I lay lashed to the mountainside, trying to defeat my evil nature and climb the chains to the Ultimate Idea? Shelley died by drowning years after his first wife died the same exact way. But weren't they all drowning from the very minute the quill was dressed with ink?

Keats had been for sure, so tortured by poor reviews of his early work that he never fully recovered—he died the youngest of the four—killed by the *belle dame sans merci* of his own beautiful words. Poor Keats, who said, "Philosophy will clip an Angel's wings."

If only he had known that philosophy *was* the Angel's wings...

I decided against trying to enlighten him here—I was badly outnumbered and poorly equipped to argue anything with these men.

Most especially Blake. He and Shelley were perhaps the most similar of any of the four, though Shelley and Byron seemed to love one another best.

I sat with them for hours, just listening—refusing to speak, all the while keeping half an eye on the slowly moving crop of hair stuck behind the book in the corner.

I noticed he had switched from Aquinas to Aristotle, without shifting his position in the least.

"Curious?" Keats asked, jerking his thumb in the direction of the silent fifth man. "That's Stephen Dedalus. Byron keeps him around because he's such a fan. Calls him the greatest poet of us all."

"He does, he does," Byron said, taking a long pull on his pipe. "Though it's Shelley the lad prefers to *quote*."

"Browning out and out liked me better, though," Shelley said with a laugh. "Once he matured."

"Perhaps so," Byron replied. "But who gives a damn about him?"

"Don't be so quick to dismiss him, George—*He's* the one buried in the Abbey with Tennyson and Dryden—the four of *us* have only memorials in the so-called Poets' Corner."

"There's no accounting for taste, Percy... There never was..."

"So you're Stephen Dedalus?" I asked, leaving the two men to parry at the table and approaching the alter ego of James Joyce.

"Have you a problem, man?" he asked, putting down the *Poetics* and taking up the *Summa theologica,* the way Van Helsing would a cross. "I am well read on your type."

"I've no doubt you are. And knowledge is power in these matters, blah, blah, blah... But we can leave the technicalities of the classification and origins of demons for another time. I have other disputes in mind."

He clutched tighter to his book. "Then I say again, and with less generosity—have you a *problem*?"

He was showing off for the others. How *quaint*.

"Not so much a problem as a few things to say on the notion of beauty and art."

"Finally—a foil for our lad," Shelley said over the lip of his goblet. "Do go on."

"Yeats should be here for this," Blake said, hard at work on a sketch.

"He'll meet the man in time," Keats said with a scowl. "You know he left here purposely when the hour struck."

Ignoring Keats' cryptic words, I explained to Dedalus in short, uncomplicated sentences just what I thought about his ideas on Desire and Loathing having no place in art—all his clever metaphors and degrees and fragments—his translations and explanations of what Aquinas called the *integritas, consonantia,* and *claritas*—wholeness, harmony, and radiance.

"It's so limiting and disingenuous," I complained, packing a freehand briar left invitingly on the table with a pungent Djubek tobacco. "Just more duality and dicotomy. More didactic bullshit. And to answer your question—the man who chops furiously at the block of wood and creates the face of a cow has most certainly created art, if anyone sees it as such."

"Hear hear!" Byron said, slamming his fists on the table. "Though I wonder—does it have to be a whole, harmonious, and radiant cow or just your average cud-loving heifer?"

Above their mocking laughter, Dedalus asked me, "And would it also be art if you saw the face of God in your own shit-stained toilet cloth?"

Before I could answer (and I was going to tell him Yes) I was back in the lodge, the horse blanket and ropes falling away as I stood. Leyton Walkingfeather sat waiting, a simply painted rattle in one hand and a pipe, a *chanupa*, in the other. I recognized the latter instantly—the red stone bowl with its seven circles and carving of the buffalo calf, the stem of wood and its adornment of the twelve feathers of the Spotted Eagle.

It was the first pipe, brought to the Sioux by Buffalo Calf Woman.

"Leyton, I—"

"Shush, *Kola*. First we smoke," he said, filling the *chanupa* with a rich tobacco made from red willow bark.

We sat in silence and smoked for hours.

"Did you have your vision?" he asked at dawn, with a look that told me he knew I had.

"I was untied... I spoke to—"

"That is not your place to say, or mine to hear. But know this, *Kola*—you must not get lost in the words of the right-hand path—words are powerful medicine, able to destroy as well as create. Demons just destroy—that is their one and only power. There is nothing of the feminine, nothing of *Unci Maka* within them, so they are Half-Things. Their leader is the Blue Man, the great violator. Of him you must beware. You can be a spirit of light, *Kola*, if you can use your words for change, for the elevation of consciousness, as those you journeyed to speak with did.

"Take this," he said, handing me the rattle. "It will not rot away as your others have. You have passed thru a sacred place in the shadow of the Crow, and the Horn cannot pierce you here. This is my gift to you, for we are now as brothers. This is our *Hunkapi* rite."

"But I have nothing to offer you," I answered, feeling the power of the rattle as I held it in my hand.

"You will be given the chance to give when the time is right, Crow Shadow. You must trust in that."

We spent the next day in the Big Horn Mountains dancing the Ghost Dance in honor of the Paiute Wovoka, and for Sitting Bull and Kicking Bear and Big Foot and those at Pine Ridge and Rosebud and Wounded Knee. Later in the day we weathered a fierce storm on Harney Peak, where we talked awhile with the echo of Black Elk, whose vision had guided our ways.

But I knew I had to return to my war and Walkingfeather, whose people had called him Wiyaka, could not leave his people's land.

"Remember what your vision has told you," he said as I pulled on my boots to begin my journey back. "Honor it, and it will serve you well."

And what had it told me? I asked myself as I walked and ran and finally flew back toward Gabriel, Mykaldaemio, and the rest.

The philosopher-poets had their power and perhaps it could be mine. I am certainly no more than they—a chronicler, an observer and commentator and perhaps, in the end, my path will be different than theirs and I will be a blood-soaked revolutionary after all.

With Parvus Cornu's head within my hands.

It's Walpurgisnacht—April 30th on the calendar most often used. A major holiday for us demons, winged spirits, and ether-dwellers, and the celebrations come in myriad, mirrored ways. It's a glorious Feast Day and we gorge until we puke, like the Roman nobles of old. The Witches' Sabbath. A time of festival and folly and poor pranks like the one I pulled at the post office. A beautifully pagan celebration like Samhain, "Hallowday"—a time without time—when everything converged and the dead could walk again. A time for dancing and fornication with Cailleach, the Grey Hag and the countless gnomes, nymphs, satyrs, and Pans recruited from the halls of Goethe's Faustian masquerade. A time to walk among the neo-Mexican monks as they chase the harvest-queen *echo* of Walpurga herself. A time to contact the oldest spirits still gathering on this Plane and bathe deeply in the wisdom pools of their Minds.

Samhain was great ... a three-day festival when chaos reigned, and cross-dressing was not just okay but encouraged, being close to the sublimated truth (and perhaps stated better as the cross-sexing of the dressers and undressers amassed around the fire). Three days when the great gates unhinged by Whitman and Ginsberg were for a time smashed to bits.

So what the hell happened?

MCA—Mother Church Absorption. The fact that the festival lasted *three days* should be a clue—that and the act of rising from the dead that wasn't reserved for some sanctified demi-god in the Samhain days but for anyone who cared to make the effort. But nothing decent lasts, and MCA suppressed, removed, grated, filtered, and reconstituted it all as Easter (a name derived from Eostra, the vernal equinox) and All Saints (meaning *Some* saints...)

St. Walpurga (thus the name Walpurgisnacht) was part of a family trinity of abbots (who *all* became saints...) who brought their English mission to Germany. Things were better before—the Brocken was our Wicca Wonderland in the Harz mountain wilderness.[12] It was our great festival in the light of the Maifeuer. And let me say in our collective defense that we never gave a good old damn about Walpurga or her sponsor Boniface (who had anything but)—MCA's report of a poor lamb of God being chased by screaming demons and cartoon broom-dancers out to fetch her soul is puerile propaganda. Take note that any rescuer of Said Damsel would receive a hefty sum of gold. Anything to shut the passion down. No more dancing naked like David at the Temple—oh no. No Bacchae or Dionysius with that bunch. But we have our means. Get up to the Brocken one April 30th with the right pair of eyes and you'll see how demons *really* dance. Demons and purer spirits and demiangels and the recently and anciently deceased and all the very many Light Beings drawn to our sacred flames.

And while I'm debunking Walpurgisnacht myths, despite what it says in Lovecraft's *Necronomicon*, no children were ever kidnapped or killed in the service of the ceremony.

This year's festival is especially good because Mykaldaemio has joined the fun, playing the newly arisen vampire to the Poets of the Night and Charnel-House in the Great Masquerade while Faust watches from the wings. A poet of content and craft, MykD was happy to speak at length with the rhapsodists and naturalists, the sentimentalists and singers of the court about the blood poems of the Nightwalker and how they just might one day bring literature back to the place of prominence and power it once so rightly held. They followed him to the village of Elend, beneath the Brocken, like the rats to the Piper, much to the attendees' chagrin, and the villagers' as well.

Then came the Graces, Fates, and Furies, there not solely to fill the gap left by the departing Poets as Goethe wrote, but instead to pave the way for the one we all came to see—great Helen, fairer than the forest nymphs, as the Homunculus said.

It had become a Classical Walpurgisnacht, attended by the Sirens and watched by a million dreaming eyes.

With a clap of his hands the Stage Manager employed by our esteemed Director (whose name I can't reveal) had the stage dressed for the wedding of Peleus and Thetis while a variety of sprites and gnomes were enlisted to play the

---

[12]For a fine description, examine Goethe's *Faust*.

gods and goddesses present for the vows. Once the play began a purple charge of energy rose from the gold and orange flames of the central bonfire and a splendid creature (whose eyes recalled to me a dream of a forsaken soul deep within the waters of a dark, fetid bog) came forth to play Eris, the goddess of discord.

"Why was I not invited to your rites?" she asked, more sadly than any of the tales have told.

"Get thee gone!" the gods and goddesses replied, more harshly than the newly cast Eris' delivery required.

"If I am not worthy to sit within your circle, I will go," this mad Eris replied, "but not before I give to you my gift."

She placed on the ground before the proud goddesses a golden apple addressed "To the Fairest" and returned the way she had come, the flames of the bonfire shooting forth a purple fury, then settling down again.

Before the transformation of the flames was complete, Aphrodite, Hera, and Athena, the most beautiful (and vain) of the goddesses, each laid claim to the apple, clawing at one another's faces and breasts in a bid to make it her own. The Director, appointing himself as Zeus, ordered them to stop and declared in no uncertain terms that Prince Paris of Troy would be the one to decide. I was called upon to play the Prince, a role suited to my skills. The three goddesses came to me, each in turn, and offered me a variety of gifts, material and carnal, so the apple would be hers. Were I to have my choice, I would have cut the apple in three and taken them all into my bed, but these plays of ours must be performed as the Director commands, so I chose Aphrodite, knowing I'd at least have Helen to soothe the pains of my by-now-throbbing cock. As I took fair Helen's hand, I saw in her eyes the swirling colors of my Anastasia's. And as I undid the clasp of her loosely hanging dress and saw the secret key that glimmered there I decided that I didn't give a fuck what kingdom would fall or what innocents would die to satisfy the wrath of the goddesses I had spurned.

I've been going and going—haven't danced to the point of collapse and breathless ecstasy in quite some time. Walpurgisnacht, Walpurgisnacht. The wicked date in 1945 when Adolf and Eva went into the restless sleep of the damned. The far less wicked but perhaps just as infamous date in 1966 when Anton LaVey formed the Church of Satan. I still get hard thinking of Manson's doll Susan dancing the go-go at his Topless Witches Review (makes ya wonder if there's any other kind…). LaVey had wonderful models for his project—the

Hell-Fire Club, Aleister Crowley, the Black Order of Germany—but he took it a step further and formed a Church.

Holy Hell, but not.

He had the right idea, but he and his clan got trapped in the dark arts and sex arts and although they mixed in some compassionate rituals of Light, they fell into the ugly old symbols of the Baphomet and fake dick and all that nonsensical flim-flam of empty worship. Satanic worship has *nothing* to do with Satan, devils, demons, or what might be called Evil. Anyone who uses the powers of the Universe for personal gain is worshipping nothing and no one but oneself, so devil worship is really *self*-worship, which is why so many rock stars are accused of Satanism. It's their self-love that's throwing you.

That, and the backwards messages...

Ironic that Satanists' chief deity is closer to the being of Light that once was Lucifer than the shadow-dwelling pig-fucker we think of when we say the name Satan. And many of their "Nine Satanic Statements" make a helluva lotta sense.

Then again, they could be the credo of the Nazis.

You'd think with less black magic and a bit more "We are the gods and what's so wrong with that?" they might get all the atheists and agnostics together and wouldn't that fine?

A pertinent aside: A few months after the founding of the Church of Satan, on July 7, 1966, The Supreme Court of Massachusetts declared Burroughs' *Naked Lunch* to be *not* obscene. This was just as major as The District Court of New York's December 6, 1933 decision that Joyce's *Ulysses* was *not* obscene.

These are two incredibly brilliant juke-rambles by two of the great authors of this Plane.

Most people can't understand anything in those books *but* the fuck-words, and I think in some fine way that's just what Bill and Jim would want.

'Cause they knew that the very hippest of the hipsters—the real cockaknockadoodle spookster-roosters—those who can see the real value in a Samhain or Walpurgisnacht—would get it all in spades.

So whattaya think? If cocks crow do crows cock?

I'll have to ask the Trixter Crow 'bout that one.

It's been an excellent Festival Day.

Now to find some clothes...

Woke up this morning, post-Nacht, with my lips wrapped around the phenomenally large breast of a Mother Goddess statue buried deep in the African jungle. Brushing an assortment of berries and leaves from my shaggy hair, I let out a spine-snapping growl-yawn that exploded the heads of a few colorful birds perched on her head.

Shit.

Throwing myself to the ground before a small stream, I saw what I had felt the moment the bones and feathers started to fly—I had been transformed once more into the Baphomet, complete with goatlike snout and especially long and curlicued horns. "OK, Cornu," I said with a smile, "if that's the way it's gotta be, so be it."

"Whatever you say, goatman. I'm game."

Someone had snuck up on me.

Fuck.

Just what I needed—some shmuck with nothing better to do in his predawn hours than stare at a Baphomet sucking stone goddess tits in the jungle deeps of Africa.

"Can I help you?" I asked, putting as much menace in my voice as I dared without exploding the heads of any more indigenous life.

"Maybe. Are you one of the fucks who fucked up my mouse?"

Christ. It was Mykaldaemio.

"How in hell did you get here?" I asked, dipping my snout in the water for a much-needed drink.

"You brought me late last night. Guess you don't remember."

"It's my policy to remember as little as possible. Keeps the body count low."

"Not including those two birds, of course."

"*Of course.*"

"So what's with the hostile transformation?"

"It's a little trick of the Cornu's," I said. "It's his way of saying 'how thou actest so shalt thou lookest,' or some crazy shit like that. He knows it pisses me off."

"So don't let it."

"Easy for you to say, you blood-sucking fuck," I said, annoyed enough to decide on Comparative Symbology as my only means of getting back to plumb: "Look at me. I'm a twisted version of a misused and badly corrupted symbol. I'm the inverted pentagram and the counter-clockwise swastika—an instrument of Evil with no predisposition inherent in its shape. Symbolic corruptions. I can't go three feet without falling on their thorns. I might as well wrap myself in a Confederate flag and make a mocking rebel yell—hang every bastardized icon in history around my neck on a long, golden chain. Take the Pentagram—in my weakest moments it burns into my vision, its horns blood-tipped and thrusting upward to deny its trinity'd lower self. It doesn't come to me as a symbol of *Satan* in those moments, but as it originally was—the manifestation of the basic principles of metaphysical and mathematical perfection. I was there in Mesopotamia 5500 years ago when the Pentagram graced the temple walls, no different than the swastika above the entrance to the Benedictine monastery where Hitler learned to love ecclesiastic things. What's a Pentagram anyhow? The five elements? The four directions? Christ's five wounds? The Pentateuch? And why does it come to me in those weak moments, burning itself first into my eyes and then into my forehead and hands—inverted on the left but upright on the right? It tells me its perfections really *can be* obtained, and all these contradictions are nothing but a game. That one morning I will wake up from my revelries not as a jungle-creeping Baphomet but as a splendid Angel of Light, as I once was."

Wrapping my wings around my scaled and hairy flesh, I sunk into the mud. Let him think I'd gone finally nuts. Who cared?

"*In hoc signo vinces*, eh?"

"Fuck you, Myk-D," I said with what might pass among goats as a pout. "Don't lay Latin on me now... It burns my pointed ears."

"I was thinking of Constantine. That crazy vision where he saw a cross in the sky before a battle with a bunch of other Roman pricks to try and secure the throne. Sucker even spoke to him—'Use this' it said. Boy did he ever. Him and every one of his kind. I couldn't even tell you the number of times some jerk with a bag of garlic and a cross has tried to ward me off. Kind of funny actually."

"I'm somehow missing the humor."

To his credit, MykD joined me in the mud. "It's probably those goat feet getting you down. They don't look half bad—they ain't Chuck Taylors, but I might give them a shot."

"Careful what you wish for," I said, grabbing a squirming fish out of the stream and biting its head off before I could stop. "Any friend of mine is a thorn in Cornu's side."

"I'm forever neutral, remember?"

He sounded unsure, and more than a little nervous.

"Sure. So ... Constantine. The quintessential Roman blood-gatherer if there ever was one... Take the Roman out of Rome and Byzantium becomes Constantinople. Fucker killed his wife Fausta in a boiling bath because she accused his first-born son of trying to seduce her. Killed him too, just in case. He and his bat-bitch mother Helena led the early Christians in ripping all the stock symbols out of their fables in the Akashic Record so they could embroider them on their flags of war, just like you said. He presided over the early quarrels over doctrine, playing the Grinning Arbiter while they killed one another over the details of how to precisely corrupt what Jesus said and did for their maximum leverage and effect."

"You finished with the history lesson?" Mykaldaemio asked, flicking his tongue into the ragged neck-hole of one of the bird carcasses that lay cockeyed against the statue. "Cause I'll give you one about us *real* vampires that won't make you feel so alone."

"By all means. A little misery in my company would be welcome. *Solamen miseris socios habuisse doloris*, right?"

"Exactly. Glad to hear you're over your bout of anti-Latinitis. Now, you know I love you—horns and all—but your co-opting of the vampiric traits as part of your fallen-angel, devilish incarnation *thing* is doing nothing for our kind. You seem to be forgetting what *Dracula* was *really* about—the Victorian preoccupation with sex, death, and violence. The *blood* exchange as signifier for the *sexual* one. And I know what I'm talking about, because I was reading that stuff as it was being *written*. Screw that shit—when I wanna fuck I fuck and when I wanna eat I EAT. Stoker was a whipped dog and *everything* was metaphorical with him. He wrote *Dracula* based on a dream for fuck's sake— that aughta tell you something about subconscious leanings! He played on the European fear of the Eastern immigrant tainting London and Western Europe. If you had half a brain you'd quit writing your cutesy little confessions and compose a story about some Iraqi vampire loose in Washington, DC. That, my friend, would make you famous—especially if he only preyed on nice WASPy Protestants. Stoker had never even *been* to Transylvania—patterned the whole deal on places in Yorkshire and things he'd read about, like the shipwrecking of the Russian ship *Dmitri* ten years before the book was published. He had plenty of models to pattern *Dracula* on—Rymer's *Varney*, le Fanu's *Carmilla*...

"What a can of maggoty mold he opened. *Dracula* pried wide the doors for Fem scholarship in all its heavy-handed glories. It's all a mess of forced interpretation. A lot of nonsense. So *what* if all the stories have a phallic, thrusting stake and juicy spewing fluids, and the cutting off of the head in order to silence the woman? Excuse *me*, but if I really wanna shut a girl up I'll just stick my rod down her throat... But this is what I'm thinking—in your Muslim vampire book, which you really have to write, you could have the female vampires killed by having some fish-smelling, cavelike apparatus inserted over their mouth and nose until they suffocate. Then the Fems will have nothing at all to complain about, right?"

"Is there anything from vampire lore that you *do* like?" I asked, mostly because it had been too long since I'd heard the sound of my own voice, corrupted by the snout or not.

"You mean like Sickle and Prevert at the Movies? Well, sure. Historically, I think Prince Vlad Dracul was a pretty good example of bloodlust gone bad."

"*Dracul* means devil, doesn't it?"

"I see what you're getting at... So, yeah—and *pokol* means Hell and a witch is called *stregoica*, and *vrlok, wampyr,* and *nosferatu* are all names for vampires. So fucking what? Murnau used those names to circumvent the fact that Stoker's widow wouldn't let him use the Count's. It's ironic that Max Schreck's over the top, zombied-out rat act is the iconic representation of Pure Evil rather than Lugosi's tux-n-tails corruption. You follow? I mean, the deeper ramifications of the collective agreement that the gentleman vampire is somehow less evil than the outright monster gets entirely overlooked. We're over a hundred years past the fabled *fin de siecle* and there's still a lot of people trying to keep everything pleasantly Victorian and buttoned down even while we're talking about murder and bloodlust. No wonder the Ripper wannabes still pop up here and there. And to answer your question, there are plenty of fictional vampires I *do* like. Lestat and his crew, Frank Langella, Bowie and Deneuve... All the rest are off the mark—though I have partied with some Lost Boys. Screw the rest. Just Hollywood/Hammer shlockfests."

"Lovely, Myk-D. So you and I are both badly represented and horribly misunderstood. At least you don't have some sick, invisible bastard pulling your strings."

"No one is invisible, Planner. You just have to change the way you see."

Just for fun, I turned to page 666 of my big black dictionary and scanned the pages for the Mark of the Beast. Sure enough, there it was—"Final Solution."

I call this "Still-life in Plastique" or "Being a Super Callous Fragile Mystic Gives Me Halitosis." Maybe it's the Joyce I've been reading or the general disposition I have toward word-rape and grammatical invention. Sound is power ("In the beginning was the Word") and once you've conquered language as a basic communicational form all that's left is to reinvent the Weil, like the Doors did with "Alabama Song."

Anyway, this is a little digg-er-ee-doo, a bit of *L'art pour L'art*, a Cobbins Corner electrospect, a curb-slam jizz-off aero-jam, and a special pill for all those practitioners of assholistic medicine. A nod to Jimmy Shelter and all his menni muddled asses.

Enjoy.

A priest folded a monk upon himself in a jagged arabesque—a bold-faceted façade—and played a cut wound into a cell of subcutaneous dungblessing. In the gauzy stillness the Nazi on the pigeoned parkbench ate a deathplank graffiti'd wind in the hare, wiping his maw sickly on bare rabbit's eyes, nose, ears, and crushed-velvet bush. His breath was a knotty rope full of Aum-choking, choirwinding ghosts. Hey padre! Amore! Garcon! The rumors are true: The one-quarter moon got 75 cents from a dollar and moved to another sky. The deepest, darkest, truest, languished, reddish secrets are the mindmad demands of the Hell-godz cree-a-shuns. Even if two rights don't make a wrong, two Wrights most assuredly make a plane. Beware the 8 great states of sickness: dollars, the re-potted dopemind, swallows, solar flares, Rome, theology, logic, and nobility. A thought: no brain, no mind, no spirit. Spend an hour with the desperado triad of Copernicus, Galileo, and Avicenna and you'll regenerate, enervate, eviscerate, contemplate, demonstrate, hate, slate, masturbate, and compensate for the golden emboldened *Hermetica* in its original gold-gild print. It's a Flash Gordian knot, noble and plucked from the pen of the cosmosonar eyesquint man, laid out so the Message lofts in onto Jupiter, onto Neptune, onto Pluto, while at home the wife of the plasmostatic tubeman finds her self-same self willingly absorbed into no man's fantasies... Spewed ink arranged on a rotten page begging for conversation—a mantric connection. They're a couple uncoupled to Saturn's but not the nocturne's rings. Glassed within a light there is a bug, a disease, a solution. A cure (?)—a late night mist shrouding a missed anniversary while she remains at home playing hockey-fork on plate—potato and steak and onions lead to only onion *breath*. It doesn't matter...no...he won't care. Him on the couch with Sunday paper crossword scribbling and it's already Saturday and tomorrow the new one comes. There is disease splashed on the wallpapered walls in fake-a-smile Christmas portraits, in broken vases, in damaged flowers that are still on shelves and not in hands; the aura, the smell, the scent of which is nowhere. Her growing agitation matching that of the machine that's made for wash, she jabs the fork into her socket, producing an eyewince/pluckbrow squeal. Hours later, still working the words in a fluorescent patch of hall, he doesn't see the creeping signs of black in the corners of the white room's no longer sterile floor. He's got no balance—no truth. Remove the wordsymbols from the tip of his rapidly dulling pencil, ever nearer to the nubbiness of the long rubbed-down eraser, and you've got what you get—a fog, a haze, a gauzy, puffed opaqueness. No wonder he won't notice the otherwise clean lab-coat pocket-pen leakage of the run and mumble overworked intern, but he oughta take care—the camera reports on a hand hidden by a hand in a cave beneath the sea on a moon ridge in the furthest place seen by a million-dollar telescopic lens.

Here's the end equation: shrug//sniffle//eyewipe + eyesquint//nibble//penpluck = cold, unceasing work.

Once the Baphomet features fully disappeared and I could go out in public without a rock-star-on-the-run disguise, I took the boys for a new tattoo. Mykaldaemio and I each have several, though it was to be Orlando Nepenthe's first. Gabriel has his wife's name written in angelic script across both wrists, though I very much doubt it was done by any earthbound artist of the ink. Even Blunt-Axe Eddie and Doubting Thomas came along 'cause "A new tattoo's the bomb-shit, brother."

Who's to argue with that?

After careful consideration, I decided we'd all get the death's-head moth (*Acherontia atropos*) on the left side of our necks, where we all favor inflicting the blood-wound. I know it's been used in some dark-side literature but those writers didn't invent the fucking thing... See my point? Cause the first tattoo artist we tried to work with didn't and gauging by the beating administered by Blunt-Axe and Doubting Thomas and the after-incident plasmic cleanup engineered by Myk-D they didn't want to hear that crap any more than I do.

So why? you ask. It's all in the name. Acheron is the river of woe and it's a waterway we've navigated over and over and Atropos is of course the Fate (one of the three Parcae) who severs the thread of life. She who has forsaken us all.

So as not to anger Atropos' sisters, we had the artist weave into the wings the names of Clotho, who spun the thread and Lachesis who measured the length, and within the thorax the names of their parents, Zeus and Themis.

Is there anybody old Z. *didn't* fuck?

I finally got Gabriel St. A. to participate in a little vengeance and retribution, though it had nothing to do with his own regrettable situation.

I was following Anastasia in the grocery store (frozen foods) as she spoke on the cellular phone she rarely uses to a mother she barely stands about an incident involving her should-be-sainted grandmother.

Before I continue I just wanna say that whoever decided no good ever comes of stalking was dead fucking *wrong*.

Dear grandma was home (probably baking cookies as should-be-sainted grandmas do) when she received a call from some sick soul pretending to be her grandson (Anastasia's older brother, who never does come home). He told her he was in the hospital with some kind of strange disease and he had to give a sample of his sperm and would Helpful Grandma be so kind as to say some fuck-words to him to help the process along?

If you have a grandma, or have even the smallest fraction of a clue about anything, you know Dear Sweet Grandmas won't deny their offspring's offspring anything they can possibly give and being that Dear Sweet Grandma knew a few or so of those very fuck-words her pretend-to-be grandson was requesting, she obliged, as should-be-sainted grandmas do.

It wasn't until a week later, when she called Grandson to see how he made out with his tests and was met with a slightly rude but perhaps understandable "What are you talking about grandma?" [Then *sotto voce* to his wife: "Shit, hon—I think grandma's got the Alzheimers!"] that Dottery Old Grandma realized she had been duped.

Grandson was furious. So was his mom.

Anastasia was in tears.

All of them so helpless.

Not me.

With a little help and supervision from Leyton Walkingfeather, I underwent another *Yuwipi* to track the bastard down. The micro details of the process beyond what I've already shared are somewhat sacred and don't matter to the story, so I'll skip to the part where Gabriel and I found him. You can probably guess what we saw—a ratty tenement pad, a stack of computer printouts with cleverly extracted links between Grandsons and Grandmothers, and lots and lots of dried, crusty spots on the worn hardwood floor that probably weren't egg white. As our three Fates would have it, he was in the middle of another of his slimy calls when we dropped in thru the window.

Being he's on the eighth floor on the side *without* the fire escape, he about yanked his dick off with fear and surprise.

"I'm _____'s Grandson, you crazy *fuck.*"

Gabriel said it and then acted on the helpless rage of countless grandsons, granddaughters, moms, fathers, cousins, and their Dear, Sweet, Should-be-Sainted, cookie-baking Grandmas.

He was a little quicker and therefore more merciful than I would have been, but we all must act out our vengeance in our own particular way.

I wanted to tell Anastasia what we'd done.

So I went once more to the window by her bed.

Wisha, won't you agree now to take me from the middle, say, of next week on, for the balance of my days for nothing (what?) as your own nursetender? (Joyce, Book II, *Finnegans Wake*; italics inDublinably his)

F itting to begin with words from a Wake, for I will tell you of a dream…

I lay beneath Anastasia's window in the mystical Maytime air, wanting to tell her what Gabe and I had done—avenging Grandma, setting something right with our claws and righteous murder, when from out the opened window, caught for an instant in a tangle of curtain before sailing just beyond, came the following dream, intercepted by the unsanctioned Dreamcatcher that is me:

Deep in the forgotten forest, at the center of the circle of the Old Gnarled Tree, there hung a tribe of apish, bony vampires; hairy once-men with shoulder blades protruding and scarred chests colored in the greyish tones of death. The thinnest and oldest, a dethroned elder with nary a tooth or claw still sharp, spider-walked his way from branch to branch, attempting to steal a scrap of blood-soaked food while avoiding the snapping jaws and swiping fingers of those he had once led. Pushed from the top by a wicked-looking female nursing a growling infant, the old ape did not fall heavily as one would expect, but floated slowly to the deeply needled floor of the forest as though gravity was a law he refused to heed. As he skulked into the brush, the others chattered mercilessly at him, waving crudely made crosses and roughly looped lengths of vine at his back like cats eager to catch a country mouse to present before their Master. As they moved in for the kill a small but vicious female appeared from a mossy hollow and tore off the head of the one closest to the spot where the elder had entered the brush. The rest turned and ran, while she began to feast upon the fallen one's flesh…

Waking from the dream, Anastasia walked in a half sleep to her computer, the brightening glow of the liquid-crystal screen bathing her perfect breasts in a pale blue light, making the key that dangles ever between them gleam with all its secret force. Peering further over the sill I saw her sign on as Whalewatcher_2, the pseudonym she uses when sending her theo-political diatribes of a coming Christian revolution to the underground members of her chat groups. Her fingers danced over the keys as though her dream had provided a needed inspiration.

It was St. George's Day, and her message was a call to arms. A passionate plea to her comrades to ready themselves for the coming of the Dragon. A call to fight the forces of paganism as St. George had done until his martyr's death in 303, riding the pale horse of Christianity against the heathen emperor Diocletian.

She then wrote the following—a hunk of meat on which I have not yet ceased to chew: "And soon we will free the tightly bound Savior—the one who will lead our War against the Devil, his pagan hordes, and their army of false gods as did Michael in days of old…"

Amazing. My pretty Anastasia, *La Ragazza di latte e Sangue*, my girl of milk and blood, my Snow not-so White, was calling forth the one-true-god–

lovers of the Christian religions to join a Crusade against the myriad gods of other names and cultures—and she had her leader, her "savior," all picked out. Whalewatcher_2 (who, I wondered, was Whalewatcher_1?)—the one strong enough to guard the Jonahs of this new age against being swallowed up should their faith begin to lag; to do her Master's will without question or doubt. She typed away with full belief in the misunderstood metaphor of the bursting forth of nature after the destruction of the world and the rising of the Christ-king, all ushered in by the dragon-slayer himself, banisher of the Adder King and other serpentine manifestations of evil beyond the lost Eden of Earth. The herder of wolves, the Lord of Horses, and spirit of protection to make the wheat grow and flowers bloom.

"Yours in the One True God—Pray for our bound and corded savior in his hour of need" she closed, leaning back in the chair as the message made its way to thousands of inboxes around the world, where it could be used and manipulated as biblical code for Anything Goes. Gunpowder in the hands of a mad group of zealots reciting a litany of exclusion lit by the fires of superiority rather than purity—after all, Light is Light—Lucifer, God—what the heck's the difference? There is none. There is only *perception*. And, at the head of the fight is a misdirected, insidiously suppressed angel calling herself Whalewatcher_2 and denying the possibility that her life is a living death.

Why is it that we deformed ones always want to couple with the one who so loathes what we are that she would kill us if she could? The Lady Van Helsings of the world are the lovers we seek to kill our vampire soul and make us whole once more. The righteous beings we blindly hope will banish their long-time gods in order to lay with their new-found and much reformed lovers. Their hatred, so divine in its source, is a toxin turned to ambrosia on our wicked tongues. It is the force of the stake entering the heart that makes it beat, in total opposition to the slayer's aims.

She is my Muse, despite her lame faith in God's Great Retribution. As Dante had his unattainable Beatrice and Petrarch had his Laura, so have I my godly Anastasia of the Dangling Key and dual pseudonyms. Like Poe's twisted Muse of Mother, Wife, and Lovers dancing in the madness of the red-mask death she is an amalgamation of so many creator spirits swirling around my days. (Freud can fuck a hole—it isn't ALL about *Mom*...) She's like the fabled daughters of Mnemosyne, whose father Oranos and mother Gaea were Heaven and Earth—the great Totality of mythic dualities consummating in ancient light to bring forth our precious Memory and treasured words so we may worship our lovely elusive Muse. Those who will only bestow the gift of Inspiration when those who worship them cast off the robes of Reason and walk naked on the ramparts of their exposed minds. Edgar Planner Poe—Anastasia's twisted poet-prince and the one who will wake her from her church-induced, mother-guarded sleep.

She and her fellows will not banish the Cornu as easily as the Antichrist falls in films. They think him nothing but an egotistical child so confident in his own Power that he charges thoughtlessly ahead. Well, that's exactly what he *wants* them to think.

Let her watch for the Whale—that's how the Lion gets his way.

Needing a place to think, I walked the etheric paths of Black Elk and brought myself to a Harney Peak of the Mind, the mountain top of pulsing spiritual power concentrated and directed into the waiting channels of the heart chakra and Third Eye.

I was thinking about Reincarnation. The disparate and yet linked origins of my own rebirth and the nature of those of my friends Mykaldaemio and Gabriel St. Armstrong beg me to ask: Does the existence of Reincarnation mean that we all have a chance at redemption or are we simply doomed to recycle ourselves in an endless series of trips to the Universal School? You see, I know *nothing* of these things, and perhaps that is for the best. I mean, I know the Basics, the Legends—the religious tracts of St. Augustine, the Hindu idea of Karma, the biblical representations of Elijah and John the Baptist being the same reincarnated soul avatars of avatars, I guess you'd say ... but none of us qualify for anything so seemingly simple as that. Gabriel won't speak of where he was, what he saw, or why he was *allowed* to come back. Then there's Limbo—Leyton Walkingfeather exists in what could be termed a Limbo, but he says little about it and seems content within its walls. Myk-D remains coolly untroubled by his own rebirth into the world of the undead and divulges almost as little as Leyton, although he says he is working on *a book*—apparently I've inspired him and one day we might know it all in full.

Then there's me—poured thru a portal in some twisted, mystic ritual, the real details of which I also know nothing. Maybe Parvus Cornu refuses to give me answers because he is as unknowledgeable as I am—just because he swung the baton doesn't mean he could play all the notes. I know he wanted me here, and he's taken full advantage of me since '68, but I have never been convinced that he's the one who got it done. He's more Opportunist than Actualizer. You have to remember that PC wants to take God's place when all the shit goes down, so he's already practicing taking credit for others' ideas of his omnipotence.

So which side do we choose? Which pseudo-deity do we serve? Do we act like Confucius, Plato, and Apollo, worshipping order and Reason and looking for an ideal based on Oppression or Servitude, or do we embrace the Individuality and Artistic and spiritual freedom (termed Madness) of Lao-tse, Aristotle, and Dionysus... This is not a choice between Good and Evil, which Blake so rightly perceived, because BOTH God and Parvus Cornu subscribe to the former.

But it's a choice I have to make.

After weeks of floating meditations trying to untangle the questions I have posed, and the occasional visit from Leyton Crowfeather and the 405 spirit powers, I emerge from a sweat lodge in the Dakota Badlands and find myself in the center of the world. Below me, in a valley of alley-asphalt civilization, I can see the crawling, grasping homeless, strung out, beaten down, looking for any thread of anything that could lead them back to some semblance of Home. The last remnants and first manifestations of the Manson Family and other wacko cults. What makes a cult different from a parish? Timeframe? Intensity? License to congregate? Advanced degrees on the leader's wall?

Deeper in the valley, where the early nightfall shadows are already taking hold, I see the bloodlust creatures that feed on the sleeping when their white light has gone out or been suppressed by the decisions of dire days. The Mischievers and other wayward idiots rallying to their idea of the opposite of God. But they are not free—to offer your soul, will, or fate to anyone, deity or devil, is the beginning of servitude. Maybe I'm a rebel because I won't serve God or the Cornu or because I don't see them as either better or worse than I, but I ask none to serve me, either. In all my countless atrocities, in every sordid tale I've told, I've never once asked anyone to do anything. You know my theories on this—but Action is everything. This is the most unpretentious and direct I can be. Better than not serving is not to *be* served. This puts the responsibility squarely on the shoulders of God and Parvus Cornu and kings and popes and presidents. What is that drive to be *followed*? Let them all fall to their deaths so that we may be Free. I'm talking Anarchy, I know. Revolution has to be at the start, as long as it then turns to something better, and that's where it usually turns to shit. Civil wars, revolutions, our little celestial difficulties—in the end there's always some shmuck who thinks he aughta be served—that he's somehow earned the right... God is as guilty as any Cromwell or Stalin or Robespierre of being about the Power and not the Freedom of others to determine their fate. I too can use the Bible to further my thesis—think of all the cities God's supposedly destroyed, kings he's punished, peoples he's annihilated. Revelation is the biggest post-revolutionary ego-trip going. A matter of perception, perhaps, but isn't that the very essence of the Free Will he supposedly gave us? Know this—God DID NOT give humans free will—*they stumbled on it themselves*. It was unforeseen on the higher Planes and not particularly appreciated. So, in the end, as I stare into the valley at all those who have forgotten that they even *have* Free Will, I shout: Serve no one, no idea, no principle, and no Creator, be it Parvus Cornu, Lucifer, money, fake titties, or God. Show him that just because he is presented as the Great White Light doesn't mean he isn't just as wrong as the rest, and refuse to fight his War.

Use the Free Will that earliest man dug from deep within his heart and do not be a slave.

Apparently when you send your thoughts so strongly thru the ether, you get responses from all directions.

I had drifted down thru South Dakota and Nebraska and cut diagonally across Colorado and thru most of Arizona when I was met in the Sonoran Desert by Mad John Gandy and a spirit acquaintance of his who called himself Percival von Grayle-Groyne.

A pseudonym, of course.

"Talkin' talkin' talkin' away in yur thinkin' words, my short-horned son," Mad John whispered playfully in my ear. "And now comes forth the dualin' angel ta makes the devil pay."

And so it began. von G-G was a major fan, a devotee, of CS Lewis' *Screwtape Letters*, as many restless and wandering spirits are and to which my own demon-prose has sometimes been compared. Like early versions of these memoirs, the book was received with either great praise or a distinct dislike and abruptly pushed away.

That's how you know you're doing something right.

"Your stuff's okay," von G-G observed, pulling a beat-up and heavily highlighted and notated paperback edition of *Screwtape* from his pocket, "but your questionable truths are no comparison to the insightful half-fictions of Master Lewis."

"Given," I replied. "His was a great conjuring mind. But this is my own experience—to hold it up for comparison is to discount almost everything I say, and to potentially miss the point."

von G-G: If there even *is* a point. And you ought to listen when someone talks—what I *said* was that there *was no* comparison. You don't have enough legitimacy as a writer to be *considered* against the Master. Just like he said of God, Lewis *has no* opposite. His work is beyond compare. My comparing you to him would be like comparing Screwtape to Michael or Gabriel—he was somewhere between department head and worker bee (the truth of which is clear, *despite* his transparent self-inflation), while as you know, *they* run the daily show while God does *godly* things…

Me: Lewis was only partially right. *Nothing* and no one has an opposite—everything is contained in both the individual parts as well as in the whole, so I counter your point by saying that Screwtape and Michael are *exactly* the same. I may be an enemy to archangels but that does *not* make me their opposite. If you've understood anything I've said, you know that we were once the same—even *God* was the same. As for his doing so-called *godly* things—sticking your nose where it don't belong is far from *godly*.

MJG: Thass the big one, Hoss! Yur on yur own now, mini-demon. I'm out to look fur some garbage pile eatage. You both have fun and keep the deep gashes to a minimum if ya wanna share a meal with me. (He exits.)

von G-G: You masquerade as a clever, poetic demon, Planner Forthright, or whatever your real name is, but you're not. I know the blackness of your heart—the ruthlessness and anger and deceit. You play yourself off as Mephistopheles—you've said so! And you play him slick and cunning, just like Lewis says about the "real" one. All that clowning around to disarm the Watchful. You *think* you're one of Milton's fallen angels but you're really more like one of Dante's. You lull the reader to sleep with your stories of meditation and vision quests and this colossal struggle of the soul and yet if you *really were* an angel, a *true angel*, fallen or not, you would appear in such a way that humans would *fear* you—even Gabriel was feared when he came with his message to Mary. You instead seek to charm—to use potty words and invoke the Beats (that talentless group of drunkards and fags!) and pick apart everything you come across. You are no closer to salvation than you were at the start, and if you had your way, all Mankind would be the very Material Magicians that Screwtape says will end the war and secure every soul for Hell. If we divorce ourselves from God and embrace only the mystical within, we are conjurers and nothing more.

Me: You're an unhappy spirit, Percival—*or whatever your real name is*. You hold your opinion up for serious consideration and yet I sense some resentment. Didn't Lewis define that as *dwelling* in Hell?

von G-G: How dare you quote him to me! You think you're smart. You're more familiar with the work of the Master than I thought. But you demons are always good at turning words around on the speaker. I just wanted you to know that your work has no strength—it won't last. It won't change a thing. You share with Master Lewis the notion that the Hell of today is nothing more than departmental office bureaucracy and that the Church itself is as much an *aid* to demons as their sham enticements and cunning ploys but a few similar philosophies do *not* make for a worthy piece of literature. Why won't you be truthful about what it is you are and forget all these literary games?

Me: Because I don't KNOW what it is I am! That's the *point*! And what do you know of it? You wander the Earth instead of swimming in the light, where you belong—where we ALL belong. What is it that you still need to get from this place? Do you fear conscription? Or are you playing your part in the War by trying to stop me from writing? Did Parvus Cornu send you?

von G-G: You'd like to think that, I'm sure. Thomas More said it, and Master Lewis put it in his book—"the devil, the proud spirit, cannot stand to be *mocked*." This way you could dismiss me as an Agent of Evil and ignore my critique. I am not trying to help your enemy. I just want this piece of garbage eradicated from the same *corpus literarium* that contains something so rich and fluid as *Screwtape*. I will have Lewis' take on Hell and the Devil over yours any day.

Me: So now we have it. You find *his* pill a little easier to swallow... Or is it that you find *his* fiction a bit more palatable because he's the better writer? That's like ranking presidents based on who gave the best speech. Let me tell you what I think about the constructs he created. First, the whole idea of a bureaucratic hierarchy in Hell is absurd. It works for Clive Barker, but he's dealing with *fiction*. That's Heaven's business, not Lucifer's. It's true that if Parvus Cornu is allowed to win, *The Screwtape Letters* will most likely be the Handbook of Hell and required reading for up and coming Mischievers looking to hold high office, but I seriously doubt it was Lewis' intention to provide a roadmap to the Wanna Bes of the lower vibrational planes. It's the take of a *Man* on the techniques of the damned, the same way that the gods of Olympus seem so human because they were invented by them! There has never been any collecting of souls, no absorbing them into ourselves—becoming a vampire on this Plane is as far as it goes. Should the Cornu get a foothold that might change, but it isn't that way now. Second, although the book is full of lots of suggestions and notes and guidelines, the fact of the matter is, and I again refer you to my own work, we CANNOT GET INSIDE. Did you ever in your life before spirit have a devil really get inside you?

von G-G: No. All my devils—and I had plenty—came from within. That became clear the minute I died after discharging a bullet into my brain. But the sordid details of my own little life have nothing to do with the question of the *supposed* truth of your work. Besides, if you had carefully read *Screwtape*, you would know that it isn't what you try to put *into* humans' minds but what you *keep out*. You, unlike Screwtape and his colleagues, seem intent on cramming every bit of knowledge humans have ever created into their heads to forge some *illusion* of *connection*, of no-sideness, or same-sideness and it's not only poorly executed but completely sophomoric and absurd!

Me: You know, Percival, I think all this ranting and raving has nothing whatsoever to do with the truth or fiction of my book, at least not in the context of your request that I not muddy up the fairly shallow waters of demon prose with my memoirs. If my words are so unworthy, so off the mark and absurd, oughtn't *that* prove the genius of Lewis all the more? Like he said, you can take these things as concrete reality or allegory, depending on your own particular beliefs, so what are you *really* afraid of with my book?

von G-G: Alright, if we have to come to that, we will. It's full of contradictions. You save one soul and drink the blood of another. You pray with shamans but you've murdered your own mother! You can only hope to confuse and seduce readers with your refusal to commit to either a life of Darkness *or* a life of Light. *Make a choice.* At least Screwtape committed himself to following the path of the devouring of souls (and despite what you say about absorption, I believe the Master and not you)—*even his own nephew's*! He at no point turned around and tried to apologize or atone for what he had done. You may put on a tuxedo and hide your horns with your shaggy hair but your red tail still shows.

Me: And who are *you* to try and pidgeonhole *me*? To say I must choose between the Darkness and the Light when I know that I am *BOTH*? That we *all* are both. And as for contradictions, *Screwtape* has plenty.

von G-G: Such as?

Me: Such as when he says that "contented worldliness" is one of a devil's best weapons and then goes on to say in the *next paragraph* that good targets are "suffering for redemption." You cannot be suffering *and* content *at the same time*. When Schopenhauer said "All life is suffering," he didn't suggest you should be *content* with it! And there are others. Any time you deal in theology there is bound to be contradiction and if I am guilty of some, it is only because there are certain lucid moments when all duality melts away and I am Whole again, so why the hell should I limit myself to a life of Darkness because I occasionally lose my way?

von G-G: Whole again? Wholly full of shit, perhaps. God—you've made me curse! AND take the Father's name in vain! Your work is dangerous and makes more than a few people afraid. Why should your struggles and pains be theirs? Why should your bitterness be theirs? Just because you were transformed into the unfortunate half-spirit, half-animal hybrid that Lucifer himself so loathed that he dared to fight against God does *not* mean that anyone should listen to you! You backed the wrong horse and now you are crying foul! Your stuff sucks! I wrote a truly compelling piece of first-person devil fiction that was a *true homage* to and furtherance of Master Lewis' work and no one would touch it! All the reams and reams of shit that get published year after year and my most worthy and important work was denied. Fuck you and your manuscript! Fuck your pitiful realities and dumb fictions!!! (He spontaneously turns into a centipede, ala Screwtape. No originality to the end.)

Me: Calm yourself, von G-G. You're revealing your true nature. Find a nice rock to live under until you are ready to go home to the light. If it's the notion of suicide keeping you here, let it go—the prison is of your own design. *You're* the key that turns the lock. Let your criticism of you—and me—go.

von G-G: Glub, blub. Gulp. (Conversation ends.)

Lewis was right—transformation truly does proceed from within. All the rest is just someone else's idea of what you should or shouldn't be.

After a fucked up meeting like that one (the product of too much deep thought—it nicks me every time...) I thought it best to do a little traveling—get out and see some stuff, study some people with more problems than a Brat Prince fallen angel like myself.

I needed a place full of hassles. A place of bad air and long lines. A place that stunk of authority abused and the sweaty balls and lurching bellies of those who had no choice but to take it. Self-important types with cell phones and laptops and lots of business to do, people to see—each the more privileged and entitled than the next and none of them getting anywhere at all.

So where does a guy go for a rippling fireball of inaction and opposing forces like that?

The airport.

I had been curious to find out what all this airport security, take off your shoes and spread your ass-checks blah-blah-blah was all about, so I hitched a ride in a fried-out Combie from some Australian guys who happened to be on their way to work at the airport in Minneapolis and booked myself a flight to my old '68 haunt—Chicago. I had some time before my flight so I taxi-cabbed with a guy named Harry to the local All-Mart, where I purchased the following items—a slightly larger-than-regulation bag to carry on the plane, which I then filled with Bic lighters, 5-oz. toothpaste tubes, 3.1-oz. hairsprays (aerosol, of course), 3 laptops with wireless Internet, and an undrilled bowling ball with a tampon string embedded in its coal black bowels. From the clothing department I purchased and put on 4 studded belts and 6 jackets with innumerable zippered and buttoned pockets that I filled with matchbooks, nail files, paper clips, spools of copper wire, a few dozen dry-cell batteries, and a putty-like substance that looked a little like plastique ... and topped myself off with 6 bulky earrings and a tongue bolt (the last in case I got the chance to do a porno in the Windy City. As it turns out, I did). I bought these mid-shin boots with about twenty feet of laces and made sure to do them up to the tippy-top eyeholes with a knot I learned from a Navy Seal.

Isn't it great that a guy like me can purchase all that different stuff in one giant supercenter the size of the Pentagon?

I got back to the airport with a chick named Nikki (a real darling) who drove a raspberry red corvette and got in line to go thru Checkpoint Charley. Gotta love those Minnesotans—slow as an 80-year-old arthritic man trying to knot baling wire in the freezing cold while standing in a bucket of ice. Airport (In)Security. The great employment alternative to real, substantial work. It's a job more worthless than the few carbon-monoxided zombies still taking quarters and dimes on the Jersey Turnpike.

It took awhile and a little bit of off-the-cuff explaining, but after about 45 minutes of waiting and 34 minutes dealing with a search of my bag and physical person (plus another 10 redoing my boots and belts after their mandatory removal), I was finally allowed access to the gate.

They didn't keep a thing.

As I was walking away I heard the tasty little bitch behind me say *"Took you long enough!!"*

Obviously a person who does not allot enough time for the *Unforseen*.

Once on the plane, I found my time was far from wasted. After crushing the shit out of some lady's bags of new purchases from some upper-echelon boutique in the process of stowing my oversized (but just *slightly*) bag, I took my aisle seat and struggled out of my six jackets while the Valium queen beside me talked about San Francisco with a guy who had lost his comb and razor but found God and was on his way to the city by the Bay as part of an Outreach program to bring other unkempt but otherwise savable souls into the fold. (He prayed frequently on approach and crossed himself as the wheels hit the ground—is that divine faith or none at all? It would have been a real theological dilemma if the landing gear had failed... Way more complicated than roofs blowing off churches and killing little girls). In the last four rows of the mid-sized jetliner were half a dozen purposefully wasting away, dyed blonde, over product'd-in-every-area bimbos on their way home from a retail clothing company's rah-rah Retreat.

Oh, the free makeup tips! Oh, the philosophical wisdom of proper hiring and management techniques ("I *had* to let Jeannie off—she had just met *the hottest guy!*"), and the promotion of the latest glitter-gold lipstick. These girls took themselves and their work so seriously, you would think they worked for RAND.

Perhaps the most interesting thing from that phase of the trip (it was too good so far to stop) was seeing Myk-D's vampiress girlfriend Racven in three different places, in similar but different outfits and a sexily moving diamond chip that was once in her lobe, once in her nose, and once just beneath her lip. She wore her hair down, black and long, each time, looking a lot like Caroline Munro, just so I wouldn't get confused.

No biggie, right? She obviously knows she's hot and I've got zero beef with that, but here's the thing—two of the three times I saw her she was in two different seats on that same plane to strip-mall hell—*at the same fucking time.*

Myk-D, you got some 'splainin' to do...

From Chicago I took a flight to Atlantic City, my favorite place to go when I want to see the very richest and very poorest of humanity co-mingling in a plastic and neon glow. The flight was empty and quiet, so I got to concentrate on watching this guy in his mid-twenties flip thru one of those men's health magazines. That is, until he came to a picture of a scantily clad cheerleader type sprawled across a bed. His eyes locked onto the page and I felt his heartbeat subtly rise, but before he could even adjust his seating position to allow for the tension in his jeans he jumped like a squirrel suddenly aware of his nuts—*Holy shit*, he must have thought—*I'm getting aroused on a nearly empty plane*! After establishing the whereabouts of both stewardesses (excuse me—*flight attendants*...) he folded the magazine in such a way that only *he* could see the picture. He didn't turn the page for a good long while.

Selfish prick.

To round my journey out, my limo driver in AC (Rock Star, baby...) smelled like curry gone bad, the origin of which was probably the walnut-sized crap-stain on his pants from some unexpectedly wet gas. The joys of travel, boys and girls.

At least, when you take the time to prep, like I do.

Blessed is the one who reads the words of this prophecy, and blessed are those who hear it and take to heart what is written in it, because the time is near. (Revelation 1:3)

I warn everyone who hears the words of the prophecy of this book: If anyone adds anything to them, God will add to him the plagues described in this book. (Revelation 22:18; possibly the first recorded incident of copyright law)

I am taking myself out of the world for awhile—forcing myself not to feed, not to play nursemaid to poor Gabriel or spend idle hours with the rest of the posse, or engage in voyeurism at Anastasia's window while she types away at her compatriots, so that I may better ready myself for what is to come, what is already solidifying itself in anticipation of the Time at Hand.

Lemme tell ya why:

While swimming in the cold acid of Iron Age peat bogs, I came across countless bodies of ancient sacrifice. Mummified bodies angelic in their sparseness and severity—only the barest essence of the physical body remained. The Bastard Bog of Matheson's *Hell House* must have been like this. Thru the spreading darkness I could see unwanted children blade-crouching in the bellies of mothers who could not keep secret their obstetric glee no matter that it meant their deaths at the hands of those who live for Secrets. In my remorse I slashed upon my arm 108 reasons for their demise until I was weak from the loss of blood, but I traveled deeper still, sharing Jung's fascination with the mystical bogs and hoping to bring Freud once more from his chair in a deep faint at the very mention of what I'd seen. On and on I went into the muck, past virgins and soldiers, chieftains and priests until I came upon the mossy spectre of a beautiful woman trapped within the living tentacles of the otherworldy plants that seemed utterly surreal in their ability to exist in such a hellish place. As I approached her, a slew of words rattled my skull—selkie, morgens, nixie, havfrau, veen, vedava, nereids, *mermaids*. She stared at me thru empty, yet familiar, eyes. In her hand she clutched the comb (in Greek *kteis*, or vulva) that was a portent of disaster in many cultures' tales of these virgins of the sea, although she had no fish's tail. Before I could turn away she mouthed the words "I am real. Do not doubt I am. And I need you to save me from *Him*."

I swam away in a fear that made the frigid water of the bogs seem warm.

I had seen those eyes before.

Her face I knew as well. The curls of flowing hair, the shape of her cheek.

She was the spirit who came forth from the flame at the Classical Wapurgisnacht in order to play Eris, the goddess of discord.

The one who dared to go against our rules and diverge from the script, if only in tone and not words.

Then I realized even more.

I had seen her visage in the works of Albrecht Dürer and countless other men of craft.

She was the Whore of Babylon the Bible bleats about.

How frail and desperate she looked… Nothing like the majestic queen the images portrayed, now that the seven heads of her fabled beast (once the pinnacle of her fame) had long since been decapitated and hung from Vatican walls.

So here I am in the Aegean, on the island of Patmos, sequestered with a sack of ancient scrolls in a cave not far from that of John the Evangelist, writer of Revelation and creator (so I had thought) of its vile little whore. Her words haunt me. It may take some time, but I will undo the knot.

What do I hope to gain? I can't say. I never can—I change moods and plans like a snake changes skin … like a slut changes boy-toys … like the ocean does the shore. I will attempt to unfold the symbols (there are over three hundred in Revelation[13] alone) that have been so carefully wedged and packed into these neatly columned texts in both their initial creation and in subsequent editions, despite John's warning to the contrary.

The easiest way to begin is to just dive on in (despite what happened in the bogs) and talk about whatever comes to mind as it relates to and weaves itself thru these mysterious and most likely insanely produced words—words that served as a pretext for the Knights Templar to go on the First Crusade against

---

[13]Notice the singular—there is no Revelation*s*—odd how a supposedly key book of such a *litura grandiosa* is often referred to wrong…

the Seljuk Turks and words that set the stage for Cornu's twisted machinations. But words, as we know, have a power almost immeasurable. After all, it's the words of some shadowy whore-ghost at the bottom of a bog that brought me here in the first place, and I know she is with me, leading me, even now, despite my best efforts to elude her.

No matter where on this island I hide, no matter how small the crevice or how deep the burrow, each morning when I awake, there are new scrolls to read and decipher, surrounded by the most delicate footprints and scented wisps of earth-kissed skin and leaf-moistened hair.

And yet, despite these favorable and deliberately left remnants, she scares me just the same.

As a way of Invocation and protection against the murderous ghosts and mad prophets I will no doubt encounter in this place (I sense she is not the only one who walks these rocky mountain paths), I turn for strength to the scrolls of the Essenes, The Brotherhood of Light. The organization that shaped and elevated Jesus in his work. The Essenes speak of the seven stars and seven candles of Revelation as angels of the Heavenly Father and Earthly Mother. It's a good start. Ancient wisdom. The raping of nature and the cutting down of the Tree of Life in Nebuchadnezzar's dream in the Book of Daniel is at the heart of the Essene metaphor. The Tree of Life, symbol of the Kabbalah, formed from Ezekial's visions. A symbol Black Elk and Leyton Walkingfeather could wrap their arms around. And something further, what I always believed until I looked into her eyes—that the whore of Babylon is nothing more than a metaphor for what Humans have done to the earth—ecologically, environmentally, politically, and if thought is energy, even spiritually, in the sense of mind gas and psychic pollution (JD Morrison—"What have they done to the earth? What have they done to our fair sister?"). But the spiritually pure will ride their white horses and redeem what has been lost. That's fine and fair to imagine—and all the more so because it has nothing to do with any devil or Antichrist. This is the cold bucket of reality that Parvus Cornu and his hordes could use in the face, but those who read the Essenes are a grain of sand compared to the endless beaches who read the Bible.

This is purely a matter of marketing, one of the Church's greatest tools.

As much as I'd love to rest my laurels on the Essene version of Revelation and leave the rest to a plethora of Percival Grayle-Groynes, I've read the evangelical take on Patmos Johnny's words as well—the Jehovah's Witnesses and Catholics and even Dante had and have their ideas and slants, especially on the meaning/identity of the Whore—and I find it wonderfully appealing that they all change around and reinterpret the words of a half-crazed would-be poet–prophet who was banished to a little island by Emperor Domitian around 81 AD *for daring to speak the word of God.* What does that say about their feelings as to the inviolability of His words? (As if anyone could possibly know what that colossal bag of light and ether means when he says anything, coming as he always has in fire and thunderheads and torrents of rain.) God *invites* interpretation—He enjoys keeping all his factions at war... It keeps them from getting lazy, from refraining to provide the daily sacrifice and weekly offerings. He likes a good metaphor, especially when the simpleminded confuse it with fact.

It's all He really has.

Revelation was created as a series of letters (circulated circa 96 AD) (which Patmos Johnny cleverly called "visions"—the product of 15 years in exile) sent to seven (note the number) churches in Imperial cities and centers of learning. It takes as its inspiration and model Daniel, a colorful book of visions, sort of like Joseph the dream-weaver's coat. Daniel was a shaman, wrapping himself in the spiritual tools of fasting, prayer, divination, and sackcloth. Johnny probably identified to the point of self-confusion with Daniel—after all, they were victims of Roman and Babylonian invasions of Jerusalem, respectively. PJ was appealing to a highly intellectual class of people with a myriad of complex symbols that the receivers could use to push forth their cause. Less than 30 years had passed since Jerusalem had been completely destroyed by the Romans after an unsuccessful political uprising on the part of the Jews, and only 20 or so since the massacre at the hilltop fortress at Masada. All that remains of the mighty temple in Jerusalem is the so-called Wailing Wall, and of Masada little more, so there was plenty for PJ and his friends to be pissed about where the Romans were concerned. Others have since taken up the cause—William Miller had half a million followers, and 7 million 7th Day Adventists and 4 million Jehovah's Witnesses take their inspiration from him. *11 million people* carrying the cross for a man who GOT IT WRONG. All of his predictions and calculations missed the mark. Shouldn't that be a clue that maybe John was nothing more than an angry, exiled zealot with a flair for the darkly poetic who should be read with that in mind? You have a shaman like Daniel interpreted by a madman who then sets down his warped visions and reworkings of Shaman Dan so that they can be further twisted by anyone wanting to show that God is on his group's side and everyone else is *doomed.*

What a fucking mess...

There are some items in Revelation I find interesting. For instance, it is wonderfully, aptly violent—the Human race at its bloodthirsty best. Such talk of swords and plagues and destruction. Also, in chapter 4, there is a courtroom containing 24 patriarchs—12 Old Testament patriarchs (a real fun bunch) and the 12 apostles. I say again—*12* apostles. That means that Judas is not only forgiven but holds a position of power, which is *what he wanted in the first place*. This shows that God loved Judas quite well and the ban in Germany on naming your child Judas can finally be lifted.

I'd stay away from Adolf though—just to be safe.

(Just 'cause I'm being somewhat scholarly doesn't mean I can't still fuck around...)

I like that Patmos Johnny used so many animals in Revelation. Animals are powerfully symbolic and are incredibly open to cultural and spiritual interpretation. We have lions, oxen, eagles (all taken from Ezekial), lambs, dragons, bears, and plenty of others.

And we have the horse—that creature of many colors and meanings in the Book of Revelation. The horse has fascinated forever—look at the demise of Catherine the Great, the hooplah of the Triple Crown, the story of Hidalgo, the myth of the super-potent centaur, and the Art—Job, Morrison's "Horse Latitudes," Pete Townshend's "Horse's Neck," Patti Smith's album "Horses," and Peter Schaffer's *Equus*. The great lures of man are all there—freedom, power, sex ... and the Book of Revelation doesn't disappoint. You have your four horsemen of the Apocalypse, those first four of the well-known seven seals—rich image there. White for the religious witness, red for universal war (enabled by technology—1 in 4 scientists work for war research, if the Jehovahs are believed), black for famine, and the pale horse for pestilence. But then there's one last white horse. The horse of the divinely clean and holy war, ridden by the White Prince himself. The heavenly sanctioned war. The death of the non-believer, the slaughter of the infidel. The kind of radical *jihad* the rest of the religious world pins on the Muslims, but which exists in all Fundamentalist patterns of thought, even in those of my precious Anastasia, the righteous Whalewatcher herself! Consider the Crusades, the warrior monks of medieval Japan, and the ongoing wars of the Middle East.

Revelation rolls along, setting up the scenarios, unveiling the first six seals and then there is silence in Heaven for 30 minutes.

What's going on? It may appear to be a mystery, but I have luckily had a vision of my own. I see the 24 judges, God, and the archangels all huddled around a widescreen plasma flatscreen watching an edited version of the Victoria Secret fashion show (without all the chit-chat)—the one that's all angel wings and tits, shorn crotches and tight little buns. Figure in some rewinding, slo-mo, and pause and you've got your 30 minutes. That's what I think.

That's the first of what I hope will be many insights that Patmos will have given me to share before I go.

Now here is where it gets a bit too real, but only because the Cornu is such a theatrical dolt. Chapter 8 goes on to say that it is at this time, while the hosts of Heaven are rubbing their silken robes to the swinging shapes of Heidi and the gals that Satan unleashes his minions, and makes an appearance as a world leader that is sort of a Frankenstein's monster made from Mao, Caesar, Alexander, Hitler, Nero, Ivan, Stalin—all the very Human creations of *Man*kind's penchant for power—the ones I believe the Cornu watched with a rivulet of drool sliding down his chin (I leave the women purposely out of this … for now). I really do think ole Parvus fancies himself the false prophet of Rev. 19:19–20, which has its genesis in Daniel's antichrist dream, which is where I found the name I've given him—the Little Horn. No lie. This tends to happen—look at that madman Manson and what he made of Revelation 9. (Not to be confused with "Revolution 9" from the Beatles.) But back to chapter 8 and onward, where Johnny inundates us with 7s—seven dooms, seven trumpets, seven angels, seven bowls, seven plagues... All these plagues and doomsday images and the Wormwood Star and all of it. A bit *too* theatrical, and not something the Hollywood blockbuster mindset would fall for any more. I hope the Cornu hasn't thought of that. If he wants to make an impression, he'll have to ratchet things up a bit. I mean, four angels killing a third of the population, that's some pretty serious shit, but given that the Mischievers are the closest thing Cornu has to Angels of Death, and AIDs and other mutant strains might very well kill *at least* that many, I see the numbers being more than a bit smaller on the Prince of Death's end. I don't really know the guy but I sense he has very little sense of scale.

Not like Patmos Johnny. He had grand ambitions. He wanted to be no less than on a scale with Ezekial—that's what that whole eat the scroll, it'll be good in your mouth but lousy in your stomach thing in chapter 10 is about. Ezekial of the wild vision of the four-headed angels with their chariot wheels, which some have called the earliest description of UFOs. Ezekial was a contemporary of Daniel's who really lived to see some shit—he served under Belshazzar, Darius, and Cyrus the Great. Rulers of two empires that figure mightily in the scheme of Daniel's book, in the form of the dreams of the mad king Nebuchadnezzar. Add the Greeks and the infamous Romans and the mystery of the giant statue is solved.[14]

Speaking of Daniel, the story of Belshazzar is one of my favorites, because I was there in the shadows as my old friend Lucifer fucked with a king. Such

---

[14] Are you checking this out or just taking my word for it? I wouldn't. I'm several weeks into a strict blood-fast and I'm haunted by a ghost of a biblical fiction who needs my help but won't tell me why, so if I were you I'd read it all first-hand, while keeping my text in mind.

palpable tension as Belshazzar called for the gold and silver cups his animal-maned, bird-feathered father had taken from the Temple in Jerusalem. How deeply he and his advisors and whores drank from them—cup after cup of perfumed wine, on and on they indulged themselves, praying to their heathen gods of substance and form until the hand appeared and wrote its words upon the wall: *Mene, Mene, Tekel, Parsin.*

It's always kind of irked me that I hadn't thought of it myself ... it was one of the great moments of intervention our kind have managed to muster, captured so exquisitely by Rembrandt van Rijn in his 1635 painting in oils. (Point of clarification—it wasn't fear that sent Belshazzar sprawling to the floor as the hand came forth, but the copious amounts of wine. He was as foolishly prideful and strong as an ancient king could be.) His conjurers, diviners, and enchanters couldn't read the writing (surprised?), so the queen called in the old wise man, Shaman Dan, who readily obliged, denying the proffered prize initially but taking it in the end.

He told the king that *Mene* meant that God had numbered the days of his reign and had brought it to an end. Not the best of news. And all the worse considering it had supposedly been written twice. In truth, I can't recall, but rhythmically, it works. *Tekel* meant that he had been weighed and had been found wanting. Amazing considering all the meat and wine he had consumed. Then there was *Parsin*, meaning that Belshazzar's kingdom would be divided among the Medes and Persians.

He was killed that night, and Darius the Mede immediately took his place.

Mystical, huh? Not really. For anyone living in Babylon with even the slightest idea of the politics at work at the time the writing was already "on the wall." Even before ole Lucifer wrote it out.

Now to return to Revelation and its key passages (at least with regard to my current circumstances)—chapter 17. Babylon's painted whore appears. She's been the subject of more scholarship and theorizing than any other part of Revelation. Who is she? What city or set of peoples does she truly represent? At first glance it is somewhat of a no-brainer that *of course* she'd be from Babylon—Rome would be way too obvious (though most of the metaphors in the book refer *directly* to Rome's emperors, past and present), and both empires had had the audacity to sack Jerusalem. The Babylonians were quite the pagans—into all kinds of blasphemies about soul survival, polytheism, talking with the dead, idols, spells—truly the devil's work. (I must mention, in fairness to the cuckoos, that *Jerusalem herself* has also been identified as the whore. It's where they killed the Christ, so they say. Some of these whackjobs quote the old and new testaments to make their case. On a continuum of overblown nonsense this might just take the cake. But if you consider that God punished Jerusalem for allying itself with tyrants, one could say that if Jerusalem wasn't the whore it certainly received a good vaginal cleansing.) But I have to think that PJ had Egypt in mind as well, being that Pharaoh Neco was the one who led his armies against those of the beloved King Josiah of Judah. Once Josiah was dead, killed near Har Megiddo (better known as Armageddon, the gathering place of the kings of the apocalypse), Jerusalem was easy prey for Babylon. Lots of choices among so many wicked enemies. So make the whore from a wicked city, and make her good and drunk (on the blood of saints no less—the cursed vampiress consuming the innocents), freshly painted and ready for a fuck. Greed and power riding on the back of the 7-headed, 10-horned beast, the world political machine (at the time revealed as the rulers of Rome)—but more generally all the horrors and travesties we've all come to know. How the Roman Empire seduced kings with riches and a little bit of power retained. How the Nazis seduced the Catholic Church. How, in 1920, Mussolini gave the Vatican its sovereign statehood. How intelligence agencies set up puppet governments and encourage rebellions in third-world countries. And, metaphorically or not, there is always a pretty lady behind the power play. The emperor's consort, the Lady Macbeths and Jezebels and all the rest—even Lady Liberty herself. A nice pair of tits can be more persuasive than an Uzi any day of the week. So we have our whore. The seduction of booze and sex and notoriety that rules politics in all spheres. The wicked woman who led the murderous Cain to build his city and Babel to build their tower and who led modern empires to build their monuments to capitalism and commerce as well.

So, in the end, maybe the whore does get undone (like in any story that caters to the false-morality masses), but then in chapter 21 a nasty thing takes place. There is talk of a *new* Jerusalem, a city of precious stones, glass, and pearls—the very adornments the whore herself once wore. So, if a city is a woman as I've heard the poets say, then the whore is merely unseated by her replacement—not a better alternative but a more cleverly disguised one—another illusion of choice, the very fuel that runs the machine of the pseudo-democracies that currently rule the planet—a mass of men so proud they would no doubt call their conquerors slaves and consider their own shaved heads and dragging chains a clever subterfuge.

Sheep looking for a shepherd, but which horse will he ride?

A sad truth: It takes an enemy at the gates for the night watchmen to feel afraid enough to truly earn their coin, and they have fallen fast asleep.

I'm getting closer to some semblance of the shape of things. It has been over a month since I came here and the scrolls have long since stopped appearing and the ghosts all seem at rest. I had plenty of visitations—writhing prophets, howling kings, even a spectral Patmos Johnny stood outside my cave but never dared to enter—but not once did I see the Whore, though I felt her near me, growing stronger as I read and thought and wrote.

I know these ancient texts are nothing by themselves. They are visions and illustrations, warnings and prophecies long since come to fruition (or not), and like the rest of the Bible, unique to the context of the times in which they were written. They are, in that way, no different than Dante's *Divine Comedy*. Like any other spiritual, religious, or philosophical system, if you remove the context the symbols lead nowhere but to speculation and, eventually, madness. (The Hopi have a detailed philosophy of the Three Shakings of the Earth and have symbolically "proven" that the first two have already come to pass and they know the harbinger of the third; if you see a "house in the sky," run like hell—especially if you're a witch and the girl in the window is holding a dog.) Isaac Newton spent much of his time trying to decipher the prophecies of Revelation alongside his interest in alchemy and I think he would have had a better chance of turning lead into gold than coming up with any definitive answers. He certainly faired no better than William Miller in unlocking the supposed secrets PJ's letters contain. Fact is, there are none. If it wasn't for the beliefs of countless millions and Parvus Cornu's clever manipulation of those beliefs and his manufactured role within the picture that they paint, I never would have taken all this time and space to work it thru the filter of what can only be defined as *his specific context*.

So here's what I think:

The Little Horn will bide his time as the world loses the last clinging remnants of its conscience in the mounting tides of war and corporate interests. He's no pimple-headed fool who goes home and whacks off to Deathmetal and his father's porn because he was jilted at the prom after springing for a sharp tux and rented car. Oh no—no impotent threats and impotent cock from this one. He's more like that very rare and precious bastard who bides his time and builds the better bomb with a recipe from the Internet and then makes a wordless but very loud statement at the high school graduation. This isn't about some paltry tug of war for Human souls or some spurned brother trying to flex his muscle and merely make a point. I've been misplaying the entire thing—thinking it was a war when it's really a *usurpation*. Parvus Cornu doesn't give a shit about souls—I've become just human enough to have stupidly bought into that particular pile of dung. It wasn't God's will that Alexander the Great, Napoleon, and Hitler didn't succeed—it was the Cornu's. Think about it—sitting in that black hole of his, watching everything that went on, he had to have known that once the world is dominated by a single human being, all that the Sole Conqueror would have left to conquer is Heaven and Hell, and he certainly couldn't risk one of these masterful men tramping on his turf. So just before they were ready to make that last great move, he beat them down and defeated them, eating up their considerable energy and storing it until he was ready to pass out of the Event Horizon and back into the game. Perhaps he had some version of the Mischievers already at work in their ranks, making bad suggestions, losing key maps…

Here's something else—having them fight all those wars wasn't just about politics by other means—CS Lewis was right. If humanity lost its faith in its farce because of a stupid thing like war, that faith wouldn't have been worth a dime bag full of pencil shavings. He must have seen where all of these warriors were heading as far as the development of technology to wage the *better* war, so he let them do their thing until the next step in the Technological Evolution of warfare was achieved. Not long after Hitler rose to power, the development of sophisticated electronics and machinery became a worldwide phenomenon. And if you're wondering why the *products* of war are more important than *war itself*, think about those bumper stickers PTAs pass out asking what it would be like if the Department of Defense had to have a bake sale every time they needed a bomb. It's the human preoccupation with *preparing* for war that has led in large measure to the economic inequality of the world. The increasing reliance on Technology has made God virtually meaningless, which has made Heaven increasingly ripe for a quiet, hostile takeover. With each new invention, each self-congratulating pat on Mankind's collective back, the tables have turned a little more. Parvus Cornu is a being of great ego and intelligence who now wants the utter Revenge of watching God *fall*.

He's been laughing uproariously at me and Lucifer and all the rest of the wayward fallen angels trying to get *back* while all the while he's trying to get *in*. The time of waiting is over and he wants the whole glob—Heaven, Hell, and everything in between, but it's best for him if you never know it's done. When the strongest leaders have been revealed he will move to destroy the truly spiritual, as it says in Daniel—the pure-hearted saints who do indeed dwell among and within you, and I'm sure he'll try and make a move to death-fuck all the angels who rise up and fly down to aid them. He'll count on God and Lucifer sitting back and doing zilch. He'll spend some time meeting in secret with the most easily corruptible of the world's leaders before seeking to undo God himself. How? By becoming his *replacement*—hence the New Jerusalem. A new likeness at the center of the Universal dollar. A quiet usurping during the chaos of an accurately manufactured and exquisitely portrayed Armageddon (courtesy of me and mine), not at all like the flashy showdown between the Big Two Hollywood always shows. A knife at the throat, a stout length of chain, a deep, dark hole, and a new God's enthroned. It'd be far better for him if the mindless minions continue to crowd the Earth, worshipping Technology and trying to puzzle out their own expansion and proliferation into the solar system. All that attention and energy focused toward him—if you know his name or not he doesn't care. It's all about the attention and energy you share. You'll almost be trading up even—God for God. With one minor difference—Cornu won't subscribe to any bullshit thoughts of Free Will. He'll have his way and have it in spades. He will be the risen king of Revelation, and like any would-be king he's searching for his queen; in kabbalistic *Zohar* terms, a Shekhinah for his Tiferet/Metatron—

Babylon's whore at the bottom of the bog.

This is clearly a case of Dr. Cornustein looking to *make* his bride, rather than find a girl who'll take him freely, as I am trying to do. Similar things have been tried before. So that's the help the whore-ghost needs. Whoever she *really* is—tortured spirit, ancient Hagatha witch, Pandora or Eris or forgotten virgin saint—because I know that she merely chose a form she knew I'd not ignore, not realizing it's *exactly what he wants*. She's been hiding from him, seeking an ally in me, of all the angels she could pick. She drew me to her for sure. And all to get me looking at these scrolls, these ancient texts of dream and myth and the tattered cords of fact. Pulling me toward the prophets, true and false—Daniel, Ezekial, John of Patmos. Obadiah. Seeking the parallels in a collection of books I no longer thought applied. Edom vs. Judah. The people of Esau vs. the people of Jacob. How the mountain city of Petra fell to the Babylonian king Nebuchadnezzar for its rulers' transgressions. God loved to punish the Jews for their bad alliances and dalliances with other gods as much as anyone, and he, being God, was far more destructive and pissy about it than any mortal king could be. The patterns of Dominion weave in and out of this. The beautiful white horse at the end of Revelation struck down and implanted with Pete Towshend's "snake the size of a sewer pipe living in its rib cage." Will Cornu take from the prophets their visions or will he instead drive them mad with false revelations, as God may have done to Patmos Johnny? There's plenty of that among the New Agers and Millennialists, and the modern monks you *used to* see in Times Square. Who will be the ones to don a sack of ashes and make their stand? I know that the whore-ghost wants it to be me, but if I lie in the city streets howling and writhing like Ezekial, I'd be carried away, locked in a tower of padded walls and numbing injections. Electric shock. No one listened to Jeremiah or Ezekial, messengers of God though they were, so who the hell's gonna listen to me, supposed spawn of the dark end of the spectrum that I am? I can play the Baphomet but I cannot play the angel of God.

But I know she won't relent and I'd find her if she did.

As much as I don't want to, I have to keep her safe.

I've returned to the Badlands, to seek healing in the ways that I have learned, having left Patmos and her mysteries blessedly behind. Leyton Walkingfeather, the shaman ghost fast becoming my closest friend, was waiting when I arrived.

That's right—another ghost. It seems I am surrounded by them now.

She is close by, but it is not yet time for us to speak. We both agree on that.

I have decided to call her Tatyana, a long-forgotten daughter of Baba Yaga, the bony-legged witch. It is clear to me now that she is no whore, and will never concede to be, for Parvus Cornu or anyone else.

And the role that I am to play in her protection just may be my greatest tale of all.

Sitting in my sweat lodge, I see in my mind a grey horse standing in a grove of mystic myrtle, singing to the winds of the Horn and the Hammer, the Feather and the Fool. He shakes his mane within the rays of the sun and eats of the new grass.

He is not afraid of his many-colored brothers.

He is mine to ride.

I had returned to the Black Hills to undertake the Sun Dance ceremony, *Wiwanyag Wachipi*, with Leyton Walkingfeather and the spirits of other Holy Men long past. It was late July, and the temperature was well over 100 degrees.

To the side of the arena stood a ceremonial tipi where we dressed in the kilt skirt and sage bracelets and anklets that we would wear during the four days of the Sun Dance. This was done following a sweat lodge ritual, during which I had agreed to undergo the piercing that would take place on the fourth day, after Leyton spoke on my behalf. The brief and respectful discussion that followed was ended when an ancient Oglala named Limping Bear, who would serve as the ceremonial Chief, quietly said:

"*Piasa* or no, this demon has a soul. Shall we not try to redeem it?"

As we walked toward the arena to the rhythmic heartbeat of the drums and the singing of the women, Leyton handed me an eagle-bone whistle and a *chanupa lutah*, a pipe of red stone. We were led by Singing Wolf, who carried a buffalo skull in his scarred and weathered hands. Beside him was a Lakota woman in a beaded white dress, who was the first to enter the sacred circle where we would dance. Upon entering the arena she danced a full circle around the cottonwood tree at its center.

The previous day, a party of fellers had gone into the woods to select the cottonwood, and one of the women among them, representing Buffalo Calf Woman, made the ceremonial first cut before they lowered and transported the tree to the arena in the prescribed way. I was told by Leyton that it was this woman who now danced. They then created the bower of pine boughs that would shade us between dances. (Being that none of the Dancers were of this world, this was for ceremonial reasons only.) They had buried a *chanupa* in the hole in the center of the arena before inserting the tree and once the cottonwood had been erected and secured they dressed it with banners in the colors of the four directions, *Topa Tate*, and of Mother Earth and Father Sky, and rawhide cutouts of a buffalo and human. They then affixed twelve chokecherry branches, symbolizing the twelve moons.

When the Lakota woman, whose face I could not see, had made her circuit, we entered the arena, moving clockwise to pay honor to the four directions, beginning with the East, *Wiyoheyapa*. When we had completed our loop, we presented our pipes to Singing Wolf beneath the shaded bower. He placed them upon a rack at the foot of the cottonwood tree and placed the buffalo skull before it, and we began to dance.

For three days and nights the ceremony progressed, the ten dancers taking no rest.

As the sun rose on the morning of the fourth day, Leyton and the others painted a crow upon my chest and several marks upon my back and I was led to a bed of sage. It was the time of the piercing. Limping Bear produced a sharp knife and made two incisions in my chest, thru which he placed an awl, in thru the first cut and out thru the second. He had gone no deeper than the skin and the pain was easily borne. Then I was called upon to give him the wooden peg, sharpened at one end, called the *canwi yuza waopo*.

"Crow Shadow, he is who is as yet without form, do you willingly undertake this journey?" he asked without speaking.

"*Hetch etu aloh*," I replied, trying not to wince as Limping Bear inserted the sharpened peg into the wound. It was a hot, searing pain, cleansing to the mind, and I welcomed it.

Had Jesus felt like this when the nails went in? Did he find the pain welcoming—cleansing, part of the path he chose?

I think he must.

While I focused my mind by concentrating on the sound of my breath, Limping Bear attached the end of a coiled rope onto a leather thong he had affixed to the ends of the *canwi*. As I was helped to my feet and gently supported as my legs regained their strength, the lone female dancer came forward, a ceremonial garland of sage and eagle feathers in her hands.

It was Tatyana.

Without speaking, she placed the crown upon my head and led me to the arena as Leyton took his place on the bed of sage.

When all ten pierced dancers were once more within the circle, we began to blow upon our eagle-bone whistles (which had been made from the left wing, nearest the heart), moving to and from the tree four times in the sacred manner as the drums were beaten with a renewed volume and insistency. I glanced back at Tatyana, who smiled sadly and turned away as we began to lean back, putting pressure on the ropes, all solidly tied to the cottonwood and our pegs. As the *canwi* began to slowly tear away the skin that held it I slowed my breath and prayed for a vision.

After several minutes the pain began to free my inner mind and I saw the Old Gnarled Tree from Anastasia's dream.

The males that constituted the bulk of this apelike tribe were sitting in and swinging from the branches of the weathered tree, beating their crude crosses against its cracked and oozing trunk while two females—the one who had been nursing the growling infant and the one who had defended the banished elder—fought among the undulating roots.

Both were bloodied and tired—the fight had gone on for hours—maybe days—and I sensed that it was fast coming to an end.

Then, from out of the brush came the elder. In his hand he held a key.

The key I knew so well.

Anastasia's.

As he came forward, the female who had defended him opened her mouth to speak.

It was then that I fell backwards as the skin of my chest gave way and as the vision dimmed I watched the blood-dressed peg fly up into the air and out of the arena, its sacred purpose served.

I knew what the female was going to say.

I had to see Father Joe.

Vexilla Regis prodeunt inferni [The banners of the king of Hell draw closer] (Dante's *Inferno*)

Fick oder kaput. (Graffiti from a prison wall in East Berlin, 1986)

I saw Father Joe.

And then I got royally fucked up.

More on him later.

One way or another, it's time for me to spew.

The only way I could deal with what he told me (preceded by what I *saw*) was to find the most loaded guy I could get my hands on and sink my teeth into his neck as fast as I could. Lucky for me, you can always find a user near a church… I closed my mind, bared my fangs, and drank the bastard dry. Whatever he was using it was laboratory based and potent as hell 'cause now I'm in some kind of seafood/porno/sex–induced rapture I can't volley with or tame. It's hitting orbs at my inner core with frightening velocity and accuracy and I can't move a psychic muscle to guard myself against its refusing-to-decrescendo derriere dance of epic scope and pressing insistence, complete with sticky palms, raspberry parfait, and an orangutan's Fuck-n-Shred disposition. A Raoul Duke/Dr. Gonzo-esque escapade in an organ-cracking carnival ride. In the midst of all the madness, I've decided it's time to pursue a vocation, and my schedule has been full. I've no (formal) license to practice ass-holistic medicine, yet there I see it hang, my neon shingle, just beyond the fuzzy yellow fog of bombardment: *Dr. Forthright's House of Melancholy Volume.* Talk therapy. Buzz and hum. Gelatin rolling on a couch of emu bone. Lay it all out in a black trail of parental misperceptions and lousy dates. Self-molestation and dinner-puking. Voyeurism and addiction to streaming cum shots on the desktop–laptop tandem. Compulsions and revulsions. Frights and over-confidences. Complexes and archetypes and the commandeered names of classical Greek tragedy. Mothers to fuck and fathers to kill and fantasies to sort and file. How I got set up in this gig I can't recall. The genesis memories are little pieces of puzzle spread out on a chipped Formica counter without benefit of having the boxtop picture for guidance.

 Not long after my return from exile, and before I had a chance to go and see the Good Priest, Orlando Nepenthe, cockeyed Nephilim and freak-about-town, mentioned something about a vacant office in a medical complex, so here I am. Special billing as an "After Hours Mental Health Clinic—Cause Crazy doesn't care that the work day's 9–5." I've always felt an ache for those poor fucks who have a psychotic episode around 9 o'clock at night and get stuck talking on the phone to some college intern more freaked out by their *own* immediate experience than the person's calling. So the line's been out the door. My form of brief therapy seems to meet a need. No application, no need for compensation—and they're guaranteed cured in a single session. I'd love to tell you how it's done, but then you'd all be hanging out the shingle and inviting me to come talk at Association conferences and write articles for all the important journals and that's a bit too mainstream for a roving sport like me. I will say it's the social sciences equivalent of the college parlor trick of rubbing some chick's temples to absorb her headache into the fiber of your soul to relieve her tension in the off chance she might rub *your* head and thereby relieve yours. If you still don't get the gist, seek me for a session. But don't delay—I am way too much of a *sponge* to make this gig long term—too easily filled with Others' psycho vibes. That's what's happening now—complete psychic cross-wiring from an eclectic mix of classic textbook cases—all jumbled and misclassified from years of formally trained therapists crammed into the tiny blue-jean crotch pocket of the pharmaceutical companies. Thoughts all the more pointed and invasive thru mislabeling. And, being an all-hours kind of operation, I get some majorly fucked up whack-nuts in here. A brief clinical sample from earlier tonight:

NUT: "Dr. Forthright, is it normal to wanna fuck your cat?"
ME: "Sure. Only *actually fucking it* is indicative of a psychological schism."

That always brings a deep release of breath and a wonderful smile of relief.
You see, I believe *Intent* is a gun full of blanks without *Execution*.
In other words, *Think* about the twisted things all you want—who you wanna kill or fuck or what you wanna possess or how you wanna behave when the curtains are drawn and the camera is rolling—the more unapologetically fucked up the thoughts the healthier you are, cause the thoughts come, bidden or not. Hell yeah they do—and you'd better let 'em dance around in that free space you've got between the ears and legs, or you might find yourself in a Southern county legislature with a KKK hood in one hand, a bootleg copy of *Kiddie Porn Fiesta* in the other (hand-delivered by a minister on his way to give Last Rites), Scripture in your teeth, and an aching bulge just below your bible-beltbuckle. One of those Jesus on a Harley mixed motifs that only work when etched on cheap metal objects. Damned if I can show you the way to your personal version of Heaven, but I know it's not thru the Three "Shuns"—repression, suppression, and oppression. That last one is tricky—oppress the shadow self and it becomes the ever-enslaving slave. So let those ponies ride.
Fantasies are our friends.
Say it with me.
Fantasies are our friends.
Consider yourself cured.
And you didn't need a pill.

Three weeks in and I'm still at it. Stick-to-it-ness seems to be my stock and trade of late. Still seeing patients, though the work makes me as bristly and ready to howl as Gardner's *Grendel* waiting in the snow outside Hrothgar's meadhall. I too can scare the lean wolves on days like this. I've a mind to, too. Tree-crash my way down to Gabriel's oak and chase his companions far into the night. I've lost patience with him—revenge has been exacted and still he wails like the silver cornet he so loves to hear. He could "move on" if he wished—the debts have been settled, but now he regrets not taking care of it himself, more directly.

My mistake there—I thought telling him about the blood-exchange thru the wolves would clear his way to rejoining his dead wife, but No—just the opposite.

Some people are impossible to please.

Screw him—let him wail. I've a mind to speak of Grendel. We are brothers of a sort—misunderstood, malformed monsters cursed with a much too active mind. We've so much in common I wonder if our father might have been the same. He had his Dragon and I have my Crow. Both of us had mothers we loathed, and Muses unable to be possessed. Me, my precious Anastasia and Grendel his Wealtheow (although I have never actually *touched* Anastasia—nor have I ever thought of abducting and/or murdering my target of impossible affection—although I'm thinking that might change, but it has everything to do with Fr. Joe and I'm still not ready to talk about it). The beauties to our Beasts—the missing pieces to our broken circles of Hope. So much in common, he and I—and perhaps the most painful commonality being our vicious, rabid, and ultimately easy conquests for blood and flesh, which leave us both more empty than if we would simply starve. Violence elevated to Art. Lunching on priests we've first toyed with to our immeasurable joy. Cursed creatures of intellect, screaming fat derision at the sky and envying the dumbest of Earth's countless beasts. What would Grendel think of Gabriel St. A., coming from the mud each night in a cycled, circular ritual of Impotent Inaction? He would have let him wallow in his own dire truths, as he did Unferth. We share a certain Existentialism, though I know that nothing is an accident—and yet nothing's ever planned. His mentor-Dragon sought to teach him that. What has my trickster-Crow ever tried to teach me other than to eat the shit the bad Lord provides? He only scolds and says "Do it again, dolt!" marking my errors in sprawling red ink without providing a single clear Instruction on how to do it *Right*. Then again, lots of what Grendel's dragon told him was pseudo-scientific bunk. I would have told him to kiss my ass in the first session. Nihilism doesn't interest me (though I have engaged in the greatest of nihilistic acts—killing my Ma); it's as unimaginative and creatively impotent as Atheism or the razor-thin mindsets of those who think Humans are the only intelligent life in the Universe. *Least* intelligent is the better bet, but that's nothing new from me.

So, in the final assessment, I can only say this about brother-Grendel and I: no matter how much alike two creatures are, they aren't much alike at all—not in how and who they handle and how they let most everyone handle them.

Grendel seemed to have it all figured out and was ultimately duped. Being that I came out of the gates as Prince Duped himself, perhaps I can see this thru without having to forfeit my "life."

Isn't that why we read another's words?

I can't put it off any more.

It's time to tell you about my meeting with Father Joe.

I knew he'd be at St. Bart's, holding court with some follower or another who was smart enough to bring a pack of smokes and a bottle of Ernest and Hoolio.

The follower was there.

I had almost figured she would be.

There through the basement window I watched as Father Joe poured over the pages of a beat-up old Bible with Anastasia. On the other side of the room, a young priest I had never seen before was loudly slamming away at a computer keyboard, the familiar wallpaper of Michael casting Lucifer out of Heaven surrounding the text box cluing me to the fact that it was Anastasia's cyber-group to which he wrote.

Whalewatcher_1, I've found your ass at last.

None of this was much of a surprise. In my sun-dance vision, right before I fell, I had heard a single word from the apelike female's lips.

Father.

And there was something about it—something in the tone and the way her eyes softened as she said it that made me realize all the meanings it contained.

Most of which Anastasia knew nothing at all about.

I concentrated in the honk and traffic night to hear better what they said.

Let me summarize, rather than share it word for word.

Father Joe was the one she had been typing about the night I saw her dream—the one "bound and corded"—the one she called their "savior."

He was the one to lead the revolution to a stronger, more intolerant church.

Turns out the young priest was a fellow Jesuit Joe had turned slowly to his cause from his position in the Diocese home office. Another strict devotee of the Elder Laws who had gotten fed up with the softening of the dogma and the continuing gap between the Shepherd and his pampered and all-too-easily forgiven sheep. It all came to a head one Sunday morning when the young priest, Father Tom, had filled in for the Youth Bible studies teacher after she had stayed out too late on a Saturday night (drinking to excess, sad to say, at a late night social in the basement of St. Bart's).

He was ready to begin the class when one of the kids—a fat, pimply bore with the last name Spork—raised his hand.

Fr. Tom: "Must you speak now, Francis? I am ready to begin our prayer."

Spork: "Sorry Father. It's just that in the nice weather we usually have class outside. Miss Jones lets us."

Fr. Tom: "Why on earth would she do that? We just renovated this wonderful room."

Spork: "Miss Jones says that the wonder and majesty of God is best experienced out in nature, rather than in here, in some oppressive and grandiose church that is built to such overblown scale to remind us how small and unworthy we all are."

That did it for Father Tom. The words and syntax used by Spork were nothing like the boy's own. Miss Jones was trying to lead the flock away, and she was doing it by rote.

That's the Church's turf, not to be used by the laypeople they reluctantly had to hire.

As he played the sentence over and over in his head while the class sat and stared, whatever small piece of him that had been resisting leaving the Diocese and joining Father Joe was finally and inexorably squashed. They did *not* have class outside that day—instead they recited the *Salve Regina* for three solid hours while their parents waited angrily outside the locked door.

Afterward, he left before he was asked to go.

But he came back to St. Bart's that night, and had been there or hiding out with Father Joe ever since.

Before I could delve more deeply into his mind, he finished his missive with a final series of emphatic key-swapps, ran the spellcheck (he had made no mistakes), hit Send, and shut the PC down.

A few words were exchanged between he and Father Joe and it was agreed that he would walk Anastasia home.

When she hugged him goodbye, Father Joe looked sad, as if she were taking a part of him with her.

No sooner had they left than he opened a new bottle of wine and grabbed a pack of Camels.

"You don't smoke in front of the flock, eh?" I asked, entering the room as the door slammed shut and the automatic locking mechanism engaged.

"I thought I sensed you."

"You wish."

"So now you know."

Did I sense relief?

"I have a feeling there's plenty more."

I sat beside him, in the chair Anastasia had abandoned, my skin flushing as it hungrily absorbed the warmth of the energy she had left. "And also that you're more than willing to tell."

Exhaling a series of smoke rings while he ran his finger around the lip of his glass, Father Joe smiled. "You should be careful what you wish for, Planner. I might just oblige, and I'm not sure you can handle what I'm about to share."

"Try me."

"Very well," he said, getting up and going to a bookshelf I had often considered but never perused. "How much do you know about the origins of alchemy?"

"I know plenty—but you know that. Do we have to indulge in games? You fucking priests, with your riddles…"

"I can see the devil's got you in an ill humor tonight—you've an excess of black bile."

"Ah," I said, settling in for what I knew would be a very long evening. "So we're to talk of Galen tonight? Very well—melancholy I am. And you are positively sanguine."

"Indeed, I am," he laughed, grabbing several books and returning to his chair. "You've read these texts, I'm sure." He spread out on a table beside him several facsimiles of well-known alchemical texts: Geber's *Summa Perfectionis*, Andreas Libau's *Alchemia*, the *Rosarium Philosophorum*, various handbooks from the Hermetic Order of the Golden Dawn, and biographies of Paracelsus, Albertus Magnus, Roger Bacon, Nicolas Flamel, Avicenna, and Newton.

"I have—many times. But, alas, I have to repeat myself—*you know that*."

"I just want to make sure we understand each other, Planner," he said. "So that we can skip the details and get to what's important. I have also studied these texts."

"Your heresy knows no bounds."

"Everything I do," he said, stubbing out his cigarette with more than a little excessive force, "everything I have *always* done, is in the service of God, and his Holy Church. We want the same things, you and I—that's why I allowed you to find me."

"Tell me about Anastasia—I know she is more to you than just a disciple—and somewhere deep inside she knows it too."

"Consider this line of questioning carefully, Angel of Darkness. I am willing to tell you the truth of things, but once I do, there will be no turning back."

Christ almighty. I needed enlightenment and he was writing bad movie dialogue. I wished he'd hurry up and get drunk—at least then he sounded more like a mere mortal and less like an Instrument of God.

"Let me make this easy for you, Father," I answered. "She's your daughter—and I don't mean that in any metaphorical sense—and further, she plays a much larger part in your plans for a Theological Revolution than she knows. How am I doing so far?"

"You're so damned smug," he said, obviously rattled that I had figured out so much. "But you don't know it all. Have you ever wondered why you aren't able to go to her—to enter her window in the night and fill her with your heat the way you have done to so many others? It's because even you, even a wayward fallen angel with very little soul, would dare not lay with his own relations."

"What the hell are you talking about?" I asked, shifting in my chair. "If you think you're *my* father, you're out of your fucking Jesuit mind."

"You know better than that. Agnes Roberta Buntz is the familial connection you share."

Careful what you wish for, he had said.

Fuckin'-A right.

"I can see from your reaction that you know my words are true," he said. "That should make the rest of this go a little easier. Are you familiar with the story of the so-called Babylon Working?"

I was indeed. And I didn't like what it meant for the conversation in which we were now engaged.

"So, what?—you intend to use Anastasia to bring forth some special child?" I asked, more than a little shocked that the pay-off was so lame. "You have to know that those OTO clowns were nuts. Maybe you understand the true meaning of alchemy—the joining of the sacred feminine and masculine and the transformation it provides—but you also have to know it's mostly all a *metaphor* for the joining of the male and female that reside inside the soul."

"Your gift for spiritual interpretation is impressive. But you're so lost in your Reasoning that you once again circle the truth but fail to peg it," Father Joe said, pouring himself another glass of wine and draining it in a single swallow. "The deed is already done. The girl you call Anastasia—whose mother and I named Elsbeth—is the product of a divine union between Sister Agnes and I."

"You're as mad as the rest of them," I said, surprised at how un-surprised I was by what he and Mother Buntz had done and how crazy and useless to me he actually was.

"All prophets and seers have been deemed mad, but I had a vision—and a visitation—when I was at Seminary where all was told to me. You will have it too, Planner, when the time is right. For now, this is all you need to know—Elsbeth is a Warrior of God. I took sole responsibility when Sister Agnes proved unworthy of the task—a tale you will also someday hear—and have taught her to walk the twin paths of Chastity and Righteousness. Her adoptive mother has never told her the truth, and never shall. She is one with our cause. Our followers are everywhere. I trust that you won't tell her either. She will learn the full meaning of her life when the time for the battle is near."

What could I possibly say?

As I walked out into the desolate night I heard the empty wine bottle fall to the floor and the cork of another being removed.

If only I could escape so easily from the truth of what he and Buntz had done.

Not able to calm my mind any other way, despite the drug-blood I had ingested after our meeting, I thought-journeyed to the house where I had last left Byron and his pals.

The ledger-scribbling Jacob Scrooge was there, scowling as before.

"Do you have an appointment?" (...not bothering to look up)

"I want to see Blake and Byron—may I go up?"

"They're not here." (annoyed sniffle) "They came only because you were coming. There are others waiting now."

(awkward silence) "May I go up?"

"Well, they aren't coming *down*."

Choking back an apt retort, I launched myself onto the ornately carved banister and, digging into the wood with my toenails, moved swiftly upward and into the main hall. The commingled smells of pipe tobacco, recent sex, aged sherry, and burnt quail filled my nose as I entered a room where last time there had been a wall.

The smoky chamber was full of drunken debauchers and their whores—carnivores at the feast. The very rabble who shadow-engineered the French Revolution and used its bloodsoaked cushions for their playground of increasing moral see-sawing, their great debauchery a grim resurrection of the Roman emperors who masked their political insecurities with elaborate shows of moral disregard. Books were burning in the half dozen fireplaces spaced around the room (all but those of Barbey d'Aurevilly, which were well thumbed and plentifully underlined), even as new ones, full of lewd sketches and false stories of the Revolution's heroes, were being writ. Shackled priests scribed pages of decency laws in the middle of the decadence, pausing their quills only long enough to snatch a scrap of fish or chicken from the jaws of roaming dogs. Decadence is truly the purview of the rich and elite, whose advanced breeding and carefully cultivated intellects allow them to maintain full morality in their public lives even while swimming in the deep waters of bestial carnality behind closed doors.

Presiding over the partygoers was none other than the Marquis de Sade (I bet you saw that coming), resplendent (I choose the word purposefully) in a bloodstained nightshirt and tattered slippers. I noticed that the fourth nail of his right hand was an inch longer than the others, and had been well used of late.

De Sade, the once-soldier and prisoner of conscious perversion who was transferred out of the Bastille just ten days before the Revolution. Arrested and institutionalized over and over for his sexual indiscretions and debts. An extremist buffoon who seemed incredibly anxious to talk to one the likes of me.

"Enter, demon," he said, covering his arm in wine as he waved his glass. "Someone lick this off at once—the inheritance from my father mustn't go to waste!"

Several of the guests snapped to his command—men and women alike.

He barely met my gaze as he spoke—doing so only as he inserted himself into the ass of a girl who looked no more than 14.

"You smell like a philosopher," he said, adjusting his position for maximum depth. "Chew on this… What is more Evil, eh—my supposedly sinister art or the real events that inspire it? I capture in ink for the book and stage what I know to happen in the libraries and drawing rooms of this entire fist-fucked land. Can a book or painting serve to corrupt an Innocent as has been the age-old accusation or is it merely the water and sun that sprout the waiting seed? Come to that, what is it that holds the *essence* of Evil—is it your horned and twisted form [All eyes on me now] or He that has cursed you with it? Is it the sun or the seed? The father or his newly conceived child? If this girl enjoys the pain, as her grip upon me says, is it really pain at all? Cut a rose to give to a sister of the Church and still it dies. If you stay with it long enough, it all comes back to God, eh?"

He thought I'd be impressed. He should only know a little of what *I've* done.

So should you all.

I've shared a lot, but held some back as well.

I left the room as he began to cum.

That was more than I could bear.

Perversion and subversion, being as they are in the eye of the beholder, bring to mind the pointed spikes of double standards and the boiling hypocrisy that is found on every corner of every city street (not to mention what I'd recently learned of the sexual coupling of a *priest* and a *nun*). True to my mode of therapy, I will say that suppression somewhere along the line is the overlooked symptom in almost all cases, leading to an explosion of raping disregard manifest in the infamous Marquis. It is the intemperate acting out for *acting out's sake*, as I have been known to do, that renders the beginning point of reaching for some semblance of freedom totally moot.

I'm giving up my practice.

As my temporary "colleagues" always say—"You'll have to read my book."

There is pumping machinery, oiled gears, smacking pistons, and lubricated timepieces beneath us, around us. Everywhere. The steam and iron rhythm to which the mindless masses dance. Endless walkways and miles-long tunnels processing, conveying, landscaping time on this Plane. Subterranean passages of clocks and carbines, drill-presses and acetylene torches. This is no service economy but one of Labor. Nothing is truly automated. Someone makes it, operates it, controls, redesigns, and adjusts it—there is someone there to fix it when it breaks. I cannot stand restaurants or casinos, where the wealthy bark orders and satiate themselves and their needs and greeds while others labor in kitchen heat and under the burdens of overflowing trays of dead flesh. I once saw a VERY pregnant girl in a short skirt and tight shirt serving drinks in an Atlantic City poker palace. The Mischievers thrive beneath the boards down there, where the handless and footless play the National Anthem on keyboards with their tongues while strapped to gurneys wheeled by ex-prostitutes too clap-ridden to work the streets. And in New York City, where rock stars and actors ascend to godliness in ornate concert halls for the tux-and-gowners while the homeless beg outside, weaving their way thru blocks of stretch limos and oversized SUVs. The painted Edens cannot hold back their shadows—the shapes of the wrenches, the sounds of turning screws, the shutting down of floodlights to clear the path for midnight arrests and insidious penetrations. Mindless repetition of the factory and corporate office tower is the Stations of the Cross transplanted into mythic Hell itself. The higher up one lives, the better (and more distorted) the view (all those pretty, pretty lights—such attainable stars), the more it costs, the less the din, the better the smell. And the less they know of what makes the world work. It's not the money, but the oil it buys. But it's not the oil, but the machinery it feeds. But it's not the machinery, but those that make it work. The uneducated, uncultured masses of shin-n-bone automatons who buzz and crackle along with their charges. Those who dwell in the dangerous subterranean underbelly of Fritz Lang's *Metropolis*. Within its heavens and death-god Satans in suits and ties, a profound truth is contained. The Inside Job, the well-connected rebel revolutionary who cannot bear the weight of his own recently denied ignorant bliss.

Enter Science—mad, tortured, out to reclaim what was torn away and cast into the flame. What thoughts and dreams can one dare to have in the iron tangles of the endlessly churning Machine? The factory, the assembly line, the rat-maze of soft-walled office cubicles where the workers hang their photocopied and email-distributed Rants. Marking time, gauging minutes, counting hours, counting beans, counting paychecks—counting every last cent Government takes to feed itself and its Ambitions while all the while squashing yours. I've seen Anastasia (excuse me, *Elsbeth*) in her flesh-colored stockings (and their inevitable run) and tennis shoes, walking up the stairs to her sterile cubicle and out-of-date computer. Handbag in the bottom drawer, lunch bag by the phone (can't use the refrigerator; some asshole has an open Tupperware full of mossy turkey and rock-hard stuffing in there from months ago, and they'll all be *damned* if they're gonna clean up after *him*) and stacks of papers to be red-inked and blue-inked and sent back stamped NEED MORE INFO! Cause that's what's needed in this age of the New Technic—endless reams of *info*. Spending habits, acquisition trends, shopping records, number of children, free-time interests in the form of online purchases and vacation destinations. Rotten little jobs all made okay with a six-pack of beer and a Sunday ball game. A few hours of vicarious living and if you're lucky, your Home Team wins. Amen Sunday brutha! How 'bout them gridiron, diamond, hardcourt, ice rink, paved oval, 18-hole heroes! And while the masses sit Entranced, the Mischievers do Cornu's dirty work for the payment of others' pain. Their weekly wage, their daily grind. They enjoy being the rabble above the rabble, the schoolyard bullies given permission by their Father to burn the playground down and all the kiddies with it. Why allow another blazing Inferno, another crumbling empire where the workers die in the streets? There must be more saintly visions to see. Something beyond the infinite parade of bald and skeletal human and spiritual trash being hurled into the glowing maw of Lang's MOLOCH! machine, so adamantly echoed in Ginsberg's *Howl*! for a whole new mass of squirming flesh. It's gotten ever easier to dismiss Art as bunk, to swim in the sea of Fictions and Entertainment without admitting it still leaves you wet and salty. It has Effect, if you let it. Demon-childe that I was, barely five, I wept when they killed King Kong the first time I saw the film (and each time after) because I understood that there must always be a Pretext to get the Big Things done and the hell with those in the way—the Holocausts, the invasions of piss-poor countries, the Mansonesque Helter-Skelters. Failed or not, the point is still illustrative—incite the masses to riot when you're poised to crush them flat. This War must be won, for anything else is mere Continuation—one flag and doctrine traded for another—new gears and pistons in the same old steam-n-grease machine. What we need is a true Armageddon—an end to *everything*—a big burning that will allow things to start anew. A *tabula rasa* like the mythic Flood, like the initial state of Being. But not for a new regime—for a purer state of Being. I don't fully know what Father Joe is up to, but I know I won't take part.

I'm thru with being a Pawn.

I have been ruminating a bit (keeps me from thinking of the Larger Issues at Hand) about the exchange between Father Tom and Francis Spork. Have you ever considered the rationale behind a massive cathedral? The sheer scale of it all? Ever wondered at the enormity of doorways and the height of the ceilings? Yeats, in "Trembling of the Veil," says that religion is an unimportant accessory to good architecture, and to the wide-eyed little girl who I once heard remark to her father as they passed a church that "They used to torture people there, but now it's a museum where they sell postcards," that's as good an answer as any, but religion for most *cannot* be separated from these madly inspired monuments to Littleness. Because Spork's Sunday school teacher was right—cathedrals are outlandishly scaled so that all who enter will feel so very small and so very, very helpless beneath the torturous visions of god and Satan and the endless parade of martyrs and saints that they cling to the priests who dwell within them as though they are the only Unafraid. In the Middle Ages, the people participated fully in the enterprise—most of the European cathedrals were built thru community zeal. The willingly oppressed, no different than the thousands who built the pyramids of Egypt's god-king pharaohs. Of course, being built and designed by those who were more zealous than handy with a plumb-bob and hammer, there was a 340-year period where no less than 8 church towers collapsed in England alone. A lot of it had to do with experimentation. Great strides were made in architecture during those years, all in the service of better praising God. In 1174, when Canterbury Cathedral burned, a French architect redesigned it to incorporate more windows. After all, if God is light, a dark, dank church doesn't do much for marketing. Churches were once the tallest buildings in a city—now the multinational and financial offices are.

Shows you where the true gods dwell and why Towers sometimes *have to* fall.

I've spent as much time in churches and cathedrals as the next fallen angel. Icons don't harm us, nor do they keep us outside the door, though for many of us they are reminders of what might have been and almost equally what *never should have been*. Not the most comfortable places for most of us, though Lucifer has rarely been elsewhere. I've even known him to take confession now and again—something about those sliding windows and their dark screens that fascinate the fool.

So when I received a cryptic message thru a fledging drug-addict of a teenage vampire while partying at Nicki's Slice a Funk that none other than Lucifer himself was "looking to take a meeting" (in the goombah parlance of North Jersey), I knew my best chance of finding him (he declined to leave details, or else the little bitch couldn't recall them) was to visit the world's churches until I found his crumpled, sobbing form and see what he had to say. I thought it'd be as good an opportunity as any to try and convince him to help me, to get him to see that what little balance we had managed to create wouldn't hold once Cornu's new configuration takes hold and that his only chance to get back home for good would be to talk to God on my behalf. Perhaps I could finally get him to see beyond that massive mound of pride and ego he's sat behind and realize that laboring in obscurity is better than annihilation. I'm tired of being fucked with. What good is trying to stay under the radar if it winds up wedged between the crack in your ass? So I resolved to seek him out. I asked Orlando Nepenthe to come with me, but he declined with uncharacteristic force ("Go fuck your mother's stinking corpse with an electric eel, cuntface," I think he said).

Lucifer has far more enemies than friends.

I started my search at the Wells Cathedral in England because its inverted arch design is richly metaphoric for a thinker like me. I've often considered on a Halloween night of inverting the long, thin crucifix that thrusts upward above the altar, but I'm usually otherwise indisposed. It'd be a cheap trick anyway, even for me (I much prefer to paint dog-shit moustaches on the stone faces of the statues that dwell on the exterior of the church at Tepoztlan, Mexico—much more subtle, and subtlety is divine). I next entered the fan-vaulted walkways of the cloister of the cathedral at Gloucester, but Lucifer was not there, though I sensed he had been just days before. Remaining in England, I stood outside the Cathedral at Exeter, staring at its western face and thinking about my appearance during *Faustus,* and its terrible ramifications for me. Needing to get out of England, I visited St. Mark's in Venice for no other reason than I like to sit atop the horses that stand sentry above its central archway. It is a tremendous Byzantine structure—Man at his most artistic and expressive. Standing near its immense columns and statue-filled tabernacle makes my heart ache within minutes, so as soon as I sensed Lucifer wasn't dwelling somewhere deep within, I made a quick flight over to the Basilica of Saint Peter, designed by the great Michelangelo (the drum and lantern dome, its most notable feature, was completed after his death. No worries—he was looking on). Saint Peter's is always so damned crowded, I never stay there long, and I knew the Child of Light most likely avoided it all together, but since I was in the neighborhood, I next went to the Romanesque cathedral in Pisa and then to the one at Amalfi, which is unique in its Sicilian Arabic style. Then I went to Florence, the seat of the Renaissance, the Medicis, Dante, and one of my favorite cathedrals of all— Santa Maria del Fiore, and her famous dome, which took the combined genius of Cambio, Giotto, Brunelleschi, and Verrocchio and 140 years to complete.

Leaving Italia, I went to Ghent, where I meditated for an evening in front of the altarpiece of the Cathedral of Saint Bavon, painted by the van Eycks. Singers and musicians offering their talents to God and the saints. Such myriad facial expressions—contemplation, confusion, concentration, and of course the tilt-headed attitude—if not the glazed stare—of religious ecstasy. I half expected them to bleed from their palms as I wept for their exoneration from entrapment in the paint. It is a masterful and sinister piece of art. Needing a dose of cathedral truth to counteract the experience, I sped to Moscow and St. Basil's, the great monument to Ivan the Terrible's victory over the Tartars. Just to be sure the chief architect would never create an even better construction, old Grozny had his eyes put out. Heading north, I entered the Gothic cathedral of Basel in Switzerland, called the Münster, the burial place of Desiderius Erasmus. I've known Lucifer to spend hours engaged in deep discussions with Erasmus' lingering essence, gleaning wisdom from "Praise of Folly," which could be his roadmap home or another trip to see the Oracle of Doom deep within Trophonius' cave.

But there were no rambling talk-a-thons that night. All was silence in the Humanist's tomb and so I went to France, walking the stone floors of Reims, Rouen, Cluny and Chartres, Lyon and Senlis, even climbing Montmartre to gaze upon the three cross-topped domes of the Sacré-Coeur basilica, but Light Bearer was nowhere to be found.

Needing a break from the Christian side of building the big buildings I went to Jerusalem to visit the Dome of the Rock. Having recently seen Saint Peter's, I couldn't help but notice the great difference in styles... I much prefer the humble simplicity of the plainer Islamic dome. The rest of the place is mad with decoration and artistic excellence in the service of Allah, but that white dome breaking the blue of the sky unhindered by ornamentation really gives me pause—the kind they were *all* designed to.

Becoming more than a little pissy at my lack of success in finding my brother Luci-loo, I beat wings across the Atlantic (calling it the "Big Pond" is stupid) and entered the sanctuary at Saint Patrick's in New York. As I passed beneath its Gothic façade I sensed he had been there not long before—hovering in the pointed architecture above its central arch like countless other real and created specters and ghouls. He has no goddamned imagination. Never has.

It wasn't a totally wasted trip, however. While I scanned the pews I watched a good-looking young teen with long blonde ringlets fix a few out of place locks using a dab or two of Holy Water.

Gotta admire the brazenness of the ultra good-looking...

But I didn't have time to stare. I had business to which I must attend and there was only one place left to go.

St. Paul's.

I could have skipped all the others and simply done the "Lucifer Loop"—Chartres, Basel, Saint Patrick's, Gloucester, and St. Paul's—if I had been in a hurry to see him. His predictability has been his wobbly wheel since the beginning. Of all the churches and cathedrals in the world I can't say why he "haunts" these five… We all have our favorite places, and St. Paul's is his number one spot.

St. Paul's, the cathedral of the Church of England, most inspired of the brilliant designs of Christopher Wren, built to replace what had been destroyed by the great fire of 1666, an event in which we were all to some extent involved, at least as far as *completely* destroying the cathedral. (In truth, Lucifer was an admirer of Wren's since his design for the Sheldonian Theatre in Oxford, patterned as it was on the Roman Theatre of Marcellus, and it seemed appropriate that since he was going to do renovations anyway that he have the chance to start from scratch.) Wren was brilliant in the way he got things done—submit a design, agree to changes, and then find a way to do it his way—surreptitiously so no one would notice until it was too late. (His favorite design for St. Paul's, the "Great Model," was rejected as being *too Catholic*, so he scaled back—and then added little by little the very things he had wanted in the first place. He's an inspiration to us all.) His design for the rebuilding of London was brilliant and aesthetic, and was rejected out of hand.

Isn't that always the way?

Passing the statue of Queen Anne, with its royal accoutrements of gold, I walked between the middle two sets of double columns in the entranceway and as I reached for the door, I felt Lucifer behind me, his breath hot and insistent on the back of my neck.

"*Not right now,*" he whispered, "*But soon.*"

I didn't bother to turn around—I knew he would be gone.

Another test. Would Planner circle the world at Lucifer's bidding, as he did back in the day?

Oh, sure—he's got nothing but time.

I didn't go inside.

St. Paul's has never been one of my faves.

Not *Catholic* enough, I guess.

And now a reading from the Goosebell according to John (but it's not either of the two you might think):

In the days before the Daze, before Sparta lost her kings, the Kundalini master, a young planner caned and able in the city of Enoch, went forthrightly forth into the desert to endure his own Temptation. Caught on the roadside with hobbled-horse demise and broken-string madrigal blues, the gone angel porter—Eden bound as angels are—sent his outta-tune words along the wire, screaming raucous folly to the Nothings—"I'm tight-room tombed; desert cornea'd in an endless puke-trail of bad-trippin' prescriptions; Reznor-burned on the cactus-needle freak's OD of triplaphonic glockenspiel low-fi and the fryin' pan finagling of my fish-a-floppin' indecisions."

Stopping the dogshit at the first leg-lift would have been simpler, but less good down the road...

And how.

Joining in a mad cocoon of mutual Imagination with his hemi-oiled, half-milin' Brother in the Bible, Planner laid down his desert road prescription for low, cheap living in the cock-n-puddle inns: "We'll eat lots of pasta and steal the robes."

Scraping/scrimping/pimping and spent, they waltzed along with waiter mime dances, cocktail wishes, and dish-soap rumblings. Top coats/old coats/no coats—with Mummers' dimes and spiders' eyes, toilet globs and fatty tissue, warm rumblings in the acid fluxing beast-belly breeze, and rancid tumors aching on the cut back of the chrysalis escapee, they were gold-guttered pan people cast off by an evolution's crude code—degrees of degrees of degrees. Loving lazily, indiscriminately, and well (as Bible boys must), they were the wet ink on the moonlit movie poster that couldn't sell the show.

Staunching the wound at the first sight of blood might have saved the soul—but cruising the sand-strand, the Gold Coast always seems so close.

So close. So close. Amen, Anon, so close.—(from Ch. 1:1–7, *The Cryptic Cyberdiary of Mad John Gandy*, the ramblin' railway ghost).

Like the horses come to kickin' while the storm is still far off, the troubled menagerie of ghosts and subterranean freak-seekers I call the Homeboyz of Hell are swirling their sick presences around me with questioning whispers and yes–no words of War since my return from the Lucifer Loop. As shown in the excerpt above, Gandy's writing his own version of what's gone down (inspired by his new pal Grayle-Groyne) and even my gone angel porter—the Dean Moriarty to my Sal Paradise—so scarce for so long, has returned, wandering the late-night hotel hallways of the places where I go when all but the oddest guests and midnight-shift marauders have either gone to bed or logged out for the night. Amid the genius lice and clerical leeches, political hack mites and despondent millipedes he scrawls his secret word-gifts of elemental consecration, leaving tiny pools of lead and eraser dust to freely mingle with the cum-puddles and booze spills on the empty, moonswept beds of the hour-rate rooms upstairs.

So far, they've produced nothing half as humanlike as me.

The porter's not alone these days—his latest mate is an almost-ghost named Chelsea Belladonna, who wears a lava-blue skinsuit woven of semi-liquid plasma and convinces everyone she's dead by the coldness of her skin and her electri-tonal voice. She is a summoner, a new-millennial Madam Blavatsky who barged into my *sanctum sanctorum* one night professing to own the key to solving all my ills. I listened with half an ear while she spoke with half a brain and when the presentation was thru I slapped her half-assed face and pushed her out the door.

If she gave even the smallest bit of shit, she didn't let it show, which impressed the hell out of a brazen skunk like me, so I invited her back and let her do her thing.

"Before I start," she said, softly caressing the pulsing red handmark on her cheek, "I want to tell you my story."

(Why should she be any different than me?)

"I was given life in a cursed house full of cracked-wall psychic energy by a woman who spent most of her waking hours slashing at swamp-and-coffin entities with a heavy Crusader's sword, speaking prayers in Latin and mumbling to God about due justice as she seared her hate into my eyes. I think my greatest victory came at thirteen years old, when, after reading Virgil's *Aeneid*, I replied with a little Latin wisdom of my own—'*Desine fata deum flecti sperare recando.*' Basically, God does what he wants no matter how much you pray. As I got older I spent less and less time under that willful gaze, wandering the rooms of the house and making friends with the specters she'd not yet destroyed. While rummaging thru a box of menstrual-stained dresses in the basement one Jesus-Easter night, I came across a blackened-leather sketchbook, thick with a decade's dust. Many of the pages had a yellowed, crumbling residue from shapes that had been pasted in and later torn out. Toward the middle were several pages of barely coherent script bled into the page with an orange marker. The writing, distorted though it was, was clearly my mother's, no doubt from one of her long-abandoned channeling events. Halfway down the final page, the letters became more elongated and misshapen, like a Wiccan's runic alphabet. As I wracked my brain to decipher them, they began to writhe upon the page, all at once moving down to the lower right-hand corner like a synchronized flock of ernes, where they intertwined like a woodcut of demons and angels from the deepest recesses of Albrecht Dürer's mind—a Middle Ages Armageddon vision that made his *Four Horsemen of the Apocalypse* seem like a drawing from a children's book.

"From the distorted edge of the picture emerged a hooded skeleton, its reddish-brown hue reminding me of an old silent movie projected in 3-D. It stared at me with its hell-pit sockets but so many years of shielding myself from my mother's athemic gaze had easily trained me for the weak vibrations the ill-formed specter was able to muster and I exploded it with an incantation I'd learned in my head long before my vocal chords were formed enough to speak it. When my mother heard and saw what I had done she sent me away to a boarding school for girls with 'misdirected' powers such as mine.

"I was there only a few days, mostly hiding out and avoiding my two fallen-Catholic roommates, when I overheard the Headmaster and his secretary speaking about a Hell-possessed specter of a little girl that haunted a room in the back wing of the school. That night after all the girls had gone to bed, I entered the hallway leading to the locked door where she stayed. As I produced the key I had stolen from the office drawer and began to turn it in the lock, a gale-force wind began to blow, disallowing me entry. Above the force of the wind I screamed 'I am here to help you!'

"It got suddenly quiet, and a strong yet gentle hand pulled me inside and relocked the door.

"In a web-filled corner of the unused room I sensed a frightened, misunderstood entity curled up in a frayed wicker crib. I felt none of the low vibration of possession, and yet there was a block between her and this world stronger than the mere fact of Death. Believing her worthy of trust I opened my mind and allowed her thoughts to come inside.

"Hers is a story you also have to hear:

"She had been forced into the room years before after a priest sent to bless the school—a friend of yours, in fact—had felt her presence and demanding her name but not understanding her inability to answer, had pronounced her a demon and had insisted she be exiled to this room, a Purgatory within Purgatory she could not escape without the added force of a mind such as mine.

"She was blind and deaf and thus had not been able to answer when the priest asked her to speak her name.

"I wonder, *Planner Forthright*, if the same could be said of you?"

[No answer from me. *Of course.*]

"I was expelled for letting her out, which was more than half the point, and I fully embraced my freedom, wandering the world as girls like me do, until I met the gone angel porter and he told me about you."

"Me?" I asked, suddenly guessing the point of her fairly uninteresting tale (save for the obvious allusion to Father Joe).

"You are exactly like that girl—an Annie-Sullivan-less Helen Keller Buntz—and I can save you, too, as you are trying to save Tatyana and the rest. As all of us with a Gift must save one another from what's to come."

That's balls.

And I can't help but be impressed by the length and breadth of what she knows about me. That fact alone has for the moment appeased my twitching hand and convinced me that I must keep her safe within my clan.

When she's not tracing nail-tip runes into the angel porter's sides or introducing me to a slew of drifting ghosts she sits in lotus position spewing long trails of JL Seagull's New-Avian philosophy ("You didn't die, you know"—she instructs our jazz-jonzed Gabriel— "you abruptly changed your level of consciousness") and charging gull-ible guests a twenty a session to stare into their eyes for 93 minutes (as with most things mystic, it's a number of which only she knows the significance). "The iris is the walkway spanning the fortress of the mind," she whispers, leaning closer. "And I am the one to love the castle guards to sleep."

To me, it's all the dream-queen's farce, though she *has* turned me on to my own private advisory board—an other-psyche Council of Twelve summoned from the archetypal theorizing of Jung; a motley group of gypsy travelers spouting unsolicited advice thru the tinted windows of a spectral white van.

No other entity, living or dead, can see their forms or hear their words but me.

I've barely gotten to know them, but here are some pencil-scratch notations:

- A scientist-visionary whose brilliant ideas were perfect for the roll-on drone of the war machine. When he refused to provide the cryptic keys to his formulaic genius he was killed on the steps of the University chapel by the DoD. Nearly a decade after his death, they still haven't decoded his work.
- A Triple-goddess rebel battling her interior aspects, which simultaneously manifest in shifting physicalities and jagged-nail cat-fights. For the briefest of moments, one of the three will dominate enough for me to get a glimpse: the strongest is a tall, thin, severe-seeming woman with short brunette hair; another is a short, chubby, red-faced cherub with stringy blonde hair and dimpled knuckles. The last is a rouged-up sexpot who does the least amount of talking but manages to get the most done for them all.
- A she-man ultra-feminist out to sabotage all things genuinely male, including dicks, balls, Iron John organizations, gun clubs, and pay-per-view sporting events of any kind.
- A handsome Shakespearian actor who took copious amounts of drugs before breaking into neighbors' houses looking for saltine crackers and sushi. He drowned himself in a Benzedrine haze in the backyard pool thinking he was Ophelia and the overnight delivery boy the finger-flipping Hamlet who jilted her for his murderous Mother's love.

- A bird-feathered Old Testament prostitute dressed in white, skilled in the martial arts, and never appearing without a shaman's elk-horn staff.
- An English once-upon-a-rock-star who in the post-spandex years produced TV shows featuring cheery-cheeked children singing falsetto background to his songs about social injustice and the need to scrap it all and start again. Judging by his spiky bottle-blonde hair and sagging tattoos he never took his own advice.
- A crippled Marijuana legalization advocate who gave up a tenured college professorship to start an access-cable program devoted to proving that all symbols are empty air and that the human mind is really a miniature spaceship carrying the progenitors of the Human race safely thru time until they can find an alternative form of fuel to power their spaceships, for now cleverly disguised as chrysanthemums.
- A high-tech wizard who used his craft to create the illusion of multinational corporations and other global entities as a pipeline for would-be investors' funds who died when his computer bank's wiring was left exposed and his twin teeny-bopper secretaries in the throes of a two-on-one spilled a bottle of champagne directly on the hot spot. He's hell to look at but an apt teacher when it comes to the fundamentals of dismantling the control rooms of the New Technic—he's the blistering, bubbling crystallization of Burroughs' Nova Trilogy—a hanging mess of cybernetic globalization and bad dick jokes (the latter of which are solely supplied by me).
- Hiding in the van as the other eleven shout suggestions and advice as I go about my way is a child-philosopher and musician from the mountains of Tibet. She plays lotus love-hymns on a silver-strung Genka and when the din of barely embodied voices gets too much for us both she plays a golden suona horn, which never fails to get the others to stop—at least for a time.
- Her full-time protector is a murdered Native American tribal sheriff from the Black Hills who carries an antique Spencer repeating rifle used during the Indian Wars. Because he's long since run out of the 56-50 cartridges necessary to give it worth, he keeps it jammed full of gelatinous green balls he says were given to his grandfather by a Lakota holy man on the eve of Little Big Horn. I've seen him trying to make mental contact with Leyton Walkingfeather several times, though Leyton can sense nothing from my advisors. [Chelsea says they are mine and mine alone.]
- The most flamboyant of the Twelve is a dance choreographer from the Caucuses who devoted his young life to the staging of pieces from classical mythology and Russian folklore. If he didn't whine like a child when he talked to me of the Greeks and Baba Yaga I wouldn't mind him half as much as I do.
- My favorite of them all is a minister to the artist-emperor Hsuan Tsung, whose foolish notions of love toppled the T'ang Dynasty in 8th-century China.

The minister, a capable poet in his elder years, spent long hours under the wine-rimmed tutelage of Han Yu and Li Shen, masters of the succinct high art that is oriental poetry.

If I can learn to separate their vibrations and isolate their particular experiential wisdoms these twelve counselors can be of use, though as it now stands, they make my fucking mind want to explode with their overlapping raps and brain-drilling thoughts.

Chelsea insists that I be patient, but that's never been my thing.

After days of trying I found a way to elude my new advisors, though it took me far north into the cold depths of the area mariners call the North Pacific Graveyard. Invoking all the power of the legendary Adamastor, master of the sea-storm, I grokked a small but potent disturbance, hoping the salt and sleet and driving winds would slap awake in me the sharp and merciless senses that have lately been lulled to sleep. I closed my eyes and quickly opened them again, trying to conjure along the rim of a thirty-foot wave—exact in every way to the one that broke the back of the *Valencia* in 1906—the stoic visage of Bergman's Antonius Block playing chess with Death, but there was only me and miles of storming Nil. How easy it would be to just play my way out—sit across from Cornu and match him move for move, exchanging new interpretations of Enoch and drinking from the same bottle of sour, poisoned wine. Or, if such a game cannot be arranged, then just Walking Away—finally forsaking all those looking to me for guidance and protection and *answers* (the biggest joke of all) and hanging every sorry soul opposed on the sharpened meat hooks of my Demon Nature. I have not gotten so soft as to be incapable of utter cruelty and despite my hatred of the Cornu and my fist-shaking impulse to see God at last on his apologetic knees I would readily lose this nothing flesh and go back to being the little splinter in the Universe's ass I once was.

This path is too unclear and I am tired of losing my way.

Watching an angel-winged wave break apart the 1600-ton mirage of the *Valencia* over and over again, I found myself thinking of the Marquis de Sade and his drunken barrage of questions in the House of Jacob Scrooge. Who is it that brings you closer to God—the one who wears the mask of death in some traveling wagon production or the one who drains your veins until you're nearly dead? Both produce visions but one is from without and the other from within. One dances in time to the shadows on the wall behind him and the other seeks to know the secrets that they hide. The player lives, but the fighter—the blood-mad killer—cannot. He is no man of vision, blinded as he is by his lack of creation. It is the artist and the Mother—just storm-grokkers like me—who know God best, though it is they who rank last on the ladder of Divine worth.

I don't think Antonius Block ever really wanted to win.

I am better off alone.[15]

Passing thru Idaho on my North Pacific return, I picked up the scent of a phantom madman on Hwy. 51 between Grasmere and Riddle. An apocalyptic Adam reinventing Eden's midnight in road-trashed boots and tattered denim, spewing forth a laugh to make rattlesnakes seek shelter in the virgin holes of potato farmers' daughters. A wandering spirit lacking any spark of originality but feeling himself "one deep, dark demon" so he's patterned his vibe on Stephen King's Walkin' Dude—Randall Flagg hisself, right down to the pockets fulla pamphlets and eyes chock full of his unwavering belief in his continuing Existence outside the 1141 pages of *The Stand*. Poetically fitting that an avid reader like him would want to be identified with such a BIG book—it takes a blackhearted piece of windblown desert dust to know the value of the Word, and this copycat was nothing if not that.

So what was this dude's deal? Like Flagg, I could sense he had powers to woo the mad 'cause he was able to share their vision—it takes a pair of abstract eyes to properly interpret and collaborate in the creation of the mental tapestries of the Unibombers and righteous revolutionaries of this Plane.

Takes a Fuck to fuck a Fuck, or something close to that.

After considering me for a moment, he walked on, like other dudes have done, sensing he might have met his match.

Smart guy.

I wasn't in the mood to test my skills.

Cutting northward into Montana, I started thinking about Flagg's pipeline-laying connection, Chris Bradenton. No doubt a composite of many scraps of tattered cloth all woven into a single hippie-liberal quilt. Was there anyone from the substate underground who *wasn't* at or near the Dem Convention of '68, drooling out the bullet sprays of Beatnik-coded poems and making tenuous links

---

[15]Planner Forthright's "small but potent storm," started though it was south of Vancouver Island in the Juan de Fuca Strait, quickly moved north, gathering strength as it swept thru British Columbian waters and 60 miles farther north into Queen Charlotte Sound, where it bested an 80-foot commercial fishing trawler, killing three of its four crewmen before finally dissipating in the apply named Hecate Strait. Planner said nothing when initially told and later whined like a Russian choreographer when he learned of this Note. *Fuck him.* (J.M.)

and inflated propositions between likeminded minds? It was all the rage in those Haight-Ashbury–Abbie–Doors days.

According to King, Flagg had been around—stirred the shit in those pre-Me and early-Me years when there was a chance to break the mold, expand the horizons, elevate instead of denigrate, but that dude's got nothing on me when it comes to stirring up the muck—I've bragged on some of it, and rightfully so—for all the pain and ache it's caused me, I might as well enjoy a little notoriety and get some credit (*I want the fucking credit*—ain't that what the Man do say?).

So here's another—December 6, 1969, Altamont Speedway, where the green-clad Black boy was killed courtesy of the Hell's Angels while "Sympathy for the Devil" bled into "Under my Thumb." It had been quite a year, '69 (that gone, sexy number), and we were out in force, watching Morrison (a devil on a stage not mentioned by McLean) on a sultry Miami night in early March become the first king of shock rock after seeing the Living Theatre's *Paradise Now* the night before. Losing Eden in an eyeblink is something no one knows better than me, and I've showed my cock a plenty in protest (which Morrison *didn't* do—all trash, no gas, sad to say—never met a successful revolutionary yet who wasn't able to hold his booze). Then, in late '69 came the Manson Family murders and December at Altamont.

So many of us were there. We could feel it happening before it began. It was the last 10 days of the Rolling Stones' tour—a free concert for 300,000 people (though more than 400,000 showed), a rush job from the get-go, a lets-do-one-better-than-the-Woodstock-show-we-missed mindset, so the fact that four people died seems an insignificantly small percentage, considering the considerable amount of hammered bitches and drugged-up mods bum-rushing the stage to get a whiff of Jagger's scented sweat. A big show of Free Love and youth rebellion caught on film in "Gimme Shelter" that Pauline Kael compared with the Nuremberg Rally staged to film Riefenstahl's "Triumph of the Will."

The whole thing was Uncle Sam meets Omega Man and the boy in the stars-n-bars tophat took the decision. Altamont was huge for Lucifer—it finally toppled the teetering Hippie mystique in one crazy night, and gave the sobbing prick a resurgence of sorts in film and song—a pound of credit he didn't deserve, so I protested and got my ass chewed by a thorny equivalent of the mythical Cerberus. We all *equally* charged the air with madness and mayhem and no one laughed louder than me at the ironic ease of things when the red and black–clad jester said into the mike: "Something funny always happens when we start that number," meaning "Sympathy for the Devil." It was a real side-splinter when he naively asked "Why are we all fighting?"

You're strutting around playing at being the devil and you profess to be surprised when the booze and drugs and Blues alchemify into evil? Come again?

No one will ever know what that crazy 18-year-old Meredith Hunter was thinking pulling out that goddamned gun. Too much bad tripping and noise and numbers... The whole thing was going sour and the Hell's Angels (they only *wish* they knew what it meant to *be* one of us) with their free beer, poor acid, and weighted pool cues didn't help. I stood by a wall of amps thinking Santana played cleaner than anyone I'd ever heard when the Jefferson Airplane came on. They did the Hippie love thing and asked the Angels to chill themselves out—Marty Balin got a shot in the mouth for that one.

Lucifer, Mr. Shaytan Rising himself, dug the press, and McLean's later tribute, fictional as it seemed, was all he needed to revive some ancient dances on the warped wood of his sanity. I hadn't seen him so happy since Rosemary rocked the cradle with love in her eyes the year before. He takes his scraps with Pride, my friends.

Between Jagger's Satan theatricals and Lucifer's credit-hogging crap, I really felt that, aside from the tunes, the whole thing was a crock.

Lots of pretenders to the throne—the wannabe Walkin' Dudes like the one I'd just met are still out and about on the ink-and-paper highway that is ID 51 between Grasmere and Riddle, levitating their self-amazed Satanic selves and thinking if the chips ever do fall as oracled they might just get their chance at being the Cheese—the second great mythic Resurrection of the Way, the Brute, and the Lies.

Totally and completely absurd. They're all chumps.

They have to be... Why else would Flagg's careful plans, all his machinations and recruitments and gleefully brutal evils be so easily unseated by such mundane paperback conventions as Light and Hope and Love?

He was a second-rate player on a sparse and splintered stage.

Trashcan Man was the real deal and the truest genius of them all.

For Him, I'd gladly give my life.

I'm hiding. Hiding from every wheel I've set in motion, every motor I gave gas and spark enough to start, every whore's pair of panties I've thumb-rubbed to produce a spreading spot of "Now I'm ready for you to Enter."

I am in my favorite place of refuge—a monastery. A cold and sterile place. One of denial and reflection. A place of simplicity and Stone and Wood and Earth. Of Mud and Straw and Fire. Unspiced food and tempered spirits. I have wandered the dirt roads, camel routes, frozen steppes, and mountain pathways to the doors of hundreds of abbeys over the centuries, seeking the solace I've seen in the paintings of tonsured monks and emaciated mendicants lost in gentle supplication to their unseen god. I have sought comfort in their ways from Nitria in Egypt to Abyssinia to Mt. Izla in Mesopotamia to the Judean desert and Monte Cassino and Nashdom, where I sat with the Benedictines, the Black Monks. I've spent time in the Buddhist Viharas and Tibetan gompas at Shaolin and Tengboche. Hidden in the shadows of the Eastern Orthodox lavras and sketes of the Holy Mountain in Greece. Prayed at Matins at Eberbach and Cluny and at Nones in Melk, Lindisfarne, and Glendalough and slept among the Cisterians, the White Monks, at Ewell after Compline. I sat beside St. Anthony, the first of the Christian monks and other anchorites and hermits sitting in solitude like the Buddha beneath his tree, and joined with 30,000 cenobites in places of vast expanse. I have sat in contemplation with Carmelites (the White Friars), Capuchins, and Augustinian friars in places long forgotten, their daily cycles of devotion offering me some small comfort on my most fractured days. I've sung the liturgy with the monks of Santo Domingo de Silos and sat with the abbey's newest members at the far end of the lower tables most distant from the high table of the Abbots to protest their insistence on Order. I've pounded the rhythm for the mortifiers in their chambers and whispered paintable and writable images into the ears of the illuminators and scribes in the cloisters and scriptoria in the hopes that their books will become at least as interesting to read as the stacks of skulls piled in their crypts. Funny that they surround themselves with books—like a nymph looking for the Cure in a whorehouse. They are seekers, monks—seekers of something Holy, something memorable and meaningful, just like me, who is brother to the Brothers. But I have been disappointed—as I have by so many things—by the strength of Hierarchy and theological debate I have found within their walls. The quarrels between different Catholic orders over the spiritual conditions of poverty and wealth. I have cheered on the splinter groups, like those under St. Bernard of Clairvaux and the Fraticelli, who sought to cling to the stricter ways despite the proclamations of such popes as John the XXII and the heated debates between the Grey Friars—the Franciscans—and the Dominicans, the Friar Preachers. And how could it be otherwise when some believed that wealth was evil and others felt that it was the only means to *fighting* it? One could not expect such a financial powerhouse as the Vatican to renounce the riches it had earned thru the Crusades and all its wars—public and secret—up thru modern time. I once heard a Minister in the Church of We Take Visa, draped in gems and gold, preaching how Joseph the carpenter, skilled as *he* was, would have been a fairly wealthy man and how his donkey was akin to a Cadillac (which he himself drove).

Blessed Be the poorer orders—the simple monks in their crumbling, leaky abbeys of stone and wood and straw and *fuck* their so-called superiors. For all their relentless prayers and chants and song I have found them to be no different from the prisoner (also in his cell) for, whether self- or state-imposed, the denial of solitude and broken off communities is an Unnatural State—prison, monastery, commune—as unnatural as me. In that way, I am more of the abbey than the Abbot himself.

I am here to pass a trio of days in mourning for a traitor, and, to add insult to my maggot-crusted injury, the face of Agnes Roberta Buntz will not leave my mind. I HATE traitors. Materialistic snakes with no conscience; only compulsion. Compulsion for the tangible, alluring, and ultimately Meaningless. They seek that which is fleeting and grasp onto it as if it were Permanence itself. They won't eat what's not choice cut; they won't fill a tank with anything other than Premium; they snort only the finest coke and shoot the purest shit; they will only fuck the golden groin ... but once their eyes are closed it's all the same wormy earth. Their penthouse in the palace fast becomes their grave—prestocked for consumption by the finest of the parasites—*asses to ashes, punks to dust, what's a squirrel without its nuts?*

I've gone and killed my trickster Crow—who in the end became a rook—a *Corvus frugilegus* in the scientific nomenclature of the academic's Naming of All. Supposedly the most friendly of all those in the crow family, but not to me.

I found my clues in *Finnegan's Wake*—a dozen different names for my nightblack trickster companion and each one glowing with a subtle red warning as my eyes scanned the page. So call him blackbird, magpie, (stately) raven, crow, or rook—the little cackling bastard was a spy for the Cornu, feeding information on what I did and said to the Mischievers, who ran it back to their boss.

It's easy to catch a spy once you know what he is, and though it snapped the young sapling that had been growing into my heart as I twisted his head cleanly from his neck, I drank his weak blood and devoured his innards, relishing the bitter taste even as my own coils of intestine began to buck and roll.

As I waited for the waves of criminal nausea to pass I picked clean my teeth with the quills of his tailfeathers, thinking back to his early lessons in the swamps where I spent my early months—his rotted beak and derisive sneer so different than the "grave and stern decorum of the countenance" of Poe's ebony bird—so unlike the silver-hued creature of Prophecy and Power that don Juan schooled Carlos Castaneda about—and growing weary of staring into its unconfessing eyes I shoved his severed head up the ass of a braying donkey at the foot of the mountain where I had caught the laughing little crow's-prick meeting with a Mischiever in the remains of a shattered temple.

Although I knew full well that he had started in the Cornu's grim employ I had come to believe that he had been my friend—loyal only to me and even a protector. Perhaps the gently guiding parent my dead Mother never had any interest in trying to be. But he was, in the end, just like the tattling Raven who rats out Caliban to Setebos in Robert Browning's eloquent poem (alluded to first in Shakespeare's *Tempest*)—all too fitting given the obvious parallel between Prospero and Caliban and the Cornu and me and come to that, Buntz as the dead witch Sycorax.

What an apt recasting we are.

So now I've killed them both. Father and mother both dead at the spoiled child's hands. That they deserved no better than they got doesn't seem to matter—something to do with that turn the other ass-cheek mentality priests and rabbis tout—and I am left with more familial blood on my hands and the dull pain inflicted by a rotted beak which I cannot take from out my heart.

I'm running short of places to go. No matter the miles, heights, or distances, there is none of Jeremiah's Gileadic balm reserved for me, and no sweet nepenthe that I can swallow to produce my own forgetting.

These memoirs have become the spear of Longinus that may finally see me destroyed.

I doubt a single soul will mourn.

I met with Lucifer last night.

There, I've said it—no beating around the bush, no stalling, no clever set-up.

Here's how it happened.

I was sitting in Nicki's Slice a Funk, talking over the finer points of vampiric multi-level manifestation with Mykaldaemio, when the power went out.

The band sucked, so no one cared, and as I looked toward the breaker box, there he was—the Old Boy himself. When he was sure he'd caught my eye he exited out the door, and I followed, surer than shit that this wasn't another case of empty Follow-Me.

He chose for our meeting a little deli up the street named Nonna Mary's that served a great squid and mussel soup.

We ordered a bowl each, a dish of bruschetta, three bottles of Chianti and kindly asked the waitress to leave us be until dessert.

"It's good to see you, brother," I said, tearing a hunk of warm bread from a basket and dunking it in the soup. "It's about time you came by."

[Note: Apparently he had just come from watching a 24-hour *Star Trek* marathon (the Original Series, of course) cause he was dressed in a subtle version of the costume from *Patterns of Force* but spoke a bit like Kirk in *A Piece of the Action*]

"This ain't too fuckin' good, Planner," he said, around a mouthful of mussels.

"The food or the situation?"

"Quitcha fuckin' around over here—I'm talkin' about the situation. You fucked this deal up good and now I gotta get involved and fix it. I'm miffed."

"Sorry to hear that, Godfather. It's just that you've been NOWHERE TO BE FOUND, so I was sort of on my own."

"Please," he said, sipping the wine. "I've been plenty busy, runnin' around like a chicken, game plannin', putting some possible situations together. So I'm here to ask ya—you wanna come on board with this thing? The door is like eighty-five, ninety percent closed, but you're my oldest friend and I thought I'd cut ya in."

"Whatcha got in mind?"

[I'm like a sponge for Mafia-speak. You'll just have to bear it.]

"I'm talkin' with some mid-level soldiers who got a beef with *Him*." I couldn't tell if he was still that upset with God or if he had bitten into a few grains of sand. "They're some dear friends of mine, in some decent positions of power. Supposebly what little control he had up there is goin' south in a hurry, you understand my point? Supposebly this Cornu chump's got them rattled."

"And you get this on good authority, do ya?"

"You're not payin' attention to what I tell ya—you gotta run your mouth all the time. Speakin' a which—I'm tired of your cuttin' me down."

"Take a number. I haven't said anything that isn't true. You led the charge, lost your nerve, rode the media machine, and now you sulk like a kid who broke his father's favorite pipe. I didn't make it up—I just told people about it."

"Fuck that writin' up my life shit, you lousy *sfacime*. And pertaining to my former state of mind, you'll see—I'm gonna fix you good on this thing—I'm already workin' on a book—*my* story, *my* way."

"Okay, Frankie—write your book. I seem to have started a trend."

"*Whateva*. All that literary situation aside, I admit I've made some errors in judgment—misplayed some hands, let *Him* get one up on me, but that's all gonna change. I'm lookin' to make a move and I wanna know if you're lookin' to grow a set a brass ones and come along. I mean, I know you got some things in the works over here, but what is it you're really lookin' ta do?"

He sat back and lit a Lucky Strike, giving me time to think.

He'd no sooner flicked his first ash into the remains of his soup [classless…] than I answered. "I appreciate the offer—I really do—but this thing is heavy and I ain't sure you're the right casino in which to play my chips. I ain't got a lotta *'scarole* to fuck around with here."

"Listen, my friend—you oughta know who you're dealin' with. Layin' low and makin' out like I ain't got the juice has always been my way—so don't make the same mistake as everyone else."

"Okay, Light-bearer, say you got muscle. Say you're ready to make a move. I'm not sure I could be of help. I gotta lot on my own plate right now—a few raviolis more than I can handle, actually, and I think it's best to look out for *me* for now."

"You do whatchoo gotta, my friend," he said, waving the waitress over and ordering each of us an espresso and a cannoli. "I'm makin' my move not too far down the road. My time ain't come and gone—all you ever talk about is them damned cult-type Armageddon films from the '60s and '70s, yada, yada, yada. You talk *nothing* about the more complex, multilayered portrayals—Pacino, Stormare, Mortensen, Byrne, Reed—these are all top-notch actors, and all of them have played *me*."

"So I've been a little unkind," I conceded, pouring two capfuls of Anisette into my demi-tasse cup and stirring away with a little gold spoon. "I'll do better in the future."

"I'm sure you will. You know where to find me, kid. You give me a ring and I'll be there in tree minutes. You bet on it. Enjoy the *cannole*. There's more meetings I gotta take. Oh," he said, pulling out a bill-clip and throwing a handful of twenties on the table, "one more ting—if you see that kid of mine, tell 'em all is forgiven if he wants to call a truce."

Off he went, giving our waitress a tap on the ass as he pulled out his cell phone [one guess which theme it played] and attempted to blow smoke up some other sucker's ass.

He can only make things worse.

From Hell ... I sent you half the Kidne I took from one women prasarved it for you tother piece I fried and ate it was very nise I may send you the bloody knif that took it out if you only wate a whil longer. Signed Catch me when You can. (Jack the Ripper letter, Oct. 16, 1888)

In a violent haze and shattered grip I gave myself over to a flame, lit by a black-robed Benedictine in the subterranean cells of Downside Abbey, Bath while the 5:45 vespers droned on above, the words indistinct yet filled with the pious praise of God. From within the tendriled smoke of the weakly flickering flame I drew to my center the sum total of its traveling, transient prayers. And they calmed me. For a day, an hour, a second, I cannot say. I'd journeyed too far on the second-hand blood of a creature nesting secretly in the heart of an English artist I'd been told about by a San Francisco collector who had bought some of my own work, and I was seeking to finally cast out his lingering presence in a place of peace. She had spoken to me of similarities, of outward expression of the deepest of inner workings, so I went and sought him out—as an artist, an intellectual, a twisted conveyor of depth-diving images—in search of a fellow prophet.

What I found was a man toiling at his craft, favoring crimson, vermilion, and cranberry interdicted and segmented into death forms by blue-tinged grays and blacks and secret-revealing oranges mixed with cuts of bladed, brilliant yellow. His studio—a ragged, spattered, Pollock-y sort of flat—smelled of cheap incense, rancid oils, and the sweat-tinged musk of inspiration, and I wandered its cramped, oppressive rooms, losing myself in his paintings, so dark and disturbing they made me feel so much less *alone*.

Perhaps his penchant for images of *seppuku* and other forms of ritual disembowelment should have tipped me to the danger of lingering therein, remaining too long in such a fractured energy, but I had a thirst on and a raging desire to feed that went far beyond physiological needs. I was *drawn* to this mysterious young painter—otherworldly darkness to Human darkness, the embodiment of evil seeking to mate with the fullest *expression* of it. His works evoked the unsettling realism of Lovecraft's R. U. Pickman, although the subject matter was not of hellish beasts but hellish deeds. Even his multi-angled reproductions of Sickert's "Jack the Ripper's Bedroom" I found fascinating—how he extended the edges of the room, revealing what was hitherto hidden within shadow with a consistency and brilliance that seemed almost psychic. It was exactly how I had always imagined Sickert's secret studios to be. His visions, burned into the canvas by his frantic hands, were of penance thru dismemberment and deliverance thru death. But the eyes that kissed the tip of the brush to the rough forms of his current canvas were not mad but lit and wise. We spoke for many hours, spewing forth our inspirations and techniques and sharing a single canvas before I could imprison my thirst no longer and I drained him—quickly and painlessly, which I considered my Gift to him for the time we had shared and the godlike brilliance I had seen.

Then I saw—an instant before I felt—the Beast that hid within.

How the creature had disguised itself I cannot say. The young artist's eyes seemed to retain their depth and clarity, even as the space created by his freefalling soul gave the Beast away, even as I had drunk my fill—even as I knew I'd be lingering within his visions and deeds for longer than a sane, mortal mind could bear. It was no accident, my meeting this demon (for that was surely what it was) in the now-abandoned husk of a man I had almost loved.

The entity inside the Man (a term I use based on the loosest biological parameters) was a butcher. A carver. A cutter. A dismemberer of women in the dark tradition and bloodlust of Jack the Ripper. He'd read about him, studied him—the documents, letters, theories, photographs, and more edgy exposés, from the early police reports to the dozens of scholarly books. I could not divine the secret of his disguise, his ability to hide undetected within the artist, no matter how far within the blood-link I swam, though about his deeds, if I were of the mind to shock you, I could write for days on end. I know you cannot understand the lines I draw between killings and atrocities, the degrees I profess exist between, for instance, my own deeds and those of this Junior Jack. I will tell you this—what he learned of anatomy he got from a $20 CD program that could be had from any children's educational center, and yet the visions showed a depth of artistry unaccounted for in most clinical displays of Human form. Like the Ripper bringing Mankind slashingly into the 20th century, his student wanted to usher in the 21st, sans the raw publicity, because this new Jack was no exhibitionist. He was no letter-writer and displayer of bodies. As to his reasons for enacting his blood-rites, instead of confining them to canvas, as his host had done, he shouted to me (once the painter's soul was gone) that it had nothing to do with Fame and everything to do with a quest to become *whole*—to repair a fracture only blood and death could patch.

He had lingered inside me, refusing to go, clutching and screaming as I traveled in desperation to the Abbey to seek out the monk I knew remained below. It was only then, with the candles lit and the prayers begun, that he fled into the ether, as roughly disembodied possessors eventually must.

And the answer to the mystery of his disguise became clear.

I could not sense his presence because it was dominated and controlled by yet *another*, far more adept at undetectable possession than any Being I had ever known.

He laughed at my slow wit and stupidity, clawing into my vertebrae and climbing its jagged footholds into my skull as he whispered: "It's me you fool—not some student, some *wannabe*, but Saucy Jacky himself, scourge of Whitechapel and environs and the Great Mystery of 1888 and onward to today."

As if to prove it, he ran in my mind a grainy, flickering filmstrip of the bladed murders of so many women—Annies and Lizzies, Marys and Frannies, Rose, and Alice and Katie and Emma—most of them scarred, disease-riddled alcoholics in their 40s, though a few almost pretty… And laid over each of their haunting, floating faces and torsos the wounds he had inflicted—slit throats, stab wounds, open abdomens, destroyed genitalia, hacked-upon faces with missing noses and ears… Despite my efforts to close my mind I saw upon the late-night streets of Whitechapel and Spitalfields, Poplar, London, and Camden Town the discarded hearts, uteruses, intestines, and kidneys that were the symbols of his hatred for those who brought forth Man.

Though they morphed and piled and became borderless testaments to one another's pain and humiliation, I could discern the essences of no less than 14 women—all victims of one entity whose face, like those of his victims, was often not the same.

"Bravo," the creature said, opening his psychic trousers and jerking forth a hot stream of piss onto my brain. "I think you're starting to get it."

"If you want to confess, I'll listen," I replied, having seen enough to know that that was his intent. "Just be quick and then be gone. Can't you see I am at prayer?"

"Very well. I am, in some earth-bound, fleshy sense, the one called Jack the Ripper—a name I came up with in September 1888, although the name is not the point. All those *whores* had other names—Siffy, Polly, Black Mary, Long Liz... You could just as easily call me Mr. Nemo, Mr. Nobody, George Chapman, Walter Sickert, Roslyn D'Onston, James Maybrick, Aaron Kosminski, Michael Ostrog, Frances Tumblety, WH Bury, Leather Apron, or Joseph Barnett—I used them all to more or less extent—Sickert and D'Onston the most. All the rest were in one way or another ... *inadequate*. Montague Druitt for instance—insanity ran in his family, a fact I overlooked. Others were too drunk or stubborn for me to coordinate their limbs, resulting in a certain *sloppiness*, and I *despise* sloppy work. Sickert, though ... he was a good one—so willing, so creative, so able to do what needed doing. And D'Onston, so drawn to the Dark Arts, *so willing to be possessed.*

"Roslyn D'Onston (born Robert D'Onston Stephenson) is worth some words. In 1887 his wife, his brother's former servant, disappeared. Many thought he killed her, but he only *wished* he had... He was educated, which I much prefer in a possession... He was also a self-professed magician and major bullshit artist who lifted the words of others for his letters and stories. He claimed to have killed a witch doctor in Africa and to have met Sir Edward Bulwer-Lytton—he merely plagiarized him. When I decided his mix of occultism and tale-telling might be useful, I brought him to Whitechapel—in July of the Great Year—and had him check into London Hospital under the diagnosis of *neurosthemia* so he'd be near.

"It was difficult to get him in and out of the hospital, even for me, so I used him mostly as a diversion. WT Stead of the *Pall Mall Gazette* thought he might be Jack (he had published one of his articles on Black Magic and knew him to be a loon who wrote under the name Tau-Tria-Delta). Poor Stead—one of the only ones involved with the investigation with any brains and he wound up going down with *Titanic*. Others thought him Jack as well, which he loved.

"D'Onston had some nicely fucked-up friends, led by that gem of an occultist, Madam Blavatsky. Their circle of friends engaged in all the best of freaky sex for forward-thinking types. Blavatsky taught them what she wished to of occult, Kabbalah, Hindu, Egyptian, and Buddhist scripture—which was her right considering she was given her wisdom thru the "Astral bodies" of Tibetan *mahatmas*. He might have done some of Blavatsky's dirty work, although it had nothing to do with me. He once showed Mabel Collins, a spiritual medium and his mistress and business partner, seven soiled ties he swore Jack used to hide the whores' organs as he carried them down the street. His other business partner, Baroness Vittoria Cremers, was a Theosophist who co-edited *Lucifer*. She met none other than Aleister Crowley in 1912 in New York and told him Mabel's tale of the soiled ties, which she said D'Onston kept in a tin under his bed. Although he was barely a teen when the murders occurred, Crowley was sharp and he could sense there was something greater at work—Jack was a life-long obsession.

"Then there's Sickert, who had studios in Whitechapel (I saw you there in '58 when Pollack had a show nearby)—places where he produced his darkest art, places where I could sit upon his desk and whisper in his ear all the things I wanted to say in my letters to the papers and police. Letters—250 of them—that have been analyzed to the point of paralysis, just like the letters I wrote 80 years later, when I took up my work again in California, *but I'll save that for another time*… I have moods the same as anyone, and literary tricks I like to play (I'm sure you know what I mean) and so what if it was at times a bit contrite, a bit artsy and over the top? It was all so much *fun*: the misspellings, the changes in grammar and syntax, the cryptograms and abbreviations, the things I wrote and then so clearly crossed thru, the addresses I blocked out with little sketches and designs. How I pretended that envelopes were reused but were really blank beneath the paste-overs. And despite what some have said, there were *plenty* of envelopes the fools in the police department tried to work with… And the postmarks and dates—that was my favorite game of all—going from town to town and even between countries in a single day to send my posts—on November 22, 1888, for instance, I sent four letters from as many towns (only three of them still exist). I sent over a hundred letters in October 1888 *alone*, though only about 80 survive—and most of those are considered frauds. Idiots and Fools! Though it's my own fault, writing as I did thru so many different arms and minds and levels of intelligence. Regardless, the most important thing was: *I was having fun*. The "Ha Ha" about jumped off the page every time I wrote it—and I indulged the flavor and speech of the one I was writing through—it is not my style to refer to the fairer sex as "cunts" but it was usual enough among commoners. And I never said a single thing I didn't mean—My knives *were* so nice and sharp and I really did find it hard to refrain from nightly work. One of my favorite little letters was addressed to 'Dear Boss', whomever the hell he happened to be at the time: 'I shant stop until I get buckled *and even then* watch out for your old pal Jacky.'

"*Even* now.

"*Especially* now.

"For, you see, my time's come 'round again. I am the 'evil one revisiting the earth' as quoted by an East End missionary in 1888, the year when I completed the best known of my work. But those few handfuls of kills were mostly nothing—just a bit of cultural extension and artistic realization while *Dr. Jekyll and Mr. Hyde* made its debut (*without* Stevenson's permission) in the summer months, playing its nightly sold-out shows at the Lyceum to that fool Irving's delight. All that Ripper business was—how might you say?—*experimentation.* You see, before I could fully enact my plans, I had to see how the damned things worked. The fools got it wrong—it wasn't someone with medical knowledge but one trying to *gain* it beyond the anatomy books and their alluring color plates. I had some experience with the female genitalia, and cadavers and parts could be had for almost nothing, but I was looking to broaden my scope and London in 1888 was the perfect place to start. Consider it—violent and grotesque beyond all human sense—you couldn't tell the vermin from the Vermin. The Thames was a waterway of shit, the air reeked of sulfur and sewage, and the great majority were poor, crazy, sick, or living in the doss-houses. Read some Holmes and Watson—the imitators more than Doyle—and you can feel it seething and pulsing beneath their tales. But I—I was *living* it! For so many of those poor bastards, the order of the day was Escapism, pure and simple—the inns like the Cricketers, pubs like the Ten Bells, The Frying Pan, and the Rising Sun, and the Music Halls! Gatti's, the Marylebone, the Alhambra….

"The people were ready for a push into the new century—I said it then and restate it now with the surety of hindsight. After I killed that whiner Annie Chapman in the rear yard of 29 Hanbury, the fine folks who lived adjacent to where she bled out charged admission to enter and see the blood-splats, and money was made at the site of Stride's death as well—this time by a social group who used the money to print their tracts. And Eddowes—they hung her body on a nail in Golden Lane Mortuary for anyone to see. So answer me this— What's worse: the butcher or the one who profits from his toils? So what if it turned out that Sickert didn't actually commit a single murder? He *painted* them … he sold some of those paintings and those he didn't he used to build a reputation—a means to good parties and fancy trips. A good seat at the music hall shows. I got caught up in Walter Richard Sickert—in his hatred of women and his malformed little prick and his robust atheism and fascination with the morbid. He also had a keen understanding of math and geometry, which was absolutely essential to my plan. I also liked his friends (I can name drop with the best of them)—Rodin, Proust, Henry James, Aubrey Beardsley... He was also chums of a sort with your butt-buddy Wilde, who visited his poor mother when his father passed in '85, although he was too jealous of Oscar's wit to be a friend and shunned him when the pillow-biter got out of jail in '97. He was ennui made flesh, much like me, and so he became my favorite vehicle, my favorite way to play. I found his disinterest in sexual consummation with the victim to match well with my own philosophy of Separation, although the big-titted fat chicks he chose to paint amused me visually no end. Though Sex and Murder are equally joyous undertakings, they are as separate and distinct as a shit and a shave. Ironic that I almost passed him by, with his head stuck in a trunk full of lice-infested hats in Angel's Theatrical Costumes. He was, after all, an *actor* ... but he had been wise enough to give up the theatre for a more important set of performances, and the spotlight he was craving was one I was also ready to use, and he turned out to be the best of the bunch. He always kept a collection of soldiers' uniforms on hand, which was helpful in a pinch. I even went back and used him nine years later on that fresh-faced Emily Dimmock (though I had been at it plenty since Mary Kelly's death—in England, Paris—as promised in my letters—and even in the great United States). In return I let Walter sketch Emily's body, the genesis for a series called the Camden Town pieces and even allowed him to paint a portrait of his bedroom and attach the Ripper's name—I forewent the usual franchise fee as he was by that time beginning to succumb in a less proactive way to his madness—he knew he was getting *help*—being *directed*; at times he even tried to expel me and once or twice he wrote in his *unauthorized* Ripper letters (Walter loved to write the papers) that "I've got someone to write this for me." Some 20 years later he engaged himself in a series of religious works in self-portrait (that self-portraiture business is something I'll talk about again). My favorite is he as Christ raising Lazarus, though "Servant of Abraham" was so ill-fitting as to be a cube of ice shoved up an angel's ass.

"What a horrible fucking joke. Worse than anything I ever had him—or anyone else—put into *my* letters. To liken me to Abraham ... quite the laugh. I have no interest in carrying out the bidding of God. I'm strictly freelance, strictly in this for Me. I don't have the same gripes as Lucifer or the other whining pukes among his boys. I abandoned God well before any of them finally did...

"Also quite unlike Lucifer and his sorrowful lot, I love the Human Form. Thus my time as Jack, thus my other excursions into the bodies of men."

"You've done this before?" I asked, feeling as though if I didn't assert my separateness from him with speech he would assimilate with my skull and remain there forever.

"Many times ... and nearly always with artists. The great god-kings of man, artists ... such keen vision, such Plane-leaping imagination. Take the highly successful Scottish woodworker and politician William "Deacon" Brodie, who I first noticed in 1785 at the Fleshmarket Close cockfights in Edinburgh. He was a wild one—a borderline sociopath, a compulsive gambler and, most appealing to me, a sex addict. Anything to fire the synapses and boost the adrenalin, serotonin, and dopamine. To me, Brodie represented real Human *Potential*. I had already made a few other in-flights, as it were, by this time, and Brodie was easy prey. He *wanted* me there, egging him on while he expanded his horizons. History tells that he turned to robbery in 1786 because of mounting gambling debts, but I was really behind the move—we both enjoyed the rush. Twelve times we did it, over a period of 18 months, always in houses in which he worked, either by stealing or forging a key. At his insistence (you know how the bastards keep control!), we worked with three others—all common thugs. I think he fancied their rugged company more than their services during a theft. No matter, now, eh? In '88 Brodie got the grand idea (*solely his*) to rob the Excise Office of Scotland. It didn't go well—and he made off with a mere 16 pounds ... hardly worth the aggravation of weathering the colossal bullshit of one thug ratting out the others for some reward money and then trying to blackmail Brodie for cash he didn't have. I wasn't with him when he initially skipped out—if I was he would have made it to America from Amsterdam instead of getting caught—but I went back to him right before his Gallows Day, and together we rigged up the little harness that saved his stupid life—he wandered Europe after that, spending some time in Paris before finally dying a dismal death.

"All in all, I consider the Brodie affair a success. As you know, he partially inspired Stevenson to write *Jekyll and Hyde*, and we both know the value of *that*. Then I got this idea in the mid-1800s to try my hand at turning a group of Victorian businessmen to my purpose by pretending I was the devil. They would sneak away from the wives and daughters they so brutally oppressed on the guise of doing charity work in the East End and I'd host some wildly debauching parties with the most pox-riddled whores I could find ... some morphia, some laudanum, plenty of wine and spirits but in the end, when I needed them to actually *do things* on my behalf, they were nothing but a trio of gutless wonders. I should have known—and if I ever had a doubt about the stupidity and unoriginality of my notion, when I saw Hammer's *Taste the Blood of Dracula* a century later, with my own bright idea blinking back at me nearly unchanged from the cinema screen, I knew for sure what a dolt I'd been.

"I never should have forsaken those who worked so well. A truly great artist can imagine Anything, and much more important, *render it into existence*— entire worlds, simple answers to complex equations, the polar opposite of whatever filth or garden he finds himself daily walking in; the enactment of truly horrific murders... And this idea—*my* idea—was embodied in a film made 25 years before *Blood of Dracula*—*Bluebeard*, with John Carradine. Do you know it?"

"Of course. He was such a handsome man. Tall, gaunt, long fingers ... he's the puppeteer and painter Gaston Morrell. *Faust* is the perfect choice for his puppet opera..."

"Exactly. It's all there—the cravat used as a garrote, paralleling the bloody neck ties kept by D'Onston, the artist tortured by his glorified model—his *Muse*—turning out to be a common street whore; the reckless disposing of the bodies and the compulsion to immortalize his victims in art... That same theme of the corrupted feminine Ideal and its effect on the artist appears in two films made 20 years apart—*Mystery of the Wax Museum* in '33 and the at times identical *House of Wax*, with Vincent Price."

"One of his best—his makeup was as good as Chaney's in *Phantom of the Opera*."

"I don't give two shits about costume and make-up, dolt—it's the *theme* that interests me! The beheading of Marie Antoinette, the gentle Joan of Arc meditating before the cross before the sticks are lit, Charlotte Corday murdering Marat ... beauty can—and must—lead naturally from violence. It's the definition of sublime... You speak of *Phantom*—the themes are similar in all these films—the disfigured genius in pursuit of his Muse—the victim of treachery who craves the Pure and washes himself in blood—that's something you know about—I know you do..."

"You're quite the cinema scholar."

"You seem surprised, yet you blather on about how thrilled that suckass Lucifer was with the antichrist films—we must be students of filmmakers as they are of us. And there are subtleties in *House of Wax* that speak directly to my work—the wax figure of the murderer Bluebeard is one ... and the other I'll reveal soon enough... Would you like to hear more of the things I've done?"

"Yes—if only you would remove yourself from my skull."

Instead of leaving he began to laugh with enough force to create fontanelles my unnatural birth had made unnecessary.

"Stop!" I yelled (whispered? moaned?).

"I go when *I* want—is that clear?"

He didn't pause to let me answer, but I felt the gaps begin to close.

"My first experience of Earth in human form was in 1529, when I entered the soul of Bevenuto Cellini. He had already killed a few people on his own, so I knew he had the knack, and such a violent temper as his amid the beauty and creation of the Renaissance had finally propelled me from being a Watcher to being an Enactor. I 'helped' him kill the man who had allegedly murdered his brother. It was so simple, so vaguely *just*, I felt stronger for the act.

"Being an artist, as I've said, I wasn't just there for the blood. In fact, I used Cellini's murderous hands to create what would be his most well-known and admired piece—a bronze of Perseus holding aloft the head of the snake-queen, Medusa. This idea of the severed head and open throat was one I would explore and expound upon for hundreds of years to come, just as DaVinci had done with the Turin Shroud.

"Despite my beautiful work in bronze, Cellini is known mostly for his posthumously published autobiography. I am amazed at you morally corrupt souls who haven't the sense to keep your ill deeds and mangled thoughts a secret. What good has it done Lestat? What good do you think it will ultimately do for you? If anyone makes the mistake of thinking you anything other than a warped fiction, your writing will be squashed and you will quickly be forgotten. And if you succeed in passing yourself off as mere shadow, no one will take it even the least bit seriously, so what will you gain? Paint great works, launch an army, decimate an entire race, start a fanatical religion … really *do something*, and *then* write your version of your life….

"My next trip to this Plane in the form of an artist came in 1606. You know the man—you've mentioned him—Michelangelo Merisi da Caravaggio. His penchant for the severed head drew me in—his Medusa (themes are the fruit of the murderer-artist), John the Baptist's worthless head, Judith beheading Holofernes… I sunk deep into his mind and because of a *spat*—a stupid dispute over a tennis score between friends—I was able to take a knife and take a life. That was nothing compared to what I did four years later—inhabiting his body to paint a portrait of David holding Goliath's head—a head that matched Caravaggio's in every detail. The horror with which he presented it to the Pope was truly a gift and the burst of low-vibration energy I received was like being back in the Millennial Lake of Fire—but on my own terms, without the chains forged by a reprobate god who thought only *He* knew the secret of—"

He stopped himself, and I felt a bony tail begin to curl around my epiglottis before resting between the creature's legs as he moved to a position just behind my eye.

"In the 1820s I chose a ruthless bastard of a fairly nothing artist named Thomas Griffith Wainewright, mostly because of his oh-so-human ability to kill loved ones in order to make a buck, though his assistance to Sir Thomas Phillips in painting his portrait of Lord Byron didn't hurt, nor his penchant for painting his victims and using pseudonyms, traits he shared with Sickert. Wainewright's evil pictures were of interest to your idol Oscar—he wrote an essay about him called "Pen Pencil and Poison in January of 1889"—just after my high-profile murders as Saucy Jack. He also shared your love of the other so-called

Romantics—Blake, Shelley, and Keats. He didn't take much convincing—as Wilde said, although he was a murderer he didn't care much for suffering himself. I didn't even alter his modus operandi—I forsook the knife and allowed him to continue with his use of strychnine, which was an education in and of itself as I watched the victim's unstoppable muscles begin to tire as they slowly became unable to breathe—all the while remaining quite aware of the pain.

"Some twenty years later, growing all the time more adept at inhabiting the body and controlling the mind and muscles of the artist I chose, I happened upon Richard Dadd while gathering concoctions in his father's apothecary shop. He was an artist who had once gotten stoned for five days on the "hubbly bubbly" Arabic water pipe while in Egypt and had himself a vision of Osiris being dismembered. Such visions appeared throughout his work, all dealing with the so-called Middle Spirits—the types who can't commit to either the halo or the horn. The kind of fence-sitters Dante so despised. *Titania Sleeping, Puck, Oberon and Titania* … such brilliance and menace! I must admit that the Osiris imagery was a major draw—his missing dick was a foreshadowing of Sickert's own sickly little dicky. You have to admit the ironic beauty of a spirited genius called upon to battle demons *by a* demon."

He didn't give me a chance to reply.

"These are the types of things that capture my attention … just like the hypnotist, I can make the subject do nothing he is not inherently willing to do. But with a sufficiently pliable subject and the properly inserted vision, the keys which fail to open so many otherwise permanently barred doors turn easily in the lock. He had quite willingly done a series of sketches of his friends with their throats slashed with nary but a whisper from me. You can read a lot of psychobabble horseshit about the Victorian pattern of psychoses—divine election and the questing of the sufferer and all of that—but in truth, crazies aren't sparked by their era—they just respond to it in kind.

"My first experiment with the possession of Dadd was less than a success … I entered him in Rome with the intention of killing Pope Gregory XVI, but it was too much too soon (I would fail again 130 years later, also with a painter—this time with Paul VI). But all was not lost. My hold was strengthening—I had him living on boiled eggs and ale (imagine the sulfuric bliss!) and I even left him now and again to inhabit his brother George (the equivalent of fucking twins). Then, August 28, 1843, a complete and utter success—he slit his father's throat with a knife and razor and dismembered the body. Such bursts of energy came forth with each slash, with each release of blood and love and soul—energy I could *use*. Dadd could have been a repeat performer—a wonderful hotel wherein I could commit my crimes—but he sensed me too clearly, and so our second attempt was a miserable failure. The stranger we chose not only didn't die, but Dadd was arrested and put in Bethlem psychiatric hospital, the infamous Bedlam itself.

"I didn't spend all those millennia in a prison of God's jealous devise just so I could visit another, so that was the end of Dadd and me, though I did give him subtle credit by making Sickert do a sketch called "He killed his father in a fight." It really should have been a painting, and with my guidance Sickert's greatest work, but that would have been more than Dadd deserved. Besides, he had *Fairy-Feller's Master Stroke*, and just for the record, his guidebook to that painting, which he so inaccurately called "Elimination of a Picture," is bullshit—*Fairy-Feller's* nothing more than an encoded record of everything I've just explained.

"As I was finishing up with Dadd, I decided to switch to music, placing my sights and eyes and claws into one Robert Schumann, a German Romanticist composer who was working on an adaptation of Goethe's *Faust*—so this should appeal to you. I plagued the man for years, piping a continuous stream of the note A5 into his ear and employing my minions to appear to him as angels and demons. What I really wanted was for him to kill his wife, Clara, but what I got were the *Geistervariationen*—the Ghost Variations… He tried to kill himself by jumping into the Rhine after warning his wife he might harm her and when he was rescued, he asked to be institutionalized, where he remained until his death. I was getting so potent, I was driving the bastards insane.

"No matter—another decade went by in the blink of a madman's eye and I *happened* upon John Wilkes Booth (and so the second subtle connection with *House of Wax* becomes clear). Skipping the details because I find your attention waning and I still have much to tell, let me say that I learned a valuable lesson with that particular man—never choose the strong willed. I wanted him to slit Lincoln's throat—the knife, the lovely, bloody necklace the wielder creates are both so crucial to helping me get my fix—but the lousy punk of an actor chickened out and used a gun.

"A fucking *gun*! I *despise* guns! No connection with the victim, no reaping of the soul-flying energies, so what the hell's the point?

"*Sic semper tyrannis* up his worm-eating ass… Now perhaps you can better understand why Sickert's being an actor nearly lost him the gig."

He whimpered as though he was a babe ill content with his mother's tit.

"My warm-ups for the Ripper games came in the form of one Thomas Neill Cream, doctor, abortionist, and poisoner of prostitutes and others in his way. I learned a great deal about the woman's lower anatomy from Dr. Cream—I certainly stared thru his eyes at enough botched abortions—the man was a hack, and an inspiration at that. He was the ultimate contradiction—a doctor who loved to kill, so I saw him as a hotel room with a comfortable bed and interesting view. He was a braggart and letter-writer who gave me my earliest ideas about how to use the press to further my aims. Cream's problem was lack of control—without me Sickert and Maybrick would have been the same—he ultimately went too far and landed himself in prison, forcing me to hit the road yet again.

"That brings me back to the Ripper years. Good years—experimental. And, to quote the demon barber Sweeney, "There's no place like London," so when it was time to really get organized, there I went. I loved the poverty and stench of the East End—the crowded streets, the Tower of London ever looming—Whitechapel. Spitalfields. Aldgate, home of St. Botolph's Prostitute Church—they'd walk in circles because, although prostitution was legal, *loitering* was not. Houndsditch (a beautiful name for a beautiful game), Ratcliffe Highway. The stench of water and dope and rampant crime, and for the collector of means, shops filled with the exotic treasures brought from around the world by sailors and other travelers. And when I needed rest, I spent my time by the springs and ponds of Hampstead Heath, where in past years I had walked among the great writers and painters of their times: Dickens, Shelley, Keats, that short shit Pope…

"But the work was done in the playgrounds of the poor. How I made my mark upon Mitre Square, Goulston, Gardner's Corner, the market along Whitechapel Road, Bucks Row, Commercial and High and Lehman Streets—the shitty little places on Flower, Dean, and Dorset where the Famous Five laid their whorey heads when they could find the scratch.

"And, lest you interrupt (I feel your tongue starting to move) I will volunteer a little truth—some researchers were onto something when they considered the occult nature of the layout of the Famous Five (and some of the other killings as well—a connection D'Onston introduced from the start)—sacred geometry, the *Vesica Piscis*, profaned crosses, the equidistant measurements between bodies, the use of the cardinal points. Whore organs are potent (you don't know just how potent, yet—but you will…) and they are absolutely vital for candles and potions when your magic lacks strength. There's plenty of bullshit, too—the carving of symbols into the eyelids and cheeks is pure theatre, as is the removal of jewelry, like I did in the case of Annie Chapman—that was a nod to the Freemasons and nothing more.

"My eyes were truly opened. Each victim a little better worked than the one before, as I mastered control of my host with each new possession. By the end, the cutting was elaborate and my tally was far more extensive than the measly 5 to 7 murders for which I'm given credit—in England alone there were 15 women and several torsos (one of which I placed in the foundation of the new Scotland Yard) and countless bags of parts. Plus two little boys and a girl."

"You mutilated children?"

"If you don't believe me, check the archives—I wrote about them in 1889... But you don't care about the means of proof—you want to know the whys and what-fors. Fine. I only chose the children when I felt like God was losing interest—his mind does tend to wander ... but holding up the heart and balls of a 7-year-old tends to bring his eyes into focus, and I needed the fool to watch, like he had at the start—like he did when I laid my hack job on Mary Kelly's face and body. When I took out her heart, I was sure I heard him cry. And in his wracking sobs I caught a small slice of God's regret about not joining forces with me while he had the chance, when he first saw I'd learned his trick. It was only then, as I lay her insides on the bedside table, that he could see what a boundless imagination I have. He'd only gotten the smallest little inkling of it when I stabbed Martha Tabram 39 times in the stomach—one gash for each lash Pontius Pilate had inflicted on the back of Jesus Christ."

"Forgive my ignorance, but you don't strike me as the type to hit back at God for what he let to happen to Yeshua ben Joseph ..."

"Don't be dense—I just wanted to let him know I'd been paying attention to his game. That I wasn't some fool of a devil trying to stretch my wings, but a Creator of equal—and now surpassing—skill. You see, I consider myself to be an Artist of no small talent. My creations and designs are multifaceted. The layouts I contrived for the organs and extremities I removed were more symbolic and meaningful than any Mason's rites. It didn't matter that no one understood—the shock value was genius itself. And look at what I accomplished with one line of graffiti on a doorjamb at the Wentworth Model Dwellings the night of the Stride–Eddowes job. I used both Kosminski *and* D'Onston that night. The "Juwes" thing set off an elaborate theory system on a Royal Conspiracy involving the Freemasons (a story later told by Sickert's alleged son Joseph), and it gave that pain in the ass credit-hogger Maybrick a place to shine (as if the watch I gave him with the victims' initials wasn't enough...), saying it really meant "The *James* are the men who will not be blamed for nothing." (I got him though—took possession of his wife Florence and killed the cocky fucker dead) and if it hadn't been for the single unfoolish thing Commissioner Warren had done thru the whole affair—getting it cleaned off the wall—there would have been a juicy religious riot to carry my game along. Warren and the Assistant Commissioner of Metro CID, Sir Robert Anderson, were one dumber than the other—totally unworthy of me. Half their suspects weren't even *in* Whitechapel during the murders. If it wasn't for his love of clocks and gardening and his dislike of extra hours (plus his inane attachment to the Royal Conspiracy idea), Inspector Abberline might have been the Holmes to my Moriarty, but it wasn't to be. He was the only one besides Henry Smith, Acting Commissioner of the City of London Police, to realize that Martha Tabram was my first victim. They never got it right—there were others—Francis Coles in 1891, Emma Johnson in 1897, that whore Emily in 1907…

"I didn't need his help, obviously, but D'Onston did his part with the graffiti, too, theorizing in the papers that it was actually *Juives*, the French word for Jew. When that didn't work he blathered on about getting the idea from the Holmes novel *A Study in Scarlet*, which was an idea Doyle got from a real case some years before. D'Onston knew Doyle—that whole Blavatsky thing. All the artists, writers, and occultists ran in the same small circles—ask your friend Mykaldaemio—he was there. But I digress. D'Onston had his office across from Holmes' fictional address on Baker Street. That kind of symmetry gets me hot."

As if to prove it, he made his cock throb just behind my eye.

"Not bad for a dozen meaningless words, eh? I was still taunting them with it in my letters nearly 10 years later. I do find it hard to let go of the good ones…

"But that was only the start. I told you I took my work abroad. In August of '92 I happened upon an angry whip of a woman trying to buy prussic acid in a Massachusetts drugstore in order to murder her stepmother. When the druggist refused her, I stepped (*way*) in and took care of the whole damned thing myself (with her consent and help, of course). Killing the old woman was easy—a piss poor excuse for a mother, step or not. I gave her 19 whacks with an axe and then waited for her husband to come home so I could give him 11 more. And just like with Eddowes I took a little off the nose…"

"*You're* the phantom killer in the Lizzie Borden case?"

"I am. And I'm also the reason she actually *got away with murder*. It was going to happen one way or another. I just helped her out. I returned to London in time to possess Cream one last time—as he put his neck into the hangman's rope for his short drop and sudden stop. Yes indeed—it was most truthfully the Ripper who said "I am Jack…" as the rope went taunt. Perhaps my greatest stroke on the entire Jackie canvas. After all, despite his being in a Chicago prison during the years I did my Whitechapel work he remains to this day a suspect. But enough about the fairly ancient past. Let's consider how much I've done in the last 40 years—almost all the modern serial killers owe some of their work to me. Bringing to life vile Babylon's whore in the form of the Technological Multinational, freeing dumbshit princes like you from your pitiful crypts and empty lives and setting you loose upon the Earth… That's right Planner, it's me—Parvus Cornu—though I'm sure you figured it out before now … I was relying on your sense of restraint in the face of a larger power to keep you quiet until the time was right, and you didn't disappoint."

"I'm pleased you're pleased, Little Horn."

"Why desecrate my name by saying it in English? It's a vulgar language, full of etymological hybrids and scraps of this and that. The Latin is so much purer and more elegant and therefore correct for beings of our stature—can't you hear its lovely rhythms coming from above? Call me Parvus Cornu, I beg you. It's so ancient and mysterious, so appropriately Biblical, and yet still hip enough for a twenty-first-century King."

"The Time of Kings is done..."

"Don't fool yourself—just because you think you've figured me out doesn't mean I can't still ram it up your ass. It was easy to lead you to London—to engineer a multi-layered possession with the Ripper wannabe and your arts and crafts chum."

"I can understand why you chose Saucy Jacky the Second, but why a young artist—more supposedly symbolic randomness like the 'extra' Ripper killings?"

"Not at all—far from it ... I chose him as carefully as I chose you—so many ideas, philosophies, visions of what's possible. And as an added bonus, he was far more controllable than you will ever be. He could only manifest as a dark image on a piece of stretched canvas—but it was just the kind of subversive artistry I knew you'd like."

"Clever."

"*Clever?*" I felt his tail break the membrane of my eardrum as he pushed its spiked length into the open air beyond my auditory canal. "I *despise* cleverness, you fool. Do not mistake all I have told you—all the games with the police and the countless machinations—as mere *cleverness*. I gave them more than they deserved, but in my own way. For instance: "Togs 8 suits, many hats I wear." And they thought I was merely talking disguise! I am learning all the time. Learning and progressing toward the actualization of my greatness. All those millennia I lay seemingly idle and forgotten since my handful of mentions in the Bible prepared me for the more active learning I've been engaged in for over five hundred years. You got the date of my breaking the Event Horizon all wrong. And other things as well..."

"So why now—I mean, I have my theories—but what is *really* going on with you?" I choked down a scream as he gathered in his tail and pushed it thru my other ear.

"Don't bother me with bullshit questions to which you know the answer! For millennia you enjoyed your immortal, supersensory existence on this Plane, so I put forth the coin for an extended stay. But the privilege of being here comes at a price, whether you had a say in it or not. As for the time I chose, has there ever been one better? There are technologies here that not even I—and certainly not that fool of a Yahweh—could have envisioned. I'm just beginning to get an idea of what it means—the hi-tech gadgetry, the gene splicing, biological and chemical warfare, the Internet and virtual reality devices—and I know you understand it—better than *you* do—because I made sure you were *born into it*—in another ten years the umbilical cord will be replaced by a USB cable so you can plug the newborn fuckers in for an on-screen APGAR."

"You fucking thief! I said almost the exact same thing months ago—but the cable went up the *ass*…"

"Yes… In some social-network *blog*, if I recall. And it was used for something else—surfing the Web, or some shit. Don't kid yourself—you've barely had an original thought or undertaken an independent action since you got here. If you had, we would have talked years ago. I sense some doubt in this piss-filled skull of yours. How about this … I know you've got a Technical Advisor—a deceased soul who exploited all the best of it to his incredible gain—that is, until the spunk sparked. And I know there are others."

"You know about my guides? You're able to see them?"

"I know when they're at work—your guides, your spies (why'd you stop at Crow?—there's another around you just as bad), your war council of disembodied outcasts—the Homeboyz of Hell, isn't it? That's a bit trite, even for you…"

"You know *everything*?"

"My vision reaches far. My only limitation is that I cannot directly manifest—the price of being one of two Genesis Beings—so just as God worked thru Jesus and Buddha-Siddhartha and Mohammad, so I chose the path to Earth thru the heart of Man. There have always been willing hosts for the manifestation of Evil, though I do think that term is unfairly limiting and as grossly misunderstood as Peace or Love. God destroys entire cities, and that's Justice, but I simply—"

"Try to supplant the accepted Devil himself…"

"Who, as you know, is like a lame duck president with a broken pecker and a closet full of secret deals gone bad. There's no saving our friend Lucifer. But that's the point—just as it is with demons, some men are more willing than others—take my most recent pupil… In most respects, an ignorant fool, but a loyal student—a studier of facts and techniques, an appreciator of the subtle ironies I've had to laboriously explain to you. His problem is that he had no interest in making his work—*our* work—*known*. He was purely clinical, caring nothing for the legacy from which he sprang. He was more of a Bundy or a Gacy than a Ripper or Zodiac—even after I made myself manifest thru him, as I did with both of them."

"Then why'd he do it?"

"Oh, that's right—he wouldn't tell you, would he? He thought you were a dolt—a godless maniac who drinks blood in order to live."

"He emulated Jack the Ripper, and he was judging *me*?"

"Easy, Planner—you take these mortal creatures too much to heart. His story is all quite typical and banal—his mother was—unspeakable thing!—a whore, a high-class stripper akin to Sickert's grandma. She also had very little interest in being a mother, so Jacky Junior spent a lot of time with his rigidly pious aunt, who filled his head with all types of damning talk about his madre, turning him into the type of tightly wound, sexually repressed half-man that becomes a killer whether I'm around to encourage it or not.

"Imagine the effect of her constant litanies on whoredom—it's enough to make a man wanna disembowel every slut he can find—which is what he did. One night he went so far as to fuck one as she slowly bled to death from half a dozen knife wounds—that was one I'd never seen. Inspiring to us both, because there was suddenly a method and a meaning to his work. He had this notion that if he were able to collect a piece from each—a liver here, a uterus there, a left breast, a right breast—each little bit wouldn't in and of itself be contaminated by whoredom, yet would contain enough of the yin-essence to slowly convert him from a motherless son to the Mother-Son itself.

"All the other gashing and ripping had to do with an ancient Tibetan ritual of dismembering the body in order to free the soul. What better model could there be than my work on Mary Kelly? I can guarantee her soul went nonstop all the way to wherever it is it chose to go, especially once it was released from her boiling heart. We left no possible obstructions on *that* finely filleted whoreflesh.

"He had such promise, but no sense of the bigger picture. He gave me some shit about contaminating the process if he went public. The bodies had to be hidden or else the soul would be drawn back—absolutely meaningless drivel no doubt put forth by his aunt and her Saturday morning bible club but the kid wouldn't make the move, and I was stuck. Another promising prospect gone awry. Our final falling out was right after he killed that bitch of a nun for me—he insisted he needed her left foot but I couldn't allow such a needless complication."

"The one who sold out Sister Agnes? I knew it wasn't me..."

"You are so far from figuring out the truth that I am beginning to wonder if I made a mistake in choosing you. But in the end, I'll bet you get some press."

"So it's all about publicity?"

"For the moment—Yes! What good is being a genius and the next leader of the Universe if no one knows who the fuck you are? You can't do dick without a press kit. But thanks to the self-serving modern media—and your little stab at prose—people are beginning to know me. They may not have guessed my name as the Mickster might say, but they know the Devil's back in town, and he ain't the pitiful angel of old.

"So that's the good word from the new book. Nearly. I must say I find it ironic that a painting by Sickert's mentor, James Whistler, marks the cover of the edition of *Dorian Gray* always stuffed into your pocket. You've no originality—Wilde carries Pater, you carry Wilde... I suppose you fancy someone one day carrying your shitty little memoirs around? You're a dolt. It's nothing more than a means to wipe a baby's ass.

"Ugh. I've got to get clear of your cluttered attic rooms…"

"You mean you're leaving? *Finally?*"

"I can only take so much of your drooly mouthed crap—but I'll be seeing you *around*. Bank on it."

My ears began to bleed the moment he left my mind, and as I began to lose consciousness and fall to the floor I watched the kind Benedictine enter, relight the flame, and begin to chant a long and ancient prayer.

I watched his lips move until my vision finally failed and I was carried into black.

It was only then I realized, I couldn't hear a sound.

A thousand-million spiders gyrate and flux as they stretch their legs in an ongoing attempt to interlock in the vast expanse of my abruptly silent hellscape, even as the thunderous impression-sounds of cats' meows and Government helicopters weave their aural imprints into what is left of my tattered-flag eardrums.

Cats' meows and black-ops blades, black-ops blades and cats' meows, and all the while Parvus Cornu dances the deaf-man's tattoo on the bleeding remnants of my connection to Sound. He's made it so I can't hear the cries of those who seek me, or the praise of those who believe me, or the advice of those who try and guide me. It is a new and frightening thing, this removal from all but the pulses and poundings of sound. If I were not a demon soul, I would not have even that.

And then there are my Eyes.

Eyes that have jumped to a new level of seeing because of the thrusting mischief done to my ears. (Ironic, given that the Cornu, who knows my love of *Faust*, no doubt took my hearing in a slick revision of the grey hag Care taking Faust's sight with a corrupted breath of air.) Everywhere I walk (I cannot seem to cease my walking…) I see the superimpositions of every car to ever motor down a highway, overlapping, bisecting, and yet not colliding (like the black-wheeled rectangles of unnatural color that represented cars in an ancient arcade game I once watched a hapless child play). In apartment rooms and hotel lobbies I can see all the furniture ever to crowd the warped-wood and stained-carpet peripheries, and the foot-traffic of every occupant, patron, visitor, intruder, or careless passer-by—it is Gurney's "Dining Room" with all the scenes played simultaneously in a moving-mouth pantomime, the overlapping characters spewing forth the hundred-million monologues to which these crowded rooms and ornate halls have borne witness, though I can hear nothing but the comical symphony of chopper blades and cats' meows that accompanies them.

That is just as well; I have learned to feel blessed by even the greatest of misfortunes and travesties to my Being, and like Odysseus, I can say, "Let this new disaster come. It only makes one more." Chelsea and Leyton and my Council have all tried to heal me, but any magickal fix is not to be. Deep within my mind will start the taunting tones of the Big Ben clockwork, but they quickly fall away and I am left in the silently blanketed Om once more. I can't say I'm surprised—Irony is the meaning of a fallen angel's life. Years ago, when I tried in varied ways to ruin this Human body in a desperate move toward suicide, I could not prevent the wounds from being healed and now, something so simple as a set of ruptured drums is beyond my own or others' power to repair.

The Cornu is out to teach me a lesson, so I will be patient and do my time. Though I cannot hear beyond the government's blades and howling kittens, I still have much to say, for I have been traveling far and wide since our meeting and have reconsidered many things.

Lying still in a deep bank of snow I struggle to recall the tortured songs the gargoyles have been known to sing to their broken, bleeding prey. Anything to occupy my mind and derail the signal I was inadvertently sending out to the group of young punks who have sensed my presence and wish to join me in what they think is some Master Plan of which they are destined to be a part. As they draw closer, almost directly above me, I feel the ground move beneath the heavy-heeled boots they wear, and I try not to breathe. It's when I am most in need of solitude that the voices roar (even now, in my deafness, I begin to hear the calls of the sinning sheep looking for a shepherd they can kiss, using all the ancient appellations for our kind), but I will not answer. They *think* they're the Essence of Evil, well-schooled as they are in ritual and lore, but they bring forth no natural Power, no understanding of the Sacred Feminine, no control of the Elements, no understanding of what it is to be Damned.

They've got me confused with the rest of Clapton's "Motherless Children," because they know of the death of Buntz, but I have nothing to say. No advice except to say "Fuck off!" I'm not looking for a daddy and I don't want to be theirs. It's a trap designed to ensnare my ego, but I'm not as dumb as I used to be. I know better than to think that I could lead. You start thinking you're a natural born leader and you're lost. It all begins with such glory and promise and then one day you're staring at the gutless visage of a 5-gallon gas can and thinking that the Burning could be good. I tried it. You know this. And even Lucifer, somewhere below the cesspool of his recent and obviously impotent stab at action, must fervently pray that Hell *was* a place of flames, where he could burn off his shame for all eternity. But there is no glory in an ill-lit flame. No glory in an ill-fought war, as much as the punks who have come to call me think there is. I lay in this snow bank hiding from promises of allegiance I know to be false, because it's clear that Cornu has sent them to test me, as Lucifer tested Christ. They promise me love and adoration and virgins on which to feast, as though I was one of those *shahids* I found myself despising after a week of watching their work. And so I've traded sand for snow, the ancient for the fleeting, the flame for the cold because I do not wish to burn any more than I wish to be the Fallen Father to motherless, fatherless sheep calling thru the ears of my heart. And since Kali won't have me and I no longer know what to make of my once-angel Anastasia, I will remain the unwed and unfathering Nothing I've become until the time I finally return to a place of Light or perish in the dark of my own self-hate.

I am sick of the inaccurate perceptions of things. Sick of the Poseurs—the bug-eyed cult leaders who sway abandoned kids into thinking we're somehow powerful and worth worshipping. If only they knew the truth about us, about Lucifer especially. Perhaps then they'd stop calling for him. He won't do anything to help me against the Cornu beyond some pop culture Mafia posturing, so why would he do anything for a few demoglyphs and a bit of corrupted Latin (so different from the new Latin of grammarians like Virgil of Toulouse…) or for the sex-craved drunkards in their scarlet robes and dangling pentacles?

We've been ignoring them for years and still they gather in their cursed churches and shout for us to come.

I blame this backwards business of trying to *summon* Lucifer—or any of us "lesser" demons (thank you, God, for that)—on the rash of Satanic films that were unleashed, as we were, in the late '60s/early '70s by studios and production companies like Hammer. I've touched on this before, though I've come to realize that the genre itself was little more than the artistic expression of *a sense of our presence* coupled with the means to make a buck. Hammer, having done their best work from '66 thru '68, holds the dubious honor of lead presenter of so many easily misunderstood images of what's just beyond the darkness, though they did things a bit more tastefully and less heavy-handedly than the producers of *Rosemary's Baby* or *The Omen*, mostly because the Brits know how to be subtle—it's not an American trait, in film, politics, or elsewhere.

Franchise fodder—that's what we've become. But who are we, really? We creatures classified as demons, vampires, and the general Unholy? To most minds we are no more than the mythological constructs and cinematic creations of gothic writers and horror film auteurs, but it gets more complicated the deeper in you go. I can't say what Cornu would look like when he's not invading someone's mind and heart—a speck of light, a ray of sunshine, a streak of lightning, the trapped energy of an atom a nanosecond before it's released. He will not be so theatrical as to come in the form of a Baphomet—that's a role for pawns like me to play. Not only has it nothing to do with truth, it has nothing to do with *him*. He's no mere demon—and far greater than the greatest of the angels, for he too is God, and more of an exact twin of G-1 than Jesus. He lives far above the cinematic images once so loved by Lucifer, and I'm sure he understands them better. The form he chose within my mind—that of a miniature Wurm—was a matter of convenience and not a nod to Human mythological art. We never see the truly Powerful of this Universe—they are forever sending their spokesmen and publicists, who in turn have theirs. But I must be clear—these second-tier propagandists are no employees of the Firm. For them to do their work, it's best to leave them thinking it's all their art, and in most cases it was their own ability to water and bring to lucrative fruition the seeds of fear and empathic lusting for blood that led them to make the kinds of films they did. Thus the good, campy fun that is the sheepsuit for the darkest, most bloodthirsty Wolf to prowl these Planes—

Humankind's ignorance of what the monsters look like and what the meaning of true Evil really is: *The embodiment of Power without Guilt.*

I think that's why we've drawn so many of the rich to seek our aid: absolution thru association. A scape*goat* in the best traditions of the Judas-blame.[16] No matter how low they sink in the Dark Prince's (supposed) service, they always have an Out: "Satan warped my mind, gave me the juice to do bad things. But when he's vanquished, I'll be released. Salvation is only a renunciation away." It's this "kill the seed and the minions are released" belief that led to the crossover genre of satanic-culture/vampire films of the early '70s. Good campy fun, but how much crucial truth goes by unnoticed as good campy fun? How many monsters have lived and worked and killed freely in society because they do not fit the type? You'd never take Mykaldaemio for a vampire having grown up watching Langella, Lugosi, and Oldman. Then there's me—on my best days, when the horns are small and my body firm and unscarred I look even less the monster than they, and those are the days of my greatest struggle, sitting in the park near a family that I could kill at any moment if the mood struck me right and wondering if their minds would *allow them* to believe what I could be. By the time it showed in my eyes, tipping them to a vague remembrance of the Dracula of Christopher Lee, it'd be too late. But not all the films have gotten it wrong. The transformation of the rebel biker, poster-boy, rock star hellions of *The Lost Boys* when the bloodlust thrives is pretty close to

---

[16]Let's be honest—that whole Judas-invoking thing is way over done. May 17, 1966, I was in the back of the hall in Manchester when Dylan was called a Judas by some brainless punk because he had dared to go *electric*. What a load of shit.

true. Simplified, sure, yet more to the facts than most of the other fables. It's all a matter of taste. If you like your energy dark and thick, the Hammer films can get you started. But if you're after a taste of the higher vibrations, the really questionable and more insidious evils, you'd better know where to look. Little towns with nasty secrets—folded over and inbred 'til everyone is kin and everyone has to cover for everyone else. Sure they have their quintessential villains but it's crucial to remember that the Andre Linoges and wicked shopkeepers of Stephen King's stories are nothing but *manifestations* of the townspeople they terrify. Incarnations of their *ill intentions*...

Power is Heaven and the path to Absolution cannot be traveled unless you are willing to go All the Way, past the cartoons and empty symbols and into the real heart of Hate. Satanism is nothing but a fuel, like murder, deviant sex, black magic. Men sit in the dark confines of Plato's cave, associating far more with Dracula than that intellectual limp-dick Van Helsing. The sexual allure, the control of the mind, the Immortality that comes with a relatively small price (conscience dies with the spleen and other organs, it seems). There is no regenerating the body once the blood-exchange takes place and the last vestiges of Humanness are expelled thru fluids that spill forth from every orifice as the Vampiric Blood takes hold.

Such mythic regeneration and redemption are best left to mythic creatures.

Humans aren't made to walk those roads.

So as I lay here beneath the snow, trying hard to ignore the pleas of those who would make me their prince, I wonder why, millennia later, a voice of Reason is *still* a voice of Treason. It's a causal loop—God hands the law to St. Peter, St. Peter to the Pope, the Pope to kings and presidents. And yet the loop splits apart at closer view because this matter of Peter is complex. He denied the Christ three times to save his hide, and he was made Pope, the foundation of the Church, in fulfillment of certain promises, so as far as that goes we are pat. But remember (and it shows the craft of the Christ)—Jesus *also* said "whomever disowns me before men I will disown him before my Father in Heaven." So who is lying to whom? Is Peter a rogue—the *real* rogue, and not Judas at all? After all, Peter stood to gain the most from Jesus' demise, his place in Heaven all but assured despite any future actions, and *Jesus knew it*. And so, in the end, I guess the voice of Reason shall *always* be the voice of Treason. God and his henchmen will continue to shut me out despite my knowledge of the Cornu—despite my knowledge of so many things ... and so he "reigns" while the pretender to his throne roams like a falsely limping wolf among the drunken sheep. It makes perfect sense that the Little Horn would bring back the whore of Babylon as the centerpiece of his scheme. It's always been easy to blame your actions on the whore who makes you drunk—whether it be on wine, power, sex, or something else. Dress her in silks and rouge her cheeks and breasts and bring her forth *to be healed by the Hand of God thru the sanctity of forgiveness and marriage*. Cornu as wedded god and second coming ready to open the crystal gates to the New Jerusalem and let all the bleating morons in.

And here I lay beneath a snow bank with everything figured out while the Innocents are led to their deaths under the guise of Communion and God won't give me a chance.

You see, the only way to get an audience with The Great Almighty is to make him think he's talking to himself and I still have too much pride to even pretend to be such a dolt as that.

Once the punks had gone (lured away by the Cornu with the commingled scents of perfume, cunts, and gin when I didn't take the bait), I made my way to Deutschland, where I sat astride a stone eagle on a Bavarian estate. It was a stern, glaring sculpture with oversized talons that evoked the Romans and Nazis and the cruel gods of the long-forgotten realms who inspired and "sanctioned" them. Since the demise of my trickster Crow I am wary of any form of avian specter anywhere near my eyes and yet there I was—heeding a summons by Mykaldaemio and Orlando Nepenthe that I thought was unusual enough to warrant my acquiescence. We were going to engage in some folly—reenact the seductions of their favorite vampire stories. (Ironic, given my latest entry.) Lure innocents, create covens, and feast upon the would-be fiancés of our chosen prey. I thought it was foolish, a waste of time (at least on the scale they had planned), and as soon as they explained the purpose of our visit to Germany (using hand signals and a mini TV when I refused to read their lips), I decided to bail, but Mykaldaemio stopped me with surprising verbal force.

"What the hell is with you, Planner?" he asked. "The shit is going down all around and it's time to be what we are—aren't you tired of fighting it? All you've gotten is dicked-with and endlessly bruised, and I'm beginning to think you're nothing but a bunch of fancy *words*."

I had to admit that on some deep-down level he was right, so I agreed to stay awhile and see how it went. We began by calling forth the bats, transforming ourselves into wolves, dissolving into smoke, and pouring our vaporous selves through keyholes and tightly barred doors. At least, Orlando and I—Myk-D's powers are somewhat more limited, being a transformed mortal and not a spirit of Air—but I had to give him credit—the little playhouses he created for our games had deftly matched components of everything from the best of the Hammer films (had he been reading my notes?) to Coppola to Carpenter. He even managed a bit of Murnau. He had arranged thru Orlando to have our myriad diversions and perversions moved to a variety of places—New Orleans, Transylvania, the English countryside, nothing towns in Mexico. We traveled by train, plane, and for a specially pointed thrill, in coffins carried by ebony carriages pulled by the four blackest horses we could find. We chased each other with long wooden stakes like the clinical Van Helsing and the passionate Jon Harker. We played Louis and Lestat and the Count in all the incarnations of which I'd recently written—Lugosi and Langella, Oldman, and the intensely eyed Lee. It was pure folly, and while Mykaldaemio had his physical limits and I my newly forged moral ones, Orlando, being a Nephilim, had none and so it fell to him to tap into the minds of the vulnerable young women—our very own Minas and Lucys—whose windows we stood before, fangs bared. It was a corruption of a corruption—I had often stood in just that way at Anastasia/Elsbeth's window. In the end, being that neither Mykaldaemio nor I would allow any Undead to be made, the mind control Orlando engaged in was essential for us to get the full effect.

We walked with lustful eyes down the Left-Hand Path, past the semi-conjured images of the voodoo chief with the yellow ping-pong eyes from *The Devil's Own* and the leader of the occultists in *Devil's Bride*. We laughed our way thru the Satanic ritual of the black cockerel and the white hen, exploring first-hand the human thought processes that use such things to juice the power of the strap-on spine into their flagging self-belief.

In the midst of the theatrics (most of which I rationalized as *research*), I had to ask myself—is there *any* shred of power inherent in voodoo, black magic, or the Tarot? Is there *any* truth to astrological readings and numerology, the reading of palms and the interpretation of one's aura? *Inherently*, I'd say no. The evil eye and the horn that counteracts it. Talismans, like rabbits' feet and the penny facing up. Drums and chants—songs to Satan (how he used to love to hear them!). Amulets and pentacles, swastikas and confederate flags—only symbols without the owner's full belief. Power is not embedded but *grafted* by the mind's desires, fears, and claims to what it wants. That's why it is wholly crap that a crucifix would repel a vamp. In order for the vampire to be afraid it would have to *believe* in its power. You don't drink blood and give a shit about another's blood ordeal, nailed to a cross or otherwise—that's literary, cinematic bunk.

The role-playing and feasting went on for almost a week before I finally asked Mykaldaemio why we were suddenly play-acting when we both knew full well the damage it could cause?

Turns out, he was *bored*.

The truth took me by surprise. He is a mere fledgling, barely thru his first century as the Dark Undead, and already he'd grown weary of the Hunt. So here we were in a manufactured, multinational Wampyrland, lurking in the shadows, luring dimwitted tourists to his elaborately constructed sets for our reenactments and blood games, all because he needed to find the Reason for his "newly" christened life.

Given this information, and despite my own feeble attempts at rationalizing the need to prove experientially what I knew to be true intellectually, I forcefully made it known that it was the wrong path, engaging in these public entertainments that hint at subtle powers so few souls, live *or* dead, can understand—what really happens when Conjurers walk among you doing their work, as Cornu has done in the guise of Jack the Ripper and thru the minds and souls of so many others.

I don't know if it was my words or something else (do we ever?) but as abruptly as Mykaldaemio started, he asked that it end. He'd experienced all the folklore, the films, the devices, and the circumstances. He was content now to just be Mykaldaemio the Vampire, whatever that might mean.

At least now one of us is closer to his truth.

I've been tunneling too deeply, deconstructing the cinema and literature that has entrapped and defined me beyond almost any hope of redemption or exoneration and yet I am coming back for more, though not of my own accord.

I spent the night in a frozen panic, listening to the vague and panicked whisperings of Tatyana, who came to me in the guise of the one known in Scandinavia as the Sleeping Hag (in Germany she is the Alp, appearing at times in the form of a shaggy animal; in other areas of Europe she is Mara or Cauchmar) because it was the only means she knew to make sure that I could *hear*, sitting squarely and heavily on my chest like one of the imps in Richard Dadd's *Walpurgis Night, Piper of Neisse, The Devil's Bridge*. She spoke to me of her friends the Brownies, who brought forth the idea of the dichotomy of the soul of Man thru the Jekyll and Hyde of Stevenson's pen. She spoke of Shelley's "Prometheus Unbound" and the creation of the homunculus in a phial over the fiery furnace by Dr. Wagner in *Faust* and the striving of the soul to escape man's riddled, evil body of animal passions and ascend to communion with the Ultimate Idea. She read to me long, complex passages from the work of Émile Zola and forced me to swallow the tenets of Hegelian dialectics and his theories on Free Will and necessity. She told me it was no coincidence that Cornu as Ripper and *Jekyll and Hyde* appeared in close proximity—if Man is to better understand his nature, he must examine—without flinching—his darkest capabilities and accept them, at least in part, as Who He Is, although not at all what he May Be.

And I must be the one to set the example; to lead the way.

"The Cornu will not leave you be if you continue to try and help me," she said with seeming concern, though her tone, clear as it was despite the palpable fear she exuded about our being discovered, conveyed that she had *every wish* to continue receiving my protection and help.

"I won't abandon you to him," I answered, though she immediately knew it wasn't a personal favor—she was a chess piece I could not afford to let him have, and whatever sentimentality I might have strived for in my voice was unsupported in my gaze.

"I need to know more about you," I said.

"Then, in time, you shall."

And then, quick as she had come, she was gone.

She had taken a colossal chance coming to see me, and as angry as I was at having to wait for answers (yet again), I was not going to discount the reason she had come.

I have been wandering for days, contemplating the fact of the Dichotomy of the Soul, and I have come to the conclusion that the most outlandish solution could also be the simplest and best. What if, instead of spending one's entire existence trying to suppress or make due with the shadow self in a bid to secure a place in Heaven, you could somehow extract out the Demon Gene and at once be done with the temptations and agonies that so shackle one to this forever-grappling state? To end the struggle by shipping one of the boxers out of the ring? I've been trying this very thing thru meditation and journeying, the following of the mystic pathways and raising of the chakra energies, rather than by employing the methods of the Theologians and Scientists, though my sensory deprivation chamber would certainly fall into the category of the latter.

In other words, what if Henry Jekyll and his Wellsian counterpart, Dr. Moreau, were right and the worst parts of us can be extracted in the lab? Stevenson and Wells were gifted psychoanalysts—dwellers in the dark and foamy places of jagged dualities and monstrous innocence that Bergman brought to vivid life in Plato's popcorn-littered cave—and the creations of their creations came straight off the table and readily joined their brothers (not *fathers*, mind you—that's where they—and Victor F—went wrong) to show the world, with a little guidance, that Salvation was at hand.

I've heard all manner of off base and self-masturbatory takes on these experiments—the most laughable being the absurd notion that the creation of the Monster in Mary Shelley's *Frankenstein* was some cryptic metaphor for male carrot-waxing. Another is that Hyde was a manifestation of Jekyll's repressed homosexuality. That just doesn't play considering Hyde's penchant for the night life. There is no doubt (and it's been made explicit on stage and in film) that Hyde, like the Ripper, killed more than one whore. It's well known among criminal profilers that a homo can't commit a sex crime against a woman—there's absolutely no release. *No point.* Talk about grasping at straws. Just the other day, as I searched desperately for answers, I read this pukish rot—supposedly peer reviewed—that said Moreau, Jekyll, and Frankenstein were envious of female reproductive power; that they actually *hated* women and used the burgeoning medical technology of the day to substitute their gadgetry for the vagina. Even if they did, how is that different than a woman using a dildo or vibrator as a substitute for a living, pulsing prick? This "scholar" said that gynecology was nothing more than the medicalizing of the female body. So then, logically, all medicine is gender exploitation... A guy in his fifties getting a finger up the ass to check the old prostate must be the medicalizing of the *male* body. The article said that the Victorian male writer was trying to eliminate the female from the world in order to enact an all-male Utopia. But let me ask—if they were so hot to kill off women by inventing some laboratory birth protocol, then why have the suggestion made through three obviously mad scientists who come to bad ends? Besides—motherhood was nearly deified in the Victorian era. Now, in a stab at fairness, I do know that there *was* some interesting shit going down on the mucking-with-childbirth front at the time these tales were spun.

In 1912 Winston Churchill and AG Bell sponsored the Int'l Congress of the Eugenics Society in London. Attendees included GB Shaw, JM Keynes, and, it's true, HG Wells, but how is selective breeding different than lezzies using sperm banks with elaborate Male Achievement Profiles to produce fatherless babies with strong genes any different? It's separate sides of the same old coin. ... And how about Hawthorne's 1837 story "The Birth Mark?"—it's the precursor to the modern obsession with plastic surgery.

Thank God for Mel Brooks' *Young Frankenstein*—the answer to all this agenda-laden academia—where the modern doc grows a conscience and actually saves and nurtures his Creation.

Let the parody set us free.

The corruption of the male form, on Moreau's island, on Victor's bloody table, in the black Burton world of the Scissorhands, and in my own unholy case—has left us all with knives for fingers and old pasta where our cocks once were. The lab is no womb, no safe passage, *unless the brother is there to help his own.* Why did Jekyll do what he did? Yellow-bellied fear of the War. It rages in each and every soul. It deconstructs falsities and makes a group of children beat the living fuck out of some crack addict and call their friends to watch and help. It's nothing but Fear of the Reflection—but I have already looked into that wall of damnable mirrors a thousand times before.

I am a child of academia, of ivy walls and cramped lecture spaces and bulging eyes splotched with ink, but I know where to stop. Everything that needs to be known is inside from the start. It's embodied in Nature if the connection can be made. The dual natures of Kali and Durga—the Monster, the Hyde, the Jackalman of Wells' tale—they all remain inside and dwell in the First Garden: Eden. The Lakota knew it, and the Sufi mystics—not men of god so much as Nature, all that she is—the unwilling battlefield where Man and his Shadow do their fighting. I once saw a 70-year-old banyan tree that was left standing though it destroyed the temple wall its roots grew beneath.

That's the better path.

Beauty IS the Beast. That's the revelation. The key to lying with the wolf and absorbing the lamb in a bloodfeast ritual. It's the equivalent of donning a sheep suit and devouring oneself. I've yet to fully find a way, me with my bad eyesight and twisted fingers, hunched over benches in borrowed labs. I've grown weary of sticking pins into butterflies. I am ready to deal scientifically with my Evil—but my work will be of a different sort than the madmen sewing bodies and playing with genes in the lightninged night. I know that if Duality is ultimately a lie then re-integration after the Procedure is the only road to being sane. It's been within me since I drank the blood of the Nazorean. The vampire feasts on flesh (following the rituals of the Church) and in so doing absorbs itself into the universal Oneness.

The means to the Extraction is all around me now—cloning, stem cell research—Frankenstein's Monster (or those of Jekyll and Moreau) is no gothic diversion any more. The seeds of their work, based on my experiences as a Person of Flesh, seem real enough to fertilize and water. Perhaps what bursts forth will be a dark, sinister flower, like those of Baudelaire, but that could still be the lesser of two wrongs. I'll employ any and all means to push the Beast out of my spine, as Jekyll was able to do.

Almost able to do. But then what? This is where I part from the Three Brothers. It is a dangerous place, this Universe, and one needs his claws, his Pure Instinct, his sense of knowing how to survive and get the things he Needs—food, blood, sex, and attention. In some mad way, it is this ruthless Self-Preservation that has allowed me to resist the furthest extremes of the Dark. If I can find a way to extract it, communicate with it, *train* it, put it to use while removing its poison from my cells, that would be a fine bit of Science—much nobler than injecting some rats with carcinogens… Then, once it was *domesticated* (following the ideas of Moreau) it would be safe to bring it back inside—to feast upon its strengths and reclaim it, as the Vampiric nature must. Perhaps then, when my battling soul is finally at peace, I shall be able to speak with the gentle wisdom and elegant verses of the Prophet of Kahlil Gibran, instead of stabbing in the dark with the curved knives of half-truths and conflicted philosophies as has thusfar been my lot.

Ironically, the skills of the cancer surgeon would serve me well to start, for what is this Germ of Evil if not a growing cancer locked deep within the healthy cells of my consciousness and my memory of the time of All? Will this growing chick ultimately breaks its egg and in the process convert itself to the horned lizard Cornu wants me to be? I've killed in horrid ways—mutilated in anger, killed my own mother, drank blood as pure theatre—and I sense the need and the capability to go further, as though hearing and seeing the details of Cornu's work as the Ripper has given an accelerated degree of bloodlust to my strengthening Doppelgänger (this no doubt accounts for some of my willingness to take part in Mykaldaemio's games). It not only wants to feed, to receive sustenance in the physiological sense, but to *be fed* by the adoring servants with which it wishes to surround itself. (I now know it was the originator of the signal that drew the young punks to seek audience with me.) To gorge itself on the energy of Worship—to draw the light to itself the way Light Itself does, for fear is a sugar-laden orgasmic rush and love, whether given toward good or ill, is the nourishment all dying cells need.

It is warring against me and my little rebellion of stricter moral rules—it is my Ego and it will not go without a fight.

But there is hope in the possibility of isolating and analyzing this growing Beast within me, to vindicate both Jekyll and Moreau to history by means of learning from their mistakes. That will be the easy task—I know the nature of the Beast inside far better than they. I have no desire to kill or even control it beyond the absolutely necessary, for its own well-being and protection, as one would with a child in the Throes of the Terrible Twos—that knowledge of Separateness that is the early manifestation of Free Will. Jekyll never once protected Hyde for Hyde's sake, but only for his own. The Beast is no longer willing to be suppressed—it wants Out, and with the right methods, I think is capable of bargaining for its own Existence. I must ultimately remove it on *my* terms or it will soon escape under its own. I had once thought that letting it out in little runs, allowing it to have its way now and again would be enough, and without Cornu's force-fed images and stories of his atrocities, it might have been, but no more. It will break free and burn itself out in the blinding light of destruction, and I will be left alone, defenseless and broken at the bottom of the stairs leading to Parvus Cornu's throne.

So it is decided: I must find a means of communicating with this Dark Essence, of monitoring its actions and thoughts, having him chaperoned and watched by my Companions in the early stages of our work lest he wreak more havoc than even I am willing to allow.

This begins a new direction for my existence among you. I must rage and rend at times, rampage and pull to tatters many among you as I give the Beast his nose, but it is all for the good, as it was for Jekyll and Moreau. It is to put the Soul back into Science, to use the knowledge now available for the betterment of all that I embark on this path. I will not damn this Frankenstein's monster of mine, as he lies still upon the table or after he is Risen and let to roam about. I will not make Victor's mistake. My Shadow Self will not gorge itself mindlessly on blood until it chokes as would inevitably be the case were I to do Nothing.

This may have once been the talk of the Mad and the Damned, but I am a far greater creature than they.

Each time I dip a living creature into the bath of burning pain, I say: this time I will burn out all the animal, this time I will make a rational creature of my own. (Moreau, *The Island of Dr. Moreau*, HG Wells)

It was on the moral side, and in my own person, that I learned to recognize the thorough and primitive duality of man; I saw that, of the two natures that contended in the field of my consciousness, even if I could rightly be said to be either, it was only because I was radically both. (H. Jekyll, *The Strange Case of Dr. Jekyll and Mr. Hyde*, RL Stevenson)

If you bring forth what is within you, what you bring forth will save you. If you do not bring forth what is within you, what you do not bring forth will destroy you. (Gospel of St. Thomas)

It's been nearly five months since I last put words upon the page, but I have not been idle. Surrounded by my Council, most of whom have assisted me in various ways and to greater or lesser degrees, I have found the means to the castle-tower heights of my theories and experiments and have bled and toiled, fought my way forward and suffered numerous setbacks and subtle deaths as I approached its darkened, guarded door and entered the Hall of the Twin.

There have been rare, precious moments when I've felt myself held tightly in the arms of the ancient Creator gods and passed back and forth, grasp to grasp, in the sweat-soaked arms of Drs. Jekyll, Frankenstein, and Moreau. I broke the code of Griffin's three leather-bound diaries and learned the mysteries of invisibility and the other dozen secrets mentioned in passing by the narrator of *The Invisible Man*. I was the great Victorian-era scientist in the throes of the sizzling voltage of my own electric mind. In other, more common moments, I felt no better than the comic-book lab-rat monkey-men—the ones trying to understand their formulaic superhero alter-egos thru the eyes of their machines. This I felt as my own were affixed to the microscope as I toiled without sleep for days at a time with the handful of assistants I'd recruited from the better research laboratories around the world. An easy task in a time when genetic research has financially boomed and the promise of even bigger paychecks lures where the golden worm of ethics might otherwise prevail.

In the subterranean laboratory beneath the facility I requisitioned years ago from an ivy-walled school, my Techno-Wiz and Scientist-Visionary counselors have overseen the efforts to make my equipment state-of-the-art. Machines for centrifuging and pummeling with gamma- and x-rays. Powerful computers with the most advanced operating platforms and statistical software packages, their data-streaming glows of blue and green bathing squinting eyes and contemplative faces in figure-etched light. Flasks, beakers, burners, test-tubes, and bottles of salts, tinctures, and liquids rise from the long, black-lacquered tables like miniature cities of rubber, glass, and cork. An array of cylinders, electrodes, tubes, disks, sockets, and switches for keeping alive an extracted human brain that comes right out of Lovecraft's "The Whisperer in Darkness" stands in a corner, more an *homage* to the The Master than anything I might ever to use. Taken together, all the apparatus makes a postmodern cityscape of precision and delicacy where the rushing commuters of figuring fingers and sleep-battling eyes have scurried to and fro in the depths of their tasks.

Apparently, being fried alive has burned away the Tech-kid's moral turpitude. That and knowing of the Cornu's interest in his work has made him wholly eager to follow my instructions and strive for a greater good than he ever thought possible before his little booze-n-fuse demise. As to his now inseparable scientist companion, he was at first unsure, but having read my latest entries and spoken at length with my Chinese ministerial advisor in moral terms only a Confucianist could understand, he agreed to run the lab. He's been invaluable, having gained his experience in gene manipulation and similar endeavors decades ago when the military was footing the bills.

Success (and in the end it was) was often hard to come by, and in those moments when we thought it best to scrap it all and find a saner way (prodded by the wheelchair-bound cable-access lecturer) I found relief and welcome diversion watching the at-first disparate artistic efforts of the retired rock star, the Shakespearian actor, and the Caucus choreographer converge into an updated score, script, and staging of "Peter and the Wolf." If Chelsea has her way it'll be her foray into the theatres of Broadway and the West End with the coming of the new season of mostly shitty shows.

It's harder to ruin a classic, so I'd say she's got a shot.

There has been a great deal of death, from the onset of operations (a word of many meanings). The involuntary sacrifice of life to create or elongate or improve the lives of others is too often the way of science—and with each passing week my assistants were gathering and bringing to the lab creatures of more and more complex cellular composition and physiological function until we were working with the very animals I had killed others for riddling with cancer and other foul diseases.

As always, Irony was alive and well and ready to catheterize my unanesthetized prick.

Staring into the eyes of a cloud-white mouse two months into our work I resolved to pull the plug. Though we had caught glimpses of the Beast in all aspects of our work I could not allow the death of mammals. A badly twisted mockery of what is normally considered morality, but the fact remains that I felt no remorse dissecting fish, reptiles, insects, or amphibians. I would have hesitated with the avian species that crossed our table were it not for memories of the traitorous Crow that still flits within my mind.

But looking at that helpless little mouse, I soon made the determination that only my own body would do for the remainder of our experiments.

It was a path I had chosen before and, contrary to what is depicted in film, no one disagreed.

I've learned a great deal about the nature of creation on my journey thru the nebulous worlds of atoms and cells, genes and genomes, molecules and chromosomes, and the myriad types of stem cells, and—using my skills as a grokker and shapeshifter—entering the pathways and conduits of the human body, with its great washes of subtle subcellular yellows and reds like those of the primordial creatures that dwell in the dark of the ocean's deepest floors. I've swum thru the viscous fluids of digestive acids and plasma, clung to the sides of platelets, and bathed in the warm wash of Green Fluorescent Protein. With the latest equipment I have probed and plucked, dissected and manipulated the tissues and organs of my body with electrodes and needles, scalpels and catheters, pumps and tubes, and a variety of fiber-optic scoping devices. I've studied the immune system and become proficient in the theories and art behind culturing, angiogenesis manipulation, allogeneic cell transplantation, histocompatibility, mutagenicity, pluripotency, and xenotransplantation (the bread and butter of the Mad Moreau). I have filled dozens of notebooks with cryptic a.m. scrawling—diagrams, schematics, equations, and the requisite graphs and tables formed from the careful analysis of reams of computer-generated paper. Scientific notation—coded symbol tucked and grafted upon coded symbol—Greek letters, superscripts, Arabic numbers, Latin nomenclature—a curved and pen-bled confluence of the Mediterranean preoccupation with communicating for consideration and posterity its thousands of years of complex thought.

I was working in my lab one morning with these pamphlets, papers, formulas, and the ethereal aspects of many different alchemists when I caught my first glimpse of the Light.

Working from Griffin's diaries and those of Drs. M and F, I produced and combined a series of tinctures from which grew forth an egg. It was first visible as a mere speck of white in a sea of greys and greens, but it soon grew to the size of a marble, then a chicken egg, then a man's fist, then a football, and so on until it was large enough to hold two tiny humanoid forms, which finally came forth after an hour of patient knocking on the inside of the egg. They were identical in every aspect, with wide, alert eyes the same deep brown as my own and generous locks of curly black hair. I could not tell them apart—each birthmark, mole, bump, and indentation upon their copper skin was the same.

For three days I sat with them in the library attached to the lab, not sure what it was I had brought forth.

Soon enough, I knew.

Sensing they were as bored with our restricted surroundings as I was, I brought the little creatures into the laboratory, where the half dozen mammals I still kept caged there began to bellow and howl as the twins approached. One of the two reached into the cage of a kitten and tore off three of its four limbs before his "brother" led him away.

Then he smelled the blood.

Suffice to say it took a week's worth of work to put the lab back in order after he was finally subdued and killed.

Not a single mammal survived.

I thought perhaps his twin could be educated—taught to actualize his higher self…

To my surprise, once he saw his brother's body, he turned out to be the more evil of the two.

Four of my six assistants died in ways that would make Attila spew.

The fifth slid a scapel across his own throat as the little imp drew near.

The last ran off.

He was, ironically, the dimmest of the bunch.

It was no joy tearing out the throat of the second of the twins, but in the end the Work must go forth, no matter what.

They had cost us time and lives, but it was clear now I'd succeed.

They were my dark before the dawn.

It was on an unremarkable night of routine vivisection (sadly lacking in thunder, lightning, or fog) when most of my lower organs had been systematically removed, biopsied, bathed in a mixture of salts and chemicals, further examined and tested, and returned to my midsection that the elusive Beast at last came forth, pulling the soul energy cleanly and thoroughly from my chakra circuit and leaving me to lie semiconscious and immobile upon the examination table.

The following is an excerpt from my journal, although I do not remember writing it: "Sleepless for 38 hours. Sweat pools on the brow, stinging my eyes…. No sleep! No food! Leave me be! I have seen a vision of the Beast transformed—skin bloodied, pricked, sliced, numbed by the sharpened blades, razor wires, electrical bursts of the Machinery as it glows and spits and hums. Oh, the Secrets kept by our so-called Teachers. The unanswered questions, the fear of provoking God by being his better. The figure moves, twitches, writhes—increase the voltage! Quick! Another hypo of the rushing fluids of Life! There is no morality other than Mine—there is no God who can do as much as I. The floors creak with the flung weight of the Beast—his claws shred the beams of his baptismal bed, this awkward newborn screaming silently at me in the tones of a damned angel awakening to his power—this animated collection of all my worst deeds, this accumulation of wars and sin and death. He shall be my savior—he shall make a better me, as I have given him the structures and poems of my mind—my sorted, collected, edited, and sanitized memories of all that I once was. He chinks the mossy brickwork of his mind in his effort to grasp his cascading bursts of thought. He stops only to try and kiss the Dark. See how he aspires where mere men dare not try? His beauty, so like a monster's, is there for the eye to grasp. Once barred entity, Come Forth into my arms! Prove the skeptics wrong—turn the Academy upon its ear! And should some blood be spilled in the name of our Progress, so be it! We shall shed no tears for there is no morality but ours, and ours shall not answer to God."

Much like Jekyll's description of the initial manifestation of Hyde, the Beast was slighter in build and far less kind of features than I—and as equally difficult for any two of us to describe in quite the same way. His arms were long and knotted with the cabled muscle of tree-dwellers and other lower-form simians, though the hair upon his body was less coarse and not evenly distributed, as he had a remarkable array of scales, plates, and feathers ranging from the sublimely beautiful to the devilishly grotesque. He was Grendel, Baphomet, goblin, vulture, dragon, and mid-transformation lycanthrope—uniquely capable of defying all attempts at rational classifications of phylum, genus, or species.

He was all of my Evil, poured into the model of semi-human physiological form—the painting of Dorian Gray burst forth from the canvas and *alive*.

He also possessed intelligence as acute as my own, and sarcasm just as sharp.

"It's about fucking time."

His voice was animal, dancing on the ragged lower timbre of one accustomed to rough living, roaring out as Hyde's did after a long suppression. It dripped of bloodfeasts, acid, liquor, and smoke. Of howling at the moon to be heard above the hurricane.

"Now that I'm free I am sure I should be asking—What are the rules of the game, brother? I've a desire to start my work."

Stepping forth under the presumption that I could not speak to the Beast even if I could hear him (my ears had long since healed) the Siouxian sheriff who normally does little else but look after the smallest of my advisors said, "You don't leave this lab without me or her" (pointing to the Old Testament prostitute), "and you stay away from the little girl."

"What about *her*?" the Beast answered, pushing to the side the Spencer repeater the sheriff had put in his face as he eyed the triple-goddess rebel, who had quickly morphed from the chubby blonde to the rouged-up sexpot the minute the Beast had talked. "She smells of fresh juice. I haven't had a good go in a long, long while. It was with a Sumerian priestess in the temple of Ninhursag if my memory hasn't failed."

I couldn't argue about the lack of sex and somehow the thought that my Evil essence's first impulse was to fuck rather than fight gave me more than a small bit of comfort that things would go just fine.

"You wanna go with *me* you'd best eat your oysters," the sexpot replied.

"Don't do it, girlfriend." This from the ultra-fem, who hadn't offered the least amount of encouragement or help with our work as the months dragged on, instead sitting by the operating table reading aloud the creation passages of *Frankenstein* over and over again. "Don't give the bastard what he wants—let him pull his pecker 'til it snaps. Keep the box locked—or if you really need a go, I can do it just as well. *Or better.*"

"Enough!" the Beast yelled, shattering a rack of test-tubes with the pitch of his voice. "I must exercise my will—sow my oats—exorcise our demons, as it were. The sooner the better for us all—especially for my poor brother lying useless on the slab."

I guess he'd seen in my eyes the mixture of relief and perplexity my mind was pulsing forth because he came close to me, so no one else could hear and I'd be sure to.

"Brother, I am grateful for my release. I am sad to say that we cannot journey together—we share but one soul, as all the other Scientifically Separated have before us, though you alone have found the trick of allowing my manifestation in a form distinct from yours and yet indivisibly connected. I am no ordinary concentration of evil any more than you are mere man. I have a name brother, a name I am most assured that you have heard.

"I am The Dark Dragon—Jaldabaoth—the greatest of the Archons and son of Sophia. I am friend to Adam, educator of Eve and champion of Cain, Seth, Esau, and Judas—names I've heard you speak with the white inflection of Truth. We have agreed on much, you and I, and differed in many ways as well, but that is the worth of our dichotomy. You have used me and I you. Just as my six brothers have migrated and manifested in other places, serving as counterbalances to the Archangels and as adversaries of the Amesha Spentas of Ahura Mazda who tried to subdue the evil of Angra Mainyu, so now must I go out into the world and learn to temper my impulses thru giving fully into them, which you so long forbade.

"You cannot take part in this, nor can your Advisors, though some will travel with me as I do the things you know I must. I will write of my blasphemies in your favorite sacred text, as Hyde did for Jekyll. I will return within weeks, my muscles, claws, and fangs all the sharper for having been so thoroughly used, and I will then be ready to take my place within you once again and perhaps forever more, though it will not be so much a cage as a bed where I take my well-earned rest in the times you need me not."

How I wished I could reply! To hear of his plans and to lay out my cautions and my sure-to-be-ignored requests that he be wise in his choice of victims and vice, but I could say nothing. I would be a seed deep beneath the soil of our soul, only peripherally and helplessly aware of all he chose to do. What new blossoming would come forth after he watered the ground with the blood of his adventures neither of us could guess.

"I want the heated bitch to come with us," Jaldabaoth said, speaking to the sheriff. "And though I will not touch her, or even look upon her unless you say, the little Tibetan girl must come with us as well. Her ancient musical instruments will be of value when my lusts grow too great for even the thickest chains and most cunning traps to stop."

Caressing the worn stock of his Spencer, the sheriff looked the creature in the eyes. "Agreed. But I won't hesitate to bring you down if you so much as brush against her with your breath."

Without another word, the traveling party—Jaldabaoth, the sexpot, the sheriff, the feather-woman, and the girl—were gone, off to either enact or be witness to the things I had set in motion and now had not a single means to shape.

All but the Chinese minister were soon gone as well, and as he read to me from the rice-paper scrolls of Li-Po and Lao and Chuang Tzu we were joined by

Gabriel St. A. and Orlando the Nephilim, who I'd asked to stay away until the deed was done. Thru the long night they stood vigil over the empty husk of me as my consciousness began to lift away and attach itself by slender silver threads to Jaldabaoth's own. Though I would not be able to experience his actions as anything more than a series of changing sensations, like the sun or wind on the face of the blind, at least I would know when the storm was abating and when the Beast would at last be free of its excess of Wrath.

As I settled into a deathlike rest, Mephistopheles' "And we, when all is said and done/Depend on creatures we have made" as quoted by Goethe, was foremost in my mind.

Out of a growing sense of propriety I will only say this about Jaldabaoth's doings over the course of what amounted to seven weeks of brutality, decadence, and chaos: if you scan the local crime sections of papers in Georgia, Illinois, and Maryland over the period of time in question, you will find stories of murders of children and other breathtaking atrocities. You will find articles in most of America's regional papers on baffling killing sprees, abductions from college campuses, and brutal rapes—all without suspects—or the *wrong* suspects. You will even find a murder strikingly similar to that of Sir Danvers Carew in *Jekyll and Hyde*—right down to the snapped cane. Evil has a cunning intelligence all its own and Jaldabaoth—at least at the start—knew how to construct a scene to muck with the modus operandi of police and forensics squads. He returned home, as it were, to preach *Jihad* and incite riots and bombings throughout the Middle East. He took up the work of long-dead serial killers to make it seem as though they had risen from the grave. This (I would like to think) was a way to say to the Cornu that no matter what he does, Jal and I can do it better and with more artistry and scale. To quote Griffin in *The Invisible Man*, it was not "wanton killing, but a judicious slaying."

As he knew she would, the little Tibetan girl proved to be beauty to his Beast and hard as it must be to believe, she kept things from being worse. The Sheriff and the triple-goddess rebel, who returned in her leggy brunette aspect (the sexpot having been thoroughly exhausted by their nightly unions within the first two weeks and the chubby blonde hiding out absolutely sickened and scared shitless at the thought of being anywhere near his throbbing cock) said very little about what they had seen or felt, though if spirits could be any paler than normal they certainly were. The Old Testament prostitute, who had gone sexless because Jaldabaoth refuses to pay for anything he can just as easily get for free, told me that one night in Madrid, after one of Jal's more vicious runs, the Sheriff had fired one of his green orbs into him to prevent him from finishing off those he'd left alive. Jal wouldn't speak of it, though I could recall a feeling at the time like being trapped in ice and suddenly being hit with a piercing heat. Whatever the effect of the mysterious green orb, his behavior began to steadily mellow, until his tastes for the dark, decadent, and violent had once more reached a balance with my own.

Upon their return, Jaldabaoth wasted little time on greetings and introductions with Orlando and Gabby St. A. before expressing his desire to return our soul to its former place and his essence with it. I suppose he missed the comfort and simplicity of the cells in which he lived the way I long to shed the false frame of a Human and become again Just Me. The re-assimilation was a quick, unscientific process—he simply squeezed himself up thru my asshole crown-first like a baby being born in reverse thru the only passage available until at last we were once again a single unit, more compatible and therefore more powerful than we had been before the split.

I can only hope that the end is justification enough for such terrible means as I have once again inflicted on the world.

Jaldabaoth had no such concerns—not once during his weeks of bloodshed and rage did he show a single sign of hesitation or remorse. Perhaps that in itself is reason enough to feel no guilt for the things I allowed him to do.

Here I am, in a place of the dead, Père Lachaise, though I have never felt more alive.

The very best of Humankind are here, spread across a hundred or so acres of gardens, statuary, and graves. One of three cemeteries created by Napoleonic decree, Père Lachaise was christened in blood—in 1814 some Cossacks camped here after putting down an uprising of Parisian students and 57 years later it marked the last stand of the Communards, 147 of whom, at last defeated at the site of Balzac's tomb, were lined up against the outside wall and shot.

As I walk among the graves of actors, writers, composers, and artists, I stop to draw inspiration from my faves—those of Moliere and Doré; of Max Ernst and Eugene Delacroix (whose grave I never fail to adorn with a single pink rose); of the American expatriates—Gertrude Stein, Alice B. Toklas, and Jim Morrison; and of Chopin (with its letterbox for secret lovers) and Wilde (with its Art Deco shapes and thousands of lipstick kisses).

But today I am no tourist and as I approach the unadorned and elegant tomb of Marcel Proust, the object of my visit appears.

Finally, one of God's four messengers has agreed to talk with me.

I have now become the center of the wheel, which the spokes cannot ignore.

It should be no surprise that it is Phanuel—father of the Prophetess Anna, who attended the presentation of Jesus in the Temple. He is said to hold the devil in his power (whoever the imp may be) and his name is synonymous with those of Ramiel and Uriel (pseudonyms all) and as such he is patron of literature and music. He is, as it were, a perfect match for me.

"It's good to see you, Brother," he says, opening his arms.

"And you as well. It has been too long."

We do not hug.

"On the contrary—the moment of our meeting is precise. Preordained. It is Perfect."

"He's trained you to think like that, you know."

"It is your function to say so, Brother. Without sin there is no repentance. How else can the power of Light prevail? It must have its adversaries."

"Sure. Lucifer, Judas, myself ... so when do we get our reward for the parts we so perfectly play?"

"I would think the human cliché of 'The journey is its own reward' answers that."

"Does it end, this journey full of 'rewards'? 'Cause I'm starting to feel like Jesus in the garden asking that the cup not pass my way even as the wine pours down my throat. I've grow weary of the walk. I'd like to call it settled."

"But you play your part so well—full of the mixed energies of the drama of angels and men. Your difficulty lies in your getting too lost in the entanglements of the physical world. It interferes with your spiritual progress."

"Then that's why you've come? To guide me to salvation?"

"Isn't that reason enough?"

"Not on a good day, when everything is stable and all the monsters sleep. You talk of the need for adversaries—you're not shy about taking that role yourself."

"'The Kingdom of God must be defended like any other.'"

"Anouilh's *Becket*—you know your literature, Phanuel. But then again, you should, being its patron and all."

"You're selfish, Brother. So consumed by your own need for completion that you forget that everything is already complete—that is the Father's plan."

"Then why all the hierarchy? Why all the energy expended on perpetuating the myth of separateness?"

"Each must play a part. You know that. In the end, the cathedral is built from myriad materials, all integrated into one single structure. But the brick is not the piece of glass, is not the Holy Sacrament, is not the Presence of God. For each piece to confuse its purpose is to risk the structure's collapse."

"You've always been good at missing the point—all of you. It only takes a match to burn the structure down."

"Man and angel must hold to their agreements, Brother. Mankind must face its adversaries. That will extinguish the flame. Not your preaching to them of Oneness. As you so wrongly think of me—they are sure to miss the point."

"Then I'm on my own."

"Only for as long as you continue to believe it."

"You know damned well I didn't want to be here."

"Perhaps it's only that you've forgotten that you asked."

As he walked away, I began to feel a spreading warmth on my thigh. Reaching into my front left pocket, I pulled out the crucifix given to me by Father Joe.

The damned thing was pulsing with a deepening red glow.

Phanuel was more involved than he'd chosen to admit.

I sometimes gaze at the twinkling carpet of the upside-down sky and wonder what might be looking down. Not the celestial, extraterrestrial, or other-Planic beings that myself and others have written of, but the beings referred to so inaccurately as *flaming balls of gas*. It might seem ridiculous that a mad bitch of a cave dweller like me would be a stargazer, but it makes perfect sense—I am relatively new to this Plane, though I am so old as to be beyond ancient, and the Ancients loved the stars—named them as gods and fallen mortals and wove around them complex, delicate myths that pervade your life to incredible degrees—you wish upon a star, know star-crossed lovers, perhaps were born under a lucky star, have gathered to watch a falling star, name the most successful and well-known among you Stars, and so on. You pay big dollars to have your fortune told based on the math of your birth and then begin to unconsciously alter your life to fit what you've found out. But it all began with the Ancients, who looked to the celestial shapes, honored the ones they burned and turned for, and found guidance and solace within their far off forms—forms that shined on pristine savannahs and plains, on villages and tribal encampments, on castle complexes and mountain lookouts, and on the conquering fleets of royal cities. And then, over time, the primitive cities became modern and postmodern and now post-postmodern and still those eternal bodies of light keep shining. I walk fogged-in bridges in movie-makers' dreams, morphing thru walls of brick and gazing at the couch zombies who don't notice the change in the ever-changing world and I marvel at their inability to draw even the slightest lesson of life from the pinpoint holes of light-year mythology shifting imperceptibly above their dull, balding heads. Only by watching the stars in their crawling near-stillness can one hope to see the natural evolution at play. These are the changes that matter—the subtle ones measurable nowhere but in the births and deaths and journeys of the stars, the one true Power alive in this conglomeration of conscious recollections and shared perceptions that unite us in the Celestial City in which all beings of all densities reside. It is the Hall of Records, where each soul's key is kept. I'm beginning to understand the constructs, the theories of chaos and quantum physics, the echoes of the alternate, simultaneous, and shadow realities, the myriad aftershocks of nanosecond concentrations of Pure Thought. Ordered and random; unique, yet transferable; replicable and able to counterbalance and complement in complete and utter Harmony. One unnamable, unknowable Source that gave birth to the stars and all Beings of Light, which knows only the countless aspects of itself as Itself in countless aspects. It is not what we call God, because the great unknowable, the *Wakan Tanka*, has no interest in Hierarchy. It is the unconscious Alpha that moves out of habit and impulses it long ago ceased to question or manipulate. If only God was so bright as to follow suit, to emulate the source of the Father–Mother and stop trying to be Father only at the expense of the Mother's wisdom and soul. Instead he's sat for eons while his angels and prophets, popes and priests have constructed the Heaven only *he* wants. But the stars will not listen, because they are not his children—they are his sisters and brothers. So gaze upon the stars, the brighter planets, the comets and nebulae, and there you will see the inspiration for the true gods, multi-named and wonderfully powerful and guiding in their role as Myths.

    I know I am repeating myself in my words and actions, although nothing is the same.

    Perhaps I am not yet Saved, but I shall no longer Fall.

P hanuel has asked for another meeting, so here I wait, without the comfort of the graves of Père Lachaise. This time, we are to meet at the shrine of an obscure saint, patron of a secret Order—the Scarlet-Shrouded Knights of St. Grotth. His grave is guarded by an alabaster angel the likes of which I have never seen. The wings of the angel are folded—cold and static, like they shall never be opened again. Its hermaphroditic form sits, head bowed, upon a throne of ancient, enduring marble. Its face is perfect, except for the black, gaping holes where the eyes should be. It chills me worse than the subterranean air to think that someone—some *thing*—had taken the eyes, perhaps to give the angel more the look of the alien seen by Ezekiel before he was carried off to Heaven.

    Surrounding the shrine is statuary that reminds me of the bog mummies I've seen in my dreams. The immortalized children of Tatyana, my troubled triple-goddess—the raped Mary Mater turned the forsaken and needing-to-be-saved Mary Magdalene, the abandoned wife left by the eager martyr. Babylon's mistaken whore—infinitely fragile and yet as blind and unyielding as the eyeless angel of this forgotten, desecrated tomb.

"He had nothing left to see, so he chose to be made blind."

Phanuel.

"I came all this way for more greeting card crap?" I asked, turning to face him.

And I thought I'd seen it all.

There before me was the face of the gone angel porter, with angel's wings and mystic hair.

He'd been Phanuel all along.

"I haven't much time," he whispered. "And I've already said too much. My reasons are unclear even to me, so asking me questions is pointless. You're closer than you think, Brother."

"To what?"

"I told you there isn't time! You will find the answers are within you, all around you, in the words and deeds of your enemies and friends. But beware—they are not who you think—any of them. Let each one earn your trust or ire, moment to moment, and be willing to let it change as often as it must."

"Who is this Saint Grotth? Are his followers still around?"

"Look to the future, Brother—not the past. This is your starting point, but you will not pass this way again. Look to the future. If you wish to save your soul and rejoin what is rent, you must not turn from what's at hand."

"You possessed that little girl in South America, right? So that means you're helping Father Joe? What about Anastasia? Tatyana?"

"Look to the future, Brother. I could tell you nothing you don't know."

Then he was gone.

And the angel's eyes had been restored.

I am desperate beyond reason, so what follows—the final words of this memoir of sorts—may yet be the oddest thing I write.

What if the maddest writers' most disturbing visions came to pass upon this Plane, instead of sticking to the etheric fringe, which makes them so much harder to find and just out of reach of the self-limited perceptions most possess? What if Stoker, Shelley, Wells, and Wilde managed to join their writers' brains with the Big Machine that runs the New Technic and produced enough juice to send across the gauzy maya of subconscious protection all the worst their creations had to offer, filling the world with a plethora of classic monstrosities and ripping the course curtain between Thought and Matter to flimsy, flapping shreds?

I mean, why *couldn't* a book manifest itself if enough people believed in it? Or, if the characters suddenly believed in *themselves*? The reality is that there *is no* reality. It's all a construct—an agreement of a trillion conscious and semi-conscious entities whirling about in weaker and stronger fields of light. If thought is energy and energy is matter at a slower, thicker vibration then isn't all that stands between the word-slap and film flick and the complete reworking of the parameters of this Plane mere tissue paper? It's nothing but Quantum Mechanics. All it would take is a mass agreement on a subatomic and yet meta-Universal level.

This isn't as absurd as it sounds (and I know you've endured some crazy shit from me…). Consider Pirandello's *Six Characters in Search of an Author*, which debuted to Roman shouts of "*Manicomio!*" ("Madhouse!") The story works like this—the characters are disembodied until the author puts them in a *context*; they are, essentially, aspects of Pirandello's brilliant mind and personal torment, seeking to manifest and be heard. It's the only way they can move from a *static* existence to the dynamics of personal change. And all stories need their characters to change—but the *converse is also true*. The characters need the *story* to change. And creating change, as anyone running up large therapy bills will confirm, is damned hard, which is why we love characters with the balls and spine to survive the myriad changes in stories—to find their same traits in ourselves. But those bastards have it hard. They get a mere *taste* of change, because when the book or film ends, so does their chance to change *further*, so they are stuck in a sort of literary Limbo—An endless cycle of the same old dramas played out over and over and over again.

And there are some characters that have it worse than others—think about the insane menagerie of artists and tortured dreamers in the tales of H.P. Lovecraft—doomed to face the Beast for all eternity with no chance to wake up and make a change.

The story, by its ending, fails them all.

If I was a character in a book (and in some ways, I am) I'd want to get out of it, if I could.

I've actually seen a few—a certain New Orleans vampire and John Gardner's vision of Grendel I've already mentioned—but there are others. Imprints and echoes of the purely fictionalized. A famous investigator of the paranormal claimed to see an image of "The Shadow" at the Greenwich Village home of his creator, Walter Gibson, in his book about the "Mothman" (which, as I've said before, at least in one instance, really was just me).

But it wouldn't *have* to be characters from works of shadow and horror, although the primal fear they dwell within resonates in the base chakras and uses the cunt or balls as a launching point—potent stuff. But it *would* have to be a tale finely crafted—the solitary writer toiling in his or her cell would have to fully embrace every aspect of the Mind to the fullest extent and pour it forth upon the page as Pirandello did—no formulas, tired plots, stock characters, *or deus ex machina*—it would have to be (for its time, at least) truly *original*.

The same outcome could be obtained by the inspired director, at work in the editing room (the stage where all good cinema begins and perhaps the conduit my crackling theory seeks). I mean, what if the macabre dreamscapes of Carpenter, Corman, or Gilliam crossed with the necrophiliac gothic of Poe and the deep resonant evil of Barker and King to such an extent that they were actually *matter-altering*, replacing the grassy greens and July 4th summer blues with the twisted metal and air-piercing towers of a spine-jolting sci-fi piece of prose? There have been works exploring the *possibility* of this, either thru a painting, film, or book, but no work has succeeded in *doing* it. And that is just as well. For if literature and cinema's greatest lunatics and monsters were to suddenly and not so secretly walk among you, the way I have—the way I believe others have—then it would not be long before they ruled. To break the boundaries of society would be a little thing compared to breaking the bounds of paragraph and book edge, celluloid and screen. And were they set free—free to write their own actions and not the good-guy-has-won drivel that drives almost all modern "art"—their reign would be fierce and sharp. They would be governed by their Will to Freedom and Self-Determination to the exclusion of all else, like teens in their freshman year of college. Take Dracula and Mr. Hyde—augmented and enlarged by how writers and filmmakers have reinvented them over the years, they would be hard to keep at bay. I've spoken of many—some by name and others by inference. I don't know what to make of it. At first, I saw them only in my journeys to the higher planes, where all such beings (an admittedly poor term) exist and, in truth, belong, for the reasons I've made clear. It's where *I* belong. This plane is Level One—the starter block for conscious life, where a being like Jaldabaoth can be nothing but a tornado in a trailer park—too much juice to do anything but major damage to your world, intentional or not. The New Technic has downplayed and done away with Instinct thru anger management and political correctness and conflict resolution and these spirits of fiction are nothing *but* Instinct when detached from the confines of the writer's cell-block tale. Their increasing infiltration and existence on the closest parameters of this Plane can only mean that Cornu's experiments in spirit transference (another inadequate term) must have somehow *created* points of entry. Doors left open when the Mischievers and I came thru. I've got this thought about the Future (which Phanuel is so insistent I focus on).

How to find and analyze it—get a step *ahead* of it instead of an hour or day or year *behind*. Get some info of real *value*, instead of empty rhetoric and trite remarks. My thought is this—there are stories of those who have come from the Future. Sci-fi is full of them. Problem is, the Future that they come from is a construct of an author from this Plane's *past*. In other words, 2 + 2 = some useless number nowhere near 4. What I need is someone who can actually go *forward*, without creating any time-looping, event-changing effects. A *fictional* character could—especially one who is Fully Liberated and making his or her own way. One of the characters I've glimpsed now and again. I would go myself but the Future is off limits to me—although I am a "fiction," I am spirit-made-flesh—I'm not capable of constructing the type of portal a work of pure fiction can with simply a thought to do so.

I need part scientist, part artist, part sneak or spy, and part Evil Incarnate to ensure that all obstacles are met and defeated. My first choice would be Gardner's Grendel but I think we're too much alike—I need not only new information but new *perspectives*. Besides, for all his delicate intelligence he hasn't the modern skills. But he can't be *too* modern, this character—modern man's wits are too damned dull.

The Victorian era will do.

So, what I need now is to *find* one and convince him to lend me his aid. God—I sound like some pimply teen on his way to a comi-con convention! But just so I'm clear—this isn't about getting a glimpse of some B-Queen's tits while getting some has-been's autograph (though I'm all for a nice set of knockers if one comes my way). The battle is fast approaching and I need to do all I can, *now*. I can't wait for one of these characters to decide to come to me. That's been my mistake from page one.

So here's the thing. I'm not the author of a Victorian-era book, nor a character in one, but I am a *reader*—and if a reader believes in a book, he can also be the Animator. The book no longer belongs to the author once it's shared. So I must find my chosen target. I know that on some level all characters must stay in contact with their creators (and though I've thus far managed to constrain myself from the Latin *ergo* I must now utter—nay—scream) *ERGO*, going to his creator could very well put me in touch with *him*.

I have just the character, and (ahem), *ergo,* just the author in my mind, necessitating a trip to France and a certain cemetery in Nice.

To get the one I want, I must speak with the essence of Gaston Leroux.

What—you were thinking Doyle and Moriarty? *Please*—he's way too English and egotistical for me. Besides, he was as much a part of the inner workings of Victoria's London as Holmes himself.

What I need is an outsider like me; someone misunderstood, who's used to working in the places where well-bred men won't go. Someone with a brilliant mind and a sense of artistic beauty. Someone who understands what it is like to love a woman beyond reason, when all the world has labeled him a monster for how he *looks*.

Someone who needs to be saved as much as I.
I must go and see Leroux.
He will know where Erik hides…

Exodus: As the Darkened Theatre Lights

I leave you with this, my poetry of the stars:

Your thoughts contribute to the path the raindrop takes
down the leaf of the banyan tree.
Child of the stars—your fathers made the gods.
What then will You be?

Now go and take a bath—it's time you washed me off.

For now.

About the Editor

Joey Madia is the author of the fantasy novel *Jester-Knight* (New Mystics Enterprises, 2009), four books on using drama and creative writing in the classroom, and many poems, short stories, essays, and scholarly articles. He is the Founding Editor of newmystics.com, an on-line literary and art site, and the Artistic Director/Resident Playwright of Seven Stories Theatre Company.

He could tell you more, but Planner won't let him.

Keeping Current with the Angel Falling Upward

Admit it… you want more. And although it's true that Planner is working on 2 more books (*Major* and *Last Confessions of an Angel Falling Upward*), his cosmic traveling and battling and fits of depression and pique make it unclear when he'll finish them.

In the meantime… visit angelfallingupward.com for blogs, multimedia selections from the book, more illustrations by N. Pendleton, and if you email Planner at planner.forthright@aol.com, he'll send you a code to access previous drafts of this odd little book going back to 2002.

Follow the Angel Falling Upward (@plannerforthrig) on Twitter.

Other great titles from:

www.BurningBulbPublishing.com

Darkened Hills
2010 Book of the Year WINNER
- *ForeWord Reviews Magazine*

Available at www.BurningBulbPublishing.com
or scan the QR code to learn more on amazon.com.

Lumberjacked

Hellhole West Virginia

Available at www.BurningBulbPublishing.com
or scan the QR code to learn more on amazon.com.

The Big Book of Bizarro

Vulgarity for the Masses

Available at www.BurningBulbPublishing.com
or scan the QR code to learn more on amazon.com.

Made in the USA
Charleston, SC
09 September 2012